Becoming Jonika

PJ Devlin

Possibilities Publishing Company

ISBN: 978-0-9861822-1-1

Published and distributed by Possibilities Publishing Company

www.possibilitiespublishingcompany.com

This is a work of fiction

In memory of my parents,
Peg and Mike Jeffers.

Author's Note

This is a work of fiction set in the Philadelphia area during the turbulent late sixties. Names, characters, businesses, places, events, and incidents are used in a fictitious manner or are products of my imagination. Any resemblance to actual persons, living or dead, is coincidental. Allusions to historical persons, places, and events may have been modified to suit the story.

The cultural change that erupted in the wake of the Vietnam War and the struggle for civil rights is best exemplified, in my opinion, by the music, films, books, and television shows of that period. I've attempted to honor various artists and their work while keeping ever mindful of my responsibility to honor their intellectual property. The best outcome I can imagine is for readers to rediscover the cultural influences of that time.

September 1, 1969

Dear Judge,

My attorney, Sally Fanelli, reminded me my record won't be expunged until you receive my comprehensive report like you ordered, so you can determine if I've been adjusted. She suggested I apologize for the trouble I caused and thank you for giving me a chance to redeem myself. Honestly, Judge, I planned to do both of those anyway.

Thank you a lot for letting me work at St. Augustine of Hippo summer camp instead of going to juvie. Even though camp was hard, I learned a lot. The best thing is — I helped every camper swim better than before. Most of them can even swim a whole lap now.

And I'm sorry for causing trouble. But I'm pretty sure the person I caused the most trouble for is me. And Ishmael. I guess we caused trouble for each other. Sometimes I'm not sure why it happened, but I am sure about this — I was messed up before I met Ishmael and started smoking weed. At school, I was a loser. I just didn't fit in. After a while, I gave up trying and felt bad all the time — until I met Ishmael and he said I was fine.

Ishmael was messed up too, you know. They wanted to make him a soldier and send him to Vietnam, but instead he came home on a psycho. I feel bad about what happened to him, even though Mrs. Fanelli says Ishmael made bad choices and I need to focus on making good ones.

What do you think about the music festival a couple weeks ago in Woodstock? Three days of peace and music — that's all Ishmael and I ever wanted.

I'm not sure exactly what you want to know, so I'm just going to tell you everything — about my parents, Redwood Academy, Ishmael, selling marijuana, getting arrested, and summer camp. I'll start at the beginning — before I knew I was a loser, before I met Ishmael, before I became Jonika. When you're finished, I hope you'll decide I've come to see the light.

Sincerely,

Jonika (Joan) Byrnes

Before

When I was little, I played hide-and-seek, pom-pom-pullaway, and kick-the-can with neighborhood kids. On playground swings I pumped my legs to go higher and higher until the chain buckled and I let go. Then I would fly, breathless and thrilled, landing on my feet and running to the arms of my friends.

It wasn't until junior high that being the youngest in class made a difference. If I didn't get invited to boy-girl parties, I didn't care much. I knew they played spin-the-bottle and truth-or-dare, and sometimes a boy asked a girl if she got her period yet. That stuff made me more shy than I already was. Instead, I went to the movies or sat in the bleachers at basketball games with other girls who didn't get invitations to those parties. Being ordinary — no one special but no one horrible either — was good enough for me.

Somehow, in April of 8th grade being ordinary stopped being good enough. After a Redwood Academy brochure arrived in the mail, my mother tacked it on the kitchen bulletin board next to the chores calendar. Every time I walked past, gleaming girls caught my eye. A few days before public high school registration, my parents sat me down at the kitchen table. Mom spread the brochure like a placemat. I stared at glossy pictures — girls playing hockey and basketball, diving into a pool, singing in choir, and talking with old ladies at a nursing home. In the center, a girl with glasses stood at a podium.

Around the border ran the words, *Redwood Academy — growing exemplary women with excellent values.* The flip side showed a young teacher at a blackboard smiling at students who looked like *Seventeen Magazine* models. On this side, the banner across the top read, *Redwood Girls are Special. Are you?* And along the bottom, *Redwood Academy empowers girls to become strong, confident women ready to serve their communities and the world.* I studied the brochure until my father cleared his throat.

"Doesn't this look wonderful, Joni?" my mother said. "Redwood has small classes and a good swim team. Since you're young for your grade, we decided it's best to send you to an all-girl school. You won't have to worry about getting lost in the riffraff at public school."

My father glanced at Mom before he started. "Private school will be better for you. Safer. Smarter. It's a lot of money, but your mother plans to work more hours at Tesses Dresses, and I'm next in line to make senior accountant. If Redwood keeps you out of trouble, it's well worth it."

Dad pushed back his chair, tapped his shirt pocket, and shook out a cigarette. After he exhaled a long stream of smoke, he looked like he might sing. Mom put her hand on his arm and he patted it. I couldn't remember the last time they agreed on anything or looked so pleased with each other. A warm feeling flushed my cheeks. Redwood girls are special. *I would be a Redwood girl. I would be special.* I couldn't wait to start high school.

It only took two months at Redwood Academy before I realized the truth — I wasn't special. I was a loser. Most of the girls came from rich Philadelphia families — society people. My parents had to work harder and cash in savings bonds to pay my tuition. They liked to remind me how grateful I should be.

During the first few weeks, I watched cliques form and tried to figure out where I fit in. Most of the girls in the cool group had older sisters at Redwood. The sporty girls met each other over the summer during field hockey tryouts. I wanted to play field hockey, but my parents had no idea about tryouts, so I missed my chance.

At lunch those first weeks, I passed by tables filled with popular girls and found a seat with six girls from Biology. Each day I unpacked a baloney sandwich, an apple, and two Oreos, while the other girls ate drippy meatball sandwiches they bought in the lunch line. As I choked down my lunch, I listened to their talk about choir and music practice. I never said much and no one said much to me. I didn't play an instrument. I never had voice lessons. I was just a girl in some of their classes. I thought that was enough.

One Friday when I got to the table, a pasty-faced girl named Scarlet slapped her hand on the one empty chair.

"Sorry, Joan, but I promised to save a seat for Trudy Evans from piano so we can talk about the fall recital."

When Scarlet smiled, one tooth protruded over her lower lip. I edged away and took an empty seat at the weirdo table. Robin smelled like burnt rubber, Paula blew her nose every few seconds, Sylvia scratched spots on her face bloody, and Marsha and Cordelia looked like football players. I told myself I wasn't like them. But same as me, they dumped their lunches out of crumpled brown bags, hunched their shoulders while they ate, and snuck glances at the other tables, desperately hoping to escape.

Later that day, I stared at myself in the restroom mirror. Because of swimming, my hair was cut short. Now I'd let it grow. All the cool girls had long hair. The Clearasil I dabbed on my forehead each morning left muddy ridges, but that was better than red blotches. My eyebrows were darker than my pool-bleached hair, but looked okay over my blue eyes. My nose was small, my cheeks wide, and my chin was kind of pointy. But I looked pretty normal. I didn't smell bad.

Each day after school, I lingered at my locker, hoping to pick up bits of gossip. I listened to cheery conversations. I studied girls who shared whispers. Soon I realized there were secret rules and inside knowledge everyone seemed to know — except me.

Each evening, when my family sat down to dinner, my mother served us pot roast with potatoes and carrots or fried pork chops with baked beans and spinach or baked chicken with rice and peas. Most days I was so nervous I could hardly eat. As soon as she sat down, Mom pegged questions at me — *How was school today? When is the fall dance? Tell me about the girls. Do any live out this way?* While she waited for my answers, she smiled like the host of Candid Camera.

Then I'd have to lie — *School was great. We started on* Lord of the Flies *in English. Dorothy Whitcomb said no one would be mean enough to call a fat boy, Piggy. But the girls who have brothers said, Oh yes they would.*

Mom expected me to become the confident, refined young woman Redwood's brochure promised. She assumed I'd be popular and run with the right crowd. When it was time to marry I'd be the perfect partner for a wealthy young man — preferably a doctor or lawyer. She liked to remind me that our next-door neighbor, Lisa White, went to Redwood Academy and married a lawyer.

Still, I thought if I just figured out how things worked, I'd make some friends and be okay. I even got up the nerve to ask my English teacher about the school newspaper and signed up for the *Redwood Reporter.* But each time I showed up for meetings, no one acknowledged my presence. For two months, I leaned against the wall while other girls worked on stories and layouts. It was like I was invisible.

Swim team was the thing that got me through freshman year. Because you have to have something or you'll go nuts.

After I asked around, I found out that you signed-up for tryouts with the gym teacher, Miss Robertson. Even though she terrified me, I made up my mind to approach her.

At the start of gym class, she barked at us to jog around the gym five times. After that, we formed two lines to shoot baskets. She stood on the court and in a steely voice called out things like — *At least aim at the backboard,* or *Do you have the slightest idea of what sweat socks and gym shoes are?* or *No more than six or seven girls out of the lot of you should even consider walking onto a basketball court.* And I wasn't one of those.

Yet when a freshman hockey player called — *Miss Robertson, Miss Robertson, look at me* — and did a cartwheel, Miss Robertson chuckled with glee.

When most girls hurried to the locker room to change, the hockey players surrounded Miss Robertson, chatting in excited voices. I fidgeted outside their circle, then got so nervous I blurted out, "Miss Robertson, can you tell me when swim team tryouts start?"

She didn't answer. She didn't even look at me. I hunched my shoulders and inched back. But one of the hockey players stared at me with a tight smile and squinty eyes.

"That girl wants to know about swim team tryouts," she said.

The gym teacher answered her, "Tryouts start October 3rd, right after school. Sign-ups in my office today."

The girl turned to me and said, "Okay?"

"Thanks," I croaked as I crept away to change into my skirt and blouse.

That afternoon, I knocked on Miss Robertson's door. When she faced me looking annoyed, my cheeks burned bright red.

"I'd like to sign up for swim team tryouts," I whispered.

"Can you swim?"

There was no missing the sarcasm in her voice. She slid a clipboard across her desk and I added my name to the dozen already there.

"Yes," I told her, hopefully. "I've been on the summer team at Meadow Swim Club since I was five. Almost every summer I make all-stars."

She inspected me like she was considering a used car.

"We'll expect you on the 3rd," she muttered before turning back to her desk.

A week later the swim team roster was posted outside the gym office. My name, Joan Byrnes, was fourth one down. Finally I had something. After that, when I walked down the hall, girls on swim team recognized me. Some even said *Hi* or smiled when I passed.

At the end-of-year athletic assembly, my name was called, and I climbed the steps to the stage where Miss Robertson shook my hand when she gave me a varsity letter — a big red R. My father bought me a

Redwood jacket and my mother stitched the letter on the left chest.

But I still sat at the weirdo lunch table and invented dinnertime stories for my mother.

During the summer, I swam with my neighborhood team. After meets, we went bowling or to the movies or to the new Gino's for hamburgers, fries, and milkshakes. I felt like a regular kid. I didn't want to go back to Redwood.

After the last meet at the end of July, twenty swimmers piled into parents' VW buses and Ford station wagons to spend the day on the amusement rides at Willow Grove Park. The fun house was dark and scary, but Billy Jensen held my hand. His family had moved to our neighborhood in January and it was his first summer on swim team. He was short, with freckles and long brown hair. I thought he looked like George Harrison. After a girl on the team told him I had a crush on him, he started to like me.

As the sun went down, he and I walked hand-in-hand toward the parking lot to meet up with everyone. Before we passed through the gate and out of the park, he pulled me behind the ticket booth. When he put his hands on my shoulders, leaned close, and kissed me, his mouth tasted like dill pickles, but I didn't mind. On the ride home, sitting in the way-back of the station wagon, he draped his arm across my shoulders.

In August, on a day when the pool was almost empty and yellow jackets swooped around us, Billy Jensen kissed me and said, "You should transfer to Montgomery High."

At home, I tried to convince my mother.

"Mom, Redwood costs too much. I'm perfectly happy to go to Montgomery with my friends."

My mother's shoulders stiffened. The smell of cinnamon and apples floated from the oven. With her back to me as she wiped the countertop, she answered in an edgy voice.

"No, Joni, we made the decision to send you to Redwood and that's the end of it. Just be grateful you have this opportunity. I wish my father had the means to send me to private school."

I was afraid to even bring up the idea with my father. Every time a carload of kids, honking and shrieking, drove by the house, his face got red and he glared out the front door. *Goddamned punks,* he'd yell then turn to me, shake his head, and say something like, *Thank God you don't have to deal with the likes of them.*

Labor Day weekend started out cold but warmed up by Monday. The day before I went back to Redwood, I rushed to the pool to hang out with Billy and the other swim team kids. But when I arrived, hardly anyone was there. I swam thirty-two laps, then leaned my elbows on the edge of the pool. The sun warmed my shoulders and the chlorine smelled like summer. I didn't want it to end.

From the hill behind the guard stand, I heard laughter and voices — Billy's I was sure. I hoisted myself out, shook back my hair, and shivered as I padded across the deck to tell Billy I was here. I know I smiled like a fool. As soon as I passed the lifeguard stand, I saw Billy on a blue towel making out with Cindy Kane. I backed away, grabbed my towel and walked home barefoot, glad my dripping hair hid my tears.

September 1967 - August 1968

So I went back to Redwood Academy for sophomore year, still a loser. And that October, I made a horrible mistake.

In English, each girl read the short story she'd written. When I stepped to the front, I blushed and my knees shook, but once I started reading, I calmed down. In my story, a bully named Chuck brings a knife to the woods to torment Joey, a little neighborhood kid. By accident, Chuck trips. He falls on the knife and stabs himself in the heart. When Joey tries to save Chuck, he pulls out the knife and gets covered in blood. After the grown-ups find dead Chuck and bloody Joey, Joey winds up in a children's insane asylum. Everyone assumes he killed Chuck.

Across the top of my paper, Mrs. Gibson marked, *A* and wrote, *Startling:* When I went back to my seat, girls were saying, *Ewww* and *gross* and *God, Joni, that's so weird.* I felt pretty good. I mean, people were talking about my story after all.

Then one of the popular girls, Elizabeth Zipley, read her story. It was about a girl whose mother is the lunch lady at her school. The girl's classmates tease her and form a club she can't join. The girl feels bad, but when a new kid who doesn't speak English transfers to the school, the girl starts hanging out with her. It all turns out just fine.

Judge, you might think Elizabeth, a cool rich girl who ignores unpopular girls, wrote a really nice story. Except I'd read an almost identical story in sixth grade — *The Janitor's Girl.* I noticed Elizabeth's paper had *A+* and *Excellent* written across the top of the page.

At first I thought I should tell Mrs. Gibson to check out *The Janitor's Girl,* but I wasn't that stupid. I mean, Elizabeth was on Student Council. Still, this was too good to keep to myself.

And that's how I made the horrible mistake. As soon as I got to the lunch table, I plopped down my brown bag and announced to my fellow losers, "Wait until you hear this."

Robin's peanut butter and jelly sandwich stopped in midair. Paula's soft pretzel dangled like a cigar. Sylvia, Cordelia and Marsha gawked, waiting for me to spill the beans. I felt like the princess of peas.

"We read our short stories in English today. Guess who stole hers from a book?" I looked from girl to girl as they guessed.

Samantha

Mary Pat

Jenny

I know, Helen Patterson.

"No, no, no, no." I couldn't keep the joy from my voice. "You ready for this? Elizabeth Zipley."

"No way," Marsha said. "She wouldn't. She's smart."

I shrugged. "All I know is it's almost the same story as *The Janitor's Girl* that I read in sixth grade. She only changed it a little."

After the last bell, I noticed Marsha whispering to Elizabeth and my stomach lurched. Marsha must have felt me staring, because she turned and grinned like the Cheshire cat. I visualized a balance scale with me on one side and Elizabeth on the other. I knew I would never measure up.

The next day, when I walked into the cafeteria, Marsha sat next to Elizabeth at the popular table. When I sat at our table, the other girls got up and left. The day after that, they moved to a different table altogether.

Redwood Academy girls, even the weirdoes, always chose a winner over a loser. And now I had that title all to myself.

Even though they called me a loser, I placed at our swim meets. Before practice, as soon as I stepped out of my grey skirt and blazer and changed into my Speedo, I felt like a bag of bricks dropped off my back. The moment I reached the pool, leaned down and cinched my fingers around the edge, I blotted out *Joni the Weirdo* and turned into a coiled spring. At the whistle's blast, I shot into the water and moved without thought — pull, kick, pull, kick, flip, kick, pull. Winner, loser, I didn't care. For those seconds, minutes, hours in the water, I didn't think about being different. I didn't think at all.

After practice, I pulled my sweats on over my wet swimsuit so I didn't have to change in front of the other girls. I didn't want anyone to see my flat chest and make fun of my body. From the locker room corner where I stowed my stuff, I listened to girls agree to give each other rides home. Before I hauled my bags across the road to wait for my father at the Wawa convenience store, I lingered until the other swimmers spilled out to the parking lot and went on their ways.

One windy day in November, just as I gripped the latch, the locker room door flew open and wrenched my wrist. Mercedes, the only black girl on the team, burst in. She stopped short, her eyebrows raised.

"You still here? I was afraid I'd be locked out." Then she stepped back and looked at me. "You can swim, Child. Why you always skittering around like a mouse?"

I shrugged, horrified but thrilled a senior bothered to talk to me.

"Thank God, there's my wallet, right where I left it. Keep swimming like you do, Girl, you be all right." Mercedes checked her lips in the mirror before she opened the door. "You coming or you plan to spend the night here?"

I followed Mercedes to the parking lot and watched her cram into the back seat of a VW bug. After the car tore out of the lot, I crossed the road to wait for my father, determined to keep swimming like I did.

On Valentine's Day, a Friday, I turned fifteen, months after everyone else in my class. No one decorated my locker. No one brought me a cupcake or sang the Redwood birthday song. I hummed it to myself — *Happy birthday to you, may your sweet dreams come true, you're a Redwood girl, Joni, and we salute you.* I snickered. The only salute the Redwood girls ever gave me was the middle finger.

At home, a heart-shaped chocolate cake and a white cardigan sweater with roses embroidered around the collar waited for me.

The truth is, I was pretty lonely. Most nights after dinner, I didn't want to go upstairs to do homework alone in my bedroom. I wanted to stay downstairs and watch TV with my family. I told my parents we were required to keep up with current events.

The Thursday before spring break, as I sat in the living room and worked on geometry, I tried to ignore the vroom sounds my brother, Tommy, made when he pushed his Matchbox cars and trucks across the floor. Dad smoked a cigarette. The TV was tuned to the evening news. After she finished the dishes, Mom came in with a basket of laundry and sat on the sofa folding undershirts and sheets.

Each of us stopped what we were doing when Walter Cronkite, his face serious and grey, broke into the newscast and reported *Dr. Martin Luther King, the apostle of nonviolence in the Civil Rights Movement, has been shot to death in Memphis, Tennessee. The bullet exploded in his face...*

My stomach lurched and my heart pounded. I noticed Mom looking at Dad with wary eyes and tight lips. I turned to my father.

"Why would they kill him? I thought Martin Luther King wanted peace. What does it mean, Dad?"

"It means trouble."

Dad leaned forward, his eyes fixed on the TV and his cigarette trembling in his mouth. A spiral of white smoke rose in the air.

"Thank God we have Frank Rizzo to keep peace in Philly," he said. As Dad left the room, under his breath he said, "What's this country coming to?"

I couldn't finish my homework that night. I stayed in the living room for hours, unable to turn away from reports about the assassination. After the TV showed Martin Luther King's 1963 speech from the Lincoln Memorial, his voice echoed in my brain — *I have a dream that my four little children will one day live in a nation where they will not be judged by the color of their skin but by the content of their character.*

The next morning, before Dad drove me to school, we paused to watch the newscast of Bobby Kennedy's speech from Indianapolis — *Martin Luther King dedicated his life to love and to justice between fellow human beings. He died in the cause of that effort... the vast majority of white people and the vast majority of black people in this country want to live together, want to improve the quality of our life, and want justice for all human beings that abide in our land.*

Once we settled in the car and pulled out of the driveway, without taking his eyes off the road, Dad said, "Bobby Kennedy is a good man, the hope for America. If everyone thought like he does, there'd be a hell of a lot less of this shooting and killing and rioting."

He shook his head and said, more to himself than to me, "But people don't think like him. And that's what we got to live with."

I rode to school in silence, confused and concerned.

In June, after I handed in my last exam, I felt like I could breathe again. No school for three months and the whole summer to convince my parents to get me the hell out of Redwood. I was overjoyed to see Dad's car pull up to Wawa. I couldn't wait to get home.

But when I opened the car door, Dad didn't look at me. His tie was loose, his eyes were red, and he smelled like cigarettes and booze. A pint-size whiskey bottle lay empty on the floor. I'd never seen him like this, and I hated it. In less than a minute, my good feelings turned to crap.

"What's wrong?" I asked in a squeaky voice.

"Don't they teach you anything at that school?" he snorted, scowling.

I didn't answer. Dad never hit me, but just then, he looked so scary I thought he might. I had no idea why he was mad, and my mind raced to figure out what I'd done. I rolled down the window and faced outside.

"They shot Bobby Kennedy in the head. The filthy sons of bitches shot Bobby and now he's dying," Dad yelled and punched the steering wheel. "Goddamn it. Just like Jack."

"Just like Martin Luther King," I whispered. Tears welled in my eyes.

"Not the same," Dad growled.

I felt small and frightened. Everyone was getting shot. Cities were burning up. The Vietnam War was always on the news. TV reports were full of riots where police bashed heads and sprayed people with fire hoses. All I wanted was to spend the summer at the pool and not worry about anything. But all I did was worry.

That summer, Billy Jensen held hands with Mary Marple. I swam with the team and passed the lifeguard certification test. The long days passed too quickly.

I dreaded returning to Redwood.

Judge, just a year ago — honestly, it feels like a lifetime — I returned to Redwood, resigned to another year as a loser.

The thing about being the school weirdo is you get to be okay with it — the same with being alone. You go to class, go to practice, go home, watch TV, go to bed, and start all over the next day. Being weird becomes easy. Being alone becomes natural. No one expects anything from you — except your parents. They always expect you to be popular and they're never okay when you're not.

Each time my mother asked why I never invited friends over, I shrugged and changed the subject. If I told her the truth — I had no friends — she'd go berserk. It was worse when she'd been drinking. Like the week before the Homecoming Dance when I admitted I wasn't going — again.

That evening, the kitchen smelled like baked apples and pot roast. Dad plunked a giant pumpkin on the kitchen table. I smiled when he called Tommy and the two of them gathered magic markers and carving knives.

"Let's make it real scary this year," my brother said.

Dad made a box with his fingers like he was framing a photograph. "Got it. We'll make it look just like you."

As Tommy squeaked the magic marker across the pumpkin's front in shaky triangles, I caught the chemical smell of the ink. I started to sit down to help, but Mom took my sleeve and yanked.

"We'll leave the men to their work. Let's go to the living room."

I couldn't help twisting my mouth and sighing. After Mom plunked down on the sofa, I switched on the TV. The theme song to *The Match Game* crackled from the set.

"Turn that off, Joni. I want to talk." Mom tipped her head and stared at me. A blush rose up my neck and my cheeks flamed as I waited for the fight. "I just don't understand why you won't go to the Homecoming dance. If you wore nice clothes instead of those dirty dungarees and old T-shirts, you'd have more friends. Boys like girls to dress cute."

That pissed me off. I was sick of hearing how my refusal to put my hair in rollers at night and the way I dressed sabotaged my chances for prep school love. *Leave me alone,* I wanted to scream. Instead, I tapped my knees with my middle fingers — my secret signal.

"Mom, no one wants to go to Homecoming with me. And you know what? I don't want to go anyway. It's all stupid rich girls in expensive dresses playing grown up. Who needs it?"

"Why do you have such a chip on your shoulder? The girls at your school couldn't be nicer." Mom knit her eyebrows and examined my face. Then she started again. "I don't like to ask you this, but I feel it's my duty. Are you on drugs? I can't help but wonder if that's why you're so disagreeable all the time. Just the other night, Harry Reasoner did a report on those hippy kids who get hooked on drugs. We sent you to Redwood Academy at great expense to protect you from the drugs and sex that goes on in public schools. But the way you act, I don't know if anything can save you. I don't know what the world's coming to."

"I'm not on drugs," I shrieked and stormed out of the living room. From the bottom of the staircase I added in my most sarcastic voice, "The only thing you're right about is nothing you do can save me."

Before I took the first step up, my father stomped after me, his blue eyes red-rimmed and angry.

"You don't know anything, Joni. It's too bad you're not a boy. At least then we could send you to a military school where you'd learn respect and motivation, things you seem to have forgotten. I don't want to hear you speak to your mother in that tone of voice ever again."

His splotchy face and bulging veins scared me. I thought he might have a stroke. Four pumpkin seeds stuck to his tie. After he shook out a cigarette and put it between his lips, his hand shook so much he couldn't tear a match out of the pack. I leaned over, took the matches, struck one, and lit the cigarette for him.

With the giant pumpkin clutched against his chest, Tommy staggered into the hallway. He glanced at me with a sheepish look then said, "I respect you, Dad. Can we light the pumpkin now?"

Dad patted Tommy's head and blew a puff of smoke from the side of his mouth.

"Joni's got the matches."

I helped Tommy carry the pumpkin — carved with triangles for the nose and eyes and three teeth in a crooked mouth — outside. He held the candle while I lit it, but I dropped it inside the pumpkin so he wouldn't get burned. As the candlelight flickered across Tommy's soft, little-boy face, I wanted to cry.

As soon as we came inside, Mom sighed and returned to the kitchen, leaving behind the smell of Jean Naté. Soon, ice cubes jangled against glass, ginger ale fizzed, and the whiskey bottle clunked on the countertop.

In silence, I joined my father in the living room where the TV sports reporter announced that the Detroit Tigers beat the St. Louis Cardinals to win the 1968 World Series in seven games.

Our first swim meet was against Cabrini High, which everyone said is in the ghetto. While the other swimmers hurried to get on the bus and claim their seats, I was last to board. Preppy seniors sprawled across the front seats, eating English muffins spread with peanut butter. My classmates, the junior girls, ignored me as I slugged past with my swim bag swaying from my shoulder. The next rows were filled with sophomores and the two freshman swimmers sat behind them. I swerved past five or six empty rows and, as the bus got underway, spilled onto the rear bench.

I made myself a seat among twenty bulging swim bags. Alone and forgotten, I observed the girls and listened without worrying about being accused of eavesdropping —

My father says the YWCA pool is a health hazard, coach told him girls who didn't come today were off the team.

Everyone gets to swim today.

Black girls can't swim.

Poor people come in from the street to use the toilets and showers.

Guard your stuff...

Up front, the senior girls slept with their heads on each other's shoulders. The juniors swayed and bobbed while they sang *Love Child* by the Supremes. That made me laugh — a bus full of preppy white girls singing about being raised by an unwed mother in a slum.

As the bus bumped over rutted streets, I stared out at shabby men with blankets draped over their shoulders. They sat on stoops outside boarded-up stores and begged cigarettes from shabby passersby. The tarry city smell oozed through a crack in the nearest window. At a red light, I studied four black teenage boys with knit caps pulled over their foreheads and ears. One of them saw me, elbowed the others, and grabbed his crotch. When I ducked out of their sight into the swim bags, the zipper across the top of the nearest bag spread open. Cradled in a towel, gold thread shimmered on a red coin purse. I checked up the aisle. Everyone faced forward, oblivious to invisible me.

Judge, you probably won't like this, but in a flash I reached in and grabbed the purse. I know it was wrong, but back then I felt like those girls stole everything I cared about. *Why shouldn't I take something for myself?*

Coins bulged against the soft silk brocade. I ran my fingers over an embroidered dragon and snapped open the triangle flap. Inside, a tightly folded clump of dollars was jammed between quarters and dimes. I figured I'd take a couple quarters for the candy machine — no one would miss fifty cents. But when I poked into the purse, something at the bottom crinkled. I burrowed through the money until my fingers touched paper. I checked the aisle again, then as quietly as I could I shook most of the coins into my lap and jiggled out two rolled cigarettes. I couldn't believe it. One of the goody-goody girls had marijuana in her coin purse. Even though I'd never seen joints before, I knew what they were. Right then I decided to keep the purse, the money, and the dope.

Sometimes at school I overheard girls talking about getting high. In the summer, the older lifeguards told stories about smoking dope and getting the munchies. And now, I could try for myself. I pulled off my denim Keds and shoved the purse into the toe of one sneaker with my socks jammed in behind it. I zippered that girl's swim bag shut and buried it under the others. After I slipped into my flip-flops, I scanned the aisle, grabbed my own bag, and moved to an empty seat a couple rows up.

When the bus lurched to a stop in front of the YWCA — an old stone building with cracked steps and an arched entrance — the coach stood and faced us. "Listen up. We're visitors here. I expect you to represent Redwood Academy as ambassadors of good sportsmanship. The Cabrini girls don't have the advantages you girls have, but they work hard and are proud of their team. Let's go win this meet like ladies."

In the lobby, black mothers sat on worn vinyl chairs. Their talk and laughter stopped when we filed in. Little black girls played patty-cake on the floor while black boys slid across the linoleum in their socks. As we waited for the coach to check in and lead us to the locker room, one little girl stared at me. Her eyes were huge and round, magnified by thick, square glasses. Braids stuck straight out the sides of her head. Even though it was pretty cold outside, her patterned T-shirt was short-sleeved and her pants were threadbare. She glanced at my feet in flip-flops and then at her own feet where a big toe poked through a scuffed saddle shoe. Dingy laces, knotted together, kept the shoes on her feet.

After our team headed down the steps to the locker room, I felt eyes on me and looked back. The girl leaned on her elbows against the steel railing with one leg swinging over the edge. When I waved, she backed up and disappeared.

The locker room smelled of mildew and sweaty socks. A row of dented, copper-colored lockers divided the space in two. Around the corner in the open showers, faucets dripped onto cracked tiles. Doors to two of three toilets had been pried off. Their metal hinges looked dangerous, ready to slash your arm if you weren't careful. On our side, Redwood swimmers made faces and whispered, *Gross*, while we pulled off our sweats and wiggled into our team Speedos — navy blue with white stripes down the sides.

A Cabrini girl stuck her head around the lockers but jerked it back when she caught my eye.

"They suits all matching," I heard her say.

The Redwood girls snorted, scooted into their flip-flops and wrapped RA-embroidered towels around their waists.

"Let's go. Bring your bags," Monica, our team captain, ordered.

I didn't like Monica. She was bossy and annoying. But we followed her to the pool and dropped our bags across the rickety bleachers.

When the Cabrini swimmers came onto the deck, we stepped back to give them room to pass. Their bathing suits were ones you'd wear to the beach. Most of them wore blue or green suits, but one girl wore a bright, purple-flowered bikini.

"They think we gonna steal they sorry stuff," a Cabrini girl said.

When the Redwood girls rolled their eyes, Coach folded her arms across her white polo shirt and glared. The smell of chlorine and the humid heat of the pool area were suffocating and I sat down, dizzy, on a bleacher bench.

"Let's go. Warm ups," Coach called, clapping her hands. "No lolly-gagging."

With my team, I lined up at one of three lanes assigned to us. At the whistle, I dove into the tepid water and swam laps — freestyle, breaststroke, backstroke, butterfly. When I pulled myself out, an oily film coated my skin. As I walked to the bleachers, a movement caught my eye.

Pressed against the tile wall, the little girl from the lobby watched us.

She'd pushed her glasses to the crown of her head. When I passed her to grab my towel, I asked, "Can you swim?"

"Nobody teach me. Weather be hot in here." She ran the back of her hand across her forehead.

I rotated my arms in freestyle stroke. "Move your arms like a windmill."

The girl looked down, scrunching her chin to her chest and whispered, "I ain't know how."

Our coach's whistle echoed in a short, shrill burst.

"I gotta go," I said and nodded toward the deck.

For the 100-meter backstroke, my best event, I jumped in my lane, grabbed the edge, and planted my feet against the wall. By then, the Cabrini swimmers had scored 46 points to our 104. Coach only filled one or two lanes for each event so the Cabrini swimmers would score if they didn't disqualify. As I waited for the start, I saw the little girl up in the stands, inching toward our bags.

Ka-bam. I pitched back, drove my head under water, kicked to the surface, and watched the puff of starter pistol fade away. My arms felt sluggish, like stroking through Jell-O, but when I lunged to touch the wall at the finish, the other swimmers had more than half a lap to go. Chatter and noise reverberated against the walls of the sticky pool area, a clatter that grew louder after I shook water from my ears.

At first, I thought the noise was applause for my win, but when I followed the sound, I saw Monica's hands on the little girl's shoulders, shaking her. The girl hugged my denim sneakers to her chest. I shot across the deck to the bleachers and made a plan. If the dragon purse dropped out of my shoe, I'd look surprised and let everyone think the girl stole it. But when I saw how scared she looked, I felt bad.

"Leave the kid alone," I called. "You're hurting her."

"I caught her stealing from our bags. Right in front of me," Monica snapped.

I made my voice sarcastic. "What did she steal?"

The girl's glasses dangled from one ear and tears trickled down her cheeks.

"I ain't take nothing, just lookin." She pushed the sneakers at me. "Don't need no honky shit."

"You take anything else?" I asked.

"I ain't take nothin.'"

With sweat beading on her forehead, our coach marched over.

"What's the problem?"

"This kid's been digging through our bags," Monica said in a nasty voice.

"She didn't take anything. Monica shouldn't pick on a little girl," I told the coach, surprising myself.

The Cabrini swimmers came over and formed a circle around us. "Can I help?" their coach asked.

"There's no problem," I whispered, shaking a little. I turned to the girl. "Is there?"

"Only wid that bitch."

The child tipped her head at Monica, who glared at her and me.

"I'll walk her upstairs to her mom." I put my hand on her back and led her to a bench to wait while I pulled on my sweats and grabbed my swim bag. Then I took the little girl's hand. When we entered the stairwell, I sat on a cement step and motioned her to sit beside me.

"I'm Joni. What's your name?"

She looked down when she answered, "Ruby."

I held out the sneakers. "You want these?"

"For Mama. They's too big for me."

"Let me get my socks out and you can have them."

My fingers shook when I pulled out the socks and the dragon purse. I tried to look nonchalant as I jammed them in my sweatshirt pocket.

"Why you give me them?" Ruby's eyes were huge behind her lenses.

"Because I like your hair."

I touched one of her braids. It felt tight and firm, so different in texture from my droopy hair.

"Your hair all yella, like wet corn flakes."

"Thanks," I said.

She was cute and I liked when she called Monica a bitch.

"You want a candy bar from the machine? You like Bit-O-Honey?"

"I like Cheese Nabs too," Ruby said, "and root beer."

When the bus pulled away from the YWCA, I watched out the window for Ruby and her mother but didn't see them among the people on the street. I tapped my pocket to make sure the dragon purse was still there, and my heart beat so loud I was sure the other girls could hear it.

At home, I tucked the purse under my mattress and wondered if anyone saw me take it. But I knew no one would report it missing.

On Election Day — Richard Nixon versus Hubert Humphrey — my father
insisted I get to Wawa as soon as possible after swim practice so he'd be
home in time to vote. With wrinkled fingers and damp hair, I sat on the
parking lot curb. As the sun went down, I shivered. To warm my hands,
I cradled the hot chocolate I bought inside. Steam rose from the white
cardboard cup and I leaned over to inhale the rich smell. But when I
sipped it liquid lava spilled down my throat. While I choked and coughed,
a woman hustled two children into the store, steering them away from my
chocolate snot and drool. Other customers glanced my way as I wiped my
nose on my sleeve. Losers don't care what people think about stuff like
that.

 After a few minutes, the people who witnessed my chocolate snot
returned to their cars and drove away. Drops of chocolate speckled my
jacket like blood. I peered down the road, willing my father's Ford to
appear. My stomach growled. I ripped a doughy soft pretzel into pieces and
as I ate one loop and then the other, flakes of salt stung my tongue. I saved
the knot for last. Each time I sipped hot chocolate, I relished the taste of
sweet and salty mixed together. It was an ordinary day but I didn't know it
then. Nothing in my life has been ordinary since.

 As I sat on the curb breaking a piece off the pretzel knot, I was totally
unaware of the car that swerved into the parking lot until I heard brakes
squeal and saw the bumper lurch at me. I scooted back and remembered
a dead raccoon I'd seen along the road, crows pecking at its guts. By the
time the VW door creaked open and dirty work boots scraped across the
pavement and stopped beside me, I was pissed but too scared to yell, *What
the hell?*

 "Sorry, I didn't see you sitting here," the guy said. "I didn't hurt you,
did I?"

 "No, but almost," I answered, staring at rumpled wool socks. He
smelled gross, like grease and burned rubber.

 "You want something? I'll get you a pie," he offered, as if that would
fix everything.

 When he went inside, I stood up and studied him through the plate-
glass window. At the cashier, he dug through his pockets and dropped a

couple crumpled bills on the counter. His hair, brown and stringy, hung below his collar. He was skinny, not much taller than me, and wearing a torn grey sweatshirt and oil-smeared jeans held up with a braided rope — a hippy. As soon as he came out, he handed me a lemon pie.

"You need a ride somewhere?"

"My dad's coming," I said. "He'll be here any minute. He wants to get to the fire station in time to vote." My teeth chattered and I shivered.

"Tricky Dick or Hubie — man, what a choice. Bummer it can't be Bobby Kennedy, you know? You want to wait in the car? You look cold."

His voice was quiet and I thought it was pretty nice after all to give me the pie. For a second, I thought about how I shouldn't get in a car with a stranger, but something about him was familiar. And I was cold. And his VW was parked right in front of Wawa. If he tried anything, I figured I could jump out. There were lots of people going in and out of the store.

Inside, the car smelled like old smoke and rotten bananas. Stuffing puffed out from tears in the upholstery. I glanced over and noticed rips in the guy's jeans at the knees and crotch. When he turned to face me, I pretended to look out the window.

"My name's Ishmael," he said while he slid back his seat.

"Joni."

I felt shy and ran my tongue over my front teeth, testing for pretzel crumbs.

"I've seen you here before." Ishmael's eyes seemed to take me in. "You always look sad and nervous."

I raised my head, surprised the guy noticed me. I guess I actually was sad and nervous, but I never realized it showed.

"I'm just tired after swim practice," I said. "I wait for my dad here."

Ishmael ate his pie in two bites and licked his fingers.

"I swam when I was a kid — summer league for Meadows Country Club. I even swam at Montgomery High my first year. Then it got too wet."

As soon as he said Meadows Country Club, I stared.

"I swim at Meadows. I don't remember anyone named Ishmael."

"I was Michael Reid back then."

He lit a cigarette and gave it to me, then lit another and dangled it from his lips.

"Michael Reid? When I was a little kid, you carried me on your shoulders at swim meets. I'm Joni Byrnes."

The slimy yellow pie filling felt good going down my throat. I swallowed the last piece.

"Little Joni Byrnes all grown up." Ishmael's eyes crinkled when he smiled.

Next to us, a horn blasted. My father, frowning, rolled down his window. Ishmael's door stuck and creaked when I pushed it and squeezed out. As soon as I hopped into the Ford, my father glared at me, his eyebrows raised.

"It's okay, Dad. That's Michael Reid from Meadows swim team."

He cleared his throat. "I heard he's back from boot camp."

At school the next day, an announcement came over the PA system: *Attention Girls. Richard Millhouse Nixon has won the election for President of the United States.*

Good old Tricky Dick.

From then on, every day after swim practice I rushed to Wawa, hoping to see Ishmael. And each afternoon, close to 5:00 p.m., the rusty red VW pulled into the lot. Then Ishmael bought two lemon pies and I waited in his car. We listened to the radio — *I am a Child* and *Bluebird* by Buffalo Springfield. He turned up the volume for *Aquarius* from the Broadway show *Hair.*

"I went up to New York to see *Hair* in August," Ishmael told me. "They get it, you know? They get it about the Goddamned war."

"Yeah," I agreed, nodding and serious.

But I didn't get it, not really. All I knew about *Hair* was the songs. And sure, the TV news always reported on Vietnam, but I didn't know much about it — just that the war upset and confused me.

After I met Ishmael and listened to him talk about it, I tried to pay more attention. One night, when my father and I watched the news, reporters showed film of US Marines after they won the city of Hue. First they lowered the enemy flag, then they raised the Stars and Stripes. My father liked that a lot. But other nights we watched reports that showed women, kids, and old people getting killed. Every time news about civilian deaths came on, my father said something like — *If they weren't killing Americans, we wouldn't be killing them.* But it was their country, right?

In the VW, when the words, *Let the sun shine in* faded, Ishmael clicked off the radio. He turned to me, all excited.

"Hey, let's take the train to New York someday. Lots of kids hang out in the city, listening to music, grooving, you know? We'll get tickets to

Hair and buy a huge sandwich at one of the delis."

"I'll be sixteen in February, maybe then."

I couldn't hide the thrill in my voice. *New York!*

"Sweet sixteen," Ishmael said, "and never been kissed."

He leaned toward me. When his lips touched mine, I got such a rush. A minute later, my Dad parked in the spot next to us. Ishmael folded his arms across his chest while I shoved open the VW door. As soon as I tossed in my bags and squirmed into the passenger seat, Dad gave me a funny look. In the visor mirror, I saw my red and blotchy cheeks.

"Gross," I said, "the chlorine's drying out my face."

"Ask your mother for cold cream," Dad said as he flicked a cigarette stub out the window.

Later that night I could hardly sleep. I mean, when Billy Jensen kissed me, it was okay. But when Ishmael kissed me, it meant something.

During those minutes in his car each afternoon, I felt grown up. Ishmael talked to me about the war, politics, books. He wanted to know what I thought, like my opinion mattered. No one else cared what I thought — not girls at school, not the teachers, and definitely not my parents.

A couple days after he kissed me, Ishmael showed up at Wawa wearing clean jeans and a green wool sweater. He'd shaved and slicked back his hair so you couldn't tell how long it was. When the Ford pulled in, Ishmael got out of his VW and shook hands with my father.

"Nice to see you again, Mr. Byrnes."

"I heard you enlisted, Michael, but you're home now," Dad said in his man-to-man voice.

"I did enlist, but I got sick in basic training down at Fort Jackson and had to come home." Ishmael shrugged and looked away.

"What happened?" Dad asked. He offered Ishmael a cigarette.

"No thanks, Mr. Byrnes. I'm not supposed to smoke. I got sent home because of asthma."

"Well, son, I'm sorry. At least you tried to do your duty, not like these kids who burn their draft cards and run to Canada."

My father shook his head with a sorrowful look.

"It was a big disappointment," Ishmael said. He paused a moment then said, "Mr. Byrnes, I was wondering, since Joni's always here when I come for a soda after work, why don't I drive her home? It's on my way and I could save you a trip." He sounded so polite. A mothball smell wafted from his sweater.

Dad cleared his throat and looked at the sky. He spat against a tire and kept his eyes on me while he answered. "We can't leave her stranded if you don't show up one day."

"I won't leave her stranded," Ishmael promised.

"Well, Joni. This young man has good values and shows responsibility. That's nice of you, Michael. As long as it's not putting you out," Dad released a long stream of cigarette smoke.

"I'm happy to help," Ishmael said. "I can start today."

While my father backed out of the lot, Ishmael leaned against the VW hood. As soon as the Ford was gone, Ishmael rolled his eyes and messed up his hair.

On those cold November days, in the time it took to hurry from practice to the convenience store, my wet hair dripped on my neck and gave me a chill. As soon as I got to Wawa, I ordered hot chocolate and lemon pies, then waited for Ishmael just inside the door. When his VW chugged into the lot, he parked along the side, where fewer people passed by.

I learned that after Ishmael's army discharge, he took classes at the community college but dropped out after one semester. His father made him take a job at the tire store.

"It's not like I needed a student deferment. Besides, college prolongs childhood. As long as you can read and write and know enough arithmetic to get by, why waste time in classrooms with a bunch of jocks and rah-rahs? People like us don't need that bullshit," Ishmael told me one afternoon. "We can figure out stuff for ourselves. Life is our teacher."

Everything Ishmael said made sense. At nineteen, he'd been through a lot and knew how bullshit the world was. Why sit in class listening to a boring teacher when you can read the same stuff yourself?

"People who go to college get caught in the rat race of more money, bigger houses, faster cars. Why do you think we're at war with Vietnam, a tiny island across the world? Who cares about that swamp? It's all a lie to force people into the slavery of capitalism, here and abroad."

When I thought about my parents and the girls at Redwood — what they cared about, what they talked about — I knew Ishmael was right. My parents fought about money every day. And at Redwood, all the popular girls talked in the same voice with the same expressions — *That is sooo cool! Like, sooo cool!* And I was the weirdo?

After I told Ishmael about the way the Redwood girls smirked and whispered, *Joni is sooo weird*, when I walked down the halls, he said, "Joni, you're fine the way you are. Those girls are a bunch of phonies. You're smart, you're cute, and they're jealous."

Whenever I was with Ishmael, I was happy. I loved to hear him talk about record albums and Herman Hesse novels. I laughed when he told stories about the tire store. In the cars, under seats or in the trunk, there'd be money, jewelry, cameras, sometimes even wallets, lost or forgotten, just waiting for him. I learned more from Ishmael than I did from any teacher.

November 27 - 29, 1968

The evening before Thanksgiving, Ishmael was waiting when I got to Wawa. As soon as I climbed in his car, he handed me a cup of hot chocolate and a pumpkin pie. While I warmed my hands, he pushed the driver's seat back and balanced his pie on his lap before he took the lid off his cup of coffee. It smelled good, sweet and creamy, different from the bitter stuff my father drank black. Ishmael sighed. He sipped the coffee, smacked his lips, then reached for his pie and ate half of it in one bite. When a glob of pumpkin filling spilled on his denim shirt he raised both hands — one holding the dripping piecrust, the other sloshing coffee — as if a cop had told him, *Hands up.*

"Shit!" Ishmael shouted, and I couldn't help laughing.

I started to wipe the pie filling with a napkin but instead I smeared it. The filling smelled sweet and cinnamony, and I leaned down and licked pumpkin off a button. Ishmael stuffed the rest of the pie in his mouth and balanced his cup on the dashboard.

After he swallowed, he pulled me close and kissed me. His tongue traced my lips and prodded until I opened my mouth. When he pushed in his tongue, I had trouble breathing. I knew it was French kissing because I'd heard girls talk about it. But it felt, I don't know, awkward, so I pulled away and wiped my mouth. I didn't know what it meant — to kiss like that. *Was I his girlfriend? Did it mean he liked me, really liked me?* When I glanced at him, I felt shy. I mean, Billy never kissed like that. I wondered what Ishmael thought, but I felt better when he smiled.

"Sweet fifteen and righteously kissed." He didn't take his eyes off me while he sipped his coffee. I still had the taste of it in my mouth. "Next time, we'll find a better place."

On the way home, when Ishmael pulled into the church parking lot instead of turning onto my street, I was afraid he wanted to make out right there. That would be too weird, at a church! But when he turned to me, he kept his hands on the wheel. His brown eyes were soft.

"What are your plans for Friday?"

"Nothing, really," I answered, trying to seem casual.

Outside the grey sky grew black and I worried my parents would yell at me for coming in late.

"You want to go downtown to the army-navy store and then to the movies? *Night of the Living Dead* is playing at the Midtown. I've been planning to see it. We could catch the early show." He sounded excited and that made me feel good.

"Sure." I hesitated, embarrassed. "I have to check with my parents."

Ishmael put on a sort of southern accent.

"I'll stop over tomorrow to ask their permission to start courting you. I'll say, Miss Betty and Mr. Fred, I would cherish the honor of escorting your daughter, Joan, to the Wanamaker's Christmas show, followed by lunch at Horn and Hardart and, finally, to the theatre where we'll enjoy the always proper songs of *The Sound of Music.* I promise to return your daughter, her honor intact, by 8:00 p.m. Whaddya say, Pops?"

I laughed my ass off. But the word courting looped through my mind. *Ishmael wanted to court me?* I hoped that meant he wanted me to be his girlfriend.

When he pulled up in front of my house, he waited until I went inside. From the window I watched him jerk the VW into a U-turn and head back down the road. I turned to find my mother, dabs of flour on her face and a spatula in her hand, right behind me. I flinched and my heart raced.

"Is that the Reid boy?" Mom asked. Her voice sounded suspicious. "I ran into his mother in the grocery store. She had no idea he's been giving you rides. But she was glad of it. She's been worried about him ever since the army sent him home."

"His mom doesn't need to worry about him. He's smart and nice." I paused. "He may stop by tomorrow so you can meet him again." I tried to keep my tone normal.

"That's nice." The smell of burning biscuits sent Mom back to the kitchen. "We're having soup for dinner tonight. Will you set the table?" she called.

Late Thanksgiving morning, the doorbell rang. With me two steps behind, Dad opened the door. I didn't recognize the boy on the porch until Dad stepped back so he could come in.

"Michael, nice to see you. Joni told us you might stop by."

I stared, too shocked to say a word. Young Michael Reid from the swim team stood in our foyer with a bunch of flowers in one hand. He was clean-shaven and he'd cut his hair back some. Even his fingernails were clipped, the tire store grime scrubbed away. When he walked past me and sat on the sofa, I smelled Old Spice, like my father used.

As soon as Mom came out from the kitchen, drying her hands on her apron, Ishmael stood up and handed her the flowers.

"Happy Thanksgiving, Mrs. Byrnes," he said, smiling and a little shy.

"Oh, Michael, how nice and unexpected. I met your mother the other day. I know she's relieved to have you home," Mom chirped like a schoolgirl. "Can I get you something to eat or drink?"

"I don't want to disturb your Thanksgiving, but I thought, since I've been driving Joni home every day, you'd probably feel better if I came by and re-introduced myself."

"That's certainly not necessary, young man, but I like your values," Dad said.

I thought he might hug Ishmael.

"At least have an eggnog," Mom offered. "It's Fred's specialty."

With the smell of turkey drifting from the kitchen, we all moved to the living room while Tommy spied on us around corners with a periscope he made from cardboard and Mom's compact mirrors. Since Ishmael sat on the sofa, I stood next to my mother's chair. I couldn't believe he went to so much trouble to look nice. He held the eggnog cup like he feared he'd drop it.

"Mrs. Byrnes, Mr. Byrnes, I've enjoyed getting to know Joni again these past few weeks. The other day, we were talking about how much we both love to go downtown each year to see Wanamaker's Christmas lights. In fact, I'm going downtown tomorrow, and I thought I'd ask if Joni wanted to come. I usually make a day of it — Wanamaker's, Horn and Hardart's, and a movie. We'd take the train, and I'd get her home by 8:00 p.m. But only if it's okay with you."

Mom glanced at Dad, then at me. Ishmael sipped his eggnog with his pinky finger out like some kind of doofus.

"I'll go," Tommy yelled.

He leapt into the room and crumpled on the floor like he'd been shot.

"Sure, Michael, it sounds like fun," Mom said, and Dad grunted his agreement.

"Great, thanks. Now, I better get going. I don't want to keep you from your family time," Ishmael said. He turned to me. "I'll see you in the morning."

As Ishmael hurried across the lawn to his car, Dad watched from the window.

"Michael certainly has good manners. You could learn a lot from that boy."

The next morning, when I skipped down the driveway to Ishmael's car, my mother called, "You're not going downtown looking like that, Joni, you need a coat."

I pretended not to hear her. The night before I spent an hour stitching flower patches on the legs of my jeans. Over a white turtleneck, I wore the virgin acrylic tennis sweater Mom brought home from Tesses Dresses in September. I liked the way I looked.

As soon as I yanked open the car door, Ishmael said, "Let's book it." As the VW jolted away, grinding from first gear into second, I stuck my arm out the window and waved to Mom, who watched from the doorway.

We parked at the train station and shoved our way through moms and kids and old people who jammed the platform. When the train doors opened, Ishmael grabbed my hand and pulled me sideways toward vacant seats in the middle of the car. Except for shorter hair, he looked like himself again — torn jeans, tie-dye T-shirt under his blue tire-store jacket, and his heavy black army boots. A light stubble covered his face. I leaned against him as the rail car swayed. Sitting with Ishmael on that train, I felt more special than I ever did at Redwood.

"I didn't recognize you yesterday. Where'd you get those preppy clothes?" I asked.

"They're clothes from high school. We had to dress up on swim meet days. They still fit. I'm a skinny guy." He leaned close and whispered, "I have a surprise for you for later."

At the I. Goldberg Army & Navy store, Ishmael dug through the bins and picked out wool gloves, socks, and a watch cap, plunking them on the counter while I looked around at all the stuff. Besides fifteen bucks I'd saved from babysitting for Lisa and Jake next door, I was shocked when Dad gave me twenty more.

After he paid for his stuff, Ishmael guided me to the stack of sailor dungarees. While I tried them on, Ishmael waited. I liked the wide legs and the way the pants buttoned in front.

When Ishmael called, "Joni, you still back there?" I came out with the dungarees draped over my arm.

With his shopping bag swinging on one arm, Ishmael showed me the long rack of coats and jackets.

"Look at these pea coats," he said. "They're really warm."

I tried on a few and when I found one that fit, Ishmael said, "You have to get it."

I didn't want to spend all my money, so I dropped the dungarees back on the table. While Ishmael looked at belts, I paid eighteen dollars for the coat. I told the man I didn't need a bag and wore the pea coat out of the store.

Outside it was cloudy but not too cold. We walked along Market Street on the way to see the Christmas display. Ishmael stopped outside a drab little building and leaned against the concrete wall. The storefront smelled like piss and sour wine. He tapped out a cigarette and lit it. After he exhaled a stream of smoke, he handed me his I. Goldberg bag.

"You want me to carry it?" I asked. I was surprised how heavy it was.

"Open it."

I hunched my shoulders and opened the bag. The sailor dungarees, folded in four, were inside, along with three watch caps, two pairs of gloves, a tan web belt with a brass buckle, and a couple pairs of socks. A flush rose up my neck.

"You got me the dungarees?" My voice was shaky but I couldn't stop smiling. "I didn't see you buy them."

Ishmael put his hand around my waist, pulled me close, and breathed his smoke into my mouth. I didn't know what he was doing. I coughed and stepped back.

"I got the army discount," he said with a smug smile.

I wasn't exactly sure what he meant. I didn't want to believe he stole the stuff, but the way he said *discount* sounded dangerous and thrilling.

We only stayed at Wanamaker's for ten minutes. Then we bought soft pretzels from a street cart and a bag of roasted chestnuts from a bum. By then it was almost noon and I was starving. Men in grey coats and dark felt hats hurried along the sidewalk. Women in bright coats lugged huge shopping bags while ordering their kids to hold hands. College girls with long hair and Weejun loafers tossed wool scarves around their necks and walked along the curb like a tightrope to avoid kids in drab army jackets and dirty jeans.

When Ishmael saw a guy with a thick mustache and long sideburns leaning on the side of a newsstand, he left me smack in the middle of the sidewalk.

"Gimme a lid," I heard Ishmael say.

After they shook hands, the guy glanced down at the folded bill Ishmael gave him. Then the guy pulled something from inside his coat. He and Ishmael nodded and shook hands again.

What was that about? I wondered. After Ishmael waved for me to catch up with him, I asked, "Do you know that guy?"

"I know everything I need to know about him." Ishmael said. He took my hand and pulled me toward the movie theatre. "We're in time for the matinee. You'll love *Night of the Living Dead.* You got enough for our tickets?"

I didn't spend all my money at I. Goldberg, and besides, Ishmael got me the dungarees, so I didn't mind paying for two tickets, two cokes, and a bucket of greasy popcorn. Almost as soon as we stepped into the theatre the lights dimmed and ads came on for soda and popcorn and hot dogs. Hardly any seats were taken.

Ishmael put his hand on my shoulder to guide me to seats along the wall in the back. Just as *Night of the Living Dead* appeared on the screen, Ishmael squirmed and leaned forward. I smelled chocolate. He pulled a napkin-wrapped chunk out of his pocket, unfolded it, and showed me a piece of chocolate-cake looking stuff. It sure didn't look like anything my mother made.

"Brownies," he whispered. "Yesterday when my parents went to my grandmother's, I told them I was sick. As soon as they pulled out of the driveway, I baked these special brownies. Go ahead, try one."

I took a bite while he watched. It tasted gritty and burned. I didn't really like it but I didn't want to hurt his feelings, so I swallowed and took another bite, wondering how to ditch the rest of it.

"Good," I mumbled.

The brownie clumped in my mouth like sand. I crumbled the last bit between my fingers and when Ishmael reached for his coke, let the scraps slide down the side of my seat. Then I took a big swig of coke to force down the lump in my mouth. I almost gagged but held it in.

On screen, a brother and sister put flowers on their father's grave. Soon, zombies attacked them, and then zombies were everywhere, killing and devouring whoever they caught. Either from the gritty brownie or the gross stuff on the screen, I got really nauseated and rested my head on the seat back. Then the seats began to spin, and I felt myself get sucked into the movie screen. A gang of zombies saw me. They chased after me with stumbling steps. I had to get away. I scooted myself back but my seat trapped me. When a zombie's hand reached out and grabbed the girl on the screen, its fingers wrapped around my wrist. I screamed, "NO!" and tried to pull away, but it wouldn't let go.

"Hey, hey, hey," Ishmael whispered.

His hand was on my wrist, keeping me in my seat. He leaned close and, with his other hand, turned my face so we looked in each other's eyes. "It's okay, it's just a movie. I'm here. I won't let anything happen to my best girl."

He kissed me then, his tongue on my lips, his hand moving up and down my thigh. I tasted brownie in his mouth. I felt confused, like I was floating, but I couldn't remember where I was.

Someone tapped Ishmael on the shoulder and in a loud whisper said, "Keep it in your pants, man."

Ishmael stopped kissing me and pitched back in his chair. He reached for the bucket of popcorn and stuffed a handful in his mouth. I looked all around the theatre, still dazed. On the screen, a handsome black guy and a white girl, Barbara, escaped the zombies by breaking into a house. Barbara acted like a terrified idiot while the black guy broke up furniture and nailed the wood against doors and windows to keep out zombies. I tried really hard to figure out what was going on. At some point, the black guy found a gun. Then two white guys and two white girls came up from hiding in the basement. The black guy told them, *I'm in charge up here.* He was the only one with a plan so that was okay with them.

By the end of the movie, sheriffs and deputies finally killed all the zombies. Inside the house, everyone got killed except the black guy. When he heard the sheriff's men coming, he thought they were zombies, so he aimed his rifle out the window. But they thought he was a zombie too, so they killed him. All his planning to protect the others and save himself turned out to be worth nothing. I was glad when the movie was over. Outside the theatre, even through the clouds, I had to shut my eyes from the light.

"Did you like the brownies?" Ishmael asked as we walked to the train station.

"They were fine."

But I didn't like them at all. The gritty taste stayed in my mouth.

"They were very fine — magic brownies, baked with love and THC," he said. "You were flying high, little Joni."

I didn't know what to say. I still felt shaky and kind of sick to my stomach. Ishmael knew I wanted to try pot some time, but I almost freaked out during that movie. He should have warned me. He seemed to think it was funny, but I was embarrassed and put out. Still, if I made a big fuss about it, I was afraid he'd think I was a baby and might not like me anymore. But then, as we climbed the steps to the train station, Ishmael put his arm around my shoulders.

"I made those brownies special for you, Joni. I wanted your first time to be with me," he said, looking proud.

That sounded so nice, I couldn't be upset anymore. I thought about our afternoons in his car talking about music, magic, and books. He loved Herman Hesse's novels — *Siddhartha, Demien,* and *Narcissus* and *Goldmund.* But *Steppenwolf* was his favorite. Ishmael considered himself like *Steppenwolf* — a middle class guy who rejects his family's comforts and instead lives the way he wants, like a lone wolf. I pretty much felt that way too. And the lone wolf made those brownies special for me.

A few minutes later, while Ishmael and I waited on a bench for our train, I noticed three girls from Redwood staring at us. I smirked and took Ishmael's hand. For the first time, I wasn't ashamed or intimidated by girls from Redwood Academy. *Hippies don't give a crap about what other people think.* I rubbed my cheek with my middle finger in the secret up-yours sign.

As if he knew what I was thinking, Ishmael slowly leaned over and kissed me.

"You're my best girl," he said.

His best girl. Not a loser. Not a weirdo. Someone special. That's all I ever wanted. I glanced up to see if the Redwood girls were watching.

December 1968

The Monday after Thanksgiving, Ishmael gave me a dragon cigarette
lighter he found under the spare tire in a Japanese man's car. It weighed
heavy in my hand. The dragon's pointed ears, mane, scales, claws, and tail
were etched in silver, with red jewels for eyes. When I struck my thumb
against the back of the dragon's head, a flame shot out its mouth.

"It's the best gift ever," I said.

"Why don't we go to my place to try it?" Ishmael's eyes sparkled.

For a moment, I hesitated. But Ishmael was my best friend — my only
friend. Even after the pot brownie, I trusted him. I was his best girl.

On the ride to his place that day, I trembled inside because I didn't
know what to expect. In about fifteen minutes, he turned into the driveway
of a stone mansion and parked his car around back.

"You live here?" I asked, astounded at the size of his home.

"Not in the house, not anymore," he said.

He opened the garage door.

"This is my place. My dad and I fixed it up after I got back from boot
camp. I got everything I need."

On the left, he pointed out the small bathroom with a tiny shower
stall. To the right, a battered washer and dryer sat next to an old
refrigerator. The creaky stairs led up to a big, open room. Clothes, towels,
and musty smelling blankets hung from the rafters. Unframed canvas
paintings of witches and ghouls and dragons decorated the walls. A
mattress with balled up sheets lay flat on the floor. Books were stacked on
shelves made from slats of wood balanced on cinder blocks. His record-
player sat on top of one of the shelves. The room smelled of gasoline,
mildew, and smoke. I felt at home there.

To get to the red beanbag chair next to his bed, I kicked clothes out
of the way. Ishmael sprawled on his mattress facing me. I leaned back and
breathed his sharp odor, like a bicycle tire in summer. When he reached
under a pillow to retrieve a flat pack of cigarette papers and a baggie of
weed, my heart raced. *This time,* I told myself, *I won't freak out.*

Ishmael took two papers, made them into a double triangle, and
sprinkled marijuana on top. His long fingers rolled the papers tight.
I remember thinking the pot looked like the dried leaves we used to

crumple in our hands after our fathers raked them into piles. After he licked the edges and sealed the paper, he glanced up with soft brown eyes and handed me the joint.

"It might take a couple tries to light it. Then just breathe in deep and hold it as long as you can."

I was ready. I knew what was coming and I wanted to try. I pressed my lips on the joint, dug the lighter from my pocket, and stroked the dragon until its breath sparked and glowed. After I took a drag, I tried to hold it but choked and coughed out all the smoke. It was way stronger than the menthol cigarettes I was used to. Ishmael grinned, took the joint, inhaled, and handed it back to me. For my second toke, I inhaled less smoke but held it longer.

God, I couldn't remember ever feeling so calm. Ishmael watched me and laughed. Then I laughed, *loud and long and clear*, like the song from Mary Poppins. I imagined Ishmael and me floating to the garage ceiling and spinning upside-down.

When the joint burned down to a tiny stub, Ishmael pinched it out and put the last bits on his tongue. Then he rolled off his mattress and ran his finger across his albums. He chose one, slid out the record, held it by the edges, and placed it on the spindle. Everything moved in slow motion. The record dropped and the needle swung into place. Ishmael flicked the album cover to me. *Grateful Dead* arched through a blue banner. Jerry Garcia — in an Uncle Sam top hat — smiled from behind a scaly monster while a ball of fire erupted.

Ishmael offered his hand, pulled me up, put both hands on my hips, and held me close. As music filled the room, I swayed back and forth, holding tight to keep from floating. I tasted his lips, felt pressure from his tool and knew at last someone cared about me. The needle moved to the next track — *Good Morning Little School Girl*. Ishmael sang in my ear, *I just can't help myself.*

"When I listen to this, I think of you," he whispered.

The following Sunday, Ishmael and I decided to meet at the park after my family got back from church. Even though it was freezing outside, I couldn't wait to see him. During Mass, I jiggled my legs and stared at a stained-glass Jesus, crystal blood dotting his chest, silicon thorns piercing his brow. It made me think of a newspaper photo I saw back in the spring — an American soldier with his arms raised to the sky and wounded soldiers all around him. I was glad Ishmael didn't go to Vietnam. When the priest turned to read the Gospel, I forgot to stand and my father elbowed me. The smell of incense drifted from the altar.

As soon as we got back home, I grabbed a jelly donut from the box Dad bought at the bakery. I checked the kitchen clock and before I headed to my bedroom to change, muttered something about meeting friends. I changed into old jeans and a turtleneck and slid my bare feet into loafers. On the way out the door, I swung my arm into the bulky pea coat and buttoned it while I ran down the sidewalk.

Near the playground, dead brown leaves crunched under my feet. The ground was hard and cold. For a moment, I stopped to study a sickly-looking white tree. Its branches were all twisted and bony, like an old man's fingers. Years ago, my father told me it was a sycamore. I always remembered its name because it looked sick.

On the metal bench at the playground gate, someone sat hunched over, completely covered with a dirt brown blanket. I wondered if it was Ishmael or a wino — or even a zombie.

"Ishmael?" I called quietly, ready to run if it wasn't him.

After he stirred and uncovered his face, I was so relieved to see him. I hurried over and sat with him.

"You look like a bum, all wrapped up like that. I couldn't tell it was you."

"I got a cold," he said.

I held his freezing, clawed hands in my mittened ones and peeked over his shoulder at the playground. The metal swings and monkey bars made grey streaks against the dreary sky, and the air smelled like cold ashes.

"It's too cold to sit here. Let's go on the swings," I said.

When I pushed against it, the metal gate screeched against the concrete sidewalk. Ishmael came up behind me and added his weight. Together we shoved it open.

With no one there except Ishmael and me, the monkey bars, seesaws, and swings seemed lost and forgotten. In the colorless sky, the sun cast a dull glow, like a flashlight shining through a pillow. Ishmael rubbed his runny nose with his blanket.

When I sat on a swing, a cold, clammy puddle soaked my butt. I grabbed the creaky chains, leaned back, and lifted my feet, rocking back and forth to get moving. As I gained momentum, I felt Ishmael's hands on my back, pushing me higher. Soon the chain screeched like a blue jay. Cold air stung my face. At the top of the upswing, I let go. My mind tangled like the branches of the sycamore. As if I were diving into the pool at the start of a race, I lowered my head, extended my arms, and straightened my legs. When I landed, my hands and face scraped the gravelly ground.

"Oh, God! Joni, you okay?"

Next to my ear, Ishmael's strained voice was soft. His breath smelled foul and sulfury. I got to my hands and knees. Blood from my nose dripped onto the ground, freezing in sticky globs. My palms and thighs stung, but my mittens and jeans saved my skin. Ishmael took my wrist and led me to the bench, where he knelt facing me as he dabbed my bloody face with his dirty army blanket. He was crying.

"I can't stand the sight of blood," he whispered.

"I'm okay. It was dumb."

I leaned to the side so the blood dripped away from my coat.

"I'll take you home." Ishmael's face was green, and he stared at the ground. "I hate this."

I pinched the bridge of my nose like my mother taught me.

"It's not bleeding much now. Let's get hot chocolate at Woolworth's," I suggested, confused and worried about the way Ishmael was acting.

On the drive, Ishmael clung to the steering wheel and looked straight ahead. His shoulders shook. The VW's heater groaned and dust that smelled like burned asphalt puffed from the vents. I coughed and wondered what I'd done to make him so upset. A rim of blood crusted the edge of my nostrils.

Ishmael fooled with the radio. A voice shrieked through the speakers until he turned down the volume. I'd heard the song before but hadn't listened to it closely. With the volume low, a soprano voice rose — singing a mother's sad questions and her son's disturbing responses, while the refrain warned, *It's hard.*

"That's Joan Baez," Ishmael said. I could tell he had calmed down. "Bob Dylan wrote the song, *A Hard Rain's Gonna Fall.* He gets it, you know? Like, how tough it is out there, no matter how much bad stuff you go through, you still got to go on." Ishmael glanced my way. "I'm sorry you fell off the swing. I feel bad for pushing you too hard."

"No, Ishmael, I jumped off." I touched his hand. "I wanted to fly."

"There's better ways to fly," he said in a low voice.

He smiled. I smiled too. I knew what he meant.

While we waited at the Woolworth's counter, the waitress served a neatly dressed man and little boy who arrived after we did. We moved to stools next to them and when the waitress asked if they needed anything else, I blurted out, "Two hot chocolates and one order of fries."

Soon, the waitress reappeared and plunked down our order. She smiled as the man paid and left with his son, then glared at us with her nose crinkled like we smelled bad. When she turned away, Ishmael cocked his head, crossed his eyes, and stuck out his tongue. I almost choked on a French fry.

We dipped our fries into the watery ketchup and stirred our hot chocolates until the marshmallows melted into soft, white globs. After we finished, flushed with warmth, I left a stack of dragon purse quarters on the counter. We strolled through the store, passing aisles of combs and hair spray, sewing supplies, crappy jewelry, and ceramic horses.

We were sorting through flannel shirts, checking out the different colors and plaids, when a family entered. Four boys, who looked like they ranged from four to ten-years-old, ran up and down the aisles, picked up toys, slid across the linoleum, and drew the attention of their parents and the single cashier.

Judge, I never expected what happened next. I don't know why I went along with Ishmael. But I don't know why I did most of the things I did back then.

"Joni, quick!" Ishmael whispered, tugging my sleeve.

When he leaned in to hug me, he shoved a couple flannel shirts into my coat, then took my elbow and steered me to the shoe section in the back, where the smell of cheap rubber vied with the fake buttery fumes from the popcorn machine. Ishmael's eyes darted back and forth, scanning the store to make sure no one saw us.

He dug through a pile of sneakers until he found black high tops his size while I grabbed some white tennis shoes. My pea coat already bulged from the flannel shirts, but we jammed the sneakers in and took another look around. I was shaking — half-scared and half-giddy. When we heard breaking glass and a man's angry voice — *Goddamn it, Mary, if you can't control your kids, leave them home* — Ishmael hustled me out the front door and into his car. Once we were on the road, we laughed so hard Ishmael had to pull over.

"I don't have asthma," Ishmael said quietly as he pulled back onto the road.

After a moment, I gave him a scrunched-nose confused look and asked, "Then why did you tell my Dad that's why they discharged you from the army?"

"They kicked me out on a psycho."

The dark circles under his eyes reminded me he had a cold. He coughed and wiped his nose on his sleeve. I sorted the shirts and sneakers on my lap while he talked.

"As long as I can remember, my dad told me I'd go into the army when I got out of high school, like he did. He said the army would make a man out of me, teach me to stand up and be counted. I never questioned him. But it was horrible. The first day, as soon as we got off the bus, the sergeant screamed at us — *Get in line, you sissy little girls! Every one of you is a worthless piece of crap, an embarrassment to your families! Why do you think you're here? You're here because you're cannon fodder!*

I glanced over and saw tears in his eyes.

He kept going. "I mean, everyone was scared, but right then and there, I pissed my pants. That was all Sarge needed. He called me Private Piss Ant and made the guys call me that too. For two weeks, I couldn't eat. I couldn't sleep. I shook all the time. Then one day I didn't get out of my bunk. When the sergeant came looking for me, I didn't care if he killed me. I'd rather be dead than report one more day for training. Even when Sarge ripped off the sheets and called me a piece of shit, I didn't move. Later, the medics came and carried me to sickbay. They made me go to the shrink for a couple weeks and then sent me home on a discharge. Dad made me promise to say asthma if anyone asked why I came home."

"I don't care," I said. "The war is bullshit anyway."

"The Goddamned war," Ishmael said, "the Goddamned war."

"Goddamned Woolworth's," I said. I tossed the flannel shirts and his high-tops onto the back seat, kicked off my loafers, and slid my feet into the new sneakers.

When I sat up, Ishmael's face was right there. As he kissed me, he moved my hand to his zipper. I didn't know what to do, so I just let it sit there until he sat back to get a joint from the ashtray. He lit it, took a drag, then exhaled into my mouth.

"My little school girl," he croaked.

After I started smoking grass, besides Ishmael, my new best friend was mary-jane. A couple tokes and I didn't care that I was different. I didn't care if I flunked the trigonometry exam. I didn't care if my swim times got slower. *I have asthma*, I'd say, and turn away to smirk.

Ishmael taught me how to squeeze out the tobacco from Kool cigarettes and refill them with pot. I always hid some in the side pocket of my swim bag.

Mornings after my father dropped me off at school, I headed around back to the pit — the only place where smoking was allowed at Redwood. I needed a buzz to face the hassle of teachers and preppy girls.

Each morning a cool senior, Jill Howard, smoked there too. She never acknowledged me — until a week before Christmas break. While I smoked my weed-laced-Kool, Jill threw back her head, blew a smoke ring, watched it disappear, and then jerked her head my way so suddenly that I dropped my smoke.

"What you got there?" she asked, her voice accusing.

After I picked up the butt and stuck it between my lips, I flashed the pack of Kools. She came closer and ripped the cigarette out of my mouth, waved it under her nose, then took a drag.

"Where'd you get pot?" she asked.

I didn't answer. She rolled her eyes.

"I'm not turning you in. I want you to get me some."

Jill stood so close I could smell her breath, nasty like she needed to brush her teeth. She gave me a shove with her left hand and grabbed the pack of Kools with her right.

"I'll take these for now. What's your name, anyway?"

At the end of the day, as I was getting my stuff from my locker, three seniors circled me.

"You selling grass?" the captain of the field hockey team whispered, her mouth close to my ear.

Her teammates, who smelled like Heaven Scent and Clearasil, pressed against me on either side.

"Maybe," I answered.

I pretended I was Grace Slick. They weren't going to scare me. The captain jammed a five and five ones into my blazer pocket.

"Get it to me Friday."

Something doughy was caught in her braces, and her expression screamed desire. She panted like she'd run a mile.

"I'll see what I can score."

I couldn't help but smile at my unexpected notoriety. Judge, you wouldn't believe the number of girls who begged me to get them pot — athletes, smart girls, popular girls, even some weirdoes. In that one day I stopped being invisible and became *Joni Juana, Reefer Girl, the stoner chick who would hook you up*. Ishmael was ecstatic.

"This is perfect. Selling to school girls is like taking candy from a baby," he said. "We'll make enough bread to put new tires on my car and buy a tent and sleeping bags. Then we'll take off and follow The Grateful Dead. We'll be free from of all the bullshit."

For that week, I was everyone's friend. Girls started calling me at home, to my mother's delight.

And each time I handed over cash, Ishmael smiled and said, "My best girl."

On the Saturday before Christmas, my father dragged Tommy and me out of bed at 7:00 a.m. so we could watch the Apollo 8 launch.

"It's a historic event," Dad grunted when I grumbled about waking up early.

I pulled on my swim team sweatshirt and sailor dungarees. After I brushed my teeth and stomped downstairs, I helped Dad set up tray tables in the living room. The house smelled like coffee and Mom's Bisquick cinnamon rolls.

Still in his cowboy pajamas, Tommy jumped from the landing to the hall floor and rolled into the living room. His blond hair stuck out all over. "What's this about?" he asked in a sleepy voice before he hopped on the sofa and rested his head on the arm.

"American astronauts will be the first humans in history to fly around the moon. We're going to beat the Russians this time." Dad turned when Mom carried in a tray of food and coffee. "Hurry, Betty, it's about to start."

"Joni, get Tommy a bowl of Frosted Flakes and a glass of orange juice, will you?" Mom asked.

Before I reached the kitchen, I heard Tommy's voice. "You mean we're sending a man to the moon?"

"Not this time. On this flight, the astronauts will fly the space ship around the moon and come right back. But soon we'll put a man on the moon. You can bet on that," Dad told him in a proud voice.

After I gave Tommy his cereal, I sat on the other end of the sofa with a cup of sugary coffee and three cinnamon rolls. I dipped my finger in the icing and licked it off while Frank Reynolds reported — *Good morning, I'm Frank Reynolds, and these are the men who will make this historic voyage around the moon, the crew of Apollo 8.* Behind him loomed photos of three astronauts with BORMAN, ANDERS, and LOVELL printed across their chests.

I thought the whole thing was boring, but Dad could hardly stay in his seat. He shifted and leaned forward each time the people in launch control announced another status check. Tommy knocked over his tray table and the bowl of Frosted Flakes splashed across the floor.

"Oh, Tommy, the new rug," Mom complained.

She ran to the kitchen and came back with a rag and club soda. While Tommy stood to eat his cinnamon roll, she sopped up the cereal and milk.

"Quiet," Dad growled. He got out of his seat to turn up the volume. "It's T-minus three minutes and thirty-seconds. Can you just simmer down for five minutes? For the love of Pete!"

Just then, the phone rang. Dad glared. Tommy hopped from foot to foot like he had to pee and Mom looked up from her hands and knees. She handed me the drippy rag.

"Joni, rinse that out in the sink before you get the phone."

"Good morning, little school girl, can I come home with you?" The lines from a Grateful Dead song came through the handset in Ishmael's voice.

"What are you doing up so early?" I asked.

Coffee in the percolator smelled burned. I turned off the stove and moved the pot to the sink.

From the other room, Dad shouted, "Joni, get in here! It's starting."

"In a minute, Dad," I called. "My father wants me to watch the rocket launch," I told Ishmael.

I pulled the cord taut and moved closer to the living room.

"There's less than a minute to launch," he yelled.

"Bring me a glass of Kool-Aid, Joni," Tommy called.

"Joni, you have to come over. I got half-a-pound of Panama Red." I knew from Ishmael's voice he'd tried it already. "I'll come get you in thirty. We'll party."

"I'll be ready," I told him, a smile spreading across my face.

"Goddamn it, Joni, you missed the launch," Dad said when I came back into the living room.

He sat back in his chair and studied his cinnamon roll.

"Where's my Kool-Aid?" Tommy demanded.

"Did you rinse that rag?" Mom asked, her voice sounding weary.

I couldn't wait to get out of the house that day.

I woke to the sound of the doorbell and Mom's voice, "Come in. It's freezing out there. Would you like a cup of tea?"

"Sure, Mrs. Byrnes thanks. Natalie's taking a nap but if she wakes up, Jake will come looking for me. Is Joni home?" I recognized the voice of our next-door neighbor, Lisa White.

"Joni, Lisa's here," Mom called up the stairs.

"Coming," I yelled down. After I hit the bathroom and combed my hair, I pulled on my dungarees and a dark blue poor boy sweater.

In the kitchen, Lisa cradled a steaming cup while, across the table, Mom leaned on her elbows, listening to Lisa like she was the most fascinating person she'd ever met.

"Hi, Joni, enjoying your vacation?" Lisa asked, her long strawberry blonde hair wavy and perfect, like the popular girl she once was at Redwood Academy.

"She certainly is," Mom answered, but Lisa ignored her and motioned me to sit next to her. I avoided my mother's eyes.

"I have lots of homework but it's better than being in school," I said.

I felt Mom frowning when I reached into the box of Frosted Flakes and dropped a fistful in my mouth.

"I remember those days," Lisa said. "It was always a relief to have a few days off. The reason I came over is, Jake forgot to tell me about the New Year's Eve dinner the partners are holding for the attorneys at his firm. If I'd known, I'd have asked you sooner, but by any chance are you free to babysit Natalie tonight?"

Mom started to answer but must have thought better of it because she pushed back her chair, went to the sink, and ran water into the dish tub. When she squirted *Joy* in the water, I smelled lemons.

"Sure, I can babysit," I answered Lisa. "What time do you want me?"

"Can you come over at five?" Lisa stood to go, cupped her hands and blew into them. She hadn't worn a coat.

"Leaving already?" Mom asked, her cheeks red and hands wet.

"You know how men get if a baby needs a diaper change. Walk me out, Joni." Lisa glanced at me as we left the kitchen. Outside, the sun made a dull glow in the heavy sky. "I wanted to talk to you alone so you wouldn't think you had to say yes. Did you have other plans for tonight?" Lisa asked, solemn and concerned.

"Not really, nothing set," I told her.

Even though I assumed I'd get together with Ishmael, he hadn't called. Besides, I loved babysitting Natalie and I wanted the money, my own money.

Lisa glanced toward her house, then turned to me.

"We won't be out too late. You can tell your boyfriend you'll be free around nine."

"What boyfriend?" I asked, frowning and nervous.

How did she know about Ishmael? I hadn't told anyone he was my boyfriend. Lisa smiled.

"I've seen you in his VW cruising around. Your folks don't know, right?"

I shrugged and looked at my feet.

"They know him, but they think he's just a friend. I'm not sure they want me to have a boyfriend yet."

"Do you like him?" she asked.

I nodded and Lisa said, "I won't say anything. It's your business. Natalie goes to sleep by eight and we expect to be back an hour or so later, so you'll have plenty of time to go out afterward."

After Lisa crossed the yard to her house, I hurried inside and shut the door against the cold. Lisa was so cool and nice, I couldn't believe she ever went to Redwood. I wished she were my older sister. I wished I lived with her and Natalie. My parents were so old-fashioned and annoying. They didn't have any idea about what my life was like or how much I hated Redwood Academy. I went back to the kitchen, got out a bowl, and filled it with Cocoa Krispies — *snap, crackle, and pop*. Mom plunked a glass of orange juice in front of me.

"I'm happy you can help out Lisa and Jake," she said while I crunched and read the back of the cereal box. "Did Lisa say what time they'll be back?"

I looked up, almost gagging on the chocolate Rice Krispies. "I'm not sure exactly — probably late. What about you guys?"

"Dad and I are going to a party at Fanelli's. Tommy's Cub Scout pack is having a get-together for the boys, so we'll pick him up just after midnight. If we get home first, we'll wait up to wish you Happy New Year."

"Don't bother," I said.

After she left, I listened to her footsteps on the stairs, heavy, like she was exhausted.

Later, when Ishmael called and I told him about my babysitting job, he said, "Solid. I'll come get you after nine. My parents drove up to the Poconos to party. They won't be back until late tomorrow."

That evening after Jake and Lisa left, I watched seven-month-old Natalie try to pull herself up in her playpen. I jiggled rattles and a soft doll in front of her. After she dropped to her knees and rolled onto her back, she kicked and put the doll's arm in her mouth. Next time I checked, she was asleep. Around 6:00 p.m., when I took her out, I noticed she felt hot. On the changing table, she whimpered but didn't squirm much when I powdered her bottom and changed her diaper.

As I carried her downstairs, Natalie dropped her head on my shoulder. When I held her for her bottle, her cheeks were shiny red. She sucked on the nipple a few times, then turned away and cried. Her head was so hot, I wondered if she had a fever. But I wasn't sure and I didn't want to call the country club and get Jake and Lisa all upset.

I dialed home to ask Mom what to do but the phone just rang and rang. Natalie cried in a sad voice and batted her left ear. I carried her from room to room, her head on my shoulder, singing *Hey Jude, Sittin' on the Dock of the Bay,* and *Stoned Soul Picnic.* Every time I put Natalie in her crib, she fussed and raised her arms to be held. I cried, too, a little. After I wiped her off with a cool washrag and gave her a bottle of sugar water, she seemed a little better. But she didn't let me put her down.

I kept my eye on the clock. The night breeze rattled the windows and I prayed for Lisa and Jake to come back. Finally, after I'd walked my legs off and rocked Natalie for what seemed like forever, just past 8:30 p.m. I heard the car pull in the driveway. I met them at the door.

"She's still awake"? Lisa asked. She put out her arms to take Natalie.

"She's hot and cranky. She couldn't fall asleep," I reported.

Jake hung his wool coat in the closet and pulled his wallet from his back pocket. He sifted through his money while Lisa examined Natalie.

"She's sick, Jake. I knew we shouldn't have left her." Lisa turned to me. "I'm sorry. I thought Natalie might be coming down with something, but when she woke up from her nap, she seemed fine."

"All she wanted was for me to walk her. I hope she's okay," I said.

I wanted to get out of there because I felt like I was about to start crying again. It's really scary to be in charge of a sick baby.

Jake got my jacket from the hook on the closet door and handed me a ten-dollar bill. "There's some extra for your trouble," he said. "Natalie will be fine. Babies get sick. It's not a big deal." He hustled me out, but not before I turned to tell Lisa goodbye and saw the angry look on her face.

"Thanks, Joni, really," she said in a pinched voice.

I hurried away.

Our house was dark, with only the front light on. Both the front and back doors were locked and I didn't have my key. On the porch, I sat on a metal chair, as cold as sitting on ice, and hugged my knees. When each car drove past, I hoped it was Ishmael. Finally, I heard a car backfiring. A moment later the red VW rounded the corner and screeched to a stop across the street. I ran to the passenger door and yanked it open.

"You waiting long? Sorry I'm late," Ishmael said after I pulled the door shut.

"I got done babysitting a little early. Natalie was sick. She cried the whole time."

Suddenly every part of me felt weak and exhausted. I didn't want to go out. I wanted to go inside, lie on the couch, and watch TV. It occurred to me I could break into our house through the powder room window — Dad always left it open a crack. I turned to Ishmael.

"You know, I really don't feel too good. I probably caught Natalie's fever. Maybe I'll just stay home tonight."

I lifted the handle and pressed my shoulder against the door. As it creaked opened, Ishmael grabbed my arm. I'd never seen him look so pissed before.

"I don't get it. You told me you wanted to party as soon as you were done babysitting. I cleaned the garage and spent a bunch of money so we'd have a nice New Year's Eve together and then drove all the way out here to get you, just like you asked. If you didn't want to come out tonight, I could have made other plans." He sat back and drummed his fingers on the dashboard. "Go ahead. Leave me alone on New Year's Eve. I thought you cared about me."

"I do care about you, Ishmael. But I'm tired and I feel like I'm getting sick. Maybe I'll feel better tomorrow. Can we do something then?" I rested my head against the seat.

Ishmael clutched the steering wheel and tipped his head to look at me. In the dark, his eyes caught the glow of the streetlights. He smelled like cigarettes and pot.

"Christ, I'm such a fool to fall in love with you. I should have known you'd hurt me."

My ears rang and my head throbbed. *Ishmael fell in love with me? Ishmael loved me.* And I loved him. I pulled the car door shut.

"Let's go. I'm okay. As long as you don't mind if I'm mopey."

The engine roared and Ishmael spun the VW into a U-turn. He put my hand on the gearshift with his on top and together we shifted into second and third and fourth. The streets were mostly empty, but lights shone in all the houses and when we passed, we heard music and laughter. As I silently chanted — *Ishmael loves me* — I knew I made the right decision to bring in 1969 with him.

I followed the smell of incense up the garage stairs. When I reached the top, light from two lava lamps shimmered across Ishmael's room. I noticed he actually did clean up — no clothes were on the floor and his sheets looked fresh.

"How do you like it?" Ishmael's teeth glowed in the weird light.

"It's great. Did you do all this?"

I turned around in a circle while Ishmael unscrewed one of the wine bottles lined up on the bookshelf.

"Boone's Farm Strawberry Hill," he said, as he filled two big plastic cups.

Even though I was nervous — the beer, wine and highballs I'd sipped before tasted nasty — I took the cup and tried it. I was surprised. "This tastes like strawberry soda."

Ishmael finished his wine in a gulp and filled his cup again and poured more for me. Then he raised his hand in a toast.

"To Joni, the little girl who rode on my shoulders, the school girl who rides my wet dreams."

When he tapped his cup against mine, some wine spilled out and stained my top. The truth is, I couldn't believe he said wet dreams. That was gross, but he thought it was funny. I wondered if all guys said stuff like that to girls, if I was a prude because I didn't like hearing it. I couldn't think of anything to say so I chugged the rest of my wine. The red lava lamp cast a strange ripple in Ishmael's eyes.

"I knew you'd like Boone's Farm. I got it special for you." He opened another bottle but before he filled my cup again, he hesitated and asked, "You ever drink before?"

"Only a couple times," I lied. I didn't want him to think I was a baby. I took a big sip and then another until I finished it. "Good stuff."

Ishmael looked pleased. He took the bottle with him when he sank into the beanbag chair. Then he motioned for me to sit on his lap.

"Glad you came?"

"Yeah, this is nice," I said. "But I gotta be home at midnight. They think I'm babysitting next door. Mom said they'd wait up to wish me Happy New Year."

Ishmael laughed. "I guess I'm the baby you're sitting. You want to powder my bottom?"

He swigged from the bottle and handed it to me. After I took a couple sips, my ears buzzed, like a swarm of bees circled my head. Ishmael pushed up from the beanbag, fingered through his albums, chose one, and put it on the spindle. I watched the record, *Surrealistic Pillow*, totter then drop. While Ishmael searched behind a bookcase, I bobbed my head to the music — *Every day I try so hard to know your mind.*

Judge, that Boone's Farm strawberry wine tasted really good going down. I sucked the last drops out of the bottle then lay back in the beanbag chair. I felt woozy but relaxed — not as exhausted as when I left Jake and Lisa's house. Ishmael zigzagged past me carrying a weird-shaped vase with a round base and long neck. He stomped down the stairs and stomped up again. When he flopped down next to me he held the vase outstretched in his hands. Water sloshed in the bottom.

He leaned forward to hold the lighter against a little bowl sticking out the side of the glass. It took a couple seconds to realize it was a bong. After he got it going, Ishmael exhaled a long stream of smoke and handed it to me.

"Joni's first bong trip. Put your lips inside the tube and inhale." Ishmael sat so close I smelled his sweat. But once I figured out the bong, the smoke slipped down my throat much smoother than from joints. Each time I exhaled, my brain exploded. After a few hits, I tried to stand up but swayed and fell back. Even though Ishmael caught me and held me close, I was sort of freaked. I wanted to get up, walk around, splash cold water on my face, do anything to feel like myself again.

"Easy, easy," Ishmael said. "Don't fight it. Let your mind expand. Welcome the light."

While the record played *One pill makes you larger*, I hung on Ishmael.

"I need to sleep," I told him. I could hardly stay on my feet.

He led me to his bed. I wanted to thank him but couldn't get the words out of my mouth. As soon as my head hit the pillow, I closed my eyes and drifted to sleep. Well, I think I fell asleep, but I felt my blouse unbutton and my bra come unhooked. I tried to sit up, but Ishmael pressed against me, put his mouth on mine, and blew smoke into my lungs.

"I'll make you feel so good," he whispered. His touches were gentle and I felt like I was floating. "Does that feel good?" he asked, his voice husky, his hand moving over my chest and stomach.

It did feel good, I can't lie. But somewhere deep in my brain, when I felt my jeans sliding over my hips, I got scared. *I have to be home soon,* I tried to say, but Ishmael ran his tongue over my lips. His hand stroked between my legs.

"Oh baby, oh baby," I heard him say.

My stomach hurt so bad it woke me up. I didn't know where I was until I saw Ishmael beside me. I rolled off the mattress and ran downstairs. In his bathroom, I puked red vomit in the toilet and all over the floor. The taste made me puke even more. I sat on the cold tiles, practically naked. Outside, the sky was dim grey, like early morning. *No,* I told myself, *no way.* I had to find a clock. I had to know what time it was. If I moved even a little my forehead throbbed and then my stomach turned and I got sick some more.

After I caught my breath, I looked for something to wipe up the vomit. Puke splattered the toilet seat, the floor, and me. Something crusty was smeared across my stomach. I tried to remember what happened last night. Why was I still here? My gut wrenched and more pink vomit splattered on the floor. There are no words for how gross it was.

I needed to be home. I turned on the sink spigot and waited for the rusty water to clear before I leaned over and took some sips. I couldn't even hold down water. I found a towel and wiped up as much vomit as I could before I heaved again. After I flushed the toilet for like the fifth time, I threw the disgusting towel in the washing machine and stepped into the shower.

There was no soap or shampoo, but water spilled over my body and I wiped away the crud with my hands. When my stomach lurched again, I stepped out to heave, then filled my mouth with shower water and spit it in the toilet too. After I stepped out of the bathroom, I stood for a moment, dripping, staring out the garage door window. The sky kept getting lighter. How could I face my parents like this? I couldn't stop crying.

Since I used the only towel I could find to clean the vomit, I grabbed a dried-out rag draped over a bucket and held it in front of me when I padded up the stairs, leaving drippy footprints on each step.

While I pulled on my clothes, Ishmael woke up, then piled pillows behind his head and watched.

"Happy New Year," he said, smiling and sleepy-eyed.

"They're going to kill me," I wept. "Please, get up. Drive me home."

"Don't be a bummer, Joni. You can't let your parents rule your life. In a couple months, we'll have enough bread to blow this place, live off the land, and be free. We love each other. Last night was just the start. 1969 will be our year."

Ishmael reached down and got his jeans and flannel shirt from the floor. I had to hold my stomach with one hand and the railing with the other to get downstairs again.

Before he opened the garage door, Ishmael looked around and said, "God, something smells awful. You blow your cookies?" He fumbled in the old refrigerator until he found a half-empty bottle of ginger ale. "Try this. It always makes me feel better after a drunk."

In the car headed toward my house, the radio announced, *It's 7:22 on this New Year's Day, 1969. Welcome to the first day of the rest of your life.*

I was scared and sick. I sipped the flat ginger ale before I whispered, "Did we go all the way last night?"

Ishmael pulled to the curb and stopped.

"You don't remember? God, Joni. Don't worry so much. I would never do anything you didn't want. I kept asking you, *Is this okay? Are you okay?* And each time, you said, *Please, please, Ishmael.* You really don't remember?" He looked sad. "Because I thought last night was beautiful."

"I don't remember much," I moaned and leaned my forehead against the cold window, trying to hold back tears. "How far did we go?"

He reached over and touched my arm. I kept my head pressed against the glass. I heard him breathing for a few seconds.

Then he said, "It hurts me that you don't even remember how great we were together. You were totally getting it on. I've never been with a girl as hot as you. I wanted you so bad, I could hardly hold back, but I wanted to make sure it would be really good for you, too. And then, well, you basically passed out. So you know, it takes two to tango. Don't worry about getting pregnant or anything, I'd never let that happen. Look at me, Joni." When I turned, he put his hands on my face. "God, you turn me on. You're so pretty. I love you. Do you love me?"

Honestly, Judge, it's hard to tell someone you love him when all you can think about is barfing. Just then my stomach turned and ginger ale gurgled in my throat. I yanked away, rolled down the window and stuck out my head to puke.

After I caught my breath, I wailed, "I'm so sick. What will I tell my parents?"

"Gross. You didn't get puke on my car, did you? Listen, just tell your parents you fell asleep watching an old movie at a friend's house. They're probably hung over and sacked out anyway. I bet they don't even know you're gone. But if they're awake, say you went out early this morning for a cup of coffee."

Ishmael stopped the car at the corner to let me out.

"Look, I love you. You love me. Why shouldn't we spend the night together? And I promise, you don't have anything to worry about." He leaned over and kissed the top of my head. "I'll see you Friday at Wawa. Everything's fine. We're fine."

After I closed door, he rolled down the window and yelled, "You want the ginger ale?"

All I could do was wave.

The one-block walk to the house felt like a mile. Just above my right eye, my head felt like someone put a bullet in it. Before I made it home, I puked ginger ale into the gutter. At the house, no lights were on. That made me feel better — they were still asleep. I walked around to the back and yanked the laundry room door. Locked. I moved to the window outside the powder room but the back door flew open.

Tommy yelled, "Mom, Joni's home!"

In her mint-green Christmas robe, Mom waited at the kitchen table. With hair still poufy from last night and eyes smudged with mascara, she looked like a bride of Dracula. All she needed was fangs. Dad, his face stubbly and wearing plaid pajamas, glared at me over the top of his coffee cup. Tommy danced around like he'd been searching all night and finally found me, but Mom and Dad looked pissed.

"Happy New Year," I croaked.

Before they had a chance to yell at me, I rushed into the powder room and dry heaved. It hurt like hell, but at least there was no more Boone's Farm on the upchuck. I was so thirsty, I cupped my hand to drink water from the spigot, even though I wasn't sure I'd keep it down.

"Are you sick, Joni?" Mom stood at the door, a concerned look replacing the angry one.

"I think I got what Natalie has. She had a fever all last night."

I took a deep breath and followed Mom into the kitchen, worried that the smell of coffee would start me puking again.

"We've been worried sick about you. I was just about to call the cops." Veins in Dad's forehead pulsed and he looked like he wanted to spit. "Where have you been?" His voice was scary.

I panicked. Luckily, my stomach clenched again and I bolted back to the bathroom to vomit. This time, watery stomach gunk came out. I felt like hell and lay on the bathroom floor with my head on the rug. After a minute, Mom came in.

"Oh, Joni. We don't know what to do with you. Why were you out all night? What is a fifteen-year-old girl doing out all night? Get up now. You can't lie on the floor."

I crawled out on hands and knees. To stand up, I had to put a hand on the wall.

"Fred, help Joni to her bedroom. But first, tell us where were you last night," Mom said, her voice shrill.

I took a deep breath and tried to look wretched. That wasn't too hard to do, you know?

"I didn't take my key when I went to babysit last night and you guys locked both doors. It was freezing, but luckily Mom's car wasn't locked, so I waited for you in there. But I fell asleep. And now I'm sick from Natalie," I lied. I lied like I never lied before. I don't even know where that lie came from.

As he took my arm, Dad exchanged a look with Mom. They didn't believe me, I knew, but at least I was home now, sick but safe. When I made it to bed, my stomach ached and my head spun like a tilt-a-whirl, but as soon as I closed my eyes, I fell asleep.

When I opened them again, my clock said ten minutes to five. I didn't want to get up. God, my head ached. I swore I'd never drink booze again. I ran my fingers real light over my stomach, trying to make it feel better.

I remembered Ishmael's fingers running over my stomach and back and legs and chest. But I couldn't remember what happened after that, no matter how hard I tried. I remembered being worried about getting home, but too drunk or high to tell Ishmael. I hated feeling that way, like I couldn't say what I wanted to say or go where I wanted to go. And then I woke up and puked my guts out. Ishmael was drunk and high too. My nose was all cloggy on top of everything else, and tears came to my eyes. I didn't know what to think.

If you love Ishmael, I told myself, *you have to trust him. He said there's nothing to worry about,* so as I lay there, I decided I shouldn't worry about it anymore. *Ishmael loves me.* I would believe him. But I also decided to tell him I didn't want to go that far again or get that high or drunk again. After I thought it out, I felt better. Well, except for facing my parents.

I smelled roast beef and biscuits. I still felt too sick to eat, but I took a quick shower, pulled on clean clothes and went to the kitchen to make a cup of tea. My parents followed me and stood in the doorway, not saying anything. That was pretty creepy. After I filled the teapot and put it on a burner, Mom took a cup and saucer out of the cabinet and dropped in a teabag. She smelled good, like soap and hair spray. I still smelled like puke and Boone's Farm. As soon as I slid into my seat, Mom sat in the chair next to me. Dad got a can of Yuengling out of the refrigerator and pulled off the pop-top. The yeasty smell made me gag, but I swallowed and took a deep breath. I got up, got a glass, and filled it with tap water. I took a long drink, then forced my feet to take me back to the table.

Mom let out a sigh. "We don't know what to believe, Joni. I talked to Lisa. Natalie is still sick. Lisa feels terrible that you caught whatever the baby has, especially because you took such good care of her. But sleeping in the car all night? It doesn't make sense. It must have been freezing. I find it hard to believe you slept through the noise of us coming home and slamming doors. You know Tommy is never quiet."

Dad drank his beer and belched. "We're keeping close eyes on you young lady," he said.

I just sat there. The teapot whistled.

Mom said, "Go back to bed. I'll bring up your tea."

The next day, I still felt shaky and sick to my stomach and it wasn't all because of Boone's Farm. I don't know if there's a way to explain how I felt — like I was blowing up a balloon, and even though I knew with one more breath it would burst, I had to keep blowing.

Friday morning before I met Ishmael at Wawa, I spent hours planning what to say. As soon as the red VW pulled into the lot, my heart felt like that balloon — ready to burst — especially when he smiled at me. No matter what, though, I had to tell him how I felt. The moment I got into his car, I blurted out everything I rehearsed.

"Ishmael, you're going to think I'm a baby, but you know, us going so far on New Year's, and me getting sick and in trouble? I don't feel right about all that. It makes me too nervous. I want to go back to talking and listening to music… but I understand if you don't want me to be your girlfriend anymore."

I started to cry. I was pretty sure I had just pushed away my only friend. But Judge, Ishmael wasn't mad at all. He was nice. He took my hands and kissed my forehead.

"Don't cry. We'll do whatever you want — listen to music and talk about books. Joni, this is real. No one will ever love you like I do. Everything I do is so we can be together. I hope you never forget that."

All the air in the balloon escaped and I was safe again. I smiled the entire ride.

When I climbed the garage stairs, my stomach clenched but the wine bottles and the bong were gone, and he'd straightened the corduroy cover on the mattress. While I wandered across the room to look at a new table Ishmael made with bricks and plywood, he lit a joint. He caught my eye and raised one eyebrow, but I shook my head no, and he nodded.

"You'll love this album," he said when he shook out a record and put it on the spindle.

I was so surprised to hear classical-sounding music coming from the record player. Ishmael chose the perfect album for the way I felt. He crossed the room and handed me the cover — *Days of Future Passed* by the Moody Blues.

Even more than the music, I loved the cover art — all swirls and flowers and horses. I'd gotten in trouble at school a few times for drawing like that all over my notebook covers. Why should a teacher care what I put on the outside as long as my notes and homework were neat? That's just another reason I hated Redwood. *Nights in White Satin* played while Ishmael lined up twelve jars of oregano on the new table.

"You know the guy at the tire store who sells me weed? He gave me a free ounce. All I have to do is deliver that pound to a dealer in the city tomorrow. Check it out."

I followed his eyes to a brown grocery bag sitting next to the record player. Even before I unrolled the top, I smelled marijuana. The bag was filled about half-way. Some of it looked like chunks of the spongy stuff florists use. But some of it was looser — green and brown dried up leaves and twigs.

"Wow," I said. It was a big bag, Judge.

"This is our chance to make some real money, Joni. If you want, I can drive you home now, or you can help me put together dime and nickel bags. You promised a couple bags to your school girls, right?"

"I can stay a little while."

"Great." He put baggies and three dinner plates on the table along with a red Velvet Tobacco can. He filled the can with marijuana, jammed in some rolling papers, then gave it to me. "I want you to hide this somewhere for our personal stash."

On a dinner plate, he mixed oregano with the rest of his ounce. "Fill twelve baggies as high as one finger across the bottom. I'll make the dime bags."

After we finished, he counted the bags and stacked them off to the side. He looked around the room like someone was watching him, then carried over the brown bag, grabbed a fistful, and replaced it with the same amount of oregano.

"Since I'm taking all the risk, I deserve more than one ounce," he said.

"I better get home. I have a swim meet tomorrow and I'm kind of grounded," I told him.

Things were turning out okay. But before he started down the stairs, Ishmael looked at me funny.

Over his shoulder, he said, "I thought you'd go downtown with me tomorrow morning to deliver that pound."

"Ishmael, I can't go tomorrow. I have the swim meet all morning and my parents want me home right after. You know they're watching me like hawks. Just go yourself. When you get back maybe I can get out for an hour and we can do something."

I was surprised he didn't remember the meet. He'd told me he'd come to watch.

"Why do you waste your time on that swim team, Joni? It's not like swimming for Redwood matters. And I need you with me." Ishmael sounded angry.

I stopped and stared, confused. "I don't get why you can't do it yourself."

He sighed and looked at me like I was the stupidest girl he ever met. "The neighborhood's kind of sketchy. The best way to deliver the stuff is with two people. All you have to do is jump out of the car, give it to the guy, and hop back in. That way, I can keep the engine running and we can get the hell out of there."

"I'm going to the swim meet," I told him.

To tell the truth, I was glad I couldn't go. I didn't mind bringing a few baggies to girls at school, but I sure didn't want to go to the city to sell pot.

"Since the day I met you, I never asked you for anything. I always go out of my way to make things nice for you. The only reason I made this deal is for you — to make you happy, to make enough money to get you away from all the shit you deal with every day. I can't do it alone. These people don't play," he said.

He turned away and stared out the garage window. His shoulders shook and I heard quiet sobs. He raised one hand to his forehead and left it there.

"I love you so much. I'm such an idiot." His voice choked.

"I love you too," I said as I came up behind him and wrapped my arms around his chest.

He moved my hands to his waist. And then lower. This time, I did what he wanted. I needed him to love me.

When he drove me home, I agreed to drive with him to the city after the meet.

The next day was Saturday. The wind blew so hard I had to push against the car door to get out. As Dad pulled away from the township rec center, I followed the Redwood swimmers into the locker room. After we entered the pool area, I sat on the bleachers, feeling drops of humidity trickle through my hair. While I waited for my event, other swimmers took their lanes. The instant the starting pistol banged, they flew over the water's surface.

This is what I love, I thought, *this is where I like myself.* But I almost missed the call for my first race — the 50-meter freestyle — and touched the wall in fourth place. When I hauled myself out of the pool, I was panting and shaky — and disappointed in myself.

Groups of girls from each team huddled together to cheer and laugh. I stood aside, wrapped in my towel, staring up at the viewing area's huge windows, searching for Ishmael among parents and friends who came to watch the meet. He wasn't there.

Since my next event wasn't for thirty minutes or so, I climbed to the top of the bleachers and made myself small. I felt old and tired. The chlorine smell and clammy air made me woozy. I looked for Ishmael again. I didn't see him, but Jill Howard was there, her nose pressed against the glass. I ducked back — I don't know why. She'd called me earlier to remind me to bring two dime bags for a party or something that night.

Theresa, a freshman swimmer, looked up, caught my eye, then smiled and waved. I sidestepped down the bleachers and joined my team.

After I positioned myself for the backstroke — in the water with hands clenched on the edge and feet planted against the wall — I studied the viewing area windows again. No Ishmael. No leering Jill. I forgot to anticipate the starting pistol. For all four laps, I lagged behind. When I touched the wall in fifth place, I couldn't catch my breath. I dragged myself to the locker room. I didn't place in a single event.

Ishmael's words played in my mind — *It's not like swimming for Redwood matters.* I didn't want him to be right. *Swimming matters,* I told myself. It matters.

Outside, my rubber flip-flops slapped the concrete pavement slick with freezing rain. After a few seconds, I couldn't feel my toes. A damp blot from my swimsuit ringed the seat of my grey sweatpants, but my nylon ski jacket kept my chest and arms warm. I scanned the parking lot until I spied the rusty red VW and let out a breath. There he was.

I hurried to the car. I didn't want to keep him waiting. When I leaned against the driver's side door, Ishmael, in sunglasses, slipped a couple dime bags inside my jacket. His lank hair hung below the dirt-brown watch cap pulled over his forehead. Across the parking lot, Jill Howard stood next to a blue Corvair.

"Hurry up and get the money from Doris Day, then beat feet back here," Ishmael said, his voice a little angry. "I want to get going with the delivery."

I pulled up my hood, tucked my hands in my pockets, and flapped across the lot. The baggies slipped down to my waist. Jill waited for me, leaning on the hood of her car.

After I shook out the baggies and showed them to her, she nodded toward the backseat of her car and said, "Give them to my boyfriend. He has the money."

A husky guy with red cheeks and a crew cut let himself out and scowled until I offered him the grass. He pulled a twenty from his wallet. As soon as I took it, he said, "Possession with intent to sell."

At first I thought he was being funny, but when I turned to go, a cop in uniform stepped out of a Dodge Dart parked a couple cars down. He wrenched back my arms and pinched ice-cold metal handcuffs on my wrists.

"You're being taken into police custody as a juvenile for the possession and sale of marijuana. Your parents will be notified as soon as we get to the station. You have the right to remain silent…"

Judge, I kept thinking Jill was playing a mean joke on me. But when her boyfriend, who was dressed in jeans and a ski jacket, showed me his badge, my knees collapsed and I fell to the ground. The uniform cop squeezed my arms to pull me up. Stunned and confused I turned to Jill.

"Loser," she smirked.

Once I realized Jill set me up, everything happened in slow motion. I tried to tell the cop, *Hey, I'm only a kid. I didn't know that was marijuana.* But my throat tightened and my jaw locked shut. I remembered what Ishmael told me — *Cops don't arrest school girls,* and *Never, ever tell them you got the stuff from me.*

With the officer holding my arm, a blue-and-white cop car appeared from nowhere, moving toward us. I scanned the parking lot, searching for Ishmael, desperate for him to save me. Just before the cop put his hand on my head and shoved me into the back seat, I saw Ishmael's red VW lurch toward the street. I felt sad and lost but prayed he'd get away or at least have time to ditch the dope. Then he could clean himself up and come get me at the police station. He'd know what to say.

His car swerved toward a group of girls, pulled left, and spattered dirty slush five feet in the air. Just as the VW made it out of the parking lot, a thousand sirens blasted and everyone turned to watch the flashing red and blue lights.

By the time we arrived at the station, from the squawking voice on the
police radio, I knew they'd caught Ishmael too. In a windowless room
without a door directly behind the front desk, I listened to the phone call
to my parents — *Fred Byrnes? This is Officer Davis. Your daughter, Joan
Byrnes, has been arrested for the possession and sale of marijuana... Yes,
Mr. Byrnes, it is your daughter...* I couldn't stand to hear any more and
covered my ears. I squeezed shut my eyes to erase the image of my father
in the kitchen, holding the phone, his face red, his hands balling into fists.

I was so scared and so cold, I shivered in a corner while I tried
to come up with an explanation for my parents. Every few minutes a
different cop came in, stared at me, then filled a cracked porcelain cup
with coffee from a huge percolator. The coffee smelled burnt, but I was
freezing and wished I could have some. My toes turned dead-looking
yellow. On the floor in my corner, I tucked myself as tight as I could. After
I bit through the rough skin around my thumbnail, the cuticle turned into
a bloody quarter moon.

Where did they take Ishmael? Was he here in another room? In my
mind, I rehearsed what he told me each of us would say if either of us
ever got picked up. Even though he promised I'd never get arrested, I still
might be questioned. Ishmael would say he hardly knew me and had no
idea I sold pot. He was only with me because he promised my father he'd
give me a ride home. I would say, *some guy I didn't know asked me to give
some oregano to his friend. I thought oregano was for spaghetti. I didn't
even know what marijuana looked like. Michael Reid? He was just waiting
to give me a ride.* But Ishmael swore cops never arrested girls like me.
And look what happened. I started to cry.

It seemed like I waited in that room forever. I doubted my parents
would come. *This will teach her a good lesson,* I imagined they decided.
How long could the cops keep me here? Probably since it was Saturday, I'd
be left here until Monday. Maybe I'd even freeze to death before someone
remembered me.

Each time I heard footsteps, I prayed it was my parents, and then I'd
pray it wasn't because I was terrified of what they'd say. I'm not sure how
long I waited until the burly cop who pushed me into the room came back
and stood in the doorway. For a moment, he stroked the ends of his thick
black mustache and frowned.

"Joni?" I heard my mother's voice and really started shaking. I pushed myself against the wall to stand up.

When the cop realized I'd been crouched in the corner, he glared at me and barked, "Let's go." Then he grabbed my arm and yanked me out of that room to the front desk where my parents waited. I couldn't meet their eyes.

"This is all a mistake, Officer. Joni's never been in trouble," my father said as soon as he saw me.

"It's no mistake, Mr. Byrnes," the cop said. He licked the edge his mustache. "She accepted money from an undercover police officer in exchange for two bags of marijuana."

My mother hooked her arm through mine. As soon as she felt me tremble and noticed my flip-flops, she went bananas on the cop.

"How could you leave her in that cold room, with no shoes? She's freezing. Fred, get the blanket from the car."

As Dad scurried down the hall to the station entrance, the cop led us to a small room directly across from the front desk. "You folks can wait in here," he said.

We sat on stiff chairs and looked at the cops through the wide window. Two cops stared back. I guess they wanted to make sure my parents didn't try to break me out. We watched my father show a cop the ratty blanket. In a moment Dad came through the door and dropped the blanket in my lap. After my parents glanced at each other, Mom cleared her throat.

"The policeman told us they arrested you for selling marijuana. Joni, tell us it isn't true."

I didn't answer. What could I say? But then Dad slammed his fist on the table.

"They arrested Michael Reid, too. What the hell is going on? How is he involved?"

"Michael's not involved. He was just there to give me a ride home. Some guy in the parking lot called me over and asked me to give Jill some oregano for her mother. I thought I was doing her a favor." My lip trembled and I wiped my eyes with my sleeve.

Dad handed me his hanky. I avoided Mom's eyes, but I could tell she wanted to believe the lie. I hoped Ishmael would be proud of me. Maybe they'd let him go. But what would happen to me? I felt sick and started shaking again. *Why did this happen? Why did Jill set the cops on me?* I didn't get it, Judge. I still don't get it.

All I could think about then was that Ishmael loved me. All we wanted was enough money to take off. We'd follow the Grateful Dead and later find a place of our own — out in the country where we'd live a simple life, away from mean people and crappy jobs. Ishmael would carve wood into forest creatures to sell at craft shows and I would have a garden. We'd plant hemp between rows of string beans and corn.

I blew my nose in Dad's hanky to keep from looking at my parents. All three of us jerked up at the sound of heels click-clacking across the linoleum. Through the window, we saw a woman with big hair stop at the front desk. She wore a scarlet-colored coat. My mother let out a breath.

"That's our friend from church, Sally Fanelli. She's a lawyer. As soon as Dad hung up with the police, I called her. She told us to sit tight, keep our mouths shut, and she'd meet us here," Mom said.

"Why do I need a lawyer?" I asked. My father snorted.

We heard Mrs. Fanelli's voice, "Where's the girl? Where's my client, Joan Byrnes?"

A cop pointed to the window and my mother raised her hand like she wanted to be called on. Mrs. Fanelli motioned for us to come out. To tell you the truth, Judge, the first time Mrs. Fanelli narrowed her eyes and checked me out, I got scared. Then, when she raised her arm, I winced, but she just put her hand on my shoulder. She smelled like damp wool and cigarettes.

"Come here, Officer, look at this girl. This is a child. She's frightened. She's cold. Don't you have the decency to keep her warm while she's in your custody? This is outrageous. I will have her released immediately to her parents' custody." I could tell Mrs. Fanelli scared the cops too. The look in her eyes when she turned to me and said, "I have to make a phone call, then I'll get you home," told me she came to save me.

My mother and I crept back to the wide-window room. As Mom draped the blanket over my shoulders, her eyes were wide open like she'd just missed being run over by a train. A minute later, a black cop stepped in and handed me a coffee in a cardboard cup. Sprinkles of Coffee-Mate swirled on the top.

"We got nothin' else hot," he said, "but I added cream and sugar."

While I sipped the weird, yellow coffee, I watched my father through the window. He marched three steps to the right, then three steps back. Each time a cop stopped at the front desk, Dad approached him and said,

"This is all a mistake, Officer. Joni's never been in trouble before."

On the chair across from me, Mom pulled each finger of her leather gloves. If she said, *Oh, Joni, how could this happen?* one more time, I'd scream. I cradled the leaky cardboard cup and took a few sips, but the coffee was gross, so I set it on the table. My feet ached deep inside. I folded my legs Indian style and hugged the musty car blanket. From down the hall, I caught snatches of Mrs. Fanelli's conversation — *parents... no risk... no way to treat a child... yes, Judge... thank you, Judge.*

At the click-clack of heels, we joined my father in the hallway. When Mrs. Fanelli reached us, she spoke directly to me. "You're released to your parents' custody. That means you go home and you stay home. Warm up and get something to eat. I'll come by after dinner to talk about what happened and what's going to happen."

"What about Ishmael?" I whispered.

"Ishmael? What, are you reading *Moby Dick?* Isn't Ishmael the only rat that survived the sinking ship?" Mrs. Fanelli asked, her voice sarcastic.

"Ishmael, he's my boyfriend. He used to be Michael Reid." From the corner of my eye, I saw my father stop dead.

"Boyfriend! You said he was just a friend. You lied to us. How old is Michael?" Dad's voice was angry.

"Did he turn you into a hippie?" Mom asked, just as angry.

Crap, I thought. I messed up. The shit hit the fan and spattered everywhere.

"Let Ishmael worry about Ishmael, and let me worry about you," Mrs. Fanelli called over her shoulder as she bustled to the desk to sign my release papers.

As soon as we got home, I ran upstairs and filled the tub with hot water. I stayed there, soaking, until Tommy knocked on the door and called, "Mom says come down for dinner." I didn't want to face my parents, but by then I was starving.

No one said a word when I carried a grilled cheese sandwich and bowl of tomato soup into the living room. When I switched on the TV, I heard Tommy say, "Why can't I eat in the living room?" After I finished, I wished I could have another sandwich, but I didn't want to ask.

After fifteen minutes or so, my parents came in. Dad switched the channel to the Huntley-Brinkley Report and I took my dishes to the kitchen, then went to my room. Tommy followed, hopped on my bed and, from all-fours, considered me.

"What you do so bad?" he asked, his voice unusually deep.

"Everything," I said.

Both of us bounced off the bed when we heard a knock on the front door and Mom say, "Come in, Sally."

I took a deep breath, glanced at Tommy shamefaced, and said, "You should stay up here."

I tiptoed down the steps and waited in the hall outside the living room. My parents concentrated so hard on Mrs. Fanelli's words, they didn't realize I was there. Mom leaned forward in her chair, her elbows resting on her thighs. Each time Mrs. Fanelli paused, Dad nodded and said, "Un huh, un huh."

After she finished with my parents, Mrs. Fanelli spoke to me. "Joan, you heard me tell your parents how the juvenile court system works, and that your intake hearing is scheduled Tuesday after next. Now I need to talk to you, alone. Get your coat."

She knew I was listening the whole time.

The beige leather seat of the burgundy Cadillac felt smooth and cold. Part of me still didn't believe I got arrested. I felt like a zombie, like nothing was real, like I died and now floated overhead, watching my old life and waiting to crash. Snow was just starting to fall. I was glad it was so dark outside.

By the time Mrs. Fanelli, cursing under her breath, backed out of the driveway, my fingers and toes were pins and needles, my heart raced, and my throat got tight. I couldn't breathe. As we drove down the street, I hugged my gut. And then, out of nowhere, I gasped and sobbed harder than ever before in my life.

"Good," Mrs. Fanelli said, staring straight ahead, "about time you showed remorse." She pushed a pack of tissues toward me and headed for the main road.

When I could choke out some words, I croaked, "What's going to happen to me?"

"That depends. Tell me everything and don't even think about lying. I hate liars and I'm the only person in this county who can help you. Get me a cigarette from the pack in my purse and light it for me. You can have one if you want."

Even though Mrs. Fanelli scared me, I felt safe, like I could trust her.

She wasn't mean or phony nice, just — straightforward or something. But Judge, by that point, I was a total wreck.

After I handed her the cigarette, it dangled from her lips, a red lipstick kiss on the filter. She inhaled and then exhaled in one long, slow breath. When I took a drag of mine, I let the smoke curl out of my mouth the way Ishmael taught me and watched it float up and disappear. Then I spilled my guts, blubbering like a little kid.

"Redwood costs a ton of money so I have to pretend I like it. But nobody at school likes me and the girls say I'm a weirdo. Then, in November, I met Ishmael and he said I was fine. That girl, Jill, who set me up with the cops? She figured out I was smoking pot one day and begged me to get her some. She told all her friends they could buy from me and she bought it, too. I even saw her smoke it. How can she get me arrested when she smokes weed herself?"

"But you smoked and sold marijuana, right? Where did you get it? What did you do with the money?" Mrs. Fanelli asked. "And that's enough crying."

I looked at her, surprised. I guess I thought she'd feel sorry for me since I was crying, but now she seemed a little annoyed. I took a deep breath, dabbed my eyes, and blew my nose.

"I'm not sure where Ishmael got marijuana. I think he knew someone from work. When I told him girls at school wanted to buy some, he gave me the baggies. Later, I gave him the money. All we wanted was enough money to move away from here."

"Move away from here? You're what, fifteen?"

Mrs. Fanelli can be pretty sarcastic, you know, Judge? I tried to sound more mature, but I felt like now she was jumping on me, too. But I tried again. "Almost sixteen. And I hate my parents. That's why I want to move away. They expect me to be this cute, popular girl, but I'm not. I'm a loser. I don't know why I have to go to school anyway. You can't learn about life in school. You have to live it to be real. Ishmael says we have seekers' spirits."

Tiny dots of snow bounced on the windshield, faster and faster. The wipers couldn't keep up with the icy smears. Mrs. Fanelli hefted herself up and hugged the steering wheel, leaning forward to see outside.

"Jesus H. Christ!" she shouted. "*Mannaggia.* I gotta get Joe to put chains on the tires. We won't go too much farther. I don't want us stuck in this frozen crap."

The snow came down so fast the road disappeared under white. The Cadillac fishtailed and crunched forward, leaving thick tracks behind.

"So let me get this right. You don't need school. Nobody likes you. But you sold marijuana to that cop, right? How long have you been smoking pot? That's what I need to know." Mrs. Fanelli lowered her window and flicked her cigarette butt outside. The cold air smelled like handcuffs.

The moment I said, "I only tried it once, but I didn't like it," Mrs. Fanelli narrowed her eyes and pursed her lips. I tried to shrink. I knew better than to try the oregano story.

"This Ishmael character, Michael Reid, got you hooked on drugs?"

"I'm not hooked on drugs. Anyway, pot doesn't hurt anyone. You don't get drunk or anything, you just feel good." My stomach turned when I said, drunk.

"You just feel good but you break the law. Joan, now is the time for you to talk to me. And believe me, Joan, if you want my help, you need to stop giving me a load of crap."

Mrs. Fanelli drummed her fingers on the steering wheel. The rear end of the car slid out again, and she tightened her grip, pulled left, then right, and we swerved down the icy road. It felt like riding bumper cars at Willow Grove Park.

After the car straightened out, Mrs. Fanelli said, "Start with your relationship with Michael Reid."

I thought for a couple minutes, trying to remember. Even though it was only two months, I felt like I'd been with him forever.

"I met him at the Wawa across from Redwood Academy. That's where my Dad picked me up after swim practice." My eyes filled with tears again and I wiped them away so Mrs. Fanelli wouldn't notice. "I was sitting on the curb and Ishmael's car almost ran into me — not on purpose." I didn't want Mrs. Fanelli to think he was a bad driver. "As soon as he realized he scared me, he came over to say he was sorry. Then he bought me a lemon pie and let me sit in his car because it was cold. After we talked, we realized we knew each other from summer swim team."

I paused to catch my breath and think. I was tired of talking. We stopped at a red light. When it turned green, the car in front of us spun its wheels and threw slush across Mrs. Fanelli's windshield. She tapped the horn and a guy came out of the car and raised both hands, like to say, *Hold on a minute.* I watched the girl in the passenger seat slide over to the driver's side. As the girl gave it some gas, the guy pushed from the back.

The wheels spun and the guy got covered in wet snow, but eventually the car drove through the intersection with the guy chasing after it.

"We better get off the road and away from these idiot drivers." Mrs. Fanelli plowed through the intersection and made a wide circle to head back. I was glad there weren't many cars. "Go on," she said.

"So after a couple days, Ishmael told my father he'd drive me home to save Dad the trouble. Most days we went to his place for an hour or so. He has a big room over the garage at his parents' house. We listened to music and smoked pot. And we fell in love." I couldn't help feeling proud when I told her that last part.

"You fell in love while you listened to music and smoked pot." Mrs. Fanelli's voice was low but tight. "And did this falling in love include sex?"

"God! Why does that matter?" I didn't want to talk about that. It's so personal. And I still felt sort of ashamed about New Year's.

"You want me to help you or not?"

"We made out." I stared at my feet. "Ishmael's gentle."

"Did you go all the way?" Mrs. Fanelli let out a long breath. She didn't look at me.

I didn't know what to tell her. You know, Judge, it's embarrassing. Besides, I wasn't exactly sure. I knew we went pretty far, though. It's awkward to have to write this, but I mean, it happened. And it's part of why Ishmael got sent to prison. Finally, I took a deep breath and told Mrs. Fanelli the truth.

"I got drunk on New Year's Eve and fell asleep, well, passed out in his bed. I didn't get home until the next morning." I swallowed and said in a low voice, "I don't think we went all the way. Ishmael told me not to worry. Don't tell my parents."

"What do you mean you *don't think?* What did Ishmael tell you not to worry about? You were there, right? What are you saying, Joan?" Mrs. Fanelli used her meanest voice.

That's when I knew I really messed up. I wished I never started talking about it. But when Mrs. Fanelli asks you a question, you can't think fast enough to make up a good lie. Now I had to tell her the rest. I sighed and let the tears stream down my face, even though I was supposed to stop.

"We went to Ishmael's to celebrate. I had to be home right after midnight because my parents said they'd wait up," I paused and looked at her. "They were at your house, remember?" She nodded. I stifled a sob.

"Ishmael picked me up after my babysitting job. He bought Boone's Farm Strawberry Hill wine special for me and we smoked from his bong. He even cleaned his room." I got so nervous no more words came out.

The back wheels swerved every time the car turned. With her eyes on the road, Mrs. Fanelli said, "Then what? I assume you didn't tell your parents you were going out with him."

"No," I admitted. "I didn't tell them because I planned to be home around midnight. But when we got to Ishmael's, even though I never drank before, I told him I had. I let him keep filling my cup. Then he got out his bong and I got really high and had to lie down. It's all my fault. He kissed me and, you know, touched me, gentle. He wanted everything to be nice, but I was scared and I needed to get home and I tried to tell him. But he was high, too, you know? After that, I can't remember anything until the next morning when I woke up in Ishmael's bed. My stomach was sick and I was freaked out because what would I tell my parents? Anyway, on the ride home I asked him how far we went, and he said not to worry because he loved me."

By then, I didn't think I could talk any more, maybe ever. So I stopped. I looked out the window and remembered being ten or eleven and playing with my friends — lying in the snow, flailing our arms and legs to make snow angels and later drinking hot chocolate at someone's house.

We drove in silence for a moment or two. I snuck a peek at Mrs. Fanelli and wondered what she thought. She couldn't understand how much Ishmael loved me. No one would ever love me as much as he did. Everything he ever did was for me. The car swerved and the windshield smeared.

"And how old is Michael Reid?" Her quiet voice made me feel better.

"He's nineteen. But age isn't important, maturity is." I felt pretty good because I thought that sounded mature.

"So, since November you've been smoking marijuana and being intimate with this man who calls himself Ishmael? And you sold drugs for him." Mrs. Fanelli sounded like she was really interested.

"I don't know what you mean, intimate. We made out and you know, touched. Is that what you mean?" I asked. I wanted her questions to stop.

Mrs. Fanelli shook her head and sighed. "What else?" Now she sounded irritated. "Tell me what happened today."

God, I thought, *you know what happened today.* But when I glanced at Mrs. Fanelli, I decided the only way to get the questions to stop was to go ahead and spill the shit. I wondered if Ishmael would be furious that I caved.

"Ishmael agreed to deliver a pound of pot to some guy in the city today in return for a free ounce. He needed me to hop out of the car and deliver the stuff so he could stay in the car. The only reason we got caught is because Jill called me last night and told me she needed two dime bags for some party." Finally, that was all of it — the whole story. My chest felt so tight, I could hardly breathe.

We were getting close to home and the worst was over. Soon, I'd be in my room listening to music and worrying about Ishmael. I never expected Mrs. Fanelli to pull into the church parking lot. I thought she might want to clear away the thick snow stuck under the windshield wipers, but she slammed her hands on the steering wheel so hard, I jumped.

In a ferocious voice, she said, "This Ishmael or Michael Reid or whatever the hell his name is took indecent sexual liberties with you, whether or not he actually raped you. And I think it's probable he did. Joan, that is not your fault. Look at me."

It took me a couple seconds. Raped me? I touched my stomach. After I moved my head so I could see Mrs. Fanelli, she said again, "That part is not your fault. I want you to say it. That is not my fault. Say it."

"Not my fault," I whispered. But I wasn't sure.

Mrs. Fanelli must have read my mind, because she took my chin and turned it so I had to face her. "Say it again, loud and clear. That is not my fault. He took advantage of me."

I had to clear my throat. "That's not my fault. He took advantage of me." I said it pretty loud. And Judge, you know, I felt better. I didn't realize how bad I'd been feeling about New Year's Eve.

"That is not my fault," I said again.

"The sex stuff, it's not your fault," Mrs. Fanelli said, nodding. "The using and selling drugs, that was your own mistake. You knew it was wrong but you did it anyway. But Michael Reid — he's a grown man. He's too old for you and he knows it. Have you heard the term, contributing to the delinquency of a minor? That man took advantage of you. He's not your friend. He's not your boyfriend. He's a criminal and when we go before the judge, that's what I'll tell him."

My teeth chattered, but not from cold. I thought how sweet Ishmael was the day we met. I remembered how good it felt to have his arm across my shoulder, the way he held me when we danced to his Grateful Dead album and how happy I was to have a boyfriend. Then I thought about the pot brownie and New Year's Eve when I wanted to stay home, but he was so hurt I changed my mind. I thought about how good I felt when Ishmael called me his best girl and told me he loved me. Then I remembered waking up in his bed, sick and practically naked. I began to sob. *Why did this happen?* But I knew the answer — because I was a loser.

"But Ishmael was nice," I whispered.

"Real nice," Mrs. Fanelli said as she backed out and headed for my home.

That night, I couldn't sleep. I wished I'd never been born. The last thing Mrs. Fanelli said when she dropped me off was: *Listen to me, Joan. Michael Reid doesn't love you. He used you. He told the judge he hardly knew you. He said you asked if you could put a box in his trunk, and he had no idea you'd stashed dope inside it. If he loved you, why didn't he protect you? He threw you under the bus. Forget Michael. Save yourself.*

But we had a plan. I'd wanted to tell her. But before I had time to explain, my mother rushed out of the house and stood by the driver's window. Snowflakes coated her hair and shoulders. The moment Mrs. Fanelli rolled down her window, my mother wailed, "Redwood Academy expelled Joni. Now what will we do?"

That should have been the best news I ever heard, but I felt even worse. I couldn't stand to hear another word, so I slipped out of the car and trudged to my room.

Sometime after midnight I got out of bed and looked out the window. I stared at the streetlights and the tiny flakes of snow glistening in their glow. I thought I'd cried all the tears I could, but so many ran down my cheeks they spattered the windowsill and trembled like dewdrops.

Now, I thought, *I'll wind up in juvie* — an exclusive girls' boarding school — where, Mrs. Fanelli told me, they beat the shit out of softies like me.

After more than a week tiptoeing around the house and doing chores like Cinderella, the day before my intake hearing I stayed in my room. I was pretty sure intake meant the police would take me in and leave me, but Mrs. Fanelli said that's just what they call it when a juvenile goes before the court. She said the court assesses juveniles to decide if they're hardened criminals or can be adjusted. I kept thinking about the time Dad's car blew black smoke out the tailpipe and he took it to the gas station to be adjusted. A few adjustments here and there and I'd be welcome again in Mr. Rogers' Neighborhood. What about Ishmael? Could he be adjusted? *Only juveniles can be adjusted,* Mrs. Fanelli told me.

To make sure I looked presentable for court, Mrs. Fanelli sent my mother to Wanamaker's. Mom came home with a plaid pleated skirt, a white blouse with a peter pan collar, a navy blue cardigan sweater, navy blue knee socks, and black loafers. I told Mrs. Fanelli I looked six years old in that outfit. But Mrs. Fanelli said it's important to show the court proper respect and wear clothes appropriate to my age. I guess that was part of my adjustment.

As I sprawled across my bed that day, my mind felt numb, like it was stuffed with cotton. I reached for the book we started reading in English before I got expelled, *The Catcher in the Rye.* Ishmael said the book was about a disgruntled rich kid overwhelmed with the wonder of his own angst, but I liked it. In the part I was reading, Holden feels like he's disappearing. I understood that feeling. Tomorrow, like Holden, on a cold, grey day, I would cross the road to the courthouse and Joni Byrnes would disappear.

Around seven that Monday night, Mom knocked on the door. "Joni? I brought your dinner. You have to eat."

The door creaked open. Mom carried in a tray with a chicken sandwich and a glass of chocolate milk. I pushed the pillow behind me and sat up.

"Turn down that music, Joni, I can't hear myself think," Mom said.

I hoped she didn't hear the last words George Harrison sang before the arm lifted and the record player clicked off — *I don't know how someone controlled you...*

After she handed me the tray and sat on the edge of the bed, some chocolate milk splashed on the sheets. I held my breath and dabbed the spill with a napkin, waiting for her to scream, *Joni, can't you do anything right?* But instead, she took the napkin, worked on the spill a second, and sighed, "I'll get to it tomorrow."

I could tell Mom wanted a heart-to-heart, but I prayed she'd just go away. While I ate, I kept my eyes on the plate and swigged down the rest of the milk.

"I know you're worried," she said. "And we are too. But Sally Fanelli has a plan."

When I choked and spit out a mouthful of chicken, Mom stood up and backed away.

"You're not impressing me with your bad manners. I was trying to be nice."

I wasn't finished but she took the tray. She hesitated in the doorway.

I knew my lines.

"Sorry, Mom. I'm just totally bummed, you know?" I used my best poor-Joni voice. *Just go*, I wanted to scream. *Leave me alone.*

"We're all bummed. Have you thought for one moment about what you've done to your father and me? Have we heard one word of apology? You got yourself into this mess, but it's up to us to get you out of it. Have we heard one work of thanks? You're not the daughter we raised, Joni. I don't know who you are." Mom turned away and slammed the door.

I listened to her heels clack down the stairs. Like always, it was all about them, what I did to them. If they really cared about me, this never would have happened. *Screw them.*

Later, I heard Mom, Dad, and Tommy laughing their asses off while they watched *Laugh-In*. I wanted to go down and watch it too — Goldie Hawn and Joanne Worley were my favorites — but after the fight with Mom, well, I stayed in my room. At some point I must have dozed off, but in the middle of night, I woke up and couldn't go back to sleep. Instead, I opened my door and stepped into the hall. I listened for a moment to my father snore and smiled to hear Tommy talk in his sleep, *Watch out, Robin!*

I tiptoed down the steps. Raindrops pelted the windows and I shivered in the chilly living room. But I relaxed. For a couple hours I could watch TV and drink a soda — Tab was the only kind Mom bought — without my parents staring and shaking their heads. Before I wrapped myself in an old quilt and rested my head on the padded sofa arm, I knelt at the TV and flicked through channels. I didn't care what I watched. I just wanted to think about something besides juvenile detention.

Across the screen, wavy white letters — *Carnival of Souls* — floated over grey waters. From the sofa, I watched a car with three women inside plunge off a bridge and sink to the bottom of a river. Soon, a mud-covered young woman emerged and staggered toward land, confused and disoriented. Eerie organ music whined as onlookers rushed to assist her. Her name was Mary, and only she made it out of the sunken car.

Mary looked the way I felt, bedraggled and stunned. Still, she went on with her life and her new job as a church organist. At random times, a man with a death-grey face stared at her. It freaked her out. Like Holden Caulfield — like me — sometimes Mary became invisible. People avoided her. Then, after Mary played disturbing music, the pastor fired her. I fell asleep but woke to hear Mary's terrified scream. I was glad my parents didn't wake up — they'd think I was screaming. I turned down the volume. Anyway, Mary wound up in an abandoned dance hall that looked like the Taj Mahal, watching ghoul couples dance a bizarre waltz. As soon as Mary recognized herself waltzing in the arms of the freaky ghoul, she bolted out of there and ran for her life. And then she disappeared, leaving only footprints in the sand. At the end, rescuers dragged the sunken car out of the river. And there was Mary in the front seat, drowned with her friends.

I felt sorry for Mary. People thought she was weird but didn't try to understand why. I understood, though. When you're invisible, you're the same as dead.

Around six in the morning, from upstairs I heard footsteps and running water. I snuck up to my room and dressed in the dopey court clothes Mom bought. When I came down, I was too nervous to eat. I watched the news with Dad while he sipped coffee and blew smoke rings. The TV showed a burly, bald-headed man while a reporter announced that Philip Blaiburg, a South African dentist who was the third person in the world to receive a heart transplant, had survived a full year with a colored man's heart in his chest.

"I'd rather be dead," my father muttered.

Dressed like a doofus with barrettes in my hair, I slid into the back seat of the Ford, shaky and nauseated. Besides not sleeping, I'd lost weight in the past week because whenever I felt hungry, my mother's expression drove me back to my room. Funny thing about food — when you're happy or even okay, food tastes good, but when the shit hits the fan, it's the last thing you want.

After Dad parked the car in the lot behind the old brick courthouse, I stepped out. Black spots floated in front of my eyes like I was high — probably not a good thing before a drug hearing. Around front, we entered the double glass doors. I felt dizzy and sick and really, really scared.

The uniformed guard, a black man with tight white hair and long sideburns, asked, "Intake?"

"Yes," Mom answered. In her purple suit and black pumps, she looked ready for church.

The guard, his forehead furrowed and his eyes narrowed, turned to me. "Who your attorney?"

"Sally Fanelli," I told him. My mother answered right on top of me.

"She tight. She take care o' you. You be all right," the guard said.

He directed us down the hall. Outside the juvenile hearing room door, I sat on a hard bench next to Mom. She sighed and sighed. My father, with his hands behind his back, paced the hall. He examined each portrait and landscape painting on the wall and studied each plaque. After ten minutes, down the hall came click, clack, click, clack and Mrs. Fanelli, in a navy wool suit and pink blouse with a paisley scarf around her neck, rounded the corner like she was being chased. As soon as I stood up, I fell back hard on the seat.

"What's going on, Joan? We're scheduled in fifteen." Mrs. Fanelli's briefcase banged her hip.

Above my right eye, a throbbing pain made it hard to think. My fingers tingled. "I didn't sleep much last night and I didn't eat this morning," I admitted.

"Get her a Coke and some peanut butter crackers," Mrs. Fanelli ordered Dad. "You didn't feed her this morning?" she accused my blinking mother, who stuttered, unable to reply.

I didn't meet Mom's eyes. She'd called me for breakfast but I couldn't eat then.

"Look, Joni," Mrs. Fanelli said, "this is the most important day of your life. You remember what we talked about? Michael Reid gave you marijuana. Michael Reid convinced you to sell it for him. Michael Reid took advantage of you."

I forced myself to pay attention while I sipped from a green bottle of Coke. I tore the cellophane off a pack of crackers with my teeth. The first cracker was so dry, I choked. Still, a few minutes later, when a man opened the courtroom door and beckoned for us to enter, I felt better — except for being worried about orange crumbs in my teeth and scared to death about the hearing.

"I don't want her in there," I whispered, tipping my head toward Mom.

"Please wait here," Mrs. Fanelli told my exasperated mother. She turned to my father. "You can come in if you remain silent and wear your poker face."

As we walked into your courtroom, Judge, I was freaking out. I tried to think about anything except what you would decide. I stared at the walls, the furniture, and the flags. Some nights I still dream about that room with its dark-paneled walls.

I followed Mrs. Fanelli down the aisle between three rows of pews. When we got to the barrier that separated the pews from two tables, she put her hand on my back to guide me to a seat on our right. At the other table, a young black guy in a brown suit sat next to the cop who paid for the baggies. I wondered if he actually was Jill's boyfriend.

When Mrs. Fanelli noticed me staring, she whispered, "The guy in the suit is Marcus Williams, the county prosecutor. I've already spoken with him."

The truth is, I was pretty surprised the county lawyer was a black guy. I turned to steal a glance at my father, dressed in his best suit, to see if he noticed. Dad blew his nose, tucked his hanky in his pocket, and bit his lower lip. He gave me a little nod — that was all.

Judge, after you walked in from a side-door, Mrs. Fanelli nudged me and I got to my feet. Your clerk — the old guy — announced, *The Honorable Michael P. Mullin.*

I can still remember exactly what you were wearing — a dark grey suit, white shirt, striped burgundy and blue tie. After you sat down on the leather chair behind the raised desk, I kept standing. I was looking at the United States, Pennsylvania, and county flags behind you. You looked up and saw me standing, do you remember? I do, because you looked me right in the eyes, like you were sizing me up. I probably blushed. Mrs. Fanelli tugged on my sleeve then, and I sat down.

For what seemed like forever, you looked over some papers on your desk. Finally, you said, "We're here to consider the actions of Joan Byrnes on January 4, 1969, wherein she accepted twenty dollars from Detective Peterson in exchange for two plastic bags containing marijuana." Then you looked up and said, "Mrs. Fanelli?"

"Thank you, Judge. This child, Joan Byrnes, has no prior arrests and no involvement with the justice system. She's a good student and comes from parents who are exemplary members of the community. The nineteen-year-old man, Michael Reid, coerced her into selling drugs for him. In addition, he gave her alcohol and took advantage of her. As you know, Judge, Joan is fifteen."

My father gasped and got to his feet. "He did what?"

When you slammed your hammer, Judge, I jumped. Mrs. Fanelli glared at Dad with cold eyes. I guess my father sat down then. I didn't dare look at him.

Then Mrs. Fanelli cleared her throat, shook her papers, and continued, "Judge, my petition includes relevant background information documenting Michael Reid's influence on this minor child. Her parents and I request Joan Byrnes be provided the opportunity for rehabilitation without the onus of an arrest record. We do not request dismissal — in my opinion and that of her parents, although she's a minor, her actions should have consequences. We request an informal adjustment as follows: Joan should be required to remain homebound to complete her studies through the end of this school year. At the start of summer, Father Vincent Luciano, Disciplinarian and Theology instructor at East Philadelphia Catholic High School and Sister Mary Immaculata, Vice Principal of Girls Catholic, have agreed to allow Joan to work as a volunteer counselor at St. Augustine of Hippo Camp under their supervision. Upon successful completion of volunteer work at this camp for poor children and a positive follow up assessment, I recommend the pending charges against Joan Byrnes be dismissed. If Joan fails to follow the terms of this adjustment, her parents and she understand she will be subject to formal adjudication to consider the arrest warrant allegation."

"Mr. Williams and Detective Peterson, do you agree to these terms?" you asked.

"Agreed, Judge," Attorney Williams said.

He and Mrs. Fanelli exchanged glances, but I wasn't sure why.

"Yes, Your Honor," the cop said. I wanted to punch him in the face. Actually, I wanted to punch Jill Howard in the face. I won't though, in case you're worried.

"Joan, selling drugs is a serious crime. What do you have to say?" you asked.

At that point, I'd been thinking about the last scene in *Carnival of Souls*, when the car gets dragged out of the river and Mary's body is limp in the front seat with the other dead girls. Eerie organ music played in my head. Mrs. Fanelli nudged me and I stood up.

"I'm sorry," I whispered.

"Do you understand the serious nature of your actions?" Your voice was scary and I was afraid.

"I do now," I answered.

Everyone laughed, but I still don't get what was funny.

Then you asked, "What was the nature of your relationship with Michael Reid?"

I didn't know what to say. I blurted out, "He was nice to me."

And then I began to cry. I'm sure you remember because I cried so hard, I bent over and gagged. I still don't know where that came from. It was like everything hit me at once. Mrs. Fanelli put her arms around me and sat me down. Then she stood up and faced you.

"This child is a victim, not a perpetrator. Michael Reid bamboozled her into using and selling drugs. She needs help, not punishment. Father Vincent and Sister Mary Immaculata will provide counseling and support to help this child return to the clean-cut, all-American life she was born to." The smell of cigarettes and perfume oozed from Mrs. Fanelli's clothes.

When you motioned for me to rise, I felt wobbly, but you looked like you felt sorry for me.

"If I accept this petition, Miss Byrnes, you must agree to the terms. Even the slightest digression will be grounds to open the proceedings and recommend you to juvenile detention. Do you understand and agree?"

"Yes, thank you, Your Honor. I'm sorry. I made a big mistake and I feel really bad about it. I'll never look at drugs again as long as I live."

The hours Mrs. Fanelli spent preparing me for that question paid off. She smiled and patted my shoulder.

Then you said, "Miss Byrnes, I want you to give serious thought to the choices that brought you before this court. I'm granting your petition for an informal adjustment. However, I will keep the record open pending successful completion of your homebound studies and a positive report from Father Vincent and Sister Mary Immaculata. In addition, Miss Byrnes, after you return from summer camp, you are to submit, in your own words, a comprehensive report that explains how you came to engage in unlawful activities and persuades me you have come to see the light. You are fortunate to have a fine advocate in Mrs. Fanelli. Use your time wisely. Go now and sin no more, Miss Byrnes."

I know I should have done better with the *sin no more part*. But right then, all I wanted was to sleep.

The morning after the hearing, I listened to music in my bedroom while I waited for Mrs. Fanelli. Just past 10:00 a.m., I heard brakes squeal and a honking car horn. From the window, I looked down as Mrs. Fanelli's

Cadillac overshot our house. She stopped the car in the middle of the road and started to back up. When an orange AMC Hornet came up the road behind her, she almost smashed into it. The Hornet driver blasted the horn. From the driver's side window of the Cadillac, an arm shot out with the middle finger raised. After another loud honk, the Hornet backed into a driveway across the street while Mrs. Fanelli jerked her car into a U-turn and arrived at our house. With a thump, the right tire bumped over the curb and the car screeched to a stop — half in our driveway and half on Jake and Lisa's lawn.

When she got out, Mrs. Fanelli's breath made white clouds in the cold air. With her hand on her hip, she studied the Whites' box shrub, crushed under her bumper. After she paused a moment to glance at the Whites' house, then ours, she gave the bush three or four good yanks. Except for a couple branches, it stayed wedged between the tire and fender. Mrs. Fanelli shrugged and disappeared.

For the first time since my arrest, I laughed. I laughed so hard I couldn't catch my breath, and I fell back on the bed with my knees tucked up. Seconds later, the doorbell rang. I heard Mom greet Mrs. Fanelli, then trudge up the steps and knock on my door.

"Yeah, okay," I coughed, still laughing.

My door creaked open and my mother hesitated in the doorway. Her right hand drifted up to her throat. She looked like Donna Reed watching a mouse scurry across the kitchen floor. Each time I tried to sit up, I collapsed back on the bed, gasping, tears spilling down my cheeks. I kept seeing Mrs. Fanelli trying to get that shrub out of her bumper.

"Joni, it'll be okay." Mom took a step toward me, her eyes narrowed.

"No, no," I said, shaking my head. I couldn't get out the words to tell her I was laughing.

"Wash your face. We can't keep Sally Fanelli waiting. She's here to make sure you understand the terms of your agreement. I know it's hard, but we pay Sally by the hour," Mom whispered.

That stopped me. She didn't care that I was upset. She cared that I cost them money.

"I'm fine." I brushed past her to the stairs.

"There you are. We thought you climbed out a window," my father said in a fake happy voice.

Since the hearing yesterday, Dad's voice had changed into this weird and strangled cheery one. I think it started after he heard Mrs. Fanelli say, *took advantage of her.* When I remembered that, my own voice got strangled. "Hi," I greeted Mrs. Fanelli and wiped my nose with my sleeve.

My mother placed a tray of tea and Oreos on the coffee table. She sat on the sofa next to Dad. The room smelled like lemon furniture polish.

Mrs. Fanelli sat in Dad's chair and I dragged in a dining room chair to sit next to her. She spoke to me as if my parents weren't in the room.

"Now that you're not on the bus to juvie, how are you?"

Besides my little brother, Mrs. Fanelli was the only person who said what she meant. I knew she honestly cared how I was doing.

"I'm glad the hearing's over. And I'm happy about the agreement. I appreciate everything you did for me. But I still think it's not fair no one who bought pot got in trouble."

God, I hated the way that came out, all whiny and pathetic, especially compared with what could have happened to me. But even so, it wasn't fair. I snuck a glance at my mother. I wondered what she thought was fair.

"Nothing in life is fair, so stop focusing on what's fair or not fair and start focusing on your future. I know you can't imagine it now, but one day this will be just a bad memory." Mrs. Fanelli reached in her purse for her cigarettes and put one between her lips.

My father got up and struck a match to light it. The sulfury smell drifted my way. She looked at me when she exhaled. I bit my tongue so I didn't say anything else stupid. I met Mrs. Fanelli's eyes and nodded.

"Now, I need to make sure you understand the conditions of the agreement. You will remain housebound until June when Father Vincent takes you to Camp St. Augustine of Hippo. Until then, you are required to complete your junior year of high school through the homebound program. Once a week, starting next Monday, a township teacher will visit to give you assignments and collect and grade your work. You're restricted to the house and yard except to go to church on Sundays with your parents or for medical or dental appointments as needed." Mrs. Fanelli sat back. I smelled her perfume, strong and flowery. "Do you understand? Do you have any questions?"

"What about the library? Like, if I want to get books or I need to look up something for school? What about swimming?" I asked, even though I knew the answers.

My mother wrung her hands. My father studied his nails.

Mrs. Fanelli shook her head. "No library. No swimming or other recreational activities. The homebound teacher will bring all the materials you need for your schoolwork. If you want books from the library, your mother or father will get them for you. This isn't vacation, Joan. It's punishment. Don't blow it. It's a few months and then camp, where you'll spend the summer outside. When you come back, if you've met the terms of the agreement, your record will be expunged — deleted — and you'll have a fresh start."

"What about Ishmael? What happened with his case?"

I couldn't help it. I worried about him. I missed him. I know he took advantage of me, Judge, and he shouldn't have. And I still feel angry and sad about that. I know that wasn't my fault. But he was my only friend.

"He's in county jail waiting for trial. The judicial process is more complicated for adult criminals. Forget about him." Mrs. Fanelli raised her right eyebrow and picked a flake of tobacco from her upper lip.

"Ishmael, shishmael," my father said in his new weird voice.

"Do you understand?" Mrs. Fanelli asked.

I nodded.

"Answer out loud, do you understand?"

"Yes, I understand," I said. That was pretty annoying.

She turned to my parents. "Do you both understand?"

They nodded, and then when Mrs. Fanelli raised her eyebrow, both quickly said, "Yes."

"And does Joan have a desk, typewriter, paper, pens — things she needs for school?"

"Sounds like a shopping spree." Dad smiled like Clifford the big red dog. "Christmas all over again, ho, ho, ho."

I walked Mrs. Fanelli to the front door. As she stepped outside, she turned to me and rolled her eyes. "Ho, ho, ho," she whispered.

From my bedroom window, I watched her car jerk out of the driveway. After she hauled off down the road, the box shrub lay crushed and bedraggled, its branches trying to spring back to shape. I probably shouldn't have laughed.

When the burgundy Cadillac disappeared, I stared out at Jake and Lisa's house. Sometimes in warm weather when my window was open, I heard them fighting — not punching or anything — just yelling, like, *You promised you'd be home to watch Natalie,* or, *I break my ass every day to earn enough money for this family,* or, *You only care about yourself, you don't give a damn about what I want* — that sort of fighting. I wondered what they'd say to each other when they saw the mangled shrub out front.

From the blue glow, I could tell the TV set in the living room was turned on. Directly across from me, on the second floor, Lisa walked into Natalie's room and out again. I sighed and turned to my records.

A little while after I shook out the *Buffalo Springfield* record Ishmael gave me, I heard a knock on the front door. I tiptoed to the top of the steps to listen.

"Lisa, come in," my mother said.

I thought Lisa was going to complain about the broken bush.

"Hi, Mrs. Byrnes. I need a favor. Jake's mother is in the hospital, so we're driving to Pittsburgh tomorrow morning to help out. Can you keep an eye on the house and bring in the newspaper and the mail? Here's the key."

"Of course," Mom said. "Is it serious?"

"She had a stroke. Jake's father never gets information quite right, but we understand she's ready to be moved to a rehab facility, and Mr. White needs Jake to sort out the medical insurance. We want to visit his mom anyway. We hope to be back by Wednesday next week."

"Don't worry. I'll keep an eye on things. Tell Jake we're thinking of him."

After the door shut, I went downstairs. "What was that about?"

I watched Mom drop the Whites' key in the silverware drawer.

"Some illness with Jake's mother in Pittsburgh. It's a long drive with a baby." Mom went to the front door, looked toward Lisa's house, and sighed.

Back in my room, I balanced the *Buffalo Springfield* album on the spindle and pressed the switch. The record dropped to the turntable, the needle arm rose, shifted, then dropped, perfect every time, on the first groove. I lay back and let the music surround me. Ishmael wasn't a hardened criminal. He was nicer to me than anyone had been in a long time. I must have dozed off. *Buffalo Springfield's I Am a Child* played in my dreams.

We didn't make the rules. We didn't say what's fair.

Monday morning at 6:20 a.m., my mother knocked on my bedroom door, but I was already awake. The typical morning sounds — water running, my father hollering about holes in his socks, cartoon jingles bursting from the TV — thumped in my head like a stereo with too much bass.

"Today the homebound teacher comes for her first visit. Mrs. Fanelli said we should make sure you keep a regular school-day schedule. Get up and get dressed."

I pulled the covers over my head and imagined Jill Howard combing her hair and dabbing on eye shadow. Just before leaving the bathroom, she'd look over her shoulder to check out her knowing-smile in the mirror. Jill would want to look perfect when she told the *Joan Byrnes goes to jail* story one more time. *Maybe you should go back and brush your teeth,* I suggested telepathically.

"Joni, get a move on," Mom shouted from the bottom of the stairs.

I rolled out of bed and knocked on the bathroom door.

"Hurry up, Tommy. Let me in."

"Coming," he hollered.

The water stopped running. When Tommy opened the door and walked past me, his dripping hair smelled funny — like mouthwash. The toilet seat was up. The floor around it was sprinkled, and Dad's bottle of Vitalis hair tonic lay on its side, dripping into the sink. After I righted the Vitalis and screwed on the cap, I showered and washed my hair. Before I went downstairs I pulled on jeans and a long-sleeved knit shirt. No juvenile detention at least, but my heart felt jumpy. The past few weeks were pretty much a blur, but now the homebound part of my adjustment was about to begin. I didn't know what to expect.

In the kitchen, Mom poured a cup of coffee. When she reached across the table to give it to Dad, the cup wobbled in the saucer. Dad looked up and set down his newspaper while he scooped two teaspoons of sugar into his cup. Just below his jawline, a bloodspot seeped through wadded toilet paper. The rust-colored dot looked like a cap for Tommy's Pony Boy gun. Cigarette smoke spiraled from the amber ashtray on Dad's right. His knife rattled around the jelly jar until the last globs spilled onto a couple slices of burned toast.

At the counter, Mom spread mustard on a baloney sandwich for Tommy's lunch. I brushed past, took a cup from the sink, rinsed it, and splashed coffee into it. She glanced at me, raised her eyebrows, and pursed her lips.

"Dad has his coffee," she said. She returned to wrapping Tommy's sandwich like a gift.

"It's for me."

"Coffee isn't good for teenagers. Eat something healthy. There's Frosted Flakes in the cabinet."

I balanced my cup on a saucer and set it on the table. Without lowering the newspaper, Dad shoved the sugar bowl my way. A dab of jelly was about to fall off his chin. I touched his wrist. When he peered around, I handed him a napkin.

"Jelly — your chin."

Dad took the napkin and nodded toward my cup.

"You'll want milk in that."

When he went back to the paper, I read the headline facing me:

NIXON INAUGURATED

ANTIWAR DEMONSTRATORS HURL BOTTLES AND BRICKS
AT PRESIDENT'S CAR

"Welcome, Tricky Dick," I said in a sarcastic voice. I added four teaspoons of sugar and filled the coffee cup to the brim with milk.

"It's a sad day when Americans throw rocks and bottles at the President! What happened to love of country, to pride in being an American? Everything comes too easy to your generation. Richard Nixon didn't start this war, Johnson did." Dad ruffled the paper. "Listen to what the President said in his inaugural address — *We see the hope of tomorrow in the youth of today. I know America's youth. I believe in them. We can be proud that they are better educated, more committed, more passionately driven by conscience than any generation in our history...* And those same American kids pelted the presidential vehicle with rocks. You hippy kids are a goddamned disgrace."

"Bullshit," I whispered, not intending for him to hear.

I sipped my coffee and added more sugar. The newspaper slapped the table and Dad glared at me. A red flush rose on his cheeks.

"You're lucky you're not in jail like your dropout druggy boyfriend. I'm leaving. Goddamned smart-aleck."

Dad plunked his cup on the table and left the room. I heard him get his coat and open the front door.

"Bye, Dad," Tommy called from the living room.

Judge, I felt really bad. I never wanted to piss off my father. Sometimes I blurted out whatever went through my mind, even though I knew I should shut up. I tried to slink away to my room and listen to records. But as soon as I pushed back my chair, Mom started in on me. At least she didn't look at me. She just washed and stacked the dishes while she talked.

"I don't know why you provoke your father, Joni. He's been on your side through this whole mess. When you go upstairs, change into something decent. The homebound teacher reports to the probation office. You need to make a good impression."

That was the most she said to me in two weeks.

I felt like one of the wacko kids from the movie *David and Lisa*, whose parents dumped them in a nuthouse. Ishmael's and my favorite scene is the one where a father, mother, and kid are sitting in the local train station when the psycho teenagers from the institution come in. After the teenagers start acting weird, the father gets all bent and ushers his family outside. From the doorway, the father looks back and calls the teenagers *screwballs, spoiling the town.* I imagined my parents thinking, *Joni, you're such a screwball, spoiling our home.* When I crept out of the kitchen and tiptoed upstairs, I felt like a criminal.

After I changed into the white, oxford-cloth blouse and plaid wool slacks Mom got on sale at Tesses Dresses, I looked in the mirror. My eyes were sunken with dark circles. My forehead was broken out, and my blonde hair hung limp around my face. I hated myself. Before I met Ishmael, I knew I wasn't cute, but he said I looked fine. Now he was gone and I looked dead, like the zombies in *Carnival of Souls.*

I forced myself to go downstairs. When the school bus honked for Tommy, I held open the door and watched him skip down the walk — happy, without a care. Next door, the driveway was empty. I hoped Lisa and Jake made it safe to Pittsburgh. Now, until the homebound teacher arrived, my mother and I were alone.

Before I turned on the TV, Mom called from the kitchen, "Joni, you know I've had to take off from Tesses Dresses for almost two weeks because of you. If I miss any more days, Tess is going to fire me, and it's the only place I'm happy. Tess depends on me and thinks I'm smart. I am smart, not that your father would notice. Not that you would notice."

When she walked into the living room, her black patent leather shoes tapped the wood floor. She paused in the entry like she wanted me to say something. Then she sighed.

"As soon as the teacher comes, I'm going to work. That means you'll be here alone. Don't screw this up, Joni. Because I will not be tied to this house one more day because of you."

Guilt-trip city — my mother's favorite destination. I wanted to scream — *You forced me to go to Redwood Academy and those rich bitches got me busted. And none of them are in trouble!*

Mom had no idea what it was like to be me. I didn't fit in and I didn't know why. And there she stood, dressed for work in a dark skirt and pink sweater with a bright scarf around her neck. The smell of lavender perfume drifted into the room. I could never be the person she wanted me to be.

Existence precedes essence, Ishmael told me. He said that meant you have to follow your own path in order to become who you're supposed to be. I didn't really understand, but whenever he said stuff like that, I felt better.

I turned my gaze on my mother. I knew she wanted me to say, *You're a great mom. I'm sorry I put you through this. Everything that happened was completely my fault.* But I sat silent, my arms folded across my chest. Lucky for me, the teacher knocked just then. After Mom threw me the *be nice* look, she opened the door.

"Good morning. I know you and Joni have scads of subjects to discuss, so I'll be on my way."

Before the teacher sat down, the front door slammed shut. From the window, I watched Mom's car back down the driveway, turn, and speed away. It took about five minutes for the teacher to explain that she visited once a week to give me assignments and collect homework. She handed me a syllabus, a pack of mimeographed worksheets, an algebra book, an American history book, an English literature book, and a general science book.

"After you study the assigned subjects, you'll complete the worksheets and write a one page synopsis of your literature reading. As long as you do your work, we'll get along fine," the teacher said. When she picked up her bag, she looked relieved. Before she went through the front door, she called, "Do you have any questions?"

"No questions," I said.

And then she was gone.

As soon as I was alone, I felt lighter. For a couple hours, I lay on the couch and watched TV — *Captain Kangaroo* and *Lucy.* I finished the week's worksheets in less than thirty minutes. The list of chores my mother left — run the vacuum, fold the laundry, scour the tub, dry the dishes and put them away — took another thirty minutes. When I sorted the knives, forks, and spoons into the drawer, I noticed the key Lisa White left with my mother.

Lisa asked us to keep an eye on things. And it was just next-door —

not like actually going anywhere. I remembered Lisa said they planned to return on Wednesday. I really should run over there, I decided, to make sure the toilets hadn't overflowed and the iron was unplugged. From the living room window, I leaned my forehead on the pane and scanned outside. No one was around. The mailman came an hour ago, Tommy's school didn't let out for three hours, and Mom wouldn't arrive home until after 4:00 p.m. I took the phone off the hook in case she or my father called to check on me.

After I made sure I left the back door unlocked, I walked across the yard and climbed over the chain-link fence into the Whites' yard. The cold air raised goose-bumps on my arms. Everything outside looked alien, like I'd stepped through Alice's looking glass. Grace Slick's *White Rabbit* pulsed in my head. My mind was moving slow.

When I put the key in the Whites' door, I felt paranoid. I called, *Hello?* My pounding heart made the only sound. Inside, the house was cold and smelled stale, like old newspapers and diapers, but other than crusty cereal bowls in the sink, it was tidy. The dining room table held neat stacks of newspapers and mail. In the living room, toys filled a red crate. On the coffee table, children's books — *Little Black Goes to the Circus!* and *The Sleepy Lion* — were sprawled open. I imagined Lisa on the egg-shaped chair with Natalie in her lap, pointing to pictures and saying, *See the lion, such a sleepy lion.* It made me sad.

After I peeked out front, I went upstairs. Baby clothes and a hooded pink baby towel hung over the side of Natalie's crib. Zinc ointment oozed from an open tube on the changing table. In the bathroom, two worn toothbrushes dangled from the wooden holder, and a double-edged razor rested in a whisker-specked glob of shaving cream. At the water line, a stain ran around the toilet bowl.

I'd never been in Lisa and Jake's bedroom before. There was a heavy smell, like clothes left in the hamper too long. Dust sparkled on the Venetian blind slats. I tiptoed to the tall chest and opened the top drawer where, among balls of black socks, I pulled out a baggie. Once I realized the round rubber bands inside were actually rubbers, I threw it back and buried it under socks. Yuck, I thought. I slammed the drawer shut.

The top drawers of Lisa's triple dresser smelled like Lily of the Valley body powder and held stockings, bright print bras, and matching silk bikinis. I imagined myself in Ishmael's room, dropping my jeans and striking a pose like Jamee Becker on the cover of the *Sports Illustrated* swimsuit issue — my father's favorite. Lisa's bras were way too big for me, but she'd never miss just one bikini bottom. Two of the seven or eight in the drawer were blue. One was dark blue paisley and the other was sky blue with soft white clouds. I jammed the light blue one in my pocket and ran downstairs, suddenly really nervous.

On my way out the back door, I noticed baby food jars lined up on the countertop — green peas, squash, applesauce, and strained peaches. Without thinking about it, I grabbed the jar of peaches, locked the Whites' door, and hurried home to return the key to the drawer.

In my bedroom, I popped open the baby peaches and dipped my finger in the jar. I closed my eyes and took my time, holding each sweet dab on my tongue. After I scooped out the last drop, I lay on my bed and cried.

The next day, after they carried Natalie inside, Lisa stopped by for the key — a day early.

For my sixteenth birthday on Valentine's Day, Mom and Dad gave me flared khaki pants and a blue cotton shirt from Tesses Dresses. They were okay, but not the hip-hugger dungaree bell-bottoms I'd asked for. Tommy gave me a *Seventeen Magazine* I knew Mom bought. Mostly I thought *Seventeen* was annoying, but this issue included an interview and pictures of Jimi Hendrix. I liked his music, ever since Ishmael played the *Electric Ladyland* album for me. Sometimes Ishmael called me *Little Miss Strange*, like one of the songs.

I thumbed through the magazine pages until I came to the interview. Jimi said some cool stuff about people needing to know their neighbors and that you shouldn't hate anyone. I thought about hate a lot. I wondered why the Redwood girls hated me. I knew I hated them. But I wasn't sure who hated who first. I surprised myself when I started a list in my head of the Redwood girls I didn't hate — Mercedes, who graduated last year, Theresa, a freshman on swim team, and a few quiet girls from each class who smiled and said hello. *Maybe I should have tried talking to them*, I thought. *Maybe they were like me.* But it was too late now.

The week before and after my birthday, I checked the mail every day. I was sure Ishmael would remember my Valentine's Day birthday and send a card or a letter. Each time the phone rang I hoped it was him, but it wasn't. It's not like my parents would let me talk to him even if he did call.

Most days, I wrote to him on blank pages from my old Redwood notebooks and decorated them with doodles. In those letters, I told him I was sorry the plan didn't work out. I hoped he was okay and I thought about him a lot. I told him Redwood expelled me. Now I was stuck at home, bored out of my mind, filling out mimeograph study sheets, listening to music, and wishing we could talk. But Judge, I didn't know where to send those letters. The one time I casually asked what happened to Michael Reid, my parents clammed up. "Don't mention that name in our house," my father said. After a while, I ripped out the letters and tore them up. But every day I wrote to Ishmael in my head.

Even though I wasn't interested in politics, a lot of time I watched the news because I had nothing else to do. Reporters said peace talks between the

United States and Vietnam were starting in Paris, but then they reported on all the fighting and soldiers' deaths and all.

Tommy and my father loved to watch the news about all the rocket ships being launched. At the end of February, America sent the Mariner 6 to Mars to take pictures and the Mariner 7, an identical space ship, would fly to Mars at the end of March. That didn't make sense. The most interesting news was that John Lennon married Yoko Ono on March 20th. She seemed sort of weird, but who was I to talk?

By then, I was dying to talk to someone besides Tommy and my parents. Four or five times a day I dialed WE 7-1212 just so I could listen to the weather report. Some days I sprawled across kitchen chairs, moving my arms and kicking, pretending to swim. Each Monday, when the homebound teacher came to pick up and drop off mimeographs, I tried to get her to stay for a cup of tea. She always looked really nervous and said she had five more students to visit.

One day at the end of the month, I was so lonely I decided anything had to be better than being a prisoner in my own home. I wrote a letter to Mrs. Fanelli. I told her I probably ought to go to juvenile detention after all. Otherwise, I might start selling drugs again. When I read that letter over, though, it sounded stupid. I tore it up and went out to the backyard. It was sunny but still cold.

At first, I walked around the yard in big circles. The wind blew through my hair. A robin pecked at the ground and green buds sprouted on tree branches. The smell of burning wood drifted in the air and steamy white smoke spiraled from a neighbor's chimney. I searched the ground for a slender stick and imagined pressing a marshmallow onto the end, then roasting it until the inside turned soft and gooey and the outside turned black. The yard smelled green and cold.

Judge, I really didn't plan to go against your orders. I just wanted to see if the red Velvet Tobacco can Ishmael filled with pot was still in the playhouse. I had stashed it there the afternoon before we got busted.

Dirt and bird doo speckled the playhouse roof and cobwebs hung in the corners. I looked around before I bent to climb in the door. Something dropped in my hair and I brushed it away. Every spring Mom browbeat my father to get rid of the old playhouse since for years no one played in it. Maybe that was in the back of my mind — I ought to ditch the can just in case this was the year Dad got around to hauling it away.

The can waited right where I left it — in the corner, covered by moldy rags. When I reached for it, a daddy longlegs walked right across my hand. I hate bugs. I zipped right out of the playhouse but after a minute I snuck back in, expecting something else to pounce. Quick as I could, I grabbed the can and scurried backward to get out. At the door I tripped and fell on my bottom. I checked to make sure no one saw me back there.

All I wanted to do then was see if the weed was still good or if water had seeped into the can and ruined it. The lid was rusty around the edges and the can had little spots on it like mildew. I rubbed it on the grass until it seemed cleaner, then I worked on prying it open.

It was hard. Ishmael jammed that lid on. I tried using a stick, but it cracked. Then, from down the street, there was a loud bang. I thought it was the cops — shooting at me. Judge, I flipped that can into the ivy behind the playhouse and crept back into the house. From the front window I looked up and down the street but all I saw was Lisa pull into the driveway, get Natalie out of the back seat, and carry a grocery bag into the house.

By then, I was totally paranoid and only able to take short breaths. *I'm not messing with that any more,* I told myself. I climbed the stairs to my room and played *Surrealistic Pillow* by Jefferson Airplane real loud. When *Somebody to Love* came on, I held my hairbrush like a microphone and pretended I was Grace Slick. *Lies were my truth.* I tried to force the Velvet Tobacco can out of my mind.

A few days later when the sun came out, I carried a basket of wet laundry outside. The neighborhood was quiet and the air smelled like damp earth. Now five or six robins pecked in the lawn. After I hung sheets and towels on the clothesline, I felt in my pocket for cigarettes, matches, and a quarter.

Judge, I hope you don't get too mad when I tell you what I did next. I stepped behind the playhouse. The vines back there tangled around my ankles. I looked down and felt with my feet for the can. I thought I remembered exactly where I tossed it, but no luck. After a while I gave up and was about to go back to the house when my toe knocked against something. That's when I spied a strip of red almost completely covered with ivy. When I lifted it out of the vines, the can felt clammy, like worms had crawled all over it. I wiped it on my jeans and went inside the playhouse.

The quarter fit perfectly between the rim and the lid. One twist and the top opened. Pot really does smell a lot like oregano, Judge. I could tell it was totally fine. I balanced the can between my knees while I squeezed most of the tobacco out of a Kool cigarette — Dad left a pack on the dining room buffet for me — then filled it with weed. Ishmael had jammed some rolling papers in the can, but I just wanted to test a little bit. And I didn't want to roll a joint for just myself.

My hands shook so much, I had to strike three matches before I lit up. Just one toke, I thought, for Ishmael. As the smoke burned in my lungs, I felt justified. After what I'd been through, I deserved a chance to relax. And somehow I felt it was a way to get back at everyone who hated me, like saying, *Who cares about you? Who needs you?*

I know I promised to stay away from marijuana, Judge. I almost didn't include any of this. But when I thought about why you wanted me to write this report, I figured it's because you want me to be honest with myself and honest with you. So this is the truth. No more lies.

Now that I decided to tell you everything, you might not be surprised when I admit I smoked marijuana more than once after that. Ok, after the first time, I smoked a joint almost every day. The only thing I'll say for myself is that being stuck at home for months is really boring. It might not be the best way to punish teenagers, you know?

By the end of April, I'd smoked almost all of the stash. I worried about what I'd do to pass the time after it was gone, but I was so bored and lonely I couldn't stop. On a Friday, I draped wet sheets over the clothesline like a theatre curtain to hide me while I smoked one of the last joints. I kept hoping the pot would mellow me out, like when I smoked with Ishmael, but by then it just made me sleepy.

As I pinched clothespins over the sheets, Lisa called from her yard, "Joni? Is that you?"

Then she hopped the fence and pushed through the sheets before I had time to ditch the joint. I held it down by my side, hoping she wouldn't see it.

"Oh, hey, I thought you'd be at work," I said.

I was scared Lisa might bust me, but I was so desperate to talk I hardly cared.

"How's it going? I know it's been tough," Lisa said. Then she frowned and scrunched her nose.

The smell of lilacs and carnations breezed from her body. I remembered a heart-shaped bottle of Wind Song I'd seen on her dresser. From somewhere, a police siren wailed, then faded. My heart beat like crazy and tears welled in my eyes. Lisa watched smoke curling up my side and sniffed the air.

"Still using?"

I shrugged. "You gonna tell?"

Lisa strolled over to our crummy picnic table and sat on a bench, even though the wood was damp and lined with green moss. She patted the seat beside her and held out her hand for the joint. I figured she'd crush it and give me a lecture. Instead, she took a toke and held it a long time.

"After our visit to see his parents, Jake started applying for jobs with firms in Pittsburgh. He told me to give up my job at the bank while he waits for the right offer." Lisa's voice was breathy and smoke-filled. "He wants me to use the time to organize the move."

"You're moving?"

I had a sick feeling they were leaving because they knew I'd been in their house and taken the jar of baby peaches...and worse. Lisa passed me the J.

"These days are hard for you, Joni. I get that. And God knows, sometimes, you just need to shut your eyes and shut out the world. You hope when you open them, things will be better, back to normal. But I think you know in your heart things never get back to normal."

I let the smoke float out of my lungs and passed her the joint.

"It will never be normal for me because I'm not normal. I'm a weirdo."

Lisa looked at me and laughed. At first I felt kind of bad until she said, "Here's the big secret, Joni. No one's normal. Everyone has a bag of crap to deal with. You're dealing with it this way." She handed me the joint. "Smoking weed, drinking booze, and lots of other stuff we don't need to talk about — they just give you a place to hide. Hiding doesn't make you happy. It makes you disappear."

Lisa stared at the ground for a long time. I dropped the joint and let it burn out. Finally she started talking again.

"So you messed up and got in trouble. So what? You have plenty of time to work your way out of it. You need to get back to school, go to college, and do something with your life. God, I wish I were your age. What I wouldn't do to have another chance." Lisa shook a leaf out of her hair.

"You'll have another chance in Pittsburgh," I whispered. *Everyone has a bag of crap to deal with,* I thought. *Lisa too?*

Lisa snorted. "In Pittsburgh I'll have a chance to have another kid, get old, get fat, drink too much, and wonder why I never did anything with my life. When I was your age, I swore I wouldn't be like my mother. She let my father run her life. Not me. I'd go to college, spend a year in France, come back and go to graduate school. I'd sing in a choir, act in plays, write a novel. But when I was a sophomore in college, I started dating Jake. He was a senior. Before the end of junior year, Jake begged me to marry him. And instead of France and graduate school, I took a job at the bank to earn enough money so Jake could finish law school. Now he's planning to move us to his hometown where he has friends and family. I'll be stuck in the house with kids and laundry and daytime soaps. I gave up my dreams for his." She leaned forward and stood up. "Don't let anyone steal your dreams, Joni. Become the person you're supposed to be."

I clenched my jaw. Dreams. I didn't have dreams. Lisa was beautiful, with thick auburn hair, blue eyes, and chiseled features — the grown-up version of the popular girls at Redwood. She married Jake, a handsome and successful man. Natalie was cute and funny, and Lisa loved her, I knew. I'd always thought Lisa had a perfect life. It was hard to believe she could ever be as unhappy as me.

She faced me and took both my hands.

"I better go. Natalie will wake up screaming if I'm not there. Look, Joni, you have a future. Don't blow it. Don't let them win. Do things your own way." She pointed to the smoldering roach on the ground. "And get over that stuff."

The next day, after I watched Lisa put Natalie in the car and drive away, I tucked her blue bikini under their backdoor mat. And then I shook the last bit of pot from the can into my palm and let it blow away.

Judge, after I'd been stuck at home four months — I know you won't believe this — I wished I could go back to Redwood. At least I'd have something to do. I asked the homebound teacher for more mimeographs and more books, but she said she had to follow school procedures. Some days I looked through the *Encyclopedias* Mom bought at the grocery store. We only had up to O. But a lot of the stuff I read was just annoying. Like, when a person wants to eat one, who cares that an orange is a species of fruit from the *Genus* citrus of the *Rutaceae* family from the *Sapindales* order in the *Plantae* kingdom? Not me. I spent a lot of time doodling — I decorated the edges of the newspaper, the papers I wrote for the homebound teacher, the backs of envelopes that came in the mail, any open space. My mother threw a hissy fit the day I doodled all over the kitchen tablecloth. I hardly remember doing it.

Each morning before she left for Tesses Dresses, Mom gave me a list of chores. Until I became the family maid, dust bunnies lived for years under the furniture. Now, once a week I sprawled on my stomach and swooshed a rag under the sofa, chairs, bureaus, and beds. When the soaps came on TV, I hauled out the iron and spray starch and watched while I pressed Dad's shirts, slacks, and hankies.

At 3:00 p.m. each afternoon, I waited at the front door, counting the minutes until the yellow school bus squealed to a stop, the doors wheezed open, and Tommy's red Phillies cap appeared on the steps. The first few months, I helped him with homework, talked about Superman, played with his race cars, and watched *The Match Game*.

But this month, the days got longer and warmer. As soon as Tommy dropped his book bag and grabbed a handful of Oreos, he was gone again. Then I'd sit on the back porch listening to the neighborhood kids play and remembering when I was one of them.

I thought about Ishmael a lot too. On May 15th — I remember the date because I was actually excited that I had a dentist appointment the next day — I started to make a peanut butter and jelly sandwich for lunch. When I reached for the bread, I noticed Mom's address book next to it. I turned to the F section and found Mrs. Fanelli's phone number. Since the hearing, I'd only seen Mrs. Fanelli on Sundays at church. But I never had a chance to talk to her there because my parents hustled me out and drove home. I wondered if she asked them about me. I imagined my parents saying, *Everything's going fine. Joni's doing fine. She does her homework and hands it in each week.*

But I wanted to ask Mrs. Fanelli what happened to Ishmael. I couldn't ask my parents. Once I casually asked Mom, *Do you ever run into Mrs. Reid at the grocery store?* You'd have thought I asked her, *Have you ever thought about driving the car off a bridge?* Another time I got Tommy to ask Dad, *Whatever happened to that guy who used to drive Joni home?* But I guess Dad figured out where that question came from. In a pretty nice voice considering he was still angry about the whole mess, he answered, *None of your business. And tell your sister to leave you out of this.*

Anyway, after I found Mrs. Fanelli's phone number, I thought, *why shouldn't I talk to my lawyer if I want?* I carried the address book into the living room. I had a right to know what happened to Ishmael. When I dialed her number, my hand shook so much my finger got caught in the dial wheel and I had to hang up and dial again.

"Fanelli and Associates, Rosie speaking," a woman said. That freaked me out. I expected Mrs. Fanelli to answer. "Hello? Hello, can I help you?"

I almost hung up but somehow managed to squeak out, "Is Mrs. Fanelli there?" It took a couple minutes to convince her Mrs. Fanelli was my lawyer.

"What is it, Joan? Are you okay?" When I heard Mrs. Fanelli's voice I was so relieved, tears came to my eyes.

"I'm okay. But no one will tell me what happened to Ishmael, I mean, Michael Reid. Did he have his trial yet?" I sounded pitiful. There was a long sigh and then nothing. "Are you still there?" I asked.

"Last week Michael Reid was sentenced to three years at Graterford prison. During the trial he testified that you provided the drugs and you arranged all the sales. And he swore you lied about your age, that you told him you were eighteen. His lawyer said Michael was just a nice guy who tried to help a messed up girl. But no one bought his story. It's time for you to close that book too and move on."

I heard Mrs. Fanelli's words, but I didn't want to believe them. The Ishmael I loved bought me lemon pies, cried because I fell off the swing, put his arm around my shoulders, and called me his best girl. But my stomach still got queasy whenever I thought about the marijuana brownie, how he always wanted me to smoke a joint, and how happy he was when

I sold pot to girls at school. I tried not to think about New Year's Eve, the wine, and the bong, or waking up in his bed and puking my guts out, worrying about how far we went.

But everything wasn't Ishmael's fault. I liked smoking pot. I sold the stuff to the girls. And even though I didn't feel like it, I went to his room on New Year's. I didn't know what to think anymore, but still, I believed he loved me. And now we both were screwed.

"Why is this happening?" I sobbed.

"Joan, you need to listen to me. You are a very lucky girl. Things could be much worse. Now, pull yourself together. I'm glad you called. I had a note on my calendar to call you next week to get you set up for summer at Camp St. Augustine of Hippo. That's just a few weeks away," she said. In my mind, I saw Mrs. Fanelli at the phone, tapping her cigarette against the ashtray and thumbing through notes on her desk. "I spoke with Father Vincent the other day. You have an appointment to meet him on Memorial Day. I'll come to your house to take you there. That way we'll have time to talk. Now, I have a meeting."

"Don't tell my parents I called," I begged, suddenly worried about what they'd think.

"Attorney-client privilege," she said.

Even after I heard the hang-up click, I kept the receiver against my ear. Grace Slick's voice rang through my head — *tears are running...* At least I knew where Ishmael was. I dug through the drawer where my parents kept pencils and pens and stamps.

When the mailman came up the walk to our house, I handed him a letter.

The week before Memorial Day, it was so hot, I dreamed about diving in the pool and staying under water until I had to come up for air. Each day, as soon as everyone left the house, I rushed through the damned chores. I washed the dishes and left them in the drying rack. Before I vacuumed the living room, I sprayed the end tables with Pledge and wiped them with a rag. I learned the hard way that if I vacuumed first, I had to do it again after I dusted. I never understood why the TV always got so dusty.

That week, after I finished the inside chores, I changed into my bathing suit before I carried out the laundry to hang on the clothesline. With the sun on my back and a breeze ruffling the sheets, I pretended it was summer and I was off from school. Soon, I'd meet my friends at the pool and we'd lie on lounge chairs to get tan.

When it got too hot, I aimed the garden hose straight up in the air and danced in the sprinkles like a little kid. I worried a little about meeting Father Vincent. But mostly I tried to figure out how to get back to the pool.

On Memorial Day, before Mrs. Fanelli arrived, I showered and washed my hair. To make a good impression on Father Vincent, I dressed like the girls in *Seventeen*. I wore blue Bermuda shorts and a red-and-white-striped sleeveless blouse my mother bought from Tesses Dresses. As I slipped my feet into the Woolworth sneakers, I wondered if Ishmael was thinking about me that very second.

While I waited in the doorway for the burgundy Caddy to bump into the driveway, my heart raced. Just the thought of driving away from the house, away from my father's silence and my mother's sighs, seemed like heaven. I needed to get out of this house. Even before Mrs. Fanelli knocked, I pulled open the front door. Heat blew in like car exhaust. Before that day, I'd only seen Mrs. Fanelli in lawyer clothes. As she took the steps to the porch, wearing red shorts and a white top with a flag bandana around her neck, I felt embarrassed, almost like seeing someone naked. I stood back to let her in. She pulled off her sunglasses and glanced into the living room.

"Happy Memorial Day, Joni. Another scorcher. Are your parents home?"

"They went to the parade. They said to thank you for getting me." I fought the urge to push past her and run to the car.

I held my breath and waited while she looked me up and down.

"You look nice. Good choices."

I followed her out the door. Once we settled in the car, Mrs. Fanelli adjusted her cat-eye sunglasses, checked her teeth in the mirror, and started the engine. The Cadillac's air conditioner blasted cold, tinny air. As hot as it was outside, after a few minutes I folded my arms against my body to keep from shivering. The radio played my favorite guitar riff from *Jumpin' Jack Flash*. I bobbed my head to the rhythm, feeling almost happy.

Mrs. Fanelli glanced over. "I don't know why you kids listen to this crap. Those Beatle people's music is weird and violent."

I started to say it was the Rolling Stones, not the Beatles, but why bother? She twisted the radio dial until she found something she liked and then sang along to an oldie — *Forget Him.*

When it ended, she sighed. "That's Bobby Rydell. He grew up in South Philly like me. We went to the same church. Lovely family. Good values. Great voice. Where's the romance in songs about spikes in heads? You should listen to those words, kid," Mrs. Fanelli said. "Forget him. Forget Michael Reid."

I squirmed. I knew I'd never forget him. But I was so happy to be outside I just nodded and looked out the window. Kids ran up and down the sidewalk waving little American flags. Red, white, and blue crepe paper decorated store windows. When we stopped at a light, the air shimmered like water. Through the breaks between the buildings, I saw parade marchers the next street over and heard trumpets blare *You're a Grand Old Flag.* I thought about all the parades I went to when I was younger — sitting on my father's shoulders, waving a flag, dripping grape sno-cone on his head and, later, going to the pool to celebrate the first day of summer.

"The pool opens today," I said, trying to sound casual.

"I don't remember the last time it hit the 90s the week before Memorial Day," Mrs. Fanelli said.

She screeched into the church driveway and lurched to a stop at the side of the rectory. When I got out, she stayed in her seat. She waved me around to her side.

"Father's office is through that door, first room on the right. Put your best foot forward, Joan. Father's a great man. He's sticking his neck out for you. Don't make him regret his decision. I'll be back in an hour."

My throat closed and I couldn't swallow. I'd expected Mrs. Fanelli to come with me. Instead, I had to face Father Vincent alone. I wondered if he'd ask me to explain all the trouble I got in and why I thought I was good enough for his camp. I wondered if he thought I was a criminal. *Why did he agree to let me work at his camp anyway?*

"Wait!" I yelled as Mrs. Fanelli started to back out.

But instead of stopping to let me in, the car zigzagged left and right. There was a loud crack when the car scraped the mailbox, but Mrs. Fanelli must not have heard it. At the curb, she paused a moment to look up and down, then swung the Cadillac onto the street.

The wooden post leaned to the side — cracked like a pencil — with only splinters keeping it from landing flat on the ground. The black mailbox dangled from one bracket. When I turned to the rectory, Father Vincent stood in the doorway. My right eye twitched. I followed his gaze to the wrecked mailbox and caught my breath, waiting for him to start yelling. But he didn't say a word. Instead, he wrapped his arms across his stomach, then bent over, choking. I thought he was so upset he was having a heart attack.

"Oh God, Father, are you all right?" I called. "I'm sure Mrs. Fanelli will get your mailbox fixed. It was just an accident."

"No, no, no, no worries," he gasped, straightening up. "Sally's the worst driver in Pennsylvania. We're lucky that's all she took down. At least for now."

Father was still laughing when he ushered me inside. His office was small and smelled like old books. On his desk, next to a pipe, sat a red can of Velvet Tobacco. It made me nervous. A roll-top desk was shoved in the corner, and next to it a two-shelf bookcase was jammed with cracked, leather-bound books. Father pointed to a chair facing him. I sat down, careful not to muss the fraying doilies draped over the seat and arms. After the chill from Mrs. Fanelli's air conditioner, this room was stifling.

While I waited for Father to talk, I figured our meeting would be like going to confession. Maybe that was why Mrs. Fanelli left me alone.

"So, Miss Joan Byrnes, we need to talk about your work at Camp St. Augustine of Hippo this summer," Father said. "Why don't you start? Do you have any questions?"

I looked at the worn carpet. A drop of perspiration ran down my back. "Why Hippo?" I finally asked. I felt really stupid.

Father looked at me sideways and cleared his throat. "Hippo's the region in northern Africa, now Algeria, where St. Augustine came from. Anything else?"

"What will I do there?" That seemed like a better question.

Father sat back. "The children who attend Camp Hippo are identified through Catholic Charities in Philadelphia. They come from families who typically live in historically black neighborhoods. In fact, most of our counselors attended Camp Hippo when they were children. Because of their families' situations, these children rarely have the opportunity to learn to swim. I consider swimming to be an essential life skill, and in past years, I taught camp swim lessons. But the truth is, I failed miserably. You see, I'm not a proficient swimmer myself. When Sally contacted me early this year about your situation, I considered you a Godsend. Finally, Camp

Hippo will have a qualified swim instructor and, according to the *Gospel of Luke, thou shalt be blessed, because they have not wherewith to make thee recompense."* Father looked at me with a pleased expression. "Sally advised me that you received your lifeguard certification last summer, is that correct?"

"Yeah. I mean, yes, Father. I took the class last August."

"Very well. And you have experience teaching swimming?"

"I helped teach the fives, sixes, and sevens at our neighborhood pool."

That sounded pretty good, I thought. I began to relax a little. Father nodded and pressed the fingers of each hand together.

"Good, good. You'll be our lifeguard and swim instructor. Most of each day, you'll be at the pool to give lessons and lifeguard during open swim times. But you'll also be a co-counselor for a cabin of twelve girls. After lessons, you'll catch up with your cabin for dinner and other activities. Does that make sense?"

It made sense but seemed like a lot of work. I hoped I'd be good enough. I didn't say anything. I just nodded.

Father Vincent leaned forward and looked at me like I was a bird in a cage and he wondered if I'd fly away as soon as he opened the door. He drummed his fingers on the desk.

"What is it that you want, Joan?"

His question surprised me. I thought about Jill Howard and the girls at Redwood. I thought about the senior, Mercedes, who talked to me once. I thought about Ishmael, Mrs. Fanelli, and Lisa White. I thought about Martin Luther King and Bobby Kennedy, both assassinated last year, and about American soldiers fighting in Vietnam. I thought about the months I'd been stuck at home. I didn't know what was real anymore. I'm not sure why I said it, except just then, it felt honest.

"I want to be real, Father."

I waited for a lecture — *the only reality is through Jesus Christ* or something. My ears pounded like Indian tom-toms. Father and the room blurred. Brakes screeched. A car door opened and shut. When my vision cleared, I realized Father was studying me.

"I believe you will find the campers at St. Augustine of Hippo to be very real. As for you, how can I help you be real?"

He stopped tapping his fingers on the desk.

"I'm out of shape for swimming, Father. I haven't been in a pool in months."

"I see." Father offered me his pack of Newports. "Do you smoke?"

"That's what got me in trouble," I said in a low voice.

Before Father lit his cigarette, there were three knocks on the door and Mrs. Fanelli entered in a rush of hot air. Sweat beaded on her upper lip, and lipstick smeared one front tooth. She looked from Father to me.

"Father, did you notice your mailbox fell down?" She made tsk, tsk sounds. "I'll call Joe and have him send someone over to build you a brick one."

I looked at Father and raised my eyebrow.

Mrs. Fanelli turned to me and asked, "Are we set?"

"We're all set, Sally," Father answered, "except Joan tells me she's out of shape for swimming. Can you do something about that? I need her ready in two weeks. Real and ready."

When Mrs. Fanelli started toward the door, I glanced at Father and returned his wink.

At noon, cars filled almost every spot in the pool parking lot. Mrs. Fanelli darted in front of a station wagon to win a spot in the far corner. Sounds of whistles and shouting and the smell of suntan lotion drifted in the warm breeze. As I headed for the pool area, Mrs. Fanelli turned left into the clubhouse. Even though I was dying to get in the water, I dreaded facing summer teammates and neighbors who knew about my arrest. I imagined a scarlet D for druggy emblazoned on my chest. After the gate girl smiled and let me pass, I threw back my head and took a deep breath.

Chlorine, lotion, and smoky hot dogs smelled ordinary and precious. Across the deck and grounds, people clustered in their regular areas — little kids by the sand pit, teenagers under a maple tree along the far fence, mothers and toddlers around the baby pool, old people sipping drinks under the canvas roof by the bar. The summer swim team coach sat in a lifeguard stand — his nose zinc-oxide white, dark hair curling over his ears, a white towel draped across his shoulders. When I called up, *Hi, Steve*, he never took his eyes off the almost empty pool. I looked for Billy Jensen and the other kids I hung around with the summer before, but none of them were there. That was probably good. Even though I missed them and was dying to be with friends, I was afraid they'd blow me off. I wasn't ready for that.

I dropped my towel on a bench and sat at the edge of the pool, testing the water with my feet. Across the deck, my parents waved to Mrs. Fanelli, and she joined them under the green-and-white-striped awning. I knew their tall glasses meant Tom Collins drinks. Dad signaled the waiter to bring one for Mrs. Fanelli.

Except for Tommy and a handful of friends, hardly anyone was in the pool. The water was too chilly for most people, but I didn't care if ice cubes floated across the top. I tightened my ponytail and adjusted my goggles.

As soon as I dove in, the cold water stunned me. A shot of chlorinated water blew up my nose. I came to the surface shivering and took a breath of bleachy air, then extended my arms and pushed off the bottom. Swimming felt more natural than walking. Stroke, stroke, breathe, flip, push off, kick, kick, surface, stroke, stroke, breathe. Each time I turned my head to the side, bleary figures in red, purple, or white glinted on the deck. After a couple laps, a blue and white mist solidified into Jill Howard. I never expected to see her that day. When I swam past, I kicked harder, splashing the deck and her legs. She stepped back. I thought about asking Tommy to creep up behind her and push her in, but I told myself to forget her. She'd done her damage. How could she hurt me now?

I wanted to swim forever, to feel cold water against my skin, to propel myself from end to end in mindless movement, but after only ten laps, my breath caught in my throat. At the deep end, I hung my elbow over the edge and gasped. This must be what asthma feels like — your heart struggling for oxygen the lungs can't supply. My muscles quivered and I worried I might drown, even though my head was above the surface. When I set my palms on the edge to push up and out like I did a million times before, my arms were too weak. Instead, embarrassed, I paddled to the ladder to climb out. Jill waited there, arms folded across her chest, her stomach, arms, and legs winter-white against her bright blue suit.

"You out of jail?" she asked in her snidest voice.

"Since the day I left Redwood," I shot back, my heart still racing and my voice croaky.

Jill snorted and curled her upper lip. As she backed away, she said, "You try to act like you're all tough and cool but you're just a pathetic druggy."

"And you're so full of shit your eyes are brown," was my best retort. God, Redwood still made me feel like such a loser.

When Jill joined three girls lying on lounge chairs, they glanced my way and laughed. After I dried off, I made a skirt with my towel and shambled to the bar, where the smell of greasy burgers and fries turned my stomach. Around the pool, kids shouted and water splashed. On the grass, Tommy smacked a tetherball with his friends. He had lots of friends.

Before they noticed me dripping outside the patio bar, my parents and Mrs. Fanelli were smiling and talking. As soon as they saw me, their expressions went blank.

My father cleared his throat. "Still got the moves. You looked good out there."

That was about the nicest thing he'd said to me in months, but for some reason it hurt. I winced and turned to Mrs. Fanelli.

"I'm ready to go," I said, shaking my hair so water sprayed out.

"I'll have her home in an hour. We need to discuss a few things before she leaves for camp."

My parents looked relieved. The less time they spent with me, it seemed, the better. Since January, the Barbie-doll daughter they wanted turned into *Rosemary's Baby*.

In the car, Mrs. Fanelli shook out a cigarette and held the red coil lighter against it before she eased out of the parking spot. She lowered her window and exhaled outside.

"How did your meeting with Father Vincent go?" she asked.

"Fine," I said.

"Fine? That's all you say to me, fine? What exactly does fine mean?" She looked like I smelled like dog dirt.

I took a deep breath, still pissed that Jill Howard wrecked my first decent day out of the house.

"It was good. Father wants me to teach swimming. He said the kids are from poor families and camp is their only chance to learn to swim. It sounds like a lot of work, though."

Mrs. Fanelli flicked the cigarette outside and stared straight ahead. "Joan, you have a chance to do some good. A summer away at camp in the country can change the lives of those poor kids. Let's hope it changes your life too." She pulled the car over and set the emergency brake. "Look at me Joan, and listen. You got involved with the wrong guy and you made bad choices. But this summer is your chance to redeem yourself. When you get to camp, as long as you follow the rules, do your best, and make good choices, then when school starts in the fall, you can put all this behind you. Forget Michael Reid. Forget drugs. Work hard, get along with the other counselors, and for God's sake, let yourself smile."

"I will," I whispered. But I couldn't imagine ever smiling again.

My last night at home, I sat at the dinner table and pulled cheese and anchovies off a slice of pizza. After one bite, I tossed the slice onto the box and spit the rest into a napkin.

"Joni, that's rude. I thought you liked pizza." Mom laid her half-eaten slice on a paper plate and ran her tongue over her teeth. "I don't know why you're so fussy."

I lost it then. I don't know why. Any other night I would make myself a peanut butter and jelly sandwich or just not eat. But that night I went bananas.

"You know I hate anchovies. The least you could do before I go away is buy a normal pizza. But why would you care? You don't care about anything I want." I pushed back my chair and stood up.

"Don't talk to your mother that way." Dad glared at me as he flipped his pizza crust into the box and brushed off his shirt. "Let's get the hell out of here, Tommy," he said in a disgusted voice.

Mom's lip quivered and her eyes filled with tears. "Before you started with Michael Reid, you were such a good daughter. Now you're all freaked out like a hippy. Why did this happen, Joni?"

I should have just shut up then and left the room but the part of me that wanted to tell her I'm sorry got buried by the part of me that hated her. So I screamed, "Because I'll never be the poufy-haired beauty queen daughter you want. I'm just me — a loser. Well, you don't have to worry about me anymore because tomorrow I'll be gone."

The anchovy smell made me gag. Until I pulled myself together enough to go upstairs, I hung on to the chair back. I didn't look up when Mom shuffled to the liquor cabinet. As I left the kitchen, ice cubes tinkled, soda fizzed, and I visualized Mom pouring a shot of whiskey with her tears spilling over the ice. I ran to the bathroom and puked.

In my bedroom, clothes, album covers, candy wrappers, empty cigarette packs, and a couple *Seventeen Magazines* littered the floor. The cover of the April 1969 issue showed a groovy girl in a swinging purple dress. To the left of the girl, my mother circled the article title — *How Can I Tell If I'm Normal?* When I kicked it, the magazine hopped and landed on a damp towel.

Like a caged monkey, I skittered around the room, picking up clothes and throwing them down, pitching everything into a bigger mess. I knew Father Vincent planned to get me at 8:00 in the morning, but I couldn't think about what to pack. From downstairs, my parents' voices rose and quieted — my mother's shrill and shaky, my father's strong and logical.

Screw them, I thought. They didn't care about me and they sure didn't understand me. Now that I'd be gone all summer, they'd be happy. I found my swim bag in a corner, smashed under books. When I unzipped the side pocket, there was the dragon lighter Ishmael gave me. I remembered the silk dragon purse shoved under my mattress and dug it out. I dumped everything out of it. Mixed in with two dollar bills and three bucks or so in change were the two joints. They were flattened and crinkly but the papers hadn't torn. I didn't think I'd need money at camp, so I put it back in the purse and left it and the lighter in my nightstand drawer. I couldn't leave the joints there, so I stuffed one in each back pocket of my cutoffs. Then I threw my blue Speedo and grey sweats into the gym bag. Tomorrow, I'd get up early and pack the rest of my stuff.

Outside, in the Whites' backyard, I heard Natalie squealing and Lisa laughing. I moved the curtain aside and watched Lisa push Natalie in the baby swing. Both of them looked so happy. I thought I might be happy if I moved to Pittsburgh with them. Most of that night, I couldn't sleep. I lay in bed listening to the Beatles' *White Album*. *Helter Skelter* and *Revolution 9* looped endlessly through my brain.

When my mother called up the stairs, "Joni, Father Vincent's here," I leapt out of bed, pulled on my cutoffs and T-shirt, and grabbed my swim bag.

I left without a word.

Father opened the trunk of his old Chevy and I tossed in my bag.

"I see you pack light," Father said.

"I guess so. I wasn't sure what to bring."

Father Vincent must have sensed I didn't feel like talking. He tuned the radio to some old people's station and listened to Andy Williams, Bobby Darin, Rosemary Clooney, and Frank Sinatra.

As we passed through the city, I stared out the window. Blocks of brick row houses gave way to car dealerships, Gino's restaurants, and shady-looking shacks with shady-looking men straddling Harleys. When Frank Sinatra's *Bewitched, Bothered, and Bewildered* came on, Father

Vincent sang along in his best Sunday Mass voice. Just then I hated Frank Sinatra, my parents, and the cops who arrested Ishmael and me. Through the rust hole under my feet, I watched dusty macadam stream by.

The cigarette ashes Father Vincent flicked out the window flew back in, tiny grey flakes spiraling onto his short-sleeved black shirt. A drop of sweat trickled from his forehead and past his nose. After he sneezed, loud and wet, Father pulled a plaid hanky from a back pocket, wiped his nose, then anchored the cloth under his thigh. When the next Sinatra song came on — *Call Me Irresponsible* — Father turned to me. His pale blue eyes were watery and a speck of tobacco stuck to a front tooth.

"Your theme song," he said, with a crooked smile.

I forced myself to smile back. Outside the city we drove over narrow roads that cut through open spaces. Heat shimmered against the windshield and bits of hay from a slow-moving farm truck floated in the open windows. I stared at green cornfields next to pastures where Black Angus cows, dirt-colored sheep, and weary horses grazed. About an hour's drive west, I knew, Graterford Prison sat in farmland like this.

I thought about Ishmael then. I wondered what he looked like with his head shaved, wearing a uniform — like when he was in the army. I figured there'd be lots of other druggies there, so at least he'd have guys to talk to. Somewhere I read that the inmates worked on the prison farm. Thinking about that made me feel better. I imagined Ishmael working outside, bulking up with manly muscles, his pale skin turning tan. I wondered if he got the letter I sent last month. I wondered why he never wrote back.

The further we drove from the city, the more I felt as if we traveled back in time. We passed red barns and jersey cows, an A&P, an ESSO station, a dingy diner, a Farmer's Supply Store, and an F. W. Woolworth's next to an ancient movie theater. From porches of clapboard houses with peeling paint and leaning downspouts, old women in faded housecoats waved as we drove by. A hand-painted sign on a big sheet of plywood advertised strawberries, raspberries, and pickles at a rickety farm stand. The air smelled like dried straw.

I reached back to touch the joints I stashed in the pockets of my cutoffs and hoped I wouldn't be subject to a strip search. Only two — all I had to make it through nine weeks. I stared down at my buffalo-hide sandals. A strip of leather ringed my toe and another crossed my instep, while the sole provided about as much protection as a layer of skin. In the rush to leave, I forgot the stolen Woolworth sneakers and everything else I meant to bring.

Just before we made a left turn onto a gravel road through a forest of pines, I asked, "Father, can I bum a smoke?"

He took the pack from his shirt pocket and flipped it to me.

"There'll be no smoking in front of the campers. Still, you'll be able to steal away for a cigarette now and again. I keep a pack in my office for the counselors."

"That's nice," I said, pressing the lighter coil that glowed like an evil eye against the cigarette.

Suddenly I was afraid. *What was I getting into?*

As the car emerged from the pines, I blew smoke out the window and squinted in the glare. Sun-bleached, low-slung wood buildings made a horseshoe around the pebbly lot where the car skidded to a stop next to a dented VW van. As we stepped out of Father's car, from behind the buildings, the sound of a ball bouncing and deep laughter broke the silence. Despite the trees that surrounded the buildings, the air hung heavy and hot.

After Father Vincent popped the trunk, I grabbed my swim bag. When I turned, I was face-to-face with a woman with short grey hair, dark eyebrows, and light eyes. Her face and arms were the same wrinkly tan as her shirt and baggy shorts. When she spoke, I heard the music of my Irish grandmother.

"We've been on pins and needles, Father, wondering when you'd arrive. And you're the little criminal, are you? Well, you're welcome here. At the end of the day you'll be good for nothing more than falling down dead on your cot. We'll work the devil out of you," she said.

Her crooked smile and kind blue eyes made me feel okay. Father Vincent introduced us.

"Sister Mary Immaculata, meet Joan Byrnes."

"They call me Mary Mac," the nun said.

I'd never seen a nun out of habit, nor had one tell me to call her anything but Sister.

"They call me Joni," I whispered.

As soon as I dropped the cigarette and crushed it, I got a chill. A picture from one of Tommy's comics flashed through my mind along with the thought, *I've entered Bizarro World.*

With Mary Mac leading me by the hand, I stubbed my toe on the steps to Hippo Hall. This is where, she told me, the campers ate their meals, chose their daily activities, and gathered each evening for Mass, dinner, and roundup.

As Father Vincent lugged a dingy brown suitcase toward his cabin, he called, "Jermaine! The new counselor's here." The sound of a ball thudding against a backboard stopped.

A tall black guy wearing a crocheted yellow, red, and green beret sauntered through the pine trees and stopped at the bottom of the steps. A lollipop stick dangled in his mouth. The man-boy looked about my age. His muscular arms bulged from his T-shirt and his face, neck, and arms glistened with sweat. As he came close, a smell like burning rubber rose from his high-top Chuck Taylors. Mary Mac dropped my hand and turned to smile at him.

"Joni, this is Jermaine, our senior counselor. Anything you need, ask him," she said.

Her face softened, like she was a proud mother introducing her son. Jermaine crossed his arms over his chest, bounced the lollipop stick in his mouth, and checked me out.

"Like Mary Mac says, anything you need. You got camp clothes? Or you gonna steal them?"

I noticed he spoke with a soft lisp, but his words shocked me. I never expected to be mocked my first ten minutes here. Was I destined to be a loser wherever I went? I felt myself begin to lose it, but in my mind I heard Ishmael say, *Mellow out. Be cool.* I remembered Mrs. Fanelli's advice too — *work hard, get along with the other counselors and for God's sake, let yourself smile.*

I scrunched my face in what must have been the most pathetic attempt at a smile ever. I took a deep breath.

With the grimace plastered on my face, I managed to say, "Why are you staring?"

"No reason. I just never met a little white girl with a rap sheet before."

I forced myself to unclench my fists. Judge, I guess I imagined I'd feel better at camp — with fewer things to worry about. But instead, just like Redwood, right away I had to keep my guard up. And that made me want a smoke, a real smoke, to calm down. Jermaine leaned against a railing to study me, the lollipop stick clacking between his teeth.

"Jermaine's just teasing, Joan, all in fun. I hope you have a sense of humor, because Lord knows you need one around here," Mary Mac said in a cheerful voice. She paused a moment and looked at my sandals and then at my small swim bag. "And did you bring camp clothes? You have other shoes, of course."

Crap, I thought, *I'm such a dope*. "I packed my swim suit and sweats, but I was kind of rushed this morning." I bit my lower lip and glanced up at Mary Mac. "Sorry."

Mary Mac shook her head and made those tsk, tsk sounds nuns like to make. "Each counselor gets five T-shirts, so you'll have those to start with. Come along. Don't worry, I keep a store with clothes and shoes and other essentials for the campers. Most of these poor children arrive with nothing — like you. You're no bigger than a pollywog. You'll have no trouble fitting into shorts and sneakers and whatever else you need. After we find you proper clothes, Jermaine will show you the pool and take you to Daiquiri in your cabin. You're assigned to Bernie — St. Bernadette's — with the tens and elevens."

By then I was nervous and confused and wondering what a Daiquiri in a cabin was. I followed Mary Mac into Hippo Hall.

"Take a look around," Mary Mac said. "I'll be a minute finding gear to fit you."

When she opened a big sliding door along the back wall, I took a quick look at the camp store — shelves filled with clothes, shoes, towels, and sheets and two cabinets with soap and stuff.

Hippo Hall was a huge, open room — bigger than the auditorium at Redwood. Weathered wood planks covered the walls and thick, exposed rafters crossed the ceiling under the sharp pitch of the roof. Fold-up chairs and tables leaned in stacks along one wall. Across the front, a stage stood three-feet above the floor. In the windows, spiders wove silky patterns that struggled to sparkle in sunlight filtered through dirty glass. My sandals crunched over sawdust and dried rodent shit. After I sneezed, Mary Mac looked up from her sorting as if surprised to see me.

"Ah, there you are. I've put out everything a girl who comes to camp with a swimsuit and sweat pants might need." She looked pleased.

My mouth must have dropped open when I saw all the clothes and supplies Mary Mac laid out for me. There were Camp Hippo shirts in white, red, blue, green, and yellow; blue and khaki shorts; white cotton underwear; red PF Flyers sneakers; a toothbrush and Pepsodent; a pocket comb; baby shampoo, and a bar of Ivory soap.

"And I don't imagine you thought to bring towels and sheets," she said.

When I glanced up with my lower lip sucked in, Mary Mac laughed. While she grabbed more stuff I asked, "Mary Mac, what goes on in Hippo Hall? Because, it's huge."

"Sure and it is that."

She plunked down stiff white sheets, towels, a corduroy bed cover, and a thick canvas bag, then scanned the room.

"There's enough space for up to a hundred campers and counselors to sit at tables for meals and attend Mass. After dinner every night, up on the stage, a different cabin leads Camp Roundup. Hippo Hall is the heart of camp."

"You ready to take the long walk?" Jermaine asked.

I hadn't heard him come in and I jumped. "Sure, just a minute."

I turned in a complete circle before I hung my swim bag over my shoulder and piled up the towels, sheets, and clothes with the other supplies balanced on top. I hardly could see when I hugged the stuff to my chest. As soon as I took the first wobbly step, the shampoo, soap, and toothbrush tumbled to the ground, like an avalanche, followed by the clothes and sheets. I managed to hold on to the towels.

Mary Mac and Jermaine stared at me with facial expressions that were either amused or appalled — probably both.

"Have you lost the brains you were born with, Child?" Mary Mac asked.

She picked up the canvas bag I'd left on the table and shook it open. Before she dug in her pocket for a black magic marker, she glanced at Jermaine. While Mary Mac printed my name across one side of the bag, Jermaine helped me pick up my mess and return everything to the table. While she talked, Mary Mac re-folded the towels, sheets, and clothes and packed them in the bag.

"This is your laundry bag. Each cabin is assigned one day each week to bring laundry to Daisy. You'll need to make sure each of your campers keeps her dirty clothes in the bag with her name on it so she gets back what she sent." She handed me a pair of sneakers. "Put these on, then be on your way. The campers will be here Saturday. After lunch you'll need to get started on the pool. The cabins and camp buildings want cleaning too."

A circle of sweat spread across the front of my shirt. I staggered out of Hippo Hall, the laundry bag slung over my right shoulder and my swim bag slipping off my left. I wished Mrs. Fanelli had found me a community service job cleaning toilets in City Hall or scraping gum off the bottom of bus seats.

"I'll show you the pool first, then we'll find Daiquiri. She's getting Bernie ready for the girls," Jermaine called over his shoulder.

I had to trot to keep up. With the bags banging against me, I followed the path through the woods. When Jermaine stopped short, I bumped into him.

"Watch out for snakes," he said, then he started walking again.

Snakes? Crap. He walked so fast it was hard to watch where I placed my feet. Silently, I cursed each time the laundry bag smacked my back. Before I caught up with him at a sign that read — **Hippo Pool: No Campers Without Counselors** — the smell of decay and fetid water hit me.

The forest ended abruptly at a chain-link fence that enclosed the wide, open area of the pool. In the middle of the leaf-stained concrete, a large, T-shaped swamp was filled with debris thick enough to walk over. At the far side from the gate, a faded sign attached to a dingy metal structure announced — **Changing Area**. Six cockeyed benches with broken planks lined the area six feet back from the swim lanes. *You've got to be kidding,* I thought, as the crystal blue waters of the country club pool coursed through my mind. I dropped my bags and shook my head.

"Ready for your first dip?" All of a sudden Jermaine lifted me over his shoulder and headed for the pool.

"No, No, No, Stop!" I punched his ear until he set me down.

"Damn, Shorty, you can't take no joke." He wrinkled his nose and covered his ear with his beret.

"That's not the pool — it's disgusting." Even I couldn't stand the sound of my whiny voice.

"It's the pool, sure 'nough, and you got to clean it by Saturday. You know how to clean a pool?" Jermaine looked pretty happy telling me that.

"I can clean a pool, but not a freaking cesspit."

My heart beat like I'd popped a couple uppers. I slumped down on the dirty concrete deck and held my head in my hands.

"Girl, you too easy. You believe whatever I say. The pool company do the first big-time cleanin' each summer. They be here later today to show you how to work the pumps and stuff. All you got to do is scrub the deck, the guard stand, and diving board. Me, Father Vincent, and Roland gonna fix the benches. You know how to swim?"

I gave him my most insulted look.

"I'm pretty sure that's why Father asked me to be the lifeguard and teach swimming. You want to see who's the better swimmer?" I got to my feet. "As soon as the pool gets cleaned, I'll race you — any stroke, any distance."

I studied Jermaine's arms, taut and muscular, so different from Ishmael's scrawny white ones.

"You don't win no prize swimmin' against me. No pools in the ghetto." Jermaine's uneven teeth somehow made his smile cute. "You gone have your hands full teaching these children. Some them rather drown 'fore they tell you they can't swim. But hear me now — they can't." He tipped his head to take me in. "I can't neither. How 'bout we make a deal — you teach me to swim and I teach you basketball?"

I swallowed. I couldn't tell if Jermaine — the first black guy I ever talked to — was teasing me or testing me. But I looked at his glistening muscles and figured, why not? "Deal."

"Come on then," he said.

I stopped hating him.

Jermaine led the way down the path to six small cabins clustered in a semicircle. In front of each building, a wooden sign hung on a chain. St. Andrew, St. Ambrose, and St. Augustine were the three closest, and signs marked St. Beatrice, St. Bernadette, and St. Brigid swung in front of the others. Inside St. Bernadette, - the middle cabin on the girls' side - someone was singing *All I Could Do Was Cry* by Etta James. I dropped my bags and let the rich voice wrap around me. Judge, the song was so beautiful I couldn't speak. Each time I heard the words, *All I could do was cry,* I felt something inside break. That should be my theme song, I thought.

When the song finished, I turned to Jermaine. "Who's singing?"

"That's Daiquiri. She the Bernie head counselor. You're with her," he said. "You sing?"

"Not like that."

"Hey, Daiquiri, I brought the criminal," Jermaine called.

I felt all the air go out of my lungs. Why did he have to be so mean? My stomach knotted up, but I looked up when a short, round, coffee-colored girl sauntered out the door.

"She don't look like no criminal to me. She look like Gidget go to camp. What you do so bad? Steal a apple pie from a windowsill?" Daiquiri flashed a questioning look at Jermaine.

For some reason, being Gidget pissed me off as much as being called a criminal.

"I sold drugs with my boyfriend," I said, trying to look like a tough city girl.

I don't know why I thought that would impress them. The air grew thick with the chicken-noodle-soup smell of sweaty bodies.

"You a druggy? That don't amount to no good, no how — trouble." From Jermaine's tone, I realized my acting all hard-ass was a big mistake.

"It was just pot," I said, like it wasn't a big deal.

"Where's your druggy boyfriend now?" Daiquiri asked.

"Graterford. I'm going to visit him after camp." I doubted my parents would drive me there, but maybe I could tag along with Ishmael's folks some Sunday.

"Graterford bad as it gets. He be ripped in two." Jermaine looked down and shook his head.

What did that mean, ripped in two? Ishmael may have sold drugs, but he would never get in a fight. He couldn't stand the sight of blood. A bad feeling brought tears to my eyes. I needed to get away for a couple minutes.

"Where's the john?" I asked. I had to go, anyway.

As I aimed at the wooden hole inside the dusty pink outhouse behind the cabins, I realized there was no toilet paper. At least Graterford has flushing toilets, I told myself. From outside, I heard mumbled conversation mixed with hoots of laughter. Before I joined them again, I waited a moment, trembling in the clean but dingy privy. I was afraid to go out, afraid of Daiquiri and Jermaine's dark eyes, afraid of what they thought of the white girl at their camp. I opened the door and stepped into sunlight and a summer of unbearable hell. A clanging bell echoed through the trees.

"Let's go, Shorty, time to eat," Jermaine called.

Before I ran to catch up, I rinsed my hands and face under a rusty spout behind the cabin. Outside showers, cold water, and blue and pink outhouses, each with four seats? I prayed Mary Mac kept stocks of toilet paper in her store.

As we entered Hippo Hall, my mouth watered at the smell of hamburgers, pickles, and onions. I hadn't eaten all day. Inside, the floors had been swept, the windows cleaned, and four neat rows of folding tables and chairs filled the room. At a table along the back wall, Mary Mac served lunch with Daisy, an elderly black woman with white hair and dusky skin. While Daiquiri joined other girl counselors in line and dropped chips and pickles on her plate, I stood back, not sure what to do.

When Jermaine passed me, balancing four burgers on his paper plate, he knocked my elbow and grinned. I watched him sit at a table of black guys. As soon as he sat down, he pointed.

"That's Bonnie. She all right," he said.

The boys at his table stopped eating to stare at me.

"Joni," I said in a small voice as I edged toward the serving table, "my name's Joni."

"Bonnie and Clyde from the suburbs come to do time with us ghetto folk," Jermaine said in a loud voice.

When the guys laughed and whistled, Mary Mac and Father Vincent — the only other white people — smiled. My face flushed. I turned away and walked out the door. *I can't do this*, I told myself. I felt even more out of place than I had at Redwood. My stomach lurched and I thought I'd puke. As I took the last step down from Hippo Hall, a hand gripped my shoulder.

"Girl, those boys funning with you," Daiquiri said from behind. "You want to get by, you got to laugh, most 'specially when the joke's on you. Come in and meet the girls. Delia got you a plate. I know you need meat on those scrawny bones." Daiquiri swung out one hip and put her hand on it, curled her lip, and squinted her eyes. "Next time you pass those boys, you give them some of this. Now come back inside or they be thinking you don't want to eat with us."

Daiquiri led me in and shot a hard look at the boys' table. Two skinny black girls scooted over to make room, and Daiquiri introduced me to her classmates from Girls Catholic High School in West Philly. With olive skin, green eyes, and long legs, Delia looked like a model. Felicia was skinny and studious-looking, her eyes magnified by thick glasses. Elizabeth, Milly, Jasmine, and Dottie smiled when I sat down. The last girl Daiquiri introduced, Turquoise, had almond-shaped eyes highlighted with thick wings. A white-and-black print bandana ran across her forehead and covered most of her hair except for curls that spilled out the back. She was big — tall and strong. She leaned back and looked at me like I was an ant.

"Why you come to this camp? You can't find no crackers to save?"

"Who else gonna teach these children who be here Saturday to swim?" Daiquiri answered.

"Father Vincent asked me to come," I mumbled, avoiding her eyes.

"You want to help poor Negroes? You can help clear my dishes so I can get the Arts and Crafts cabin ready."

Turquoise shoved her empty plate across the table to me.

"I don't mind," I said.

If you want to know the truth, Judge, I was scared to death. I even thought I might faint. And I was really hungry.

"Don't pay her no mind," Delia said. She patted my hand. "You stay right here, Bonnie."

"Joni," I whispered.

After the screen door shut behind Turquoise, I let out my breath and looked at my plate. I shook a glob of ketchup onto my hamburger and put dill pickle slices on top of that. I didn't want the girls to think I was a pig, so I forced myself to eat one bite at a time. Then I finished my potato chips and sipped the cotton-candy-sweet red juice.

"Nasty," I said, but I drank it all.

Delia laughed. "That old bug juice sure is nasty. Feel Bonnie's hair."

The girls gathered around to run strands of my straight blonde hair through their fingers. I looked up to see Mary Mac smile and I smiled back. I actually smiled. When the girls touched my hair, it felt like they saw me as a real person, not a loser. Since the arrest, hardly anyone had touched me — only Tommy and Lisa and Mrs. Fanelli. Now it felt weird, but nice. The girls moved back to their seats when Father Vincent came by. He leaned over the table and smiled benignly, the smell of cigarettes and onions on his breath. Between the buttons of his Madras shirt, Father's chest hair showed. I blushed.

"Can you girls get our swim teacher in shape for the campers?" he asked.

The girls made positive sounds and Daiquiri answered, "Joni be all right, Father, I'll show her the way."

I put Turquoise's paper plate on top of mine and dropped both in the trashcan. Before I made it back to the table, a hand grabbed my elbow.

"My boys say I'm too awnry to learn to swim, but I say don't be doubting Shorty." Jermaine plunked his knit beret on my head and gave a satisfied nod. "Now you hardcore."

Jermaine totally confused me, but I listened while he introduced me to the boys. Derrick, Wilson, Roland, Terrell, Michael, James, and Lincoln played basketball with Jermaine at East Philly Catholic, where Father Vincent served as Vice Principal. All but Terrell were tall.

"You still mad, Bonnie Joni?" one of the guys, Roland, asked.

He was skinny, with hazel eyes and long lashes. He turned to pitch his rolled up napkin toward the trashcan and missed. I grabbed an empty paper plate and flicked it in the same direction. By some miracle, it tapped the wall and dropped in.

"Maybe you can take basketball lessons too," I said, a little surprised at myself. I wondered if I might have a chance of making it to August 9th.

"Ooo, Roland, she hurt you. Man, don't mess with Bonnie and Clyde," Lincoln said.

Roland clutched his heart and winced. Jermaine beamed as if I were his little white Frankenstein's monster.

From behind us, Mary Mac announced, "Time to get this Hippopotamus ready for the campers, Gentlemen and Ladies."

When the counselors left Hippo Hall, joshing and pushing, I followed behind. Somehow, despite Turquoise's hostility, I felt okay. Maybe it was the magic wedge in the new PF Flyers that made me feel like I could run my fastest and jump my highest. Too bad they didn't make swim suits. I trailed the other counselors until, in pairs or alone, they broke off to clean and prepare the archery range, the music room, the basketball court, the summer school cabin, and the sleeping cabins.

From inside the arts and crafts building, I heard a rich and resonant voice — Turquoise's, I realized — singing *Trouble in Mind.* Ishmael and I had listened to Janis Joplin sing that song, but from Turquoise it sounded like a hymn. Her voice, as wonderful as Daiquiri's, echoed through the pines, powerful in its sorrow. I didn't know if Turquoise had a troubled mind, but I did. As I headed to the pool, she shouted out — *The sun's gonna shine.* Would the sun ever shine for me? Jermaine's beret weighed on my head like a hand. I thought of Ishmael. I wondered if he ever felt bad about what he'd done to me.

As I approached the pool, the low rumble of a motor and the smell of diesel fuel told me cleanup was underway. Before I talked to the white guys working there, I took off Jermaine's beret and set it on a bench. One guy shoved a commercial vacuum across the pool bottom while another skimmed the surface with a huge net. I went up to the sweaty guy at the pump house.

"Hi, I'm Joni. I'm the lifeguard," I said. "I'm supposed to know how this works."

"Butch." The guy wore a flag bandana tied across his forehead. "Watch and learn," he grunted and got back to lubricating the motor and replacing the filter.

After an hour, the water began to clear and fresh water splashed in from the spigot under the diving board. While I trailed Butch, trying to remember everything he showed me, I kept thinking about Jermaine saying they'd rip Ishmael in two. Why? Why would anybody do that? I wondered if Ishmael dreamt, like I did, of the afternoons we spent smoking dope and listening to music — or if he hated me because I just got stuck at home for a few months before I spent the summer teaching swimming at camp, but he wound up in prison.

No matter how hard I tried to put it out of my mind, I still felt nervous and disturbed about New Year's Eve. I was glad Mrs. Fanelli convinced me that whatever happened was not my fault. I just couldn't remember what that was. I guess what bothered me most is that Ishmael didn't take care of me. He should never have let me get so drunk and high. He should have made sure I got home on time. But instead he said everything was fine because he loved me.

I was so lost in my thoughts I was surprised when the pool company guy, Butch, called my name.

"Hey, Joni, I'll show you how to backwash the filters and then we're pretty much done here."

After he demonstrated the steps, he taped a company card to the pump room wall.

While the other guys rolled up their hoses and packed their equipment, Butch and I sat on the edge of the diving well with our feet in the water. It smelled like chlorine and looked unbelievable compared to earlier in the day. Butch unrolled a pack of cigarettes from his sleeve, took one, and offered one to me. It was nice to sit and relax. "I thought this was a colored camp. What're you doing here?" he asked.

"I'm the swim teacher."

"We clean lots of nice white pools you could teach at. Probably better pay too," he said and let out a long stream of smoke.

I started to tell him about the whole arrest deal, but that would take forever. Instead, I shrugged and blew a smoke ring.

The truck motor started up and a guy called, "Let's go, Butch. We're done here."

Before he stood to go, Butch looked me in the eyes and said, "Watch yourself. Leave a message at the office for Butch if anyone messes with you."

"Sure, thanks," I said.

As the truck pulled away, I smiled. *Butch is no match for Turquoise*, I thought.

Billowy clouds crossed the sun, fresh water splashed into the pool, and the blue sky reflected off the clear water. The air smelled bleachy and woody. By late afternoon, when Jermaine came to get me for dinner, sweat glued my shirt to my back. My arms glowed from sunburn and my knees and hands were raw from scrubbing the deck. Tomorrow, after I cleaned the lifeguard chair and diving board, I'd get in the pool to scrub the tiles along the edge. The water shimmered clear and cold.

"I guess you know how to work, Shorty. But damn, Girl, look at your arms," Jermaine commented as he came in the gate. "Didn't you never hear of Coppertone? Get some from Mary Mac after dinner."

I looked down and winced, knowing I faced a night of unbearably hot skin and shivers. The clean water offered immediate relief. I plunged in and swam with sweeping strokes and frog kicks. After I reached the diving area, I rose and waved to Jermaine, my T-shirt billowing like a float. The cold water soothed my burned arms, skinned knees, and aching shoulders.

"Come in, or are you chicken?" I yelled.

This day was turning out better than I expected. Just being in the pool let me feel like myself.

"You crazy? We be late for dinner and get stuck with the leftovers."

But Jermaine kicked off his Chucks and twisted out of his shirt. With one hand on the edge, he lowered himself into the shallow end with his arms raised above the water. I dove under and surfaced with a mouthful of water to spray on his chest. He ducked under and came up sputtering, drops of water sparkling in his hair. I dodged his grasp, swam to the wall, made a flip turn, and swam butterfly stroke back, splashing as hard as I could.

"You gonna teach me to swim like that?" He sounded impressed.

"I'll try, but you got to want it, bad."

At the edge of the pool, I put my hands on the concrete lip and pushed myself up and out, welcoming the stress on my muscles. I ignored my exhaustion and sunburn. Right then, I felt clean and almost happy.

Each summer, Daiquiri told me, on the Friday before the campers came, Daisy made a special dinner to eat outside on picnic tables. After another day working my ass off, I was sunburned, exhausted, and starving by the time the dinner bell rang. I never looked forward to eating as much as I did then, especially hearing the other counselors' comments —

You go on, Daisy.

Been waitin' all year for your catfish and cornbread.

Keep spoonin' it on, there enough for seconds?

Even before I reached the serving table, my mouth watered and I licked my lips. The smell was warm and rich and salty. Judge, maybe you'll think this is strange, but I'd never eaten fried fish before.

After she slid two golden pieces on my plate next to a heap of coleslaw and sweet-smelling cornbread, Daisy glanced up. I must have looked like an anxious puppy — if I had a tail I'd be wagging it — because she chuckled to herself and dropped three pats of butter on the cornbread. I hurried after Daiquiri and sat next to her at the table with Father Vincent, Mary Mac, Roland, and Jermaine.

There wasn't much talking at any of the tables — just serious eating going on. I buttered my cornbread and broke off a piece. The top felt stiff but inside the bread was sweet with moist corn kernels that gave it an unusual texture. I could have eaten a whole pan of it. Before I tried the catfish, I watched Daiquiri eat hers. Like everyone else, she picked it up with her fingers and took a bite. The crunching sound and the way she closed her eyes made me crazy to taste mine. Just before I bit into my first crispy piece, Daisy carried her own plate over and sat with us. She smelled like hot oil and sugar.

"Go on, Child, don't let my cookin' get cold."

I hesitated a moment before I took a bite. "Oh my God," I said. "I never tasted anything so good."

The spicy, crisp coating over the sweet, white fish blended into a delicious flavor. I tried to take my time so I could savor each mouthful.

"That's right," Daisy said.

I could tell she enjoyed her own cooking. Daisy's voice was strong and richer than I expected for someone so old. Her curly white hair was brushed back from her pecan-colored face, but her eyebrows were dark over her wide-set, deep brown eyes. Daisy was about my height, five-feet-four, and her arms were as thin as a child's. That evening she wore green pedal pushers and a short-sleeved flowered blouse.

I finished my first piece and started on the second. I probably let a moan of satisfaction escape because when I looked up, everyone at the table was smiling.

"You never eat fried catfish before? Girl, you missing something out in the suburbs," Jermaine said. He licked his fingers and wiped his mouth with a paper napkin.

"Wait 'til you try Daisy's sweet potato pie," Daiquiri said. She collected the empty plates and dumped them in the trashcan on her way back to Hippo Hall. When she returned, she delivered what looked like a pumpkin pie to each table.

Mary Mac sliced our pie with a pointy spatula and passed around the pieces. Everyone waited while I cut a small orange triangle from my piece and raised it to my mouth. I shook my head from side-to-side as the creamy taste, actually a lot like pumpkin, lingered on my tongue.

"Daisy, this is the best," I said, nibbling on the crust rimmed with blackened sweet potato.

"Know why this tastes so good?" Roland asked from across the table. I shrugged.

"Because it's got Soul!"

I knew their laughter was with me, not at me. I let myself smile, at least for a moment.

Father Vincent wiped his mouth with his handkerchief and shoved it in his back pocket. He cleared his throat. "Counselors, most of you know each other, but let's make a circle so we can introduce ourselves to Joan. Each of us should say something about why we're here or what we hope to accomplish this summer."

As soon as Mary Mac and Daisy spread blankets on the ground, the counselors arranged themselves like they had designated spots. I felt awkward standing there, searching for a space big enough to plop down in. Daiquiri looked up like I was her responsibility, shimmied over, and tapped the space next to her. I squeezed in, feeling my bottom press against hers on one side and Terrell's on the other.

"Who would like to start?" Father Vincent asked.

Daiquiri raised her hand. "My name is Daiquiri, like you alls know.

I'm back at Camp Hippo 'cause the company's so good. And because someone got to be here to look after these children."

That got things started, because then the others just jumped in.

"I'm Jermaine. I'm here to keep yous in line and get a tan."

Everyone laughed.

"I'm Turquoise. I'm here to make some money and so my Mama have one less mouth to feed." She paused. "And because nobody can teach these campers to sew and mend and fix their zippers like me."

Unh hunh, that's right, various voices agreed.

"I'm Terrell. I'm at camp because I like nature and every day I discover something new and special." He turned and looked at me.

I swallowed. "I'm Joni. I'm here because I'm a little criminal who knows how to swim."

At first, they lowered their eyes. The only sounds were buzzing and rustling. Then Roland slapped his knee and laughed, and Father Vincent and Mary Mac smiled. "You funny, Joni," Roland said.

Everyone joined in then — *She's the criminal. You hear her say that?*

"No way to top that. I'm Roland, and I'm at Camp Hippo 'cause this place would fall down if I'm not here to fix what gets broke. And stuff gets broke every day, right, Father?"

"Indeed, Roland, I don't know what we'd do without you," Father Vincent agreed.

Mary Mac smiled. "I'm here because I dearly love to be out in the woods with the likes of you and with dozens of children to make our lives interesting. And of course, to enjoy Daisy's sweet potato pie."

Ain't that the truth? Un hunh. Me too.

Daisy spoke next. "I just do what I do."

After everyone had a turn, Father said, "I'm Father Vincent, and I come to Camp Hippo every summer because you and the campers give me joy. When Jesus said, *Suffer the little children to come unto me,* he showed humankind the vulnerability and the wonder of our little ones. Let's pledge to give these children the best summer of their lives. Now, counselors, you may relax for one last time before our charges arrive."

We stood up and brushed ourselves off. Jermaine gathered the counselors around him.

"I seen a big snake down by the cabins this afternoon. I chase after it but it slither under the outhouses 'til I couldn't see it no more. Daisy gave me this bag of marshmallows to catch the snake before the campers come."

I was horrified. "Wait, there's a snake in the outhouse? What are the marshmallows for?"

"Marshmallows the only thing what works," Delia said. She could be on the cover of *Seventeen*, I thought.

The other counselors looked serious and stoic. "She don't know what marshmallows are for," Jasmine whispered to Millie.

Lincoln looked at the girls wide-eyed and shrugged.

"Don't they teach you nothin' in the suburbs?" Jermaine's expression was sad and pitying. "Every city child know you catch snakes with marshmallows. Soon's a snake snap his fangs in a marshmallow, you got him. He can't open his mouth no more. Come on, now. We got to trap that snake."

I followed the counselors down the path to the cabins. Wilson and Michael prodded long sticks into bushes and brush along the way. Elizabeth, Dottie, and Felicia strolled along behind the rest of us, quietly talking. I wondered if they hated snakes as much as I did. In the lead with Jermaine, whatever Turquoise was saying made him laugh real loud.

Just before we reached the cabins, I asked Daiquiri, "Are there lots of snakes around here?"

"I guess you got snakes in the grass wherever you go," she said.

That didn't make me feel any better.

Roland, Michael, James, and Derrick waited outside the cabins, squinting in the streaks of sunlight that slipped through the trees. Roland handed me a stick with a marshmallow on one end.

"Here you go. You want to stay three feet back. If the snake come at you, toss it the marshmallow and use the stick to keep it back."

I studied the stick a moment, then gave it back.

"I'll be too scared to use it. I'm just going to run. Aren't you guys afraid?"

I looked around. The girls sat on the steps of Turquoise's cabin — St. Beatrice. Everyone called the youngest girls assigned to that cabin the Honey Bees.

"Terrell's the only one what like them," James said. His voice was deep but he looked at the ground. He seemed shy.

We heard shouts and banging from behind the cabins. I followed the boys to see what was going on. Jermaine crawled along one side of the outhouses, poking his stick underneath and yelling, *Get out of there.*

Hunched over on the other side, Terrell sidestepped along, poking in openings and slapping his stick on the wall.

"I don't want to be here if they catch the snake," I said, and I jogged back to the front of the cabins.

Every time I heard a shout or a bang, I jumped. My heart raced. I felt like I must be a total coward, because the other girls didn't even look up. A drop of sweat ran alongside my nose and I flicked it away. A few minutes later, the boys came back and draped themselves on railings or sat on cabin steps.

"Couldn't catch him, but at least we scared that old snake off into the woods," Jermaine said with his soft lisp. "We alls heading up to play some B-ball 'til lights out."

The boys, leaving behind their sharp, sweaty smell, followed Jermaine up the hill. As I watched the girls joke and chat, I felt out of place. But only Turquoise scared me. I promised myself to stay out of her way. Tomorrow, the campers would arrive — that made me nervous too.

When it began to get dark, my head dropped and jerked. I wondered if anyone noticed I fell asleep standing up.

"I'm going in," I called to Daiquiri.

"Wait a minute," she said. "Hold on, I'll come with you."

After that, most of the girls wandered to their cabins except for two girls who started up the path toward the basketball court — to hang out with the guys, I supposed. I felt bad that I broke up their conversations.

Daiquiri took a step my way but Turquoise called her back. They put their heads together and whispered. I assumed they were talking about me and that hurt my feelings, especially because so far, Daiquiri had been really nice. I decided to just go inside myself.

When Daiquiri realized I was at our cabin door, she called, "I'm coming, Joni, what's the big rush?"

I wondered if she thought I'd mess with her stuff if I went in without her. She must believe I'm a criminal after all. *They think we gonna steal they sorry stuff* ran through my mind. That's what the black swimmers said when we went into the city for the meet in the fall. I felt guilty for how those girls felt, and for how I felt now. I decided to wait on the steps, holding my tired head in my hands.

Finally, Daiquiri left Turquoise and we went inside. I was so exhausted, my head felt stuffed with cotton. I needed to lie down and close my eyes. I got under the covers in my T-shirt and sweat pants.

"You going to sleep already?" Daiquiri asked as my light flicked off.

"I'm beat." I muttered, then I dropped my head on the pillow and stretched my legs.

When I turned over on my side, my foot pressed against something. I kicked at it and shut my eyes, wondering if I'd left my goggles or sandals on the cot. But when my toe touched it again, it felt smooth and firm, not like goggles or sandals at all.

It couldn't have been more than a few seconds before an image slithered through my brain. My heart almost exploded.

I fell out of bed, then jumped to my feet, hollering, "The snake! The snake! It's in my bed!" I grabbed Daiquiri and dragged her to the front door.

As soon as we got outside, a bright light blinded me. Still clutching Daiquiri's arm, I raised my other hand to shield my eyes. A roar of laughter rose from the open space in front of the cabins. Daiquiri freed her arm and the flashlight beam dropped away from our faces. I followed Daiquiri down the cabin steps, anxious to get as far away from the snake as I could, but I tripped on the last step. Jermaine caught me and helped me stay upright.

"You found the snake in your cabin? That ain't no good. I best go get it."

He made sure I saw his long stick with a marshmallow stuck to the end.

Trembling and trying not to cry, I saw other counselors bunched together, laughing and whispering. This wasn't funny. What if there were more snakes crawling around the cabins?

Jermaine came out then, dangling a thick, green snake by the tail.

"I got it. You safe."

But the snake swung up and wrapped itself around his neck. Jermaine reached up and tried to pull it off. I was horrified. No one went to help him. I leapt up the steps and yanked the snake off him, then flung it on the ground. Jermaine hopped down after it and picked it up again. I was so confused.

The snake dangled like a heavy piece of rope. I inched backward toward the cabin door, but I was afraid there might be more snakes inside.

"Come on down, Shorty. This snake ain't gonna hurt no one never again," Jermaine said.

"No, I don't want to see it. Take it away," I begged.

There was more laughter and eyes sparkling in dark faces. Daiquiri took the snake from Jermaine and climbed the steps to show me.

"It's fake, Joni, rubber. Each new counselor got to face the snake."

In the darkness, the counselors, now silent, watched me. I studied the snake in Daiquiri's hand for a second, then as quick as I could, grabbed it and flung it at the counselors. Someone squealed.

I moved to the steps and sat down, shaking and laughing.

"You got me. You got me good. You scared the living daylights out of me. Look at my hair — it's gone white. Oh God, look at my skin. It's white too. What will my parents say?"

Jermaine took my hand, helped me stand, and brought me to the huddled counselors who smiled and patted my back.

"She gonna make it," Roland said.

"You mad?" Daiquiri asked, her eyes watchful.

"I'm not mad, but I might never stop shaking. I got snaked good," I said. As I stood in the shadows with the counselors, Turquoise returned to her cabin. She paused a moment under the door light, her hands on her hips. Then she went inside. All the others, still laughing, disappeared up the path or into their cabins.

"No more snakes tonight," Daiquiri said, and we went inside to our stalls.

After I checked the sheets and settled down, I thought about Daiquiri's question — *You mad?* And I wasn't. I wasn't mad. It was a new feeling.

Only by the grace of God, Mary Mac insisted, was camp ready Saturday when diesel-spewing buses loaded with kids from what Jermaine called *the projects* crunched up the driveway. Seventy-two campers — boys and girls ages eight to thirteen — spilled from the school bus doors. Some dragged suitcases held together with rope, others lugged beat up book bags. A few campers hugged brown A&P grocery bags to their chests. About half hopped down the bus steps with nothing in their arms.

The eight and nine-year-old kids looked scared. They moved away from the bus only after Daisy took the hand of one boy and one girl and led them to a spot in the shade of Hippo Hall. The oldest campers — the twelves and thirteens — chewed gum and looked bored. Like they knew their way, they sauntered toward Jermaine and dropped their bags on the lawn while they waited. The campers I pegged as being the tens and elevens turned in circles to take in the trees, buildings, and counselors. But the moment a camper noticed me, he or she stopped and gawked, then whispered to friends and pointed.

Wearing our green camp T-shirts, Daiquiri and I put our heads together to review the names of the dozen ten and eleven-year-old girls assigned to St. Bernadette cabin — Joyful, Tiara, Francesca, Josephine, Sharone, Crystal, Raven, Jailyn, Keesha, Yvonne, Angel, and Lady. To me their names sounded like music — the songs of their births.

As Father called out names and cabins, the campers gathered around their counselors. The Bernies packed close to Daiquiri, keeping their distance from me — except Lady.

Daiquiri waved her arms. "Give me space, Children. Miss Joni's not gonna eat you."

"That white girl not my counselor," one girl said.

"Indeed she is," Daiquiri said. "You might as well get used to it."

The girl stared at the ground and the others glanced from one to the other. I forced a smile.

"Hi," I croaked. Lady turned to me with concern.

"We are the Bernies," Daiquiri said. "We're spending the whole summer together. The first rule you got to learn is Bernies look out for each other." She raised her eyebrow at two squirming girls until they caught her eye and quieted. "Our jobs are to watch over you and help you have a good summer. Your jobs are to listen, cooperate and behave. Can you alls do that? Yes? Then the first thing we do together is line up behind the Honey Bees to get your camp shirts and new sneakers."

As the girls jostled for partners and lined up, I noticed a little girl talking to Turquoise and gesturing toward me. I let out a sigh, resigned to stick out like a white thumb. I heard Turquoise's voice rise.

"Un unh, you don't know no white girl."

When I turned to look more closely at the little girl, our eyes met. I recognized her immediately.

"Ruby?" A smile, a real smile, spread across my face.

In a weird way, I felt like I found a long lost friend. Ruby smiled back. She hadn't changed at all since I met her in the fall. Her thick glasses still magnified her round brown eyes. Her upper teeth rested on her lower lip, and her hair stuck out in three braids.

"How you know this child?" Turquoise snapped, narrowing her eyes and tilting her head.

"We met at the Y." I knelt so I was eye level with Ruby. "This summer, I'm going to teach you to swim for real."

"For real," Ruby nodded. She turned back to Turquoise. "See. I tole you I know that white girl."

Turquoise spit out a short breath. "That don't make no sense. Come on, Miss Ruby."

Back in line, Daiquiri gave me a questioning look and said, "You just full of surprises, ain't you?"

"I'm pretty surprised myself," I said, but the Bernies seemed less standoffish after that.

While the Honey Bees and the Bernies collected their camp stuff and packed everything in their laundry bags, every minute or so Ruby turned to catch my eye and flash a giant grin.

As we trailed the Honey Bees down the path toward the cabins, Daiquiri led the Bernies, and I took up the rear. Lady, the tallest girl, with long, elegant limbs and hair braided tight against her scalp, lagged a little behind the girls to walk beside me. Her face was oval-shaped and her features, or maybe her facial expressions, made her seem older than eleven. I felt curious and pleased that this young girl seemed to accept me, maybe even like me. Mary Mac had told Daiquiri and me that as soon as

Lady's mother put her on the camp bus, she was flying to Haiti to care for her own mother, sick with cancer. She wouldn't be back until camp ended in August.

"Miss Joan, there snakes in the cabin? 'Cause I'm mightily scairt of snakes," Lady said, her eyes wide.

"I'm mightily scared of snakes too. So, if we ever see a snake, we'll run the other way. Together."

I bit my lip so she wouldn't think I was laughing at her, but I wondered what she'd say if she learned about the snake in my bed the night before.

When Lady slipped her soft, cool hand in mine, a thrill ran through me. For a moment, I felt strong and maybe even good. Ahead, girls laughed and chatted, voices echoing through the pines, their shoves and jostling followed by — *Oh no, you di-int. I'mma getchoo when you not look-in.* I found their loud and rowdy behavior unnerving.

My only experience with controlling and disciplining kids came after I got my lifeguard certification and sat on the stand for a couple weeks last August. When country club members' kids misbehaved, I whistled and benched them — ten minutes of time-out on a bench behind the diving boards. A kid who was really bad got kicked out for a day. That always worked. No pool mom wanted to be stuck babysitting her kid — that meant no golf or tennis or afternoon card games drinking high balls on the patio with friends. But this camp and these girls were completely new to me. How would I get these city girls to behave?

When Crystal shoved Raven, a chubby girl with wild hair, into Daiquiri, I got my first lesson. Daiquiri stopped short and scowled at each girl until the jostling and jiving quieted like the hush before the preacher speaks. No one moved. After everyone was still and quiet for almost a minute, Daiquiri looked from girl to girl and asked, "Which of you alls is ready to move on?" Twelve hands went up. Mine started to go up, but I managed to keep it at my side.

On the quiet walk from there to the cabin, Lady looked up at me with her eyebrows raised and her lips pressed tight. I returned a serious look and a nod.

After we showed the girls how to make up their cots, Daiquiri sat them on the cabin floor to go over the rules. With the look, Daiquiri got complete quiet and only a little squirming.

"We are your counselors but we are not your mothers. This summer, I expect you to behave like young ladies. We gonna have fun, but you got to follow the rules. Most important camp rule — do what your counselors tell you. If I or Joni tell you, pay attention, then you pay attention. We tell you, time to shower, you get your towels and go outside to wash up. We tell you, line up, you line up. Nobody go anywhere alone. You need to go to the john, you tell me or you tell Joni. You understand? Now here are the Bernie rules — Take care of each other. Share. Be nice. Don't hit. Clean up. Have fun." Daiquiri looked from girl to girl.

"I want to go home," Tiara whimpered.

"I miss my Mama." Tears welled in Keesha's eyes.

A few other girls forced out tears and sniffled. But not Lady.

"I miss Mami, but I ain't no crybaby. Mami say, *Lady girl, you go have fun at camp.*" With her lips pursed she glanced at me. "So I'mma have fun."

"You can cry or you can laugh, but this cabin is your summer home. You might as well get used to it," Daiquiri told them as she got to her feet.

"I'm hungry," Raven wiped her nose on her arm.

"You best go on outside to wash up," Daiquiri directed, "then change into your camp T-shirts and shorts. The quicker you do that, the quicker we go to lunch."

Hippo Hall hummed with noise from the bright-shirted campers who lined up for food then sat at tables, eating off plastic trays. Standing fans blew the smell of sweaty children and hot dogs and beans throughout the big room. I spied little Ruby in her yellow camp T-shirt, legs dangling from her chair, swinging her head from side-to-side with a hot dog clutched in one hand. Across from her, Turquoise smiled at the Honey Bee campers and turned to call something to Jermaine. When she turned back, she caught my eye and scrunched up her nose and mouth. I sucked in my lower lip and felt like I'd done something wrong. For a second, I wanted to cry and tell Father Vincent I wanted to go back home.

After lunch, we lined up our girls to follow the map and schedule Father Vincent gave each cabin so the campers got a chance to see the different activities and learn their way around camp. It was my first time learning the entire layout too.

With Daiquiri in the lead and me taking up the back, we marched the girls toward our first stop — the archery range. On the narrow paths through the woods, three girls lost their footing and landed on their palms and knees. Lady and I pulled them up.

"I went and burned my hands," Sharone said, showing her scraped palms and holding back a sob.

"You got to look afore you leap," Lady told her.

When I helped Angel to her feet, she didn't have a scrape, but a drop of blood oozed from a tiny cut on Keesha's knee.

"We'll get you a Band-Aid when we get back to Hippo Hall," I promised, "but I know you Bernie girls are tough."

Keesha looked up from smearing the blood across her knee. She wiped her hand on her pants and said, "It's aight."

"Tough enough," Lady said, and Keesha smiled.

On the narrow path through the woods before we reached the hill to the archery range, we passed the Auggies — the oldest boys from St. Augustine cabin — and bumped shoulders with them. I felt a hand touch my hair, then another give it a yank. I called out, "Hey!"

When I turned to see who pulled my hair, I felt a wet splotch on my ankle and heard boys' laughter. I grabbed the arm of their counselor, Michael.

"One of your kids spit at me," I said.

"Nah, no one do that," Michael said, shaking his head.

"Someone did."

"You just got bird bombed," he insisted, keeping his eye on his campers who were getting ahead of him.

"From a big walking bird," I grumbled. I knew it was one of the boys.

As Michael trotted to catch up with his kids, Daiquiri stopped the Bernies and called, "You got a problem, Joni?" Twelve pairs of girls' eyes fixed on me.

"I guess not. Let's move on," I said, but I felt really pissed.

From above, a crow cawed. As the Bernies left the woods, I watched it flap its shiny black wings, and soar out of sight. A bird. I wondered if Michael was right. As the girls ran or rolled down the grassy hill to the archery field, I followed. I remembered what happened at Redwood after I told the loser lunch table about Elizabeth's borrowed short story. If the kid spit on me, he knew it, and his friends knew it. And they knew it was wrong, same as Elizabeth knew she'd cheated. *Screw it*, I decided. *Let it go.*

At the range, Lady waved like mad for me to hurry down and join them. Jermaine walked along the white shooting line with bows in one hand and a quiver of arrows on his shoulder. He and Daiquiri lined up four girls facing the four targets.

"Joni, you gonna stand there watchin' or you gonna come on down here and help?" Jermaine shouted. He turned to the girls. "Safety the most important part of archery. Two rules: One shooter at a time, and don't shoot until I give you the signal. Today, each girl get one try. You gone see it ain't easy."

Jermaine positioned each girl with her forward foot pointing toward the target. I chuckled when Daiquiri handed out four toy bows and suction-cup tipped arrows.

"The hardest thing to learn is to hold the bow and arrow," Jermaine announced as he demonstrated the proper stance with a real bow. Then he showed them how to notch their arrows against the string.

The first few times the girls tried, their toy arrows dropped or flopped before they released the bowstring, but they kept at it until Jermaine was satisfied.

"Now, when Daiquiri tell you, shoot, you shoot — one at a time. See here," Jermaine took the stance, held his bow, drew back the bowstring, and let his arrow fly. It thudded into the straw-filled target.

At best, the girls' arrows landed a few feet down their lanes. Each wanted another turn, but we had our schedule and ran out of time. Daiquiri rounded up the Bernies, but I lingered. I was dying to shoot an arrow. Jermaine must have seen the longing in my expression.

"You want a shot, Shorty?" he asked.

I turned to Daiquiri and raised my eyebrows.

"Go on. I'll get these children moving. You think you can catch up?"

I nodded. From the woods up the hill, boys hooted and hollered as they approached. I showed Jermaine I knew the stance and he handed me his bow. He stood behind me and moved my hand to the proper grip. All I could think about was his body, warm and damp, pressed against mine.

"Keep your eye on the target," he said. "Shoot."

The bowstring's twang vibrated near my ear. I watched the arrow arch high then land in the grass, tip down, a third of the way down the lane. It really was a lot harder to shoot than I'd guessed. I thought about how much Tommy would love to shoot a real bow and arrow. As I handed the bow back to Jermaine, Roland's cabin, the Andys, swarmed up to the shooting line.

"Not bad for your first time," Jermaine said.

I ran to catch the Bernies. When I glanced back, I caught Roland watching, but before I could smile and wave, he turned away.

Later that afternoon, dark clouds formed and a breeze came up. Campers gathered outside Hippo Hall, sweat beading on their foreheads, elbows flying as they raced around trees playing tag. The way the kids gaped at me, I felt like this was a circus and I was Jo Jo the Dogfaced Girl. While I leaned against a tree and listened to the counselors talking and laughing, I couldn't imagine being comfortable enough to join them.

Ruby swung around my tree and slid in front of me, her breath coming in short gasps. "What you doing?"

"Just hanging around." I scrunched down so we were face-to-face. "What you doing?"

"Theys tryin' to get me," Ruby said in her high-pitched voice. She swirled around to see if she'd outrun her pursuers.

"Do you like camp?"

Ruby's little girl smell — sweat and Ivory soap, dirt and pine needles — rose from her body like steam. "It fine," she squealed and ran to join the Honey Bees lining up for dinner.

When Lady came to drag me to the Bernies' line, I was smiling. We ducked inside just before the rain. Inside Hippo Hall, boys and girls sat at their cabin tables, drumming their plastic knives and spoons while they waited to be called to the dinner line. When it was our turn, I watched Mary Mac and Daisy fill the Bernies' plates with ham, macaroni salad, and what looked like spinach.

Lady nudged me and nodded her head toward the steam table pans. "I'mma get me some greens."

The racket from the hungry, excited kids grew deafening. After Lady's plate was filled, Mary Mac put ham slices and a scoop of macaroni salad on my plate. I hesitated in front of Daisy, then started to turn away, but Lady spoke up, "Joni want some greens too." She turned to me with a serious expression. "Mami say you got to eat your greens."

As we headed to our table, above the clatter, a sweet falsetto voice sang — *People get ready.* Except for random bursts, once they heard the song, the campers quieted and sang along, swaying their heads to the rhythm. From the stage, Terrell, almost pretty as he stood there, led the singing. When he finished, the campers clapped and the noise level returned to a joyful drone.

Daiquiri smiled like she'd had a vision. "My man, Curtis," she said.

I frowned, "Isn't his name Terrell?"

"Say what? *People Get Ready* — that's Curtis Mayfield's song. You don't know that?" Daiquiri shook her head and sighed.

"Eat your greens, Joni," Lady said. "We don't be wastin' food."

I took a deep breath, balanced a clump on my fork, and put them in my mouth. The girls laughed when my eyes squinted shut. The greens were drenched in vinegar and tasted peppery and a little slimy — but interesting. I took another forkful and swallowed, trying not to make a face. I wanted to be a good example for the girls. By the last forkful, I realized I liked greens. My mouth felt clean and hot. Lady wore a smug smile, as if she'd successfully accomplished her mission.

When Daisy delivered plastic cups of butterscotch pudding to our table, she checked my plate.

"New girl like my cookin'," she said, a note of approval in her voice.

"She be eatin' greens from here forward," Lady told her, and they smiled like conspirators.

By the time the campers cleaned their tables, the ground had turned soft and mushy from the rain. The kids were rambunctious, running around and spattering mud on each other's legs. A small boy from the Andys cabin hurled into me and knocked me down. He looked really nervous when he said, "Sorry, Miss."

I patted his arm and said, "I'm okay. It's just a little mud."

But when I got up, my legs and the backside of my shorts were wet and filthy. I heard a burst of laughter, then boys' voices — *Look at the white girl!* The little boy who knocked into me shrugged his shoulders and backed away.

My first thought was to run to the cabin, take a shower, and change my clothes. But then I looked toward the archery range and the long, gently sloping hill we trudged up earlier. I hesitated, then decided, *screw it.* They could think whatever the hell they wanted about me, but I was wet and dirty and about to have some fun for the first time in months.

I took off running, then dove head first onto the sparkling wet grass at the top of the hill. I slid almost all the way to the bottom. My face, clothes, legs, and arms were covered in mud and grass. When I started to climb back up, Daiquiri, Jermaine, and Roland waited on the crest, shaking their heads.

"You one strange white girl," Roland called down.

"Look what you did to the grass," Daiquiri yelled. A long slick of crushed and torn grass marked my slide.

"Shorty look good all messy and stuff," Jermaine said.

Kids and counselors started to line the top of the hill.

"What you doing down there, Joni?" Lady called, her voice concerned, a worried look on her face.

"Mudslide!" I shouted, "Dare you!" As I reached the top of the hill, it started raining hard.

"Geronimo!" Roland yelled, then he jumped feet-first and skimmed down the hill on his back. He looked like a dead bug with his arms and legs tucked close to his body.

Lady grabbed my hand when I reached the top. All around us, kids were saying — *White girl crazy.*

"Joni not crazy," Lady told them. That warmed my heart, but when she let go of my hand and slid down the hill, I was completely shocked. At the bottom, Lady called up, "Hey, you alls, it's fun."

Lady's words were like the blast from a starter's pistol. As Roland took Lady's hand and helped her up the hill, Jermaine whooped and dove down headfirst. Soon so many kids and counselors were running and jumping and sliding, I got a sick feeling there would be a horrible crash, kids would get hurt, and I'd be to blame. But before I had time to figure out how to stop the wild mud-slide, beautiful Delia clapped her hands and called, "Honey Bees and Bros come over this side, Bernies and Andys over there, Bridges and Auggies move on over to give these little ones room."

While the guy counselors slid down the hill, Millie, Felicia, Delia, Daiquiri, Jasmine, Dottie, Elizabeth and me sorted out the kids and made them take turns. I'm not sure where Turquoise was then, but she wasn't with us.

Within ten minutes, the grass was uprooted and the whole hill turned brown and mucky. I felt really good, like I showed the whole camp a new way to have fun, until I heard Mary Mac.

"For the love of Pete!" she hollered, her voice loud and exasperated. "What will Father say when he sees what you've done to his grass?"

I felt my stomach drop. Then I saw Father hurrying our way.

"Children," his voice boomed. Everyone quieted and looked at their feet. "Enough of this. Everyone off the hill! Now."

Father turned away as we pulled the kids off the hill. Scared out of my mind, I kept looking at Daiquiri and Delia, especially after hearing a loud whoop that sounded like, "Banzai!"

Father Vincent raced toward the hill and before I had time to swallow, pitched himself down the hill on his back, mud spattering all around him. When he reached the bottom, he got to his feet and waved. *Was that for real?* I asked myself. But everyone cheered.

Before Father made it up the hill, the Bernies surrounded me and pulled me with them to the top. We slid down in a jumble of arms and legs and mud. The hill was so slick by then, we had to crawl to get back. I didn't even see Ruby coming until she sideswiped me and I spilled down the hill again.

"I got you, Joni," Ruby said. Her glasses were coated with mud. I tried to wipe them with my shirt but all that did was smear them more.

Just as Ruby and I made it back up, a khaki lump swished past us. The kids chanted, *Mary Mac, Mary Mac, Mary Mac.* When she rolled onto her hands and knees at the bottom and got to her feet, she called up, "I've never in all my days seen the likes of this."

After a few more runs, drenched and muddy, the kids got chilly and the counselors lined up their campers to return to the cabins. A small figure marched to the crest of the hill and everyone made way.

"Now who you think got to clean these muddy clothes?" In the rain, Daisy stood as tall as her five-feet-four frame let her, a yellow bandana covering her hair.

I felt bad. I never imagined the whole camp would wind up with muddy clothes. "I'm sorry," I said.

"You be sorry enough, I don't get my turn," Daisy said. My mouth hung open.

The campers cleared back from the muddy hill and cheered. With Mary Mac waiting at the bottom, Daisy looked down, prayed, "My sweet Jesus," and jumped feet first. By then, the hill was so wet and the paths so worn that she flew to the bottom and kept right on going to the edge of the archery range. "Lord, Lord," we heard her call.

When Mary Mac and Daisy finally climbed to the top, Michael and his Auggies — the same boys I thought spit at me earlier — raised their arms to make a tunnel for the women to pass under. After they came out, Mary Mac clapped her hands and said, "Jesus, Mary, and Joseph, if your darling mothers could see the likes of you now. Walk down the path in orderly lines and each and every soul among you must have a good wash before you go near your beds."

On the paths to the cabins, the trees shielded us from the heaviest rain, so the campers stayed covered in mud until they hit the showers, fully dressed for their first rinse. Then, while Daiquiri made sure our girls washed with soap and rinsed the mud out of their hair, I collected their filthy clothes and draped them on every railing I could find. So many campers took showers at the same time, the water spurted and trickled, but one by one, the girls came into the cabin clean and wrapped in their towels. While they changed into pajamas, I listened to Daiquiri assure them the scratches and scrapes covering their backs and legs *weren't nothing*. Outside, I packed our girls' sneakers with old newspapers Father sent to each cabin.

My bottom hurt and my knuckles were raw, but I thought Mrs. Fanelli would like what she saw.

Within a few days, camp activities became routine, and there were fewer stares and comments about my being white. Mornings, the girls woke early. While Daiquiri watched six girls straighten their cots and cubbies, I led the others to the toilets and made sure they washed their faces and brushed their teeth. Then we switched. After the girls dressed, we joined other campers on the path to Hippo Hall. Before breakfast, counselors took sick, itchy, scratched, and blistered campers to Mary Mac and Daisy, who tended their ailments then sent them back — itches pink from calamine lotion, cuts and scrapes covered by *flesh*-colored bandages. Any kids who were actually sick spent a day or so in the infirmary, where Daisy kept an eye on them.

Each morning after the blessing and breakfast, Father announced cabin order for choosing activities. Campers who needed remedial work on spelling, reading, and arithmetic spent the first two activity hours each morning in the school cabin with Mary Mac. While Father and Mary Mac supervised activity selection, the counselors congregated outside to complain about the kids and decide which cabin would perform at Camp Roundup. Then the instructors rushed to their assignments to wait for the first groups of campers.

On the first day of swim lessons, before I finished testing the chlorine, I heard Roland's twelve Andys — at eight and nine-years-old, the youngest boys — splash into the pool like bison driven over a cliff. Not one of them could swim.

I rushed to the deck and shouted, "Everyone out!" and turned to Roland, my voice tight. "Hey, you can't let them in until I say so. What if something happened?"

"I knew you were back there. Anyway, nothing happened." He grinned, his teeth even and white.

"Next time, don't let them in the water until I'm here. Look, Roland, I can't teach and guard at the same time. I need your help." I looked at his camp T-shirt and shorts. "Wear your swim suit next time," I added.

Thank God, the pool was designed for non-swimmers. The twenty-five-meter-long swim area was only three feet deep. But the diving area, separated by a rope, was fourteen feet deep — off limits to everyone who couldn't swim, which meant everyone except me.

For the start of the swim lesson, I jumped in the pool to face the campers who sat on the edge with their feet in the water. "No one goes in the pool unless I say so and no one ever goes in the deep end. Each time you come for a lesson, line up on the edge like you are now. Who's had swim lessons before?"

A glistening boy with close-cropped hair and big ears raised his hand. "I don't need no lesson, I can swim."

He gave me a smug look and jumped in.

While the others laughed, the boy, with his eyes closed tight and his chin up, beat the water, splashing everywhere. One after the other, the boys hopped into the pool and started splashing and flailing.

"Hah, you can't swim for nothin', Antoine," a boy taunted. Water dripped like tears down his face.

"Back on deck!" I yelled, angry and afraid. These city kids would never obey me.

Roland stepped to the edge and frowned. "You heard teacher, Andys. Get out, now. Sit right there, like she tell you."

While the boys squirmed onto the pool's edge, I offered my hand to a chubby boy, the only camper who didn't jump in after Antoine.

"I want you to show everyone how to hold their breath," I said.

The boy looked up at Roland before he reluctantly dropped down into the pool.

"Tell me your name," I said.

The boy looked away but said, "Robert," in a quiet voice.

"Robert's going to help me show you how to hold your breath under water, like this." I squatted down until my head was completely submerged, then popped up after a few seconds.

I offered both hands to Robert, but since he didn't take mine, I took his. "Robert, keep your eyes on me. Do you know how to hold your breath?" He shrugged one shoulder. "When I count three, hold your breath and dip under with me. Ready? One, two, three."

With Robert's hands held tight, I dropped under. Robert bent his knees but dipped only as far as his chin, jerked away, and struggled to climb back on deck.

"I don't want no water in my ears," he whined.

As he scooted away from the edge, I said, "That was a good first try, Robert. Who's next? Is anyone brave enough to go under?"

Antoine slipped in, turned to leer at the other boys, and took my hands. With his eyes fixed on mine, he waited while I counted — one, two, three. Then we dipped under. Antoine immediately shot back up, water gushing from his nose.

"I ain't never seen no one swim like that. You don't know nothin'," he snarled.

"It just takes practice," I said, my voice drowned by hoots and laughter.

This was impossible. As soon as I began to feel like I'd make it through the summer, a bunch of little boys shot me down. I wanted to shout at them to never come back. I wanted to stomp away from the pool, walk down the long driveway to the road, and hitchhike away from here. I wanted to call Butch from Watermark Company to come and get me. I wanted to smoke a joint and mellow out to the Moody Blues. The words to *Nights in White Satin* circled my brain — no one knew what I was going through. I took a deep breath, hopped out and motioned for the boys to follow me across the deck. I checked the clock to see how long until this class was over and glanced at Roland.

"Listen to teacher," he said.

I thought he was smirking, but at least the kids quieted down and looked at me.

"Since you're not ready to put your heads under water, we'll start with dry-land work," I said.

After I lined them up, I bent at the waist and swept one arm after the other to demonstrate the motions of the freestyle pull. Even though they complained, they mimicked my movements. As soon as a camper's arm-sweeps looked close to what I wanted, I told him to swim-walk across the deck to Roland. After everyone had a turn, I led the boys back to the edge of the pool.

"Now that you're expert dry-land swimmers, I want you to show me how far you can splash moving your feet one at a time."

As they kicked and splashed, I walked back and forth in the pool. "Good. Strong kick. Now you have it," I said.

When the camp bell gonged and Roland herded the boys to the changing area to get ready for their next activity, they groaned and begged to stay. At least the lesson ended better than it started.

Since I had a few minutes before the next group arrived, I dove in to swim a few laps. At each end, I tucked into a flip turn and came out with a different stroke. When I finished and stood in the water, I saw the boys hanging along the gate, staring.

"Teacher, I wanna swim like that," Robert called.

Other boys shouted, *Me too! Me too!*

"Dang, white girl can swim," Antoine said, shaking his head.

Five minutes after the Andys left, the Bernie girls arrived singing *Baby Love* in sweet, clear voices. They shimmied onto the deck, self-conscious in bathing suits. Keesha's white two-piece was streaked with green bug juice. Joyful wore a deep purple suit with ruffles along the waist. Raven's blue flowered one-piece stretched tight over her shoulders and caught in her crack, too small for her pudgy body. The other girls wore red cotton-knit suits from the camp store, except for Lady. The V-neck and padded bra of Lady's turquoise suit made her flat chest look developed. Thick straps ran over her shoulders, and the waist narrowed to a panel skirt. I suspected Lady's mother sent her to camp with her own best suit.

After the mess with the Andys' lesson, I decided the girls would practice dry-land exercises before they went in the water.

But first, I asked, "Do you want to see me swim?"

"Joni gonna show us to swim," Sharone announced.

Francesca followed me to the edge of the pool, but stepped back just before I dove in. I swam a lap of freestyle, made a big splash on the flip turn, and returned swimming backstroke. I still wasn't in shape, though. I had to take a minute to catch my breath when I got out of the pool.

"That's good," Tiara and Lady said at the same time.

"Dang, Joni, you gone teach us that?" Yvonne asked, taking her thumb from her mouth.

"No way, uh uh, I ain't getting in there. I got washed last night," Crystal said, taking a step back.

"Why you care about you got washed? That ain't a tub. We gone learn to swim," Jailyn said, wide-eyed.

When I grabbed my towel and led the girls to a grassy area, Lady hurried to walk beside me. While the girls spread out, Lady jiggled from foot to foot, glanced at Daiquiri, then took my arm and pulled me close. Her face was pinched with concern, and I wondered for a moment if she was going to tell me she had her period.

Instead, she whispered, "Mami take hours on my braids. They got to last 'til she come back from Haiti. I mess them up if my hair get too wet."

I put my hands on her shoulders, leaned down, and whispered back, "Your Mami does wonderful braids. Don't worry, for now you can just dip your face in. Come on, we better get over there before Daiquiri gets suspicious."

Lady nodded. She hurried to join the girls and I followed, rubbing my hair with a towel.

"Before we go in the pool today, we're going to practice right here, on the deck," I told the fidgety girls.

I arranged them in two rows so everyone could see me and I could see them. Daiquiri stood off to the side, but I noticed she followed along with the exercises. First, we practiced holding our breath and squatting down, then letting out the air as we rose to standing. Only a few of the girls managed to time their breath-holding with the squat and breath-blowing with standing. Lady did it perfectly, even the first time.

When I showed them the freestyle stroke, they did better after I told them to pretend they had to dig their way through Jell-O. After twenty minutes, they started to squirm, giving each other little shoves. A few of them sank to the deck and fanned themselves. When Daiquiri gave me her dead-eye stare, I realized it was time for the water.

"Okay, Bernies, sit on the edge of the pool. From now on, when you come for a lesson, that's the first thing you do. Never go in the water unless I tell you to. That way everyone stays safe. Now, hop in!" I looked to Daiquiri for approval, but her watchful eyes gave no hint of what she was thinking.

I demonstrated crouching down under water and coming to the surface. Then I showed them how to blow bubbles in the water. When I let them in the pool, Tiara ducked under and then burst back up, coughing.

She climbed to the edge, saying, "I can't do it, Joni."

Lady watched, leery-eyed, as Angel dipped under repeatedly and came back up, announcing, "That ain't so hard."

Joyful, Crystal, Raven, Francesca, and Keesha dipped their faces in, if only for a second.

"Sharone, Jailyn, Josephine, Lady, will you try?" Each one of them shook her head no.

I looked at Lady, then splashed water on my face and raised my eyebrows. She shrugged and sprinkled a few drops on her neck.

"That's a start," I said. "Now, who remembers the freestyle stroke we practiced?"

Lady's hand went up first, followed by all the others.

"Good. Let's have a race across the pool, just for fun, using the stroke you learned." I glanced at Lady's stricken face. "But I want you to keep your heads above water the entire time."

To show them what I meant, I leaned over with my chest above the water and rotated my arms so my hands cut through the water with each stroke.

Lady made a tiny nod and set her mouth, determined. I knew this idea turned out to be a good one. As I lined up the girls in a straight line, shoulder to shoulder, they squealed and jostled. I hopped out of the pool and waved for their attention.

"Wait for the whistle, then stroke-swim to the other end." I made a circle of my thumb and forefinger, stuck it against my tongue, and whistled for the start. While most of the girls headed across the pool, splashing and laughing, four of them stood in place, staring at me.

"You teach me that whistle?" Francesca called.

"Only if you get to the end of the pool," I called back, gesturing for them to get going. When I looked up, Lady was moving fast, rotating her arms exactly as I taught them. She reached the other end and watched while the other girls flailed to the finish.

"Well done, Bernies," I shouted. *It really was*, I thought.

"Time to get changed. Get a move on," Daiquiri called.

As Lady passed, I smiled. "You got the moves, Lady. You'll be a good swimmer."

She mumbled, "I don't know," but gave me a sideways look and smile.

When the girls lined up to leave, Jailyn yelled, "Show us how you swim again, Joni."

This time, I swam a lap of breaststroke, flipped, and returned swimming butterfly.

Dang, someone said, *she like a fish in the ocean.*

That evening after dinner, Daiquiri and I led the Bernies to the front for Camp Roundup. Using the extravagant gestures we'd rehearsed, we chanted:

Nobody likes me, everybody hates me, I'm gonna eat some worms! Fat ones, skinny ones, short ones, tall ones, my how they squiggle and squirm! Bite their heads off. Suck their guts out. Throw the skins away. I'm a Happy Hippo when I eat… Worms! Three times a day.

From the stage I peered into the seats where campers squirmed and counselors chatted among themselves. In the front row, Ruby leaned forward, her eyes big as saucers behind her specs. I winked and smiled. With a wide grin, Ruby turned to the camper next to her and pointed at me.

As soon as the Bernies formed a line to sing their rendition of *Jimmy Mack* — fully choreographed by Daiquiri — I moved to the wings. I noticed Turquoise in an aisle seat, arms folded across her chest. Her hard expression made me uncomfortable.

A few minutes later, with the words to *Jimmy Mack* thrumming through my head, I followed the Bernies off-stage to grab seats for the Andys' performance. I slowed down to tell Ruby, "See you at swim tomorrow."

As I continued toward my seat, I looked back at Ruby, pleased to see her smile. I never saw a foot jut out in the aisle, but I heard Turquoise snicker when I tripped and landed on the plank floor. My palms stung from tiny splinters. I felt someone take my arm and help me up. Just another reason for everyone to make fun of me, I thought.

"Y'all right?" Roland asked.

His eyes were crinkly, like he was trying not to smile.

"Thanks, I'm fine."

My voice was husky. God, I was so embarrassed. After Roland dropped my arm, I looked around and pretended to smile in case anyone was watching. When I slid into the seat between Daiquiri and Lady, their eyes were on me.

"I tripped is all. No big deal. I'm just clumsy," I said.

Turquoise looked back and shook her head. "Got to watch yourself.

Got to watch your step."

There was a rustle when Jermaine walked up the center aisle. When he passed me, he reached over Daiquiri to flick my hair. I liked that. I mean, guys only flick hair of girls they like, right? After he passed, I scraped the splinters out of my palms.

Turquoise motioned for the Honey Bees to slide down a seat. "Jermaine," she called, and patted the empty seat next to her.

As he sat down, Jermaine threw me a smile. I stared at Turquoise's back and knew I better watch my step.

After the first two weeks, I began to relax. The Bernies grew more comfortable around me too. One night before bunk-down, the girls gathered around Daiquiri's and my stalls. Keesha scratched a mosquito bite on her neck until it bled. As she looked at the rim of red under her fingernail, she asked, "Why your name Daiquiri?"

"'Cause nine months after Daddy drank five daiquiris to celebrate his promotion to warehouse supervisor, I was born. He told the nurse — *That's my Daiquiri girl*, and she wrote it on my birth certificate — Daiquiri Girl Williams. Why your name Keesha?"

"Cause my Mama di-int want to name me Debbie Reynolds," Keesha said.

The girls leaned into each other, howling with laughter. Raven spilled onto the floor.

"Why your name Joni?" Lady asked me, her voice quiet and shy.

I looked up and stuttered, words refusing to come to my mouth. The truth is, I had no idea why my parents named me Joan.

Daiquiri looked from girl to girl and answered, "'Cause her Mama didn't know her real name Jonika."

Joe-neeka, the girls screamed. *Your real name Jonika. Thaz good. Un hunh, that's right.*

I nodded, grimacing into a half-smile.

Lady squeezed next to me on my cot. She took my ponytail and sifted her fingers through the long, straight hair. "Soft and smooth," she said.

The girls swarmed me, undid the elastic band, and petted my head.

Raven said, "It feel like my Mama's nightgown."

"Like baby hair," Yvonne whispered.

Even Daiquiri reached over to touch it. "Limp like cooked spaghetti."

"I'mma give you cornrows," Lady decided.

"Me too," Raven squealed.

Raven and Lady knelt on either side of me. From drawers and bags and off heads, rubber bands and barrettes and bobby pins mounted in a pile on my pillow. With a tug and a warning to hold still, Lady pulled back my hair. She parted it with my comb and gathered a section on top.

"Yous gonna need to Ultra Sheen that hair if you want cornrows to last," Daiquiri advised.

After she dug through her cubby, Daiquiri handed a jar to Raven. While Raven scooped out a glob, rubbed it in her palms and then through my hair, Lady wielded the comb with confidence and concentration. Some girls danced and sang to the tinny music squawking from Daiquiri's AM radio — *Heard It through the Grapevine* and *R-E-S-P-E-C-T* — while others took turns braiding sections of my hair, their coppery body smells mixing with the mild earthy scent of Ultra Sheen. By the time my blonde hair transformed into narrow rows of braids, my scalp throbbed. After universal approval of the new look, Daiquiri got the girls calmed down and into their bunks.

Finally, the girls stopped giggling and their soft sleeping sounds floated through the cabin. I grabbed Jermaine's beret from my cubby and turned to Daiquiri.

"Okay if I go to the basketball court? I'll stay in tomorrow night so you can go out."

"You showing your braids to Jermaine?" Daiquiri's voice was firm.

"I thought I would. Shouldn't I?"

I felt embarrassed and foolish. I touched my hair.

"Might as well, theys all gonna see your new 'do sometime, 'less you take it out and break the Bernies' hearts. You giving Jermaine back his tam?"

The question felt like an accusation. I realized she thought I crossed a line and needed to cross back.

"Yes," I told her, "I keep forgetting to give it to him."

"Joni, Jonika," Daiquiri called quietly as I reached the door. She tiptoed over and stepped outside with me. "You know 'bout Jermaine and Turquoise?"

I shook my head.

"They got history," Daiquiri said. "And you can't change history."

As I crunched up the path toward the dull light of the basketball court, my heart pounded and I rubbed my tongue over the back of my teeth. I'd planned to arrive with Jermaine's beret perched over my braids, but now I was afraid the boys would mock me. Maybe they'd think it was disrespectful or offensive. When I reached the court, friendly jeers, deep-voiced laughter, and the sound of the ball thumping on macadam and thudding against the wooden backboard pulsed the air.

For a few moments, no one noticed when I came into the light —
beret in hand, braids whipping my neck — and sat on a log to watch.
Roland saw me first. He dribbled the ball between his legs, spun, and took
a shot that bounced off the backboard. Jermaine grabbed the ball and
dribbled to the other end of the court while Roland strolled over and sat
next to me.

After his jump shot swished the net, Jermaine skipped backward to
the half-court line. When he noticed me with Roland, he tipped his head
and gave me a funny look. I tossed him the beret like a Frisbee. He caught
it with one hand and put it on his head.

"Shorty, you ready to play?" he called.

"Girl gone native," Roland said.

He offered his hand and pulled me to standing.

"Now you wearing braids?" Jermaine's lisp sounded soft and cute.

Next to him, quiet Terrell with the gorgeous singing voice looked at
me with a blank expression, like I was a new specimen he'd found in the
woods and now needed to classify.

"The Bernies did it," I reported. I felt both proud and awkward.

"New girl got her hair all corn-rowed," Jermaine announced.

"Looks good," Roland said. "Not so Wonder Bread."

Roland joined Terrell and Lincoln on the court, where they jived
and shoved each other while James took shots from the free-throw line.
I got a bad feeling and realized I shouldn't have come. But I fought my
inclination to run, took a breath, and stepped onto the hardtop. Jermaine
plucked down a rebound and held out the ball.

"Shorty think she ready to ball. Shorty, me, Lincoln against James,
Roland, Terrell."

Jermaine tossed in the ball from the half-court line. The boys played
around me like I was a little kid — dribbling between their legs, handing
me the ball only to pull it away, holding the ball over my head while I
jumped for it. Still, I tried, running up and down the court but keeping to
the outside so I wouldn't get bumped. Every few plays Jermaine or Roland
passed me the ball, and the boys let me take a shot unguarded. The one
time I heaved the ball at the basket and it spun around the rim a couple
times before it dropped through, the boys cheered and clapped.

But Jermaine said, "You just throwing the ball. You got to shoot it.
You got lucky that time."

When Mary Mac rang the first lights-out bell, I lingered as the boys started back to their cabins. Terrell hesitated at the edge of the court before he turned and followed the guys into the woods.

"Jermaine, is there time to teach me to shoot?"

Again, I wondered *what was I thinking, why did I come?* I mean, of course, I know why, but I felt really awkward.

"If Mary Mac keep the lights on." Jermaine ran through the trees to Hippo Hall and came back after a few minutes. "She say, fifteen minutes then lights out for real."

When Jermaine placed my hands on the ball in proper position, I smelled his breath — sweet from Juicy Fruit gum — and his body — bitter, like tar melting on asphalt. I liked the heat from his body so close to mine.

"Spread your fingers against the ball. Use your left hand to guide. Lift your elbow, aim, and shoot. Push up with a flick, like this."

He took the ball from my hands as he spoke to show me how. I tried to follow his instructions, but my hands felt weak and small. When I shot, the ball made a tiny arc and dropped. It seemed like it was only a minute or two before the camp lights flickered. I tossed the ball to Jermaine and wondered if he thought I'd acted stupid.

I didn't want to go back to the cabin yet. I imagined sitting on the log in the dark and Jermaine taking my hand. I'd put my other hand on top of his and wait for him to kiss me. But Jermaine looked like he wanted to get going.

"S'all right, Shorty, we play again some time." Jermaine put his beret on my head. "I got to see Father Vincent. You good to get back to your cabin?"

"No problem," I said, more confident than I felt. "Come to the pool after breakfast tomorrow. Your turn for a lesson."

I wiped sweat from my forehead and entered the woods, my heart pounding like I'd just finished a 500-meter swim. Through the deepening haze, I stumbled down the path. With each rustle from the trees and bushes, my brain felt squeezed in a vise, and I worried I'd lost my way. A scene from *Carnival of Souls* — Mary running away from the ghouls — came to me then. I forced it out of my mind. *Why didn't I ask Jermaine to walk back to the cabins with me? What was I trying to prove?* I took a breath. *Stop being a baby,* I told myself. *You walked down this path dozens of times.* Still, my pulse throbbed in my ears. A low buzzing on the right got louder. Visions of zombies hurried my step.

Ahead, two specks of iridescence glimmered in the dark. As I leaned forward and stared, trying to figure out what they were, the specks drew closer, and two red orbs glowed like the coils of a cigarette lighter. I froze and shut my eyes.

When I opened them — it's still so scary, Judge, I can hardly write the words — something shaped like a tall bell, without arms or legs but with glowing red eyes, floated toward me. Its smell, as disgusting as vomit, made me gag. *This can't be real, you're imagining things,* I chanted silently, but I inched back, my heels crunching up the path. I held out my right hand like I was signaling a dog to stay.

"Stop," I whispered, but the thing floated closer.

A branch snapped under my foot and I fell on my backside, hard. Still, it drifted closer. I pushed away, my palms stinging, my eyes fixed on the red, shimmering eyes. A cry rose in my throat and strangled there. I wanted to get up and run, but I was too afraid. *Please God, someone, help me,* I prayed. I wanted to be home in my bed listening to music. If I got away from this monster, I'd even go back to Redwood Academy. *I'll never complain again,* I promised the woods.

The thing, brown and musty, hovered an arms-length away, like it was examining me. When an owl hooted from a nearby tree, the creature receded like a wave, flowing backwards and dissolving in the dark. My brain screamed — *RUN!* — but I couldn't move. I became a statue, frozen in a marble base. I could hardly breathe.

"Jonika, you out there?" Daiquiri's voice came to me like she was talking through a tin can.

Whatever spell held me, broke then. I pushed myself up and lunged down the path, gasping in short, shallow breaths until I reached the cabin steps where Daiquiri waited. Her round face showed concern, but her eyes were suspicious. I felt lightheaded and ill. I swear, I've never been so frightened in my life. It was like living in a horror movie. My teeth chattered and I felt chilled.

"Why you still out after lights out?" Daiquiri asked.

When I collapsed on the steps in tears, she sat beside me, our shoulders touching.

"One them boys do something to you?" Her voice was deep and quiet.

"No, we just played basketball," I answered between sobs.

I knew she'd never believe what I saw, but I had to tell someone.

"When I was walking back on the path, a horrible thing came floating at me. It had red eyes and smelled disgusting. I was so scared, I couldn't move until I heard your voice. I'm sure I imagined it, but God, Daiquiri, it was terrible."

Daiquiri sat back. "Two red eyes? Floating? For real?"

"Yeah, that's exactly what it looked like," I said, in shock. *How could she know?*

"Those boys tell you 'bout the *Manetu*? They get you all upset so you seeing things? Every summer they tell that story to new counselors. They used to tell it to the campers 'til Father Vincent put a stop to it."

As Daiquiri spoke, I felt my pulse slow and my breath settle into its normal rhythm.

"No one told me any stories like that. The only scary stories I've heard are the ones they tell at Roundup. Daiquiri, the thing I saw was real. I smelled it. I saw its horrible eyes. I'm never going out alone after dark as long as I live," I swore. I took a deep breath and asked, "What's a *Manetu*?"

In the dark, Daiquiri's eyes glinted in the glow from a porch light. "It's supposed to be the spirit of some old Indian brave whose tribe lived and hunted in these woods. A couple hundred years ago when the whites moved in and forced the Indians to give up their land, one warrior refused to leave. They say he roamed the hills in a bearskin. Whenever a white family moved onto the land, he stole their children and killed their cattle. Now they say the *Manetu's* spirit roams these woods. He must of seen your white face and thought you come to steal his land. We'll tell Father Vincent tomorrow. Maybe he can do an exorcism or something. Don't say a word about this to these children or you'll scare them white."

"But is it for real?"

"No one knows," Daiquiri said. "But you not the first person to see it."

Later, as I lay in bed, still trembling, I thought I would have a heart attack unless I blew some weed. Even though I'd smoked pot almost every afternoon with Ishmael, and whenever I could during my house arrest, here's the truth-- since I came to camp, except for the first few days, I hadn't missed it. I didn't even think about it until that night, when my brain screamed for escape. I needed to calm down. I needed a J. But even though I was desperate to snuff out the red eyes that glowed in my brain, I knew if I got caught smoking pot, I'd be sent to juvie.

Judge, I kept thinking that if that *Manetu* Indian was hanging out in the woods, juvie didn't seem all that bad.

The next morning, I woke groggy and shaken. As soon as Daiquiri and I herded the Bernies to Hippo Hall for breakfast, I looked for Jermaine. I heard his voice before I saw him — circling the girl counselors' table. Each one said something to him and he smiled like she was the funniest girl he ever met. I knew they loved Jermaine flirting with them as much as I did.

When Turquoise put her tray on the table, she said, "Ain't the brother workin' it today?"

Then Jermaine moved behind her, reached his arms over her shoulders and took a piece of toast from her plate. After he ate it in three bites, he pulled a lollipop from his pocket. As he handed it to Turquoise, to everyone's amusement, he sang, *I got sunshine on a cloudy day*, before he made his way to the guys' table.

"Jonika, stop staring and go tell Father 'bout the *Manetu*." Daiquiri's voice drew my attention away from Jermaine.

I was embarrassed and wondered who besides Daiquiri noticed my focus on Jermaine and Turquoise. But I shrugged and dumped my breakfast trash before I approached Father Vincent and Mary Mac. I cleared my throat. "Father, a scary thing happened last night on my way back to the cabin."

He and Mary Mac turned to me with concern.

"About half-way between here and the cabins, some weird thing came at me. I don't know what it was, but it had red eyes and smelled really bad."

Father patted my hand. "No need to worry, Joan. I'm sure what you saw was a raccoon, but I'll walk down the path and look around." Father tapped his chest pocket where he kept his cigarettes.

"Thanks, Father," I said. "Can you spare a couple cigs? I think a smoke will calm my nerves."

"You know the rule — don't let the kids see you."

After he shook out a cigarette for me, Father carried his coffee mug to the oldest boys' table. Mary Mac motioned for me to follow her to the clinic. Inside, she closed the door and put her finger to her lips. After I sat down by the window, I put the cigarette in my mouth, but my hands shook so much I couldn't light it. Mary Mac struck the match and held it while I inhaled. I took a deep drag and blew the smoke out the window.

"Child, I am not one to dismiss visits from ghosts and fairies. Sure, I remember well a picnic in Ireland on a warm spring day when I was a lass of eight years. After we finished our egg-mayonnaise sandwiches and biscuits, my parents lay back on the blanket and dozed. I spied a butterfly, wondrously shimmering with big ovals that looked like lovely blue eyes on each of its red wings. I chased it for what seemed like eternity, enticed by those blue eyes like they were my very mother's. The beautiful creature flitted away the instant I was certain to touch it. Not until the sun's rays darted like spokes behind the mountains and the butterfly settled beyond my reach on a hedge did I realize I was lost. I began to cry. A small boy in strange clothes — a rough brown tunic with a rope belt — crawled out from the hedge. He smiled and his bright eyes sparkled with fun. Without a word, he motioned for me to join him. I got to my hands and knees to follow him into the thicket. Just as my hand reached into the shrubbery, I heard Mam shouting my name — Ashling, Ashling, Ashling! As I turned to look, my arm was yanked into the hedge so hard my face dragged against the ground. *Mam,* I cried, *Mam!* And then everything went black.

When I came to myself, I was on the picnic blanket next to Da, bundled in my mother's arms. Mam rocked back and forth, wailing, *It's the Lurikeen, the little people, come to steal our Ashling.* A few weeks later, we flew from Shannon Airport to Philadelphia, where Daida joined his brother's roofing business. Until today, I've never spoken of the boy in the hedge."

Mary Mac's face drooped with exhaustion, as if telling her story wore her out. She handed me a silver flashlight.

"When you traipse about after dark, shine this to fend off creatures of the night. Don't they hate the light? Now don't be telling Father Vincent or anyone else my story. Sure, they'll think I'm bats."

"Thank you," I said, grateful she believed me but thinking Mary Mac was bats.

But then so was I.

On the path through the woods to the cabins, I caught up with the slow-moving Honey Bees. Ruby, dragging the tips of her sneakers through pine needles and dirt, lagged a few feet behind. Her legs and arms looked like sticks, and her braids were tied with green ribbons. I aimed the flashlight at the shady ground in front of her and jiggled it so the light danced at her feet. Ruby squealed and leapt at the streaking beams. After she heard my chuckle, she turned and skipped to me.

"Whazzat, Jonika?" she asked.

She pushed her thick glasses closer to her eyes.

Jonika? That surprised me. The Bernies must have talked at breakfast about last night's cabin conversations. As we walked, I let Ruby hold the flashlight. Wide-eyed, she twirled it between her hands. When she found the switch, she clicked it on and, with a huge smile, turned in a complete circle to shine it against the trees. Just as the beam reached the back of Turquoise's head, I grabbed it and turned it off.

"What you alls doing back there?" Turquoise called, her brow furrowed.

"Just following you to the cabins," I answered.

"Catch up now, Ruby," Turquoise said, turning back to the path.

I looked down at Ruby and put my finger on my lips. Ruby nodded and sniffed, then scurried down the path. Before she caught up with the Honey Bees, she turned and waved.

"See you for swim, Jonika."

I liked Jonika more than I ever liked Joni.

July 4 – 11, 1969

As soon as the kids heard rumors of fireworks after dark, the whole camp went bananas. All morning, campers ran from activity to activity, crazy with anticipation for the evening cookout and campfire. Ten minutes after I checked the chlorine and skimmed the pool, a high-pitched *Yankee Doodle Dandy* echoed from the path. Before I put the skimmer in the shed, Honey Bees and Bernies in rainbow colors sat on the pool's edge, kicking their legs to splash each other. The air thickened with squeals and screams and calls of — *When you gonna let us in, Jonika?*

After I returned from the tool shed, Lady scurried over, her eyes serious.

"Mami say the 4th of July be my day, cause I'm born American."

"You're an all-American girl, Lady. Mami must be so proud of you."

I smiled and put my arm across her shoulder as we walked to the pool where Ruby, squinting without her glasses, jiggled and kicked.

Water splashed our legs, and Ruby's voice rose above the others. "Jonika, we ain't waitin' no more!"

I turned to Lady. "I need someone I can count on to help me today. Will you keep an eye on Ruby when she's in the pool?" I bent close to her ear and whispered, "She can be a little rambunctious."

Lady smiled in her sweet, shy way and nodded. I stood on the edge of the pool while Lady squeezed in next to Ruby.

"No lessons today, just fun swim. Fun and safe. I want each Bernie to buddy with a Honey Bee. Bernies need to take care of their Honey Bee buddies," I said.

I watched Lady take Ruby's hand and felt proud when each Bernie took a Honey Bee buddy.

"That's bossy enough," I heard Turquoise tell Daiquiri.

"Jonika allowed to be bossy at the pool," Daiquiri answered.

"Who your buddy, Turquoise?" a Honey Bee called.

"Ain't no one my buddy but Daiquiri," she answered.

"You need a buddy, Jonika," Raven called.

"You're all my buddies. Jump in." I stepped back, but water from twenty-three bodies drenched my T-shirt.

"Will you help watch the girls?" I called to Daiquiri and Turquoise.

While I walked around to the lifeguard stand, Daiquiri stood and moved to the deck near where the girls were splashing, but Turquoise just rolled her eyes.

"Now I'mma supposed to do your work?"

From the guard stand — positioned at the diving well — I scanned the pool left to right and back again, tooting the whistle whenever girls drifted into the deeper area near the rope.

Keesha cannonballed off the side to splash Turquoise and Daiquiri. But in the wake of Keesha's jump, I saw Ruby pitch forward, face down. Without her feet on the bottom, she thrashed and splashed. I dove from the guard platform into the diving well and under the rope, surfacing in the middle of a cluster of girls. But before I reached Ruby only seconds later, Lady had pulled her up and set her on her feet. Ruby rubbed her eyes and snorted water from her nose.

"I save her, Jonika, like you say," Lady said.

"Good job, Lady," I said. "You did real good."

I scooped up Ruby, carried her to the side of the pool, and sat her on the edge facing me. The other girls crowded close and Turquoise loomed over us all.

"When you got knocked over, did you hold your breath like we practiced?" I asked.

Ruby shook her head and sneezed.

"I di-in't see no baby Honey Bee when I jump in," Keesha wailed, tears welling in her eyes.

"It's a accident, Keesha," Lady said. "I be right here to save Ruby."

"Lady's right. It was an accident, and Lady saved Ruby, and that's why we always swim with a buddy," I told the girls.

But my heart was racing and I could hardly breathe. I felt like I swam twenty laps instead of across the pool.

"'Cause you sure 'nough didn't save nobody," Turquoise said.

"Jonika be here fast as she can. Ain't that right, Daiquiri?" Lady glanced at me with downcast eyes, then looked up at Daiquiri.

"Jonika dove right in," Daiquiri said in her confident voice. "And Lady be by Ruby's side. You fine now, Ruby."

"I drown-did," Ruby cried. "I'mma tell Mary Mac I drown-did." Her eyes were squinty and red. She pawed the deck for her glasses until Lady hopped out and retrieved them from a bench.

"Honey Bees, y'all come on out of there. Time we get dressed for lunch," Turquoise called as she turned her back to the pool and walked toward the changing area.

As the Honey Bees filed out, Ruby pushed her glasses back, turned to me, and smiled her big-toothed grin.

"I drown-did," she announced, turning her head to make certain everyone heard. "I drown-did."

Before she herded the Bernies toward the gate, Daiquiri said, "Don't worry none on Turquoise. She just plain mean some days."

I sat at the edge of the pool, running Ruby's dunking through my mind, trying to decide if I could have handled it any other way.

On her way to line up with Daiquiri, Lady patted my head as if I were a child.

Roland's cabin of Andys had whooped, hollered, and splashed out so much water, I didn't need to hose down the deck after I blew the whistle and closed the pool at 4:00 p.m. The boys hopped out and hurried to line up, still wet in their swimsuits, wild with excitement for the cookout. Before locking the gate, I policed the area. I piled towels, underpants, and shirts in a plastic lost-and-found tub and threw wadded napkins into the trashcan. From the across camp, random shouts and gleeful chants of *fireworks! fireworks! fireworks! fireworks!* rang through the trees, like cheers from an arena on game day.

After six hours of sun, noise, and berserk non-swimmers splashing in the pool, I was so exhausted I couldn't walk straight. As I staggered down the path to Bernie, I considered staying in my bunk during the cookout and campfire. I imagined being in Ishmael's bedroom, lying on his mattress, my head propped on two pillows, my knees bent to support a copy of *Rolling Stone*, while the sweet smell of marijuana encircled me. Overhead, the staccato chop of a helicopter drowned out the buzz and rustle of the woods. I recognized the chopper sound from TV news reports that showed US Chinook helicopters evacuating wounded American soldiers in Vietnam. One thing I didn't miss was news about the goddamned war.

All the way from the archery range, the oily, chemical smell of charcoal lighter fluid drifted up the path. Around the cabins, boys and girls in red, white, or blue T-shirts ran in circles, screeching, *I got you, you it!* The oldest girls, the St. Brigids, or Bridges, as the campers called them, sat on their cabin steps, some playing jacks, others doing the hand jive in rhythm, without music.

When I entered Bernie, Lady was sweeping the floor and singing along with the AM radio to *Mixed Up Shook Up Girl*, by a group from Philly — Patty and the Emblems. I sang along, feeling mixed up and shook up too, especially about Ishmael. When I least expected it, I'd think about him and miss him. But right behind that thought, I'd remember Mrs. Fanelli's words — *You got involved with the wrong guy and you made bad choices.* My memories really were all mixed up. I stumbled to my cot, almost too weary to smile at Lady. As I lay back, I wondered what she would think about Ishmael and me, and I was ashamed. When the song ended, Lady leaned over the divider and beamed.

"Your braids look good, Jonika."

"Thanks. Where's everyone?" I asked, raising my head from the pillow.

"They all somewhere," Lady said, "runnin' an' hollerin'."

"Daiquiri let you stay in the cabin alone?"

"She let me come back when she saw you on the path. I tole her I need a break from the noise."

I rolled off the cot and joined Lady. As she walked the broom to the closet, I put a hand on her shoulder.

"You took good care of Ruby today. She's special, like you."

Lady's eyes opened wide. They were so round and deep, I felt like they took in the whole world. With a shy smile, she lowered her gaze and continued humming to the radio. Whenever I looked at Lady, I felt at peace.

I hardly remember lying down on my bunk again, but pushes and jabs on my shoulder and anxious voices — *Jonika, wake up. We missin' the cookout. Daiquiri say we don't leave widout you. Please wake up* — pulled me from a deep sleep.

"You think you might be ready to join us?" Daiquiri said, hands on hips, lips pursed and head tipped. She reminded me of a stern teacher.

"Okay, okay, I'm coming. Give me a second," I begged as the girls dragged me off my cot, spilling me onto the floor. "Go on, I'll catch up."

The girls were out the door in a snap once they made sure I was awake.

As soon as I pulled on fresh clothes, I ran along the path to the archery range, following the cooking smells. On a level area just below the hill, Father Vincent and Daisy stood over two grills, tapping hamburgers and hot dogs with tongs and forks. Red-checked vinyl covered three folding tables where big aluminum pans held baked beans sweetened with brown sugar, mustardy potato salad, and runny coleslaw. Plastic knives, forks, and spoons stuck out of vases from Mary Mac's office, and a stack of paper plates was held down with a fist-sized rock. Huge cans of Charles Potato Chips and bowls of Fritos rested on a square card table. Steel tubs filled with ice, Pepsi, root beer, and orange soda stuck out from under the tables. Up the hill by Hippo Hall, Mary Mac, in a red-white-and-blue-striped apron, stood by an ice cream freezer and doled out cherry and grape popsicles, orange creamsicles, fudgesicles, and ice cream cups to stained and sticky campers.

After the Bernies filled their plates, I followed Daiquiri to the counselors' table, balancing two hamburgers and a mound of corn chips on a paper plate. I trapped my soda in my armpit, its icy cold welcome against my sweaty skin. Jermaine and Roland made room for me between them and helped themselves to my chips.

"Jonika got the jungle fever," Turquoise sneered from across the table.

Delia elbowed her and frowned. I thought Turquoise was commenting on the way my face and shoulders throbbed red with sunburn. With campers coming in and out of the pool all day, I'd forgotten to slather on the Coppertone.

"What you say that for?" Roland sounded annoyed.

"'Cause white girl like brown sugar," Turquoise answered, "like that song, *chocolate-flavored love*."

She made an air kiss toward Jermaine, who shook his head.

"I don't know what get into you, Turquoise. You ain't never act like this before."

"We ain't never had no white girl come to our camp think she can boss us around before. She took over my Honey Bees today like they hers. Almost drowned one, too." Turquoise glared at me.

A corn chip stuck in my throat and I grabbed the soda to wash it down. After I took a big swig, I coughed and brown fizz came out my nose and dripped down my chin. Terrell pushed a napkin across the table and twitched when Turquoise bumped his shoulder. I bent over and Roland pounded my back. But Turquoise didn't stop.

"What, Pepsi too strong? I thought you a hard-ass criminal."

"I didn't see you jump in after Ruby," I croaked when I caught my breath.

Turquoise pushed her empty plate across the table, swung out her legs and stood up. "You don't know nothin'," she said. When she saw Father coming our way, she stepped aside and waited. Father Vincent, smelling like charcoal and grease, took Turquoise's seat.

"Everyone ready for the campfire? Be sure to keep the little ones at least ten feet back. They have such a fascination with fire. Be smart, be safe, and be alert. And if you want ice cream, you better get it now before Mary Mac runs out." Father turned to me. "Jermaine tells me there was a drowning scare at the pool this morning. You're aware, aren't you, that you must report all significant incidents to me?"

My face flushed when I said, "Father, there was no incident to report. I was on the guard stand and saw Ruby get knocked off her feet. I dove in to grab her, but Lady pulled her up in the second or two it took me to get there. Kids go under like that all the time. Lady was Ruby's swim buddy and did exactly what she was supposed to do."

With his eyebrows raised, Father turned to Turquoise. Her features hardened and she narrowed her eyes.

"Turquoise was right there too," I said. "She had her eyes on the Honey Bees the whole time they were at the pool."

"It weren't no thing," Turquoise said. She flicked her head.

"Ruby insisted she drown-did," Father said with a smile. "I'm delighted it weren't no thing."

After Father headed back to douse the grills, Turquoise reached across the table and grabbed her empty plate. She and I reached the trash bin at the same time. As we dumped our scraps, her napkin and fork dropped on the ground. I picked them up and flipped them in without saying anything. We avoided each other's eyes.

Turquoise headed to the campers' tables, clapped her hands, and called, "Honey Bees, time to buzz back to the Queen."

While Turquoise watched the Honey Bees climb on the big rocks and boulders on the far side of the archery range, I crept away, thinking about the things she said — *jungle fever, brown sugar, chocolate-flavored love.* Humiliation stuck in my throat like the corn chip. I couldn't go back to the counselors' table, and I didn't want to go anywhere near Turquoise. I wanted to disappear. From up the hill at the ice cream freezer, Mary Mac waved and I headed up.

"It's been a wonderful holiday," Mary Mac said when I reached her. Sweat stained the neck of her red camp T-shirt. She wiped her face with a rag and untied her apron. "Will you be having a treat, Jonika?"

Although I felt a little queasy from the sun and Turquoise's scorn, a popsicle sounded pretty good. "What you got left?"

Mary Mac broke into a wide smile. A heartbeat later, two hands covered my eyes.

"Guess who?" a falsetto voice asked.

"Jermaine?"

The hands dropped. "You killin' me, always thinkin' 'bout Jermaine," Roland said, his face scrunched as if in agony.

I felt awkward and bad, but I turned and smiled.

"Got you!"

"You funnin' me, Shorty?"

"You too easy," I said with a half-smile.

Mary Mac handed each of us a chocolate and vanilla Dixie cup and a wooden spoon. "It's not the 4th of July without ice cream. Roland, will you help me bring the freezer back to Hippo Hall?"

Roland tossed his ice cream back in the freezer and grabbed the handle. Before he started to push, he craned his neck toward me and grinned.

"Save me a seat at the camp fire."

As the sun dipped lower in the sky, I headed down the hill, ears ringing with squeals and shrieks of dozens of excited campers. Daiquiri and I gathered the Bernies and lined them up to march back to the cabin to wash up. Along the path, the girls' complaints echoed through the trees like bird-calls —

Why we gotta come back here?

They cooking the marshmallows!

We jes gonna get dirty again.

Boys be lucky, they pee in the bushes but we got to walk all this way to the toilet.

After the girls hit the outhouse, in record time they washed their faces and arms at the spigot and changed into clean T-shirts. On the way back to the campfire, I took up my place at the rear and Lady walked with me, rolling her eyes whenever one of the girls would whine. She seemed so adult, so respectful. The others recognized Lady's reserve too. *You a church lady, Lady,* they sometimes said.

"Jonika, do I still be Ruby's buddy?" Lady asked, after we'd gone more than halfway to the archery range.

"Whenever the Honey Bees and Bernies are at the pool together, you can be Ruby's buddy just like today."

"Who her buddy the other time?"

"I don't think anyone is. Turquoise is her counselor," I said. "Why?"

"'Cause after the cookout Ruby go off by herself. She say she goin' up the cabin to get her a flashlight 'cause she don't like the dark. She say she big enough to go by herself," Lady said. "I guess she's back at the campfire now. Didn't see her up the cabins."

"When did she leave the cookout?"

"When you gettin' your ice cream with Roland."

Cold sweat tingled on my forehead, yet my cheeks burned with dread. "Stay in line," I told Lady, then I ran up to Daiquiri. "Lady just told me Ruby left the cookout before we did to get a flashlight from the cabins. But Lady didn't see Ruby up there. What should we do?"

Daiquiri glanced at the girls. Her body smelled like warm soup and ivory soap.

"Why Lady wait 'til now to say something? Well, it don't matter. Could be Ruby sitting with the Honey Bees eating marshmallows and drinking bug juice. Let me get these girls back to the archery range and I'll check with Turquoise to be sure. Best you run back and check the Honey Bee cabin — check all the cabins — then meet us at the campfire. Not like a city girl to go wanderin' through the woods. I 'spect she's with Turquoise."

With my heart pounding, I forced myself to walk past the girls and back to Lady.

"I'm checking the cabins. Will you keep up the rear and make sure everyone stays together? I'm glad you told me about Ruby." I tried to smile.

As soon as Lady nodded, a look of concern on her face, I bolted, my breath coming in painful bursts, like trying to breathe under water. The voices of the Bernies faded by the time I reached the cabins. When I looked in St. Beatrice — the Honey Bees' cabin — clothes and bedding were scattered on the floor and the room smelled like sugary pee.

"Ruby, you in here? It's Jonika. Come out so we can go to the campfire," I called, trying to stay calm. I looked under the bunks and around the room, but if Ruby had been there, she wasn't now. I thought I heard something, but you always hear things in the woods. "Ruby?" I called.

Since we'd just been in the Bernie cabin, I checked the three boys' cabins and St. Brigid's. After I came back outside, I heard a scuffling sound in our cabin and pounced through the door.

"Ruby, where are you? You're not in trouble, I just came to walk you back to the campfire."

Oh God, I wanted that little girl safe. I walked around the cabin. In my cubicle in the middle of the room, my cot was as I left it, but the stuff stowed under it was spread all over the floor. I heard a sneeze.

"Ruby?"

When I got on my knees to look under the cot, huge round eyes magnified by thick glasses stared back at me. The silver flashlight Mary Mac gave me glowed dull and flickering.

"Ruby! Come out of there! Everyone's worried about you. We thought we lost you." My voice was high-pitched and angry.

With dust in her pigtails and her T-shirt streaked with mud, she shimmied out, my flashlight clutched against her chest.

"I ain't done nothing," she said. She pushed back her glasses and curled her upper lip. "This ain't no good, it don't hardly make light."

I grabbed the flashlight.

"Dang, girl, what were you thinking? You know better than to run off by yourself. Come on. We got to get back to the campfire," I scolded.

When I reached to take her hand, Ruby pulled away.

"You ain't my boss, Turquoise is. You just a cracker," Ruby shouted.

Like a cat springing onto a tree, Ruby burst out the cabin door running. It took me a moment to realize what happened. I was exhausted from the sun and the pool and worrying about Turquoise, and now Ruby called me a cracker. I always thought she liked me.

The girl was fast. By the time I got out of the cabin to chase after her, Ruby was a spot of red T-shirt far down the path. I ran as fast as I could, sucking wind. Even when I turned my ankle on a root, I kept running, pain shooting to my brain like an electric shock. Ruby was a miniature Wyomia Tyus, the runner I watched win the 100-meter gold medal for the US in the Olympics last year.

As we got close to the archery range, tendrils of smoke curled in the air and the smell of burning wood grew strong. When I reached the place where the path broke out of the trees before dropping down to the archery range and the campfire, I saw Father Vincent, Mary Mac, Turquoise, and Roland running to intercept Ruby. Campers stood and cheered. Like a puppy determined to evade capture, Ruby stopped short, then veered away, running toward the fire. Her glasses flew off and crunched on the ground.

Now Ruby ran blind, her legs driving her toward the red-orange flames and curtains of smoke.

It was a straight line from where I stood to Ruby's path. There was a chance I could stop her. I leapt down the hill like I was leaping off a high dive and landed on my twisted ankle. I righted myself and sprinted, ignoring the pain. Screaming boys and girls scooted back to make way for me.

With horror I watched Ruby, a few steps ahead of me, reach the edge of the fire and trip into it. Without breaking stride I caught my breath, followed her into the flames, grabbed her, and carried her out the other side. We must have gone through the campfire in a second or less. As soon as we were well clear, I dropped to my knees and lay Ruby down on a patch of grass. I smelled burning hair. Tiny red threads sizzled through one of her pigtails. *Holy crap, her hair was on fire!* I cupped the pigtail with my hand and squeezed to smother the flame. Crusty ashes disintegrated in my fingers.

All my thoughts were on Ruby. When Father Vincent pushed me aside, I was shocked. Like in a dream, I watched him wrap Ruby in a sweatshirt and hold her tight against his chest. After a few moments, she wailed.

As Father and Mary Mac examined Ruby, the campers and counselors formed a tight circle around them. I wobbled over to a tree and leaned against it, shaking my hand and blowing on my fingers. Hair on my arms was singed. Blisters formed on my palm and between my fingers. My T-shirt was filthy and the rubber on my sneakers looked melted. When I sneezed, snotty soot blew onto the ground. My ankle throbbed, but I was okay. I slid to the grass, my legs too weak to hold me up any longer.

"You burned, Jonika? You hurt?" Lady loomed over me, tears in her eyes.

I patted for her to sit with me. "I'll be okay, just some tiny burns."

Lady looked at my hand and recoiled. "Oh, Jonika, I don't like burns. Mami puts butter on burns. You want I should get some butter?"

"Butter on white bread?" I said.

"Go on," Lady said, smiling but crying too. She dangled Ruby's spectacles, lopsided and with one lens missing. "Ruby gonna need new glasses."

"You're a good buddy, Lady," I told her. "Look, Daiquiri's getting the Bernies together over there. We better go."

Together, we walked to Daiquiri. When she looked at me and raised her right eyebrow, I showed her my hand and shrugged.

"Girl, you all about saving Ruby — first water, now fire. We're gonna have to call you the White Wonder or something. You best go up the clinic and take care of that hand. We don't need no more excitement. You done good, Jonika."

The girls giggled but their expressions looked nervous.

Is Jonika hurt? someone asked.

"Just some tiny burns," Lady answered.

I looked at Daiquiri. "Are you okay without me?"

"I'll manage," she said. When she motioned me over and hugged me, the girls swarmed me too.

I ain't never seen no one run through a fire afore, a Bernie said.

I left the girls to check on Ruby. Melted marshmallow stuck on my shoe. Close to where I'd carried her, Ruby lay on a blanket, her head in Mary Mac's lap. I sat with them while Father Vincent strode toward the bonfire and faced the campers and counselors still milling around. Behind Father, flames licked the coppery sky and the fire burned bright as a sunset.

"Let's say a Hail Mary together in thanks for Ruby's deliverance from the flames. Afterward, counselors, take your campers back to the cabins. We've had enough fireworks for one day." Father Vincent stretched out his arms, *Hail Mary, full of grace...*

I stayed until the Bernies hiked out of sight. All around me, sounds of the snapping fire and counselors lining up and counting their campers for the walk back to the cabins seemed far away. The air smelled of smoke and sugar.

My palm and finger webs were stiff with painful blisters. Next to me on the blanket, Ruby sat up, squinting and crinkling her nose. I rested my other hand on Ruby's head and asked Mary Mac, "How is she?"

"Thanks be to God and you, Joni, Ruby's got some scrapes and bruises but you pulled her out before much burned but her pigtail." Mary Mac made the sign of the cross and bowed her head.

I felt a hand on my shoulder.

"You brave, Jonika," Turquoise said. Light from the flickering flames rippled across her face. Turquoise dropped to her knee to look at Ruby eye-to-eye. "You doing aight, Ruby? Mary Mac say you best stay in the clinic tonight. But you come back tomorrow. Honey Bees need their Ruby."

Before I had a chance to thank Turquoise, she walked away and joined the rest of the Honey Bees on the path to the cabins.

Roland jogged over from the group of squirming Andys.

"You hurt, Shorty?"

I held up my fingers. "Just a little."

Mary Mac got to her feet. "Roland, tell Lincoln to manage your campers. I need you to carry Ruby to the clinic. You come too, Joni. I need to take care of that hand."

Trying not to limp, on the hill to Hippo Hall I stopped to watch Father Vincent, Jermaine, and Terrell douse the bonfire while the last group of campers trudged back to the cabins. As black smoke rose in the air, two burning embers flared like devil eyes. I shivered and turned away.

The clinic was a section of Daisy and Mary Mac's cabin enclosed by drywall that stopped a foot or so above my head. Instead of a door, wooden beads hung from the frame and clacked whenever someone stepped through. After Roland put Ruby on one of the two cots, he sat with me on the other. My head bobbled and a curtain of black dropped over my eyes. When I felt myself sway, I willed myself to consciousness, shook my head, and took a deep breath. Roland twirled Ruby's glasses with his left hand and the vibration felt like trembling.

"I hung the beads so I can hear the sickies breaking out," Mary Mac said when she noticed the direction of my gaze. She sat on a rolling stool next to Ruby. "There will be no running from my clinic, my cheeky baby."

"I be fine wid a flashlight, 'cause a flashlight mean you don't be scairt in the dark," Ruby told Mary Mac in a serious voice.

Without her glasses, Ruby screwed up her face like she smelled something bad and turned her head from side-to-side to look around the room. Her left pigtail, which survived the fire, stood up like a tiny boxwood shrub. Her right pigtail had burned down to a short stump and smelled sulfury, even across the room.

"So it's a flashlight you need to keep you in one place, is it, Missy?" Mary Mac said. "Indeed, I may have just the ticket. Roland, can you do something with Ruby's glasses? The child's near blind without them."

As the beads rocked and rattled, we heard Mary Mac chuckle. While Roland bent the eyeglass frame back into shape, I slid over to Ruby's cot. I put my left hand on her knee, rough with dried blood and dirt. A bumpy scrape ran across her left cheek and along her ear, but I didn't notice burn blisters. Ruby raised her shoulders and tucked her head into her neck.

"Sorry I run away, Jonika." She touched the pigtail stump, pulled her hand back and scrunched up her face again. "My mamma give me a lickin' she see my hair."

The beads clacked. Daisy, white hair escaping the edges of her green bandana, came into the room.

"Honey, don't you worry none about a lickin'."

Daisy pulled a silver flashlight from her apron pocket and handed it to Ruby.

"Sister Mary Mac talking to your mamma on the phone right now. Your mamma ain't mad, Child, long as you don't go runnin' into no more fires. Now, let me just take a good long look at you. Un hunh. You be all right. I'mma give you a bath, put some nice lotion on those scratches, find some clean pajamas, and put you to bed. Tomorrow, we goin' to town to get you new glasses and a haircut. What you think about a natural for Ruby, Roland?"

"I think a natural be perfect," Roland said. He set Ruby's glasses on the stool, checked to see if they balanced, then picked them up and continued his work.

"I want me some nice glasses. I don't want big ole black glasses no more."

Ruby flicked on the flashlight and shone it in my eyes, then aimed it at Roland.

Roland placed Ruby's glasses on her nose. On the left side, with no lens, they tilted up. Ruby squeezed shut her left eye, and her right eye looked like a monster's. But as soon as she realized she could see with that eye, her face softened and she smiled.

"Child, you think you can walk to the washroom?" Daisy asked. "You can soak right in the laundry tub like the delicates."

Ruby jumped into Roland's arms and he set her upright on the floor. As she followed Daisy through the beads, she turned to shine her flashlight at us, a look of satisfaction on her face. Roland and I laughed.

"What about you, Jonika? That hand hurt bad?" Roland took my burned hand and studied it, gently pressing the blisters. "Burn bubbles."

Mary Mac click-clacked through the beads.

"Let me see to Joni-Jonika." She held my hands palm up. "They don't look so bad, but I bet the blisters hurt."

"I twisted my ankle," I told her. "That hurts more."

Mary Mac took my leg in her hands and poked the swollen skin. She unlaced and pulled off my sneaker. Dirt rimmed my toenails and my foot smelled gross, like a dead skunk. I peeked up at Roland, knowing he smelled it too. Mary Mac removed my other sneaker and tossed both through the beads. When she doused a thick piece of cotton with witch hazel and started to clean my feet, I felt embarrassed.

"You shouldn't wash my feet," I said and pulled one leg back.

"When our dear Lord washed the feet of his disciples, he told them, *As I have done for you, so you should do for others.* Would you deprive me of the grace to follow our Lord?" Mary Mac asked.

I'm sure I made a face like, *Yikes.* Even though the cool cloth felt really good, I still worried about grossing her out. I mean, we called her Mary Mac, but she's really Sister Mary Immaculata. Maybe that's why she didn't seem to mind. After my feet were clean, Mary Mac put a pillow on the cot and I was happy to lie back. The room buzzed.

As I closed my eyes, I heard Mary Mac like she was very far away, say, "Roland, find an Ace bandage, gauze pads, and adhesive tape in the first-aid cabinet, and get a jar of honey from Daisy." She wiggled my big toe. "We'll fix you up, Jonika. I'll wrap your ankle and make a honey salve for your burns. Do you want to stay in the clinic tonight?"

It took all my strength to raise my head.

"I'll go back to the cabin. The girls will be worried. I can walk back with Roland."

I dropped my head on the pillow and concentrated on breathing slow and rhythmically. I felt confused but grateful — relieved, I guess. But I felt bad, too, like I was unworthy of all this care.

"Thank you, Sister." I murmured.

As she tugged the Ace bandage tight on my ankle and foot, Mary Mac looked up with a surprised smile.

"You're most welcome, Joan of Arc. Now if you're ready, Roland will help you to your cabin."

With my ankle wrapped and my right hand smeared with honey and covered in gauze, Roland took my left arm to help me down the cabin steps. We stood back to let Daisy lead Ruby, clean and in new pajamas, through the door. Ruby tilted her head to look at us through her lopsided glasses.

She opened her mouth to let out a long, sighing yawn and said, "Are yous getting married?"

I was too flabbergasted to answer, but Roland laughed.

"Could be," he said.

Father Vincent declared the day after the 4th of July a play day — instead of scheduled programs, the oldest boys and girls organized games and fun activities for the younger campers. Because I was sore and uncomfortable, the pool stayed closed the whole day. After breakfast, the Bernies scattered — some joined a group of boys for wiffle ball, a few decided to visit the classroom to watch Saturday morning cartoons on a color TV, others went off to play Frisbee. Early that morning, Mary Mac and Daisy drove Ruby in the old VW van to the closest town.

I sat in a fold-up beach chair outside Hippo Hall, my ankle propped on a step. Across the back, a strip of broken green-and-white webbing flapped against the aluminum frame. In front of me, Lady paced back and forth, taking a few steps toward the Frisbee players and then, on tiptoes, peeking in at the TV watchers, then moving away and staring at one cluster of campers after another.

"Lady, why don't you find a group to play with?" I called. The blisters between my fingers oozed like tears and made gluey spots on the gauze.

"I can't find Ruby, Jonika. She go to the *hopital* last night?" Lady's wide, brown eyes rimmed with tears. She wrung her slender fingers between her palms.

"I'm sorry you worried, Lady. Ruby scraped her knees and scratched her face, but only her pigtail got burned. I thought you knew Daisy and Mary Mac took her to town to get new glasses. Remember, you found her busted ones?"

Lady's expression softened, and I felt tears well in my own eyes at this young girl's concern. She sighed and sat on the step, running her finger over the ace bandage on my ankle.

Shouts reverberated through the pine trees from the different play areas. When I started to stand up, Lady gently placed my foot on the ground. Overnight my ankle had swelled a lot. Before Daiquiri rewrapped the Ace bandage this morning, I pretended that the cloud-shaped black and blue mark that ran from the top of my foot around my ankle and up my shin was no big deal. But honestly, Judge, I worried that I broke it. Five fat toes stuck out from the thick binding. When I put pressure on that foot, the pain — like when you bite your tongue — made me cringe. Once I got moving, though, the stretchy band gave me enough support to walk, especially with the walking stick Roland carved from an oak branch. And Mary Mac promised she'd buy me a cane from the drug store in town.

"Let's find something fun for you to do," I told Lady. I felt bad she wasn't playing with the other kids.

With a serious face, Lady hung my arm over her shoulder. I bit my lip to keep from smiling.

"I see Jermaine and Terrell on the basketball court. You want to go there?" I said.

"You want to play with Jermaine?" she asked.

I stopped walking and looked at her.

"I can't play anything with this ankle."

So tall she stood almost eye level with me, Lady gave me a school-teacher frown.

"Jermaine playin' you."

I caught my breath. Jermaine looked our way and waved. I waved back and pretended I didn't understand what Lady meant.

"Look, some of the big girls are over by the swings. And they have bubbles! Doesn't that sound like fun?" I made my voice sound cheery.

Lady looked at me sideways, shrugged, ducked from under my arm, and ran to the swings. Her movements were graceful and effortless. A few minutes later, I heard the crunch of gravel and smelled car exhaust. I waited for the old VW bus to emerge from the driveway and screech to a halt.

"Jonika! I got new glasses. Daisy say I need ruby red ones cause my name Ruby," Ruby squealed from the back window.

As soon as Daisy opened the door for her, she jumped out. She wore a fabric hat made of six triangles in bright colors sewn together and splayed at the bottom. Red cat-eye glasses sat perfectly on her nose. With glasses that fit her face and lenses that showed normal-sized eyes, she looked fabulous. It made me angry to realize how awful her old glasses were.

"And I got a new do. Mr. Tony say my natural look good!"

I leaned on the fender to study Ruby. She jumped and jiggled but stayed still when I took off her hat and brushed the top of her hair with my left, uninjured palm. Then, I ran a finger over the scratches on her face.

"I love your glasses and your hair looks cute. You're beautiful."

Behind me came the scritch-scratch of footsteps on gravel. Lady reached down and pulled Ruby close for a hug.

"Been worryin' over you, Child. Dang, you pretty enough for *The Julia Show!*"

"Ruby's well and good, and now she even sees better. With her new glasses she got every letter on the chart right," Mary Mac said. "You children run along and play. Keep your eye on our little rascal, Lady."

While Daisy carried grocery bags into the cabin, Mary Mac twirled a light wood cane like a dancer in an old-time variety show. She slapped it down, clicked her heels, handed it to me, and grabbed the last grocery bag.

"Come inside," she said. "Give me a couple minutes to wash up and then I'll check your burns and ankle. Are you feeling on top of it?"

Sweat showed on her forehead and darkened her shirt collar. In her go-to-town black cotton blouse and long skirt, Mary Mac looked nunnish and uncomfortable. I followed her through the door. The cabin she and Daisy shared smelled of Jean Naté — the same citrusy cologne my mother wore. While Daisy bustled around, putting away laundry detergent, packs of bandages, bars of Ivory soap, and a carton of cigarettes, I sat on a ladder-backed chair and grabbed a magazine from a stack in a wooden box on the floor. From the enclosed outside shower I heard Mary Mac sing *Danny Boy* with great gusto.

"The post office had a box for you," Daisy called. "I'll get it from the car."

I studied the cover of the June issue of *Ebony* magazine. On it, Betty Shabazz — who looked like a movie star — wore an animal print dress, a smart red turban, and hoop earrings. In the background, the image of Malcolm X stared from behind thick, black glasses. The upper right corner read, *The First Generation, The birth of black America* and in the lower right corner, the words touching Betty Shabazz's arm said, *The legacy of my husband Malcolm X by Betty Shabazz.* Curious, I flipped open to the article. What I knew about Malcolm X was sort of scary. He preached black power and called white people devils. A couple years ago, he'd been gunned down. I remembered watching the news of his assassination with my father. His comment ran through my mind — *Devils come in all colors, Mr. X.*

Before I started the article, I looked at the photographs. There was one of Betty Shabazz surrounded by her six fatherless daughters, another of her shopping with friends, and one where she was dressed elegantly in a powder blue dress and matching coat. The photo I liked best was of Betty on a cold day at a playground with her daughters. As she pushed their swings, she smiled.

"Miss Joan, you gone burn a hole in my magazine, you look at it any harder," Daisy called.

I jumped. I hadn't heard Daisy come back in. A brown-paper-wrapped box tied with twine sat at my feet.

"Sorry. This magazine has good stuff in it."

"Uh hunh. You surprised?" Daisy asked.

I shrugged my shoulders, a little embarrassed.

"I never thought about it."

"You like Betty Shabazz' article?"

"I'd like to read it. So far I only looked at the pictures, but I like them," I said.

"Well, then, that's that. Go on, take it," Daisy said. "Maybe you learn something you don't know."

Mary Mac, her grey-streaked brown hair wet and slicked back, came into the room in fresh camp clothes. I smelled Ivory soap. After she looked from Daisy to me, she pulled up a stool, sat facing me, put my leg on her lap, and unwrapped my ankle. The Ace bandage imprint wound up my leg like a vine. A rank odor like a towel left in a swim bag rose from my foot and I blushed. At least it wasn't as gross as the night before.

"How's it feel?" she asked, lightly touching the bruised, swollen skin. "Can you wiggle your toes?"

My swollen toes moved up and down in a reluctant wave. "A little sore."

"And the hand?" Mary Mac asked as she unwound the dingy gauze. "Ah, your fingers are raw where the blisters broke."

"I can deal with it," I said, but I grimaced when air hit my burns.

Mary Mac dabbed the raw skin with Johnson's burn cream and covered my hand with fresh gauze. She cleaned my foot again with witch hazel and wrapped my ankle with a new Ace bandage from the drugstore.

"We'll see if Daisy can get the dirt out of this one," Mary Mac said, dangling the old bandage away from her like a dead fish. "The pharmacist gave me a canvas brace to go over the wrap. It has a soft sole so you can step lightly without fouling the bandage."

She opened a slim cardboard package and wiggled the brace over my ankle. I bit my lip to keep from crying out when my ankle moved the wrong way. After Mary Mac finished lacing the brace, I let out my breath.

"There, all done," she said.

"That feels better, thanks," I told her. "Ruby's new glasses are nice. They look expensive."

"Thank God for people's generosity." Mary Mac said. "Father Vincent has a way about him. One phone call and people are happy to help. John Kelly, the optometrist, examined Ruby's eyes and let the child pick out frames. His son grinds the lenses for the shop and he finished Ruby's glasses in two hours. Meanwhile, we took Ruby to the barber, Tony Mazetti, who gives our campers haircuts whenever we ask. Ruby was a little afraid to have a white man cut her hair, but Mr. Tony promised her a lollipop if she sat still. Then, while we waited for her glasses, Ruby, Daisy, and I went grocery shopping, bought Ruby her new hat, and stopped at the drugstore. Before she leaves for home, Mr. Kelly promised to make another pair of glasses for Ruby — just in case. And didn't Mr. Tony remind us to bring him our campers any day of the week for a trim? Most people are good."

"The new glasses fit much better than the old ones. They don't make her eyes all googly," I said.

Mary Mac nodded. "I'm afraid our poor children are not often well-served. It's a blessing Mr. Kelly was so generous."

With the cane in my left hand, my right hand well wrapped, and the canvas brace over my sore ankle, I balanced the box from home under my right arm and staggered back to the empty cabin. After I reached my cot, my arm and elbow ached. I should have asked for help carrying the box, but I wanted to be alone in the quiet cabin while the girls enjoyed play day.

As soon as I pushed the twine over the edges and tore off the wrapping, I opened the package. Right on top was a box of Tampax. I shoved it in the back of my cubby behind my camp T-shirts. Mom sent Coppertone, Breck shampoo, Pepsodent toothpaste, and Mr. Salty pretzels. Under a new blue towel, I found a cellophane-wrapped package of brightly colored days-of-the-week bikini underpants — seven different colors with an embroidered weekday on each. I guess she worried about dirty underwear. Still, I liked them a lot. I looked back in the box and was shocked to see a transistor radio and a pack of batteries. That was a lot cooler than I expected from my mother. Especially since Daiquiri's radio died after one of the girls knocked it down.

The June issue of *Seventeen Magazine* lay flat on the bottom. On the cover, five models in mod clothes bounded forward, heads tilted up, smiles brimming. The cover promised articles titled, *where to PERCH when you leave the nest, how to write to a BOY, and FASHION PLENTY UNDER $20.*

I compared the glossy teen mag to Daisy's *Ebony*. I don't know, *Seventeen* seemed frivolous or something. I tossed *Seventeen* back in the box, grabbed the cane and the transistor radio, and limped up the path to the pool with *Ebony* squeezed under my arm.

On the far side of the pool in the shade from towering pines, I pulled up two chairs — one to sit in and one to put my legs on. As I smeared Coppertone on my face, legs and arms, the scent reminded me of my family's annual seashore vacation the week of the 4th of July. That's why my mother sent the package — she must have felt guilty that they went away without me. The pool water gleamed clean and blue, with three pine twigs navigating the ripples like tiny surfboards. I fooled with the radio tuner until I found the Boss Jocks from Wiffle radio shooting some tunes over the airwaves. *Grazin' in the Grass* came on and yes, I could *dig it*. The music rose, fell, and even though it was scratchy, I liked it.

As I read Betty Shabazz's article, my chest grew tight. She described her husband as a family man whose Muslim faith compelled him to reach out to American Negroes to persuade them to seize their constitutional rights — *black people in America must form our own destiny*. Mrs. Shabazz portrayed Malcolm X as likable if driven. I was reading Mrs. Shabazz's comment about young black Americans — *Against staggering odds, as if by a miracle, they have gone beyond such crippling historical facts as racism and found themselves* — when something cold pressed the back of my neck. I jerked and turned.

Roland stood behind me, smiling and offering a can of Pepsi. "Thought I find you here," he said. "You sure must like what you reading 'cause you didn't never hear me come in."

"How'd you get away from the Andys?"

"They playing wiffle ball with Father Vincent and Mary Mac. Mary Mac sent me to make sure you don't get in more trouble. What you reading?" Roland tipped the magazine toward himself. "*Ebony?* I never knew white girls read black magazines."

"Daisy lent it to me. I'm reading this story about Malcolm X. He was different than I thought."

Roland pulled up a chair, wiped sweat from his forehead, then took off his T-shirt and draped it over the back of the chair. His dark chest glistened. "You think black folk all be scary criminals, right?"

Before I answered, I set the magazine in my lap. "I don't think that.

But some black people are scary criminals same as some white people are. scary criminals."

"Oh yeah, I see that. All them scary black folk in colored sheets and hoods going round burning *Wall Street Journals* on white men's lawns and keepin' white children out of their schools," Roland snorted.

"Wait a minute," I said, hurt and angry. "I was reading about Malcolm X because I'm interested in his story." I tossed *Ebony* to him. "Sorry for trying to learn something."

Roland raised his eyebrows and licked his lips. "You like all white people. You listen to the Supremes, Smokey, Aretha, but you don't want them movin' in next door."

I smelled his sweat. His eyes looked angry, like I'd never seen before. It didn't matter where I went or what I did, I always made people hate me — now, even Roland, who'd always been really nice. I slapped a mosquito on my arm and a speck of blood spurted out. My ankle throbbed and I just wanted to be left alone.

With him just sitting there, staring, I got really mad. "You don't know anything about me. You have no right to say I'm like all white people or who I want living next door. Are you like all black people? Are all black people the same? Do you hate me like Turquoise does because I'm white?"

I leaned back and closed my eyes, feeling the sun on my face. Right then I felt more white, more different, than the first day of camp. I mean, what did I do wrong? Read *Ebony*? I let out a sigh.

Roland's chair scraped the concrete and I heard him get up. *Good,* I thought, *leave.* I counted the days left until camp ended. But when I felt his breath on my face and his hand rest gently on my burned one, I opened my eyes.

He squatted next to me, his clear hazel eyes looking sorrowful. "I don't hate you, Jonika, and neither does Turquoise." He stepped back and moved his chair to face me.

"Could have fooled me. Look, Roland, I was just sitting here by myself, not trying to make anyone mad. Earlier today when I was up at the clinic, I started reading the article and Daisy let me borrow the magazine so I could finish it. No one told me white people shouldn't read *Ebony*. In fact, Daisy told me maybe I'd learn something."

His face softened then. "You really want to learn about black folks?"

I nodded and shrugged at the same time.

"You know what this camp's about? What camp means for these

children? For me? For Daiquiri, Turquoise, Jermaine? It means freedom. It means for these weeks, we are free. We got a place to sleep, food, and clothes. It means Ruby gets a new pair of glasses when hers break. It means Jermaine gets to teach basketball and archery and no one look at him like they afraid he's gonna rob them. It means Daiquiri can teach little girls what it means to be a black woman — how to behave, how to get along, how to sing, and to clean up after yourself. It means when these children need to talk 'bout things — family, school, being scared, hate and hunger — someone listens. It means after Turquoise shows little girls how to sew and mend, they don't go to school with holes in their clothes. It means I can teach these children to make things with their own two hands. They can build a birdhouse, they can build a bookcase, they can build a table and that table will stand. It means no one follows you when you go in a store to buy a record or a bag of chips. It means white people don't cross the street when they see you coming or move closer to the driver when you board a bus. For us, that's freedom. For you, camp's a prison. That's the difference." Roland wiped his face with his shirt.

Roland's words shimmered like lightning bugs and I reached out to catch one. But when I opened my fist, it disappeared. He looked at me like I was crazy. You know, Judge, in my whole life, no one, not even Ishmael, talked to me like that, explaining everything and making it real.

"I'm sorry. There's lots I don't know about these kids, or the counselors, but I'm beginning to understand. And camp's not my prison. I feel free here too."

My brain buzzed and black spots floated in front of my eyes. I thought I might faint but, as if he realized how I felt, Roland fanned me with his T-shirt. The air smelled like pine, chlorine, and him.

After I looked him in the eyes and gave him a weak smile, he draped his shirt over his chair and took my burned hand. With a gentle touch he unwrapped the gauze, looked at my burns, and rewrapped the bandage. He grimaced and said, "Looks sore."

"Roland, I didn't know what to expect when Father Vincent first talked to me about camp. I was scared and worried, but it turned out much better than I ever hoped. Almost everyone seems to accept me now. I just don't know what I did to make Turquoise hate me."

"Turquoise don't trust white people. Truth is, none of us do. You talk more than a minute to any one of us, you soon hear about white people acting like we all stupid and gonna steal something. Why you think Ruby go up to that cabin looking for the flashlight? 'Cause after the girl see you got a nice flashlight from Mary Mac, she think, why can't I get that? Every day, that baby got to scrape to get by. But she know where to find that flashlight and she know how to run. She know not to trust a white girl. But she learning to trust you. And Lady, that girl so lonely. Her mama work night shift at a old folks' home, tending white people what treat her like a slave. She gets home after Lady go to school and go to work soon as Lady go to sleep. Most of these children be taking care of themselves by time they five or six. But at camp, they got counselors to look after them. They got food on the table. They got bandages when they skin their knees. And they allowed to have fun. Freedom."

He moved closer and undid the Ace bandage on my ankle. "Bruised," he said as he propped my foot on his knee. He rubbed my arch, my heel, gently pressed my toes, and worked on my ankle like he was kneading bread. "Hurt much?"

"Where'd you learn to do that?" I asked. "It feels better already." I felt my face flush.

"GoGo, my grandma, rubbed our bumps and bruises like this. She say, *You got to rub the swelling out fore it will heal.*" Roland looked in my eyes. "Jonika, Turquoise don't hate you. She say you did good, running for Ruby in the fire. But she don't trust you. Jermaine and Turquoise, they together in the city. When Turquoise come to camp, she see a white girl all over her man. It don't sit good. Turquoise been hurt. Her daddy drink and lose his job and her mama got to work at the dry cleaners every day 'til she can't hardly breathe. If her mama don't work, she don't get paid. Turquoise blame the white owners 'cause they don't care what her mama be breathing, long as she run the machine. White man got the money, her mama do the work, and her mama get the cough."

Roland moved his palms up and down my calf, hard over the muscle, then soft on my ankle and foot. The dinner bell gonged and he stood up.

"I'm sorry about Turquoise," I said. There was so much I hadn't known, so much I still didn't know.

"She be all right." Roland put out his hand to help me up. "You be all right too."

Days later, my ankle felt stiff when I woke up, but the swelling went down. Though I didn't need help, the Bernies pushed and shoved to be my crutches. Girls practically knocked me over when they draped my arms across their shoulders and bumped their hips against me during the walk up to Hippo Hall for breakfast.

When we reached our table, Lady directed me to sit in one chair and pulled out another to prop my injured ankle on. Then she stepped to the front of the breakfast line, politely announcing she had to get Jonika's food. She returned and set down a tray filled with Rice Krispies, milk, a banana, and red bug juice. "You want more, you ask," she said.

"I get you food too, Jonika," Raven called out.

I get you food, Jonika, a chorus of voices assured me.

Their faces beamed with pride and possession. One Bernie spread a napkin on my lap, another peeled the banana, and all of them watched to make sure I took my first bite.

From the other end of the table, Daiquiri said, "Your mamas be proud to see you take care of your counselor. You good girls."

The Bernies grew quiet and looked at each other, suddenly shy. Lady coughed and glanced from Daiquiri to me. I thought about my conversation with Roland and I wondered how often these rambunctious, brassy, noisy girls heard themselves called good.

"I don't know what I'd do without you. Thanks to you girls, my ankle feels much better. Who remembers the Bernie rules Daiquiri taught us the first day of camp?"

Most of the girls looked puzzled, but Lady waved her hand.

"Go on, Lady, say the rules," Daiquiri said. She looked at me with interest.

"Be nice. Don't hit. Take care of each other," Lady said.

I knew that. Oh yeah, I remember. Un hunh, and other sounds of agreement came from each girl.

"In fact, from what I've seen, the Bernies take care of whoever needs help." I smiled at each girl, one at a time. When last I turned to Lady, I hoped she knew my smile for her was special. "You're the best Bernies I ever met."

I let Sharone take my tray and as the girls tidied up the table, I announced, "I need to get to the pool now and check the water, but I'll see you all for swim lessons in a couple hours."

On the way out the door, I passed Daisy, sweeping under the serving table. She stopped and leaned the broom handle on her shoulder.

"I read the article by Betty Shabazz," I said, "I'll bring your magazine back at dinner."

"I guess you learned something," Daisy said.

I smiled and nodded. "I guess I did."

I hobbled to the pool, looking forward to the cool, soothing water. My ankle still ached, and the skin between my fingers stayed shiny red after the blisters peeled, but I felt pretty good. As I wrenched open the pool gate, the metal bottom grated across the concrete and I thought of the wintry day Ishmael and I scraped the playground gate to reach the swings. I could hardly visualize his face any more, but his smell — of car tires and burned weed — came over me as if he were standing right there.

I tried to picture him at Graterford, in a tan uniform and slip-on sneakers, with stubble for hair. I thought about how nervous he was the day he admitted he'd pissed himself at boot camp. I got a horrible feeling he probably pissed himself at prison too. I felt bad for him. I felt bad about everything to do with him.

I remembered the first time he told me, *Existence precedes essence.* Now my existence amounted to the woods, the pool, and the campers and counselors. *What,* I wondered, as I backwashed the filter and fished out debris with the skimmer, *is the essence of all that?* While most days I didn't think about home or Ishmael, sometimes memories washed over me. And those were the times *loser, loser, loser* drummed through my head. Those were the times I craved the mellow feeling from smoking a J.

I drew a deep breath of bleachy air. Even before I tested it, I knew the chlorine level was too high. I opened the faucet under the diving board to dilute the water. Over the summer, the chlorine turned my hair white-blonde with green highlights. And even though my nose was always red and peeling, my skin no longer glowed white. The Bernies delighted in comparing my tan back to my white bottom when they caught me in the shower.

Shortly after I hopped in to scrub the tiles, I heard high-pitched voices singing *Somewhere Over the Rainbow.* By the time I stashed the brush and cleanser in the storage box, the Honey Bees swarmed in, striking wide-armed poses and shouting, *Why can't I?*

Ruby, with her tulip hat covering her short fro and her new glasses resting perfectly on the bridge of her nose, flapped across the deck in pink flip-flops.

"Jonika!" she called, "Where you at? Guess what? Dorothy dead!"

I dropped the kickboards and put my hand to my throat, horrified.

"When? What happened?" I turned to Turquoise, "I just saw Daisy this morning."

"Daisy? Nothin' happen to Daisy. Ruby talking 'bout Dorothy — from *Wizard of Oz* — you know, Judy Garland." Turquoise whispered so the girls couldn't hear. "OD-ed on red devils couple weeks back."

That surprised me. Not just that Judy Garland died, that was sad. But that Turquoise talked to me like I was a regular person. I nodded and smiled while my mind screamed, *Wow!*

"Mary Mac and Turquoise say we gonna play-act *Wizard of Oz* for Camp Roundup next week. You ever see them lions and tigers and bears, Jonika?" Ruby asked.

"*Oh my. Follow the yellow brick road,*" I answered. "But now it's time to swim."

The Honey Bees sat along the edge, kicking water high in the air. Drops landed on the concrete in little splatters, then dried almost instantly. As fresh water poured in, the chlorine smell faded. I was glad. When the chlorine got too high, the kids' eyes got all red and weepy. I jumped in and dipped to my shoulders. Over the past week the sun warmed the water more than I liked. Already the added water made it cooler and refreshing.

"Jonika, who you think should wear the magic slips?" Ruby called. The other girls' splashes sprinkled on her face and she whipped her head around and yelled, "Stop wettin' me!"

"Someone named Ruby?" I asked.

"Un hunh, that right." Ruby kicked as hard as she could to splash the other girls.

I'mma flying monkey. I'mma Toto. I'mma Munchkin. I'mma Winkie. Turquoise be a scairt lion, Honey Bee voices rang out. *Whachoo be, Jonika?*

"I'm the Wicked Witch of Camp Hippo." I made a witchy face. "Who's ready to swim?"

"Get your scrawny selfs in the water and don't nobody go telling Jonika 'bout the surprise," Turquoise said. She pulled off her T-shirt and stepped out of her khaki shorts, revealing a red bathing suit from Mary Mac's store. "We gonna see if Jonika all that. See if she can teach me to swim."

It took me a moment to realize what Turquoise said. I couldn't believe it, but I sure liked it. I wondered if Roland talked to her, and that made me a little nervous. But I didn't have time to think about it, because Turquoise hopped in the pool.

"It's too cold, Jonika," the girls complained, jumping up and down and wrapping their arms across their chests.

"Munchkins aren't afraid of cold water," I told them. "Kickboards today. Line up." I handed each girl a kickboard and said, "Go!"

With Turquoise right there, no Honey Bee dared complain. Each one clutched her board, leaned her chest on it, and kicked like crazy. I smiled when I handed one to Turquoise.

"Ready or not." She heaved forward, her feet dragging on the bottom.

I checked the Honey Bees to make sure they were safe and kicking. Then I turned to Turquoise.

"Kickboards can be awkward until you get used to them. If you don't mind putting your face in the water, the best thing to start with is the dead man's float. You just hold your breath, lean into the water, let yourself go, and relax."

After I demonstrated, Turquoise practiced floating while I worked with the girls. From time to time I caught her eye and gave her a thumbs up. I thought about what I told her — *Let yourself go and relax.* That was something I needed to learn too.

After the camp bell gonged, the Honey Bees scurried to the changing area. Before she followed them, Turquoise paused a moment to say, "Mary Mac have the *Wizard of Oz* book in the school cabin. After dinner this week, the counselors gonna read to the campers — the real story like the man wrote it."

As the Honey Bees lined up and started through the gate, Turquoise called, "You alls forgettin' somethin'? What you say to Jonika?"

Thank you, Jonika, twelve little voices chanted.

"Thank you, Jonika," Turquoise repeated.

Thank you, God, I silently prayed.

Each evening, one of the counselors retrieved the old book — the copyright said 1900 — from the school cabin. *The Wonderful Wizard of Oz by L. Frank Baum, Pictures by W. W. Denslow* ran across the top of the dusky, buff-colored cover. Below the letters, a lion in glasses with a green ribbon tied to his mane walked through a wide, green band. The top and bottom of the spine had rubbed rough, and the pages were separating from the binding. No one wanted to be responsible for finally wrecking the book, so we handled it with care.

During the day, campers talked about the story. As soon as they finished dinner, the kids picked up their trash, helped fold tables and chairs, and hurried to the basketball court where they sat cross-legged on blankets Daisy retrieved from the back of the storage closet. Even the most rambunctious boys and girls settled down when that night's reader, with the book in outstretched arms, led a procession of counselors to the court. As soon as the reader sat down, the campers cheered.

Turquoise read the first night. She sat in a webbed lawn chair, scanned the campers, and said, "Honey Bees, move on up here."

The Honey Bees crawled up front and arranged themselves on the blanket Daisy spread for them. Ruby turned around and around like a cat, grinning at whoever caught her eye, before she plopped down at Turquoise's feet. In the hot, humid air, campers fanned themselves with their hands. I sat on a log on the far side of the court. When Jermaine sat next to me, I blushed. I didn't know if I was more pleased that Jermaine sat so close or more worried about pissing off Turquoise.

The moment she cleared her throat, all sounds of shuffling bodies and even the low insect drone grew silent. Her rich voice, with each word enunciated like she was an actor in a play, drew me deeper into the story with every sentence. I realized Turquoise didn't just read *The Wonderful Wizard of Oz* — she performed it. Each time the campers sucked in their breaths or commented, *That's right, uh hunh, she done kilt that old witch,* Turquoise included the campers' responses as part of her show.

After Turquoise read — *The feet of the dead Witch had disappeared entirely, and nothing was left but the silver shoes* — she looked at Ruby. "That bad witch wore silver shoes, not ruby slippers," she said in her everyday voice.

Ruby stood up and slapped her forehead with the palm of her head. "Silver slips? Dorothy wear silver slips? They supposed to be ruby slippers."

"Book say silver. I guess Roland got to make Dorothy silver shoes. Let me go on." Turquoise resumed reading in her story voice, the words ringing through the pines like a song.

A few evenings after Turquoise's reading, inside Hippo Hall Jermaine, his lisp adding softness to his deep voice, read the final chapter. Wind rattled the windows and rain pattered the roof. Thunder rumbled in the distance. A crack of lightning flared like a whip in the dark sky. A couple weeks ago we'd had two days of downpours, but the weather stayed dry ever since. Not this night. When Jermaine shut the book and said, "The end," the lights flickered.

Behind the stage curtains, the Bridges, Bernies, and Honey Bees waited to perform while Mary Mac pussyfooted across the stage.

"Camp St. Augustine of Hippo campers, welcome to the City of Emeralds. A long time ago on a night just like this, a terrible storm blew through Kansas and spun a young girl named Dorothy, her dog, and her house high into the air, twirling and spinning in a cyclone, only to land with a great thump."

Mary Mac stamped her foot on the stage. A gasp rose from the audience and kids put their hands over their mouths.

"Dorothy and her little dog, Toto, found themselves in a wonderful place, as wonderful as Camp Hippo, but far, far away. We all enjoyed listening to our counselors read about Dorothy's adventures in Oz. Tonight, Delia, Turquoise, and Daiquiri will bring Oz to you. Are you ready for Oz, campers?"

Yeah! Yay! Campers shouted and clapped. Backstage, the girls giggled.

"When Dorothy's house landed, who met her?" Mary Mac asked.

Silence.

Mary Mac looked from side to side. "Does anyone remember?"

"I remember. Theys peoples be Munchkins and they all-as wear blue clothes," Antoine called out.

"Yes, indeed, Antoine," Mary Mac said. "Wait, do you hear that?"

Roland turned off the lights. Jermaine and Terrell pounded upside-down trashcans. Campers murmured and a few called out — *What's happening?*

The trashcan pounding stopped and the lights flicked on. Delia led the Bridges onto the stage, wearing blue T-shirts and hats they made from newspapers. While the Bridges stomped and clapped, Turquoise came out from the wings to chant —

Oh see that house, y'all — oh see that house, y'all —
oh see that house, y'all — fall out the sky...
It kilt the witch dead — it kilt the witch dead — it kilt the witch dead
— she dead and gone.

Ruby, in a white shirt and blue shorts with a blue-checked bandana on her head, carried a stuffed dog in an Easter basket as she skipped onto stage. Turquoise's voice echoed through Hippo Hall —

Out come a girl, y'all - out come a girl, y'all - out come a girl, y'all —
with a little dog —
Give her silver shoes, yeah — give her silver shoes, yeah — give her
silver shoes, yeah,
From the witch what died.

With a final stomp, the Bridges stopped and faced the campers. The kids stood and cheered. Ruby sat on the upended milk crate Daiquiri set out, while a Bridges girl knelt and put silver-painted sneakers on her feet. After Delia and the Bridges ran past me to find seats in the audience, Daiquiri led the Bernies onto the stage.

Lady, with straw leaking from her sleeves and pants, propped herself against a pole. Josephine, a quiet, chubby girl, had whiskers drawn across her cheeks and a thick rope tail drooping from the back of her shorts. Tiara, with green eyes and coppery skin, wore a tin cook pot balanced on her head. They moved stage left near Lady.

On center stage, Ruby zigzagged through green-shirted Bernies who clutched apples and held their arms high like tree branches. After Ruby crossed through Bernie forest, she stopped in front of scarecrow Lady and cocked her head.

"What you doing up there, Scarecrow?" Ruby asked in a loud, screechy voice.

"Just hangin'," Lady answered.

The campers hooted and hollered. I was pleased she projected her voice so well. Ruby turned to Tiara, whose cook pot tilted to the left.

"What you doing, Tin Man?"

Tiara muttered something, and Lady gave her a nudge. "Waitin' for my wife," Tiara replied, louder this time.

"What she look like?" Ruby said, grinning at the audience.

"She big and grey and wear glass slippers." Tiara looked at Daiquiri who nodded.

"What her name?" Ruby shouted.

CINDER-ELEPHANT! the campers yelled. Elephant jokes had taken over the camp the past week.

Ruby turned to Josephine, who prowled across the stage and roared three times.

Ruby asked, "Why you roarin', Mr. Lion?"

"Cause I'm hongry," Josephine answered with an extravagant roar.

"Why don't you get something to eat?" Ruby said.

"Cause I only eat on CHEWSDAY," Josephine growled.

The campers booed, but they were boos of amusement, not mean-spirited.

"Scarecrow, Tin Man, and Lion, will you come with me to see the Wizard of Oz?" Ruby strutted across the stage, facing the audience.

"I'm too scared," Josephine said in a deep voice.

"I don't have the heart," Tiara whispered. Lady nudged her. "I don't have the heart," she shouted.

"I don't have no brains," Lady made a silly smile and dangled her head from side to side.

The Bernie trees skipped off stage and Daiquiri and Turquoise brought out the Honey Bees. They formed a ring around Ruby, Lady, Tiara, and Josephine and began another stomp, clap, chant dance. This time, it was Daiquiri's voice that rose above the others —

You got to move, you got to move, you got to move,
When the time is ready, you got to move.
You may be tin, you may be small,
you may be scared, you may be straw,
You got to move, you got to move, you got to move.
When the time is ready, you got to move.

"The road to the City of Emeralds is paved with yellow brick. The time is ready. You got to move," Daiquiri called in a commanding voice.

The Honey Bees hopped off stage and sat on the floor in front of the first row of chairs while Roland flicked the lights on and off, leaving the room in darkness.

In the wings, Ruby, Josephine, Tiara, and Lady huddled around Turquoise and Daiquiri, their expressions joyful and expectant. I felt invisible. Not even Lady looked my way. I shuffled farther back into the curtain, wondering why Daiquiri insisted I remain in the wings — *Just be ready case we need you.*

Hippo Hall pulsed with anticipation. Rolls of thunder grumbled in the sky and rain hit the windows like a million pebbles rapping glass. After five minutes, Roland flicked on the lights and the campers shielded their eyes. When they lowered their hands, their faces gleamed.

On stage, Father Vincent sat in a straight-backed chair facing the audience, with a long hand-saw balanced on his lap. In the wing, Roland teetered on a ladder, adjusting a spotlight to shine on Father.

Earlier in the day, I sat with Roland while he made the spotlight from an empty can of Folgers. First, he opened the bottom with the can opener. Then he flattened the metal edges on both rims with pliers. In the storage room, Roland found an old lamp, unscrewed the light bulb, yanked out the socket, and unhooked the wires. He braced the socket and plug in the coffee can with a round piece of dark wood. After he checked the wiring, he screwed in the bulb and pushed the plug into an outlet. I was horrified he'd get electrocuted, but the bulb lit in the can and made a perfect spotlight. *It ain't scary if you know how to do it,* he'd said.

Now, on stage under Roland's spotlight, Father propped the saw handle between his knees and showed the campers his violin bow. When the bow ran against the blade, an eerie, frightening sound, like the banshee's wail from the movie *Darby O'Gill and the Little People,* saturated the hall. Campers sat at the edge of their seats with their hands clasped over their ears. The saw rang, *WANG, WANG, WANG.*

Then a large figure draped in a black cape from head to mid-calf leapt onto center stage and swung around to face the audience. Roland turned the spotlight on him and I noted the brown legs and well-worn sneakers. Father eased off the chair and backed into the wings.

"I am Oz, the great and terrible. What do you want, visitors?" the caped figure bellowed in a deep, lispy voice.

A hush spread over the campers. Ruby, grinning, entered stage with toy Toto clasped tight against her chest, followed by the scarecrow, the tin man, and the lion.

"I want a brain," Lady said, her melodious voice projecting like I'd never heard before.

"Young Lady," the Wizard answered, "all campers who spend the summer at Camp Hippo prove they have brains. Now go and do three smart things every day."

"I want a heart," Tiara whispered. Josephine nudged her this time. "I want a heart," Tiara cried.

"Tin Girl, by coming to Camp Hippo, you show you have a heart. To make your heart grow, you must do three nice things every day."

When it was Josephine's turn, she roared, "I want courage."

"It takes courage to come to Camp Hippo. It takes courage to try new things. Try three new things every day and your courage will grow."

Roland turned the spotlight on Ruby.

"Mr. Wizard, I want to go to my cabin." Ruby hit her forehead with the palm of her hand.

"You have already learned the way to your cabin," the Wizard replied. From under his cape, he pulled out a small flashlight. "Shine this light and your way will always be clear."

In the audience, the campers stood, clapped, cheered, and whistled. Ruby ran to the wings, took my hand, and pulled me toward the stage.

"Wait, no," I whispered, confused.

But when I walked out in front of everyone, the Wizard said, "Jonika, for your conspicuous bravery in saving Ruby from the fire, I award you the Lollipop of Valor. You are now an official, for real, Camp St. Augustine of Hippo counselor." Jermaine dropped his cape and handed me a giant lollipop.

I was embarrassed but thrilled. My head buzzed — whether from the applause or anxiety, I couldn't tell. Ruby pranced around me. I curtsied, since I had no idea what else to do, then crept off stage where Daiquiri waited, smiling and calm. After Jermaine followed me, Daiquiri and Turquoise re-entered the stage and stood behind Ruby, Lady, Tiara, and Josephine.

Ruby squeezed her eyes shut, clicked her silver sneakers three times, and shouted, "Sweet chariot, swing down to carry me home."

Turquoise and Daiquiri motioned for everyone to stand. Their voices and the campers' voices pulsed in my heart.

Swing low, sweet chariot,
Coming for to carry me home,
If you get there before I do,
Coming for to carry me home,
Tell all my friends I'm coming too,
Coming for to carry me home.

Everyone sang the last line really loud. Campers called out, *That's right. Un hunh. You know I'm comin' Lord...*

The rain had mostly stopped by the time the campers started down the soggy path to the cabins. I stayed behind a few moments to see if Daisy needed help setting up for tomorrow's breakfast. I pulled out a couple tables before she ordered me to go on.

No swim medal ever meant as much as the Lollipop of Valor. I kept hearing Jermaine's voice announcing that I was a *for real Camp St. Augustine of Hippo counselor.* It was the best day of my life. Then it got better. Jermaine came up behind me as I hopped off the bottom step outside Hippo Hall.

He took my hand and whispered, "Come up for B-ball after the Bernies go to sleep. I be waiting."

When I burst around the building, I almost bumped into Terrell. I assumed he was waiting for Jermaine.

"Sorry," I said.

Tiny raindrops trickled down his cheeks.

Before I started down the path, I waved to Mary Mac, who stood in the door of her cabin.

"Be careful with that ankle," she called.

"It's much better, thanks to you," I called back.

The air weighed heavy, as if a cloud hovered just above the ground. With every breeze, leaves spattered water on my head. At camp, each time it rained, the trees smelled like the mint jelly my mother served with lamb for Easter dinner.

As I hurried to catch the Bernies, I slipped on the wet pine needles and slid into Lady. We both landed on our rumps. When one of us tried to get up, she knocked the other down again. Daiquiri and the girls watched.

"How much longer you two intend to roll in the mud?" Daiquiri asked in her most impatient voice.

"We be slipping," Lady said.

"Stead of trying to stand straight up, get to your hands and knees, then squat, then stand," Daiquiri ordered.

By the time Lady and I got ourselves upright, Keesha, Raven, and Jailyn sprawled in front of us on the path. Behind us, other campers slipped and slid and fell.

From the cabins, Turquoise's voice rose. "You-uns gonna slide to the cabin or you gonna walk? I don't know how my little girls be all down here without falling but the Bernies be rockin' and rollin' down the path."

It took a couple minutes to get everyone up, and we side-stepped the rest of the way. As soon as we reached the cabin, Daiquiri and I led the girls around back to the showers. Since I was covered in pine needles and mud, I supervised while Daiquiri waited with towels. In the dull light from a single bulb, the girls jiggled and squealed while the chilly water spilled over them. They all loved to rub Ivory soap into a thick lather on their bodies, then watch the frothy water swirl down the drain.

After the girls were dry and in their pajamas, Daiquiri tossed me a towel and shampoo and I stripped off my clothes to wash up. I wanted to smell fresh for Jermaine. By the time I came inside, the girls had turned on my transistor radio. Like most days, the music came in scratchy. I had tuned it to the only station I could get that played the music Ishmael and I liked. The girls scrunched up their faces as if the radio insulted them. Circus-like organ music introduced Jim Morrison's deep voice and the hypnotic refrain of *Light My Fire*.

"Why you like that song, Jonika," Lady asked, "singing all 'bout starting fires? It nasty."

"You'd think Jonika have enough fire," Daiquiri said. The girls laughed.

"I like the beginning and I like the singer's voice." I tried to sound convincing.

Daiquiri snorted, but Lady thought about what I said.

"Jonika, that man sound like a devil when he sing. I think he Satan, be *tryin' to set the world on fire.*"

Girls looked up from their cat's cradle games. One girl looped string through her fingers and then transferred the string to another girl's fingers, back and forth, making different patterns, like Cat's Eye and Fish in a Dish.

"That man a demon," Jailyn said in a deep and serious voice. "He sing demon songs."

"Why can't we play soul?" Angel asked, squirming around to look at me with round, dark eyes.

I glanced at Daiquiri. When she shrugged, I handed the radio to Angel.

The girls gathered around and took turns moving the dial. After a minute, Angel pulled it away from them and said, "Jonika give it to me." She fiddled until a strong voice burst from the radio — *Make-a no mistake-a Jake-a, I'm Sonny Hopson, the Mighty Burner, and you listening to W-H-A-T radio. I'll take my sound on the way down, Foxy Mama.*

As soon as Sly and the Family Stone came on, the girls danced around the cabin and sang, *Different strokes for different folks, and so on and so on...*

When the hands on the wall clock moved to half-past nine, I panicked. I didn't want Daiquiri to know I planned to meet Jermaine, but I had to get to the basketball court before lights out at 10. Would the girls ever go to sleep? I looked at the clock again and sighed. I'd never make it. Daiquiri must have seen me checking, because when *It's Your Thing* by the Isley Brothers ended, she turned off the radio.

"You-alls had a long day. Time for bed," she announced.

I expected the girls to complain and beg to stay up, but each one hopped on her cot and pulled up her sheets.

"You Bernies were terrific tonight, each one of you — the scary forest trees, Tin Man Tiara, Courageous Lion Josephine, and Scarecrow Lady. And I'll never forget my Lollipop of Valor," I said.

Night, Jonika. Night, Daiquiri — their sleepy voices called.

In five minutes, the last restless camper's breath grew quiet and regular. Daiquiri clicked out her reading lamp. I fumbled my flashlight out of my cubby and snuck Jermaine's beret from under my pillow.

"I might sit outside a while," I said. "I don't feel tired at all. That okay?"

"Un hunh," Daiquiri said, her voice groggy like a drunk.

Before I left I checked the girls, then eased out the door and tiptoed down the steps. I sat on the bottom step for a few seconds, my heart racing. I worried about what Daiquiri and especially Turquoise would think if they found out where I was going. There wasn't much time before lights out, and I worried Jermaine would think I stood him up. After I made certain no one was around, I headed up the path, careful not to slip. If I stayed along the edge of the trail, away from the muddy middle, my soggy sneakers gripped the ground a little better. Every few steps my ankle protested, but I managed to keep going.

Before I got to the basketball court, the lights-out bell gonged and, one-by-one, the craft cabins glinted and dimmed. In another minute, the court lights would blink out. As I continued toward the court, the sound of guys' voices rose then quieted and the ball-bouncing stopped.

Just before the spotlight over the backboard flicked off, Roland took a final shot while Derrick, Michael, and James started down the path to the cabins. On the far side of the court, in the last blink of light, I noticed Jermaine and another person duck behind the storage container and disappear. It must be Turquoise, I realized. I was furious. *What was Jermaine trying to do by telling me to meet him? Did he want to make Turquoise jealous?* It was just wrong. I ripped Jermaine's beret off my head.

Footsteps — Roland's — came toward me and I backed into the trees, praying he wouldn't see me. I felt embarrassed, angry, and jealous. I waited five minutes after Roland passed before I started in the direction Jermaine went — to the archery range.

Every buzz, every caw, every rustle and snapped twig fed my anger and envy. I knew I should call it a night, go back to the cabin, and go to sleep. But *Light My Fire* spun through my head like an incantation, driving me on. I wanted to know. I had to see for myself.

Ever since the day I met him, Jermaine — with his self-confident teasing and flirting, even his lisp — attracted me. He wasn't movie star handsome but his muscles bulged from his shirts and the way he played basketball, ran, even the way he walked, looked smooth and effortless.

The more I think about it now, the more I have to admit that I believed if the little white girl became Jermaine's girlfriend, everyone at camp would accept me and even be impressed. It sounds dumb now. But Jermaine was the coolest guy at camp. Each time he flirted with me, I thought I could grab the brass ring. I could win the prize. Some nights, before I fell asleep, I wondered how shocked my parents would be if I had a black boyfriend, like in Janis Ian's song, *Society's Child.*

A breeze rustled the leaves and heavy drops landed on my shoulder. I hoped it was water. Bird-doo had bombed everyone at camp at least once. *Birdy, birdy in the sky, dropped a doo-drop in my eye, I'm just glad that cows don't fly* — I chanted the silly rhyme to myself as I crept closer to the archery range. My right eye twitched. Part of me wanted to go back to the cabin, but another part had to see what Jermaine and Turquoise were doing. I know that sounds horrible, but I figured if they were making out, then I'd know I didn't have a chance. But if they were just talking, maybe I did. My foot turned in a rut and my ankle screamed.

A wet, mulchy smell like rotting wood rose from the path. Lightning bugs flickered their tiny green luminescence, but clouds blocked the moon and stars. Among the trees, I moved through the darkness like a blind girl, snapping on my flashlight for a second or two, then turning it off so I wouldn't be discovered. The spongy ground sucked at my sneakers.

As I reached the crest of the hill above the archery range, a dank breeze swept through the trees. In the sky, grey clouds heaved like ocean waves. When a patch of clouds floated away, a veil lifted from the face of the moon and the night brightened. Three stars formed a triangle in the summer sky. From behind a tree I peered down, seeing at first only shadows and shapes. Then, on the flat top of the boulder, a single silhouette appeared in the moonlight. The figure rested on his elbows, looking up at the sky. I felt a rush of joy — Jermaine waited there for me.

Clever things to say ran through my head — *Are you the cowardly lion or the king of the forest? Winken, Blinken, and Nod one night sailed off in a wooden shoe.* Or, I could dance over, singing — *I heard it through the grapevine.* I thought of Daiquiri's powerful version — *with some other guy that you knew before.* I wished I could sing like her.

I took a step toward the boulder, about to call out — *Jermaine! I'm here!* But then I heard voices. I couldn't tell what they were saying, but I recognized Jermaine's lisp. I stopped, inched back into the trees, and watched, determined to see who was with him.

A slender body pressed against Jermaine and their faces came together. When I realized it couldn't be Turquoise — her build was bigger — I wondered who was with Jermaine. Was it Delia? But whoever it was, they came out here for privacy and I felt ashamed to witness their kisses and quiet moans. Even though the scene mesmerized me, I forced myself to turn away.

I'd taken a few steps back along the path when Jermaine's voice rang out in the dark, "You flexin' on me, Terrell? Cause I show you a flex for real."

For a moment, I didn't move, disbelieving what I'd heard. *Terrell? The soft-spoken boy who led nature hikes? Terrell? With his face nestled in Jermaine's neck?* I was wrong to come. I had no right to spy. I hurried away.

My heart pounded so loud I was afraid they'd hear. But as I made my way back to the cabins I realized how isolated and narrow my suburban life had been. There was so much I knew nothing about. What I did know was Jermaine and Terrell must never find out I was here.

I stumbled along the path. When a cloud floated across the moon, it became so dark I couldn't see my hands. I forced myself forward. My clothes, wet from rain and sweat, stuck to my body. I trembled, disoriented and angry with myself. My brain felt stuffed with cotton.

After I tripped and landed face down in a mushy mess of pine needles, dirt, and rotting leaves, I wanted to stay there, with the smell of decay a punishment for my stupid crush. But when the thrum of tiny wings vibrated in my ear, I got to my feet like someone yanked me up and I scurried as fast as my legs would go. I didn't care about anything but reaching my cabin, my cot, and my campers.

A strong skunky smell, like burning rubber, filled the air. My heart stopped. I knew that smell. *No, no, no,* I silently screamed. When I forced myself to look through my mud-spattered eyelashes, two red orbs glowed, flickered, and floated toward me. Nothing would save me this time. *Nothing should save me,* I thought. I hated myself and every act, every memory, every desire that festered under my skin for sixteen years. *Loser, weirdo, druggie, criminal, cracker* — I couldn't think of enough ways to describe my wretched self. "Come get me," I sobbed.

It makes no sense, but just then Lady's image came to me, saying — *She be eatin' greens from here forward.* Somehow, I knew no matter what faced me, I couldn't let down that special, caring girl. As the *Manetu* loomed closer, I backed away on my hands and knees, searching my pockets for my flashlight — front pocket, back pocket. As soon as I found it, I dropped it.

The creature's smell stole my breath. If I reached out, I'd touch its filthy coat. I felt like a kitten, crouched in a corner with no way out. My hands scrabbled across the path, desperate for the flashlight. When my fingers brushed against it, I grabbed it.

After a couple tries, I managed to flick the switch and aim the beam at the demon eyes. As it veered away, a terrible howl, like a wolf caught in a trap, echoed through the trees.

I was soaked and shivering, too scared to cry. In the distance, I heard an owl hoot. I scanned the light across the path, not caring anymore if someone saw it. The way was clear to me then — I'd made it to the turn in the path. The cabins were just beyond.

By the time I reached the cabin steps, my knees shook and I couldn't stop crying. I had no idea what time it was, but I was covered in muck and as disgusting as the creature. I went around back, stepped out of my clothes, turned on the shower, and tried to scrub away sixteen years.

Finally, I padded across the cabin floor, naked and dripping. A few girls stirred and Daiquiri sighed. I sunk onto my cot, pulled on a T-shirt and day-of-the-week undies, and collapsed. The closing words to *Araby* —

a story I'd read at Redwood before my expulsion — drummed in my brain.

Gazing up into the darkness I saw myself as a creature driven and derided by vanity; and my eyes burned with anguish and anger.

"Jonika, wake up. Jonika, why you cryin'?" I opened my eyes to Lady's worried brown ones looking down at me. "Your face all scratchy, Jonika, and you been cryin' in your sleep," she whispered.

My brain felt foggy, and a bitter taste, like after drinking Boone's Farm wine, coated my tongue and teeth. The cuts on my face stung, my nose was clogged, and my throat felt raw. Lady sat on the edge of my cot, studying me. I felt like I'd let her down, and that made me want to puke. I took a breath, sat up, and swung my legs over the side.

"What wrong, Jonika?" Lady asked. "Look, your braids all mess up." She leaned in and started to unweave my frazzled hair. Just by sitting close, she comforted me.

"I had a bad dream," I croaked. If only last night were a dream.

Daiquiri looked over the separator between our cots. "You all right, Jonika? You look kind of peaked."

"Jonika have a bad dream," Lady reported.

The other girls, out of their beds but still in their shorty pajamas — tiny flower-dotted white cotton button-down tops and elastic-waist briefs — crowded into the tight space around my cot or leaned on the four-foot separator to look in.

What you dream, Jonika? someone asked.

With a deep breath, I shook my head to clear my brain so I could come up with something to tell these girls I'd come to love. I grabbed a tissue to blow my nose and tried to smile.

"I dreamt the fighting trees from *Wizard of Oz* reached out their branches to grab me." I thought of those floating red eyes. "I was really scared."

"Was they grabbin' us too?" Lady asked.

"They tried to grab all the Bernies and throw us out of camp. But the Bernies had courage."

Somehow, while Lady worked on my hair and the other girls squeezed close to listen, I began to feel better.

Lady turned to look at me. "I surely know I be scared of grabby trees."

I be scairt. I be scared, girls chimed in.

While she got dressed, every minute or so Daiquiri looked at me with a concerned expression. As soon as Lady undid the last braid, I ran a brush through my hair and pulled it back in a ponytail.

"The Bernies weren't scared, they were brave. When the trees reached down to wrap their branches around us, every Bernie found rocks and sticks to throw at those mean trees. *Don't you be grabbing at us, nasty trees,* you yelled. And those trees raised up their branches and acted like they didn't know a thing about trying to grab us," I told them.

"We were brave. We didn't let no fighting trees get us," Raven said with satisfaction in her voice.

"Maybe the fighting trees ain't gonna get you all, but I sure will if you don't get yourselfs dressed and ready for breakfast," Daiquiri said.

With a stern expression, she looked from girl to girl. As soon as they scampered away to use the privy, wash their faces, and brush their teeth, Daiquiri turned to me with her lips drawn tight. "Why your face all beat up? What you been up to?"

"In the middle of the night I went out to pee and didn't bring my flashlight. I tripped and scraped my face. It's nothing," I lied.

I stepped into my swimsuit, then pulled on shorts and a T-shirt over it.

"Look like a lot more than nothin' to me. Girl, we more than halfway through camp and you still be wanderin' the woods lookin' for trouble. And when you look for it, trouble will find you," she said in her knowing way.

"I'm done looking for trouble, for real," I told her, and I meant it. "Let's get the girls to breakfast."

Jermaine's beret, damp and smelly from my fall last night, poked out from under my cot. I folded it like a napkin and clenched it in my fist. As we hiked up the path, the warm, sweet smell of waffles drifted through the air. My stomach rumbled and my legs itched. Overhead, branches rustled.

"Them trees gonna get us," Keesha shouted.

The other girls squealed and ran for Hippo Hall. At the top of the path, Lady waited for Daiquiri and me to catch up.

In the breakfast line, I poured syrup over my waffles, put a banana on my tray, and reached for a cup of orange juice. Mary Mac looked up from refereeing two Andys fighting over a box of Trix and touched my arm. "What happened to your face, Jonika?"

I felt myself blush and stutter. I couldn't seem to come up with an answer.

Next to me, with her tray filled exactly like mine, Lady leaned forward and in a loud whisper told Mary Mac, "Fighting trees."

The nearby Bernies burst into laughter and shared my dream story with any camper who would listen.

"Now that's a horse of a different color," Mary Mac said, shaking her head and scooping scrambled eggs onto the next camper's plate.

"Can I get a cup of coffee?" I asked her. "I didn't sleep well."

"Up all night with the fighting trees?" Mary Mac asked. "Sure, and I'll bring one to you — sugar and milk?"

As I turned away from the line, I bumped into Jermaine.

He took a waffle off my plate and bit into it. "Sweet and soft, the way I like them." I heard snickers from the boy counselors' table. "Missed you last night," he whispered. Then, in a louder voice he asked, "You ready to teach me to swim?"

"I give lessons all day. I teach whoever comes." I hoped my voice didn't sound as shaky to him as it did to me.

While Jermaine cut to the front of the breakfast line, I left my tray on our table and walked to the boys' table.

"That Jermaine's seat?"

"I guess it is, the only empty one," Roland answered.

He looked at my face and started to say something, but instead cleared his throat.

"He misplaced his tam," I said as I lay the beret on the plastic chair.

"You hurt your face?" Roland asked then.

"Attack of the fighting trees." It was as good an answer as any. And maybe even true.

After the campers hustled out, Daisy and Mary Mac sat and sipped coffee with me.

"Young girl don't need be drinking coffee," Daisy said. When she raised her cup, her pinky finger stuck out delicately. "Don't need no joe at your age."

Mary Mac nodded. "Yet didn't me own mam fill our baby bottles with milk and tea? *Ach, it's never too young to learn to love tea,* she'd say. Myself, I prefer tea through the day, but I'll take a cup of coffee in the morning. Now Joan, tell me the name of the fighting tree who scratched up your face."

"Just me. I tripped in the bushes on my way to the bathroom in the dark. I guess I'm a goofus."

We sat awhile, silent. As soon as she finished, Daisy gathered our cups and headed to the kitchen.

"Out with you too," Mary Mac said. "There's little time for dawdling."

Down at the pool, I checked the pH and chlorine levels and the pump pressure, killing time before the campers arrived for lessons. Then I skimmed leaves and bugs until the water sparkled, as clear and blue as the sky.

When the deck clock read half-past nine, I climbed on the diving board and tested the spring, then hopped off and turned the gear to get more bounce. Back on the board, I took three steps into a hurdle, raised my arms and sprang straight up, bent and straightened, and cut the water with hardly a splash. Again and again, I flew from the board into straight dives, back dives, and flips. Each time I plunged into the cool water, I felt free from everything but my body's flight and descent. If only I could drown the memory of my pathetic pursuit of Jermaine.

I pulled myself out of the water, hopped back on the board, and visualized a jackknife dive. I had taken the first step when loud clapping and whistling stopped my approach. Roland and twelve little boys clambered through the gate.

"Jonika, look at me," Antoine called, running toward the pool.

As I stood rooted to the board, Antoine cannonballed into the diving well. Six feet under water, he uncurled, his outstretched arms swaying like a ghostly orchestra conductor's. I dove under, grabbed him, and kicked to the surface, taking a pop to the nose from his elbow. Roland reached over to lift Antoine out of the water while I rested my elbows on the edge, watery blood spilling from my nose. After I heaved myself out, I knelt in front of Antoine, who sneezed and spit. I checked his stomach to see if he swallowed water, but he was okay. I'd gotten him out in seconds. We stared at each other for a few moments before he reached out to touch my upper lip.

"You bleeding, Jonika." He looked at the drop of my blood on his finger, "same blood as mine."

"Same," I said.

I kept my hands on his shoulders while Roland watched.

"Sorry. He got away from me," Roland said, looking guilty. "Now you go and bust up your nose. You a mess, Jonika."

"No big deal. And Antoine's okay. Right, Antoine?" I called. When he nodded, I asked Roland, "Can you get the boys lined up and keep your eye on them? I need a minute."

While Roland barked at the kids, I trotted to the benches near the shallow end, sat down, leaned my head back, and swallowed coppery blood. Then I pinched the bridge of my nose and pressed a towel under it until the bleeding stopped. Before I got in the pool and waded to the campers, I rinsed my face and hands with the garden hose. My nose felt tripled in size. *Another bloody day at Camp Hippo*, I thought.

"Does everyone know the deep end rule?" I asked.

"Don't never go in," Robert chanted.

"But Jonika, I been practicin'," Antoine said. "I saw you divin' in, I thought I could too."

"That was a mistake, wasn't it, Antoine?"

"Yes," he said, drawing out the word.

"Even though all of you are getting better and better at swimming in shallow water, no deep end. Agreed?" I said.

Yes, they answered in chorus.

"Okay. Antoine, bring the boys over to the grass and get them started with dry-land practice while I get the kickboards. You're in charge. Make sure no one gets in the water."

With a confused look that changed into a confident one, Antoine swaggered across the deck with the boys following. He was much more bossy than me, but his demonstration was decent and the boys copied his windmill arms.

After I signaled for the boys to jump in the water and practice with kickboards, most of them hugged the boards but kept their feet on the bottom as they moved the length of the pool. Only Antoine sprawled on his kickboard, lifted his feet off the bottom, and kicked with determination.

"Get your feet up," he ordered. "Do what Jonika say. We learnin' to swim."

Roland took off his shirt and sneakers and splashed in next to me. He cupped his hands and spilled water over his arms. The smell of chlorine against his grassy scent rippled through the air.

"Girl, you all beat up. Every time I see you, you got somethin' else bleedin' or bruised or scratched. What you do to your face?"

His finger traced a long scratch on my right cheek.

"Keep kicking. Feet off the bottom, like Antoine," I called to the boys before I turned to Roland, surprised when tears welled in my eyes. "I tripped. Wherever I go, I trip myself up. The only place I know I won't fall is right here, in the pool."

"You a fish out of water," Roland said, splashing me. "So stay in that water like a fish and teach me to swim."

"For real?" I asked.

After he nodded, I offered him a kickboard. As he took it, his hand clasped mine and he held it for a heartbeat. Our eyes met and I remembered his hands on my sore ankle, his hands molding Ruby's old glasses into shape, his hands threading the light through the coffee can.

"We got a few weeks left," I said. "You sweep the water under your body with your hands like this..."

As I extended his arm and shaped his hand, I held it for a heartbeat.

On Wednesday, July 16th, as Hippo Hall thrummed with breakfast chatter, Father Vincent stepped onto the stage. He wore his version of a camp uniform — a short-sleeved Madras shirt, black Bermuda shorts, black dress socks, and black leather sandals. He cleared his throat, but the noise from dozens of campers drowned him out — *I'mma getchoo for that! Unh uh, no you won't.* Two trays clattered on the plank floor.

Mary Mac marched to the front of the room and clapped her hands. "Campers. Campers! Father has an important announcement, if you care to give him your attention. Counselors, see to the quiet — the word is QUIET — table cleanup while everyone listens to Father. Amen, campers?"

"Amen," the kids roared.

Father tugged on the collar of his sport shirt the same way he tugged his clerical collar. He'd slicked back his salt-and-pepper hair, now so long it covered his ears.

"Who knows what happens today, Children?"

"Hamburgers tonight!" Ruby called.

When her eyes found mine, she grinned.

"Saturday is hamburger night. Today is Wednesday," Father's eyes roamed from table to table as if he were looking for a friend.

"Free play day!" Antoine shouted.

The campers stomped and clapped.

"Children, children, please." After Father raised his voice the kids quieted down. "Something happens today you will remember the rest of your lives. Today, the United States launches Apollo 11, a giant spaceship, to send American astronauts to the moon. Since time began, men, women, and children have gazed at the moon and dreamed of flying there. Today, that journey begins. As soon as the tables are cleared, I want you to line up in cabin order and march to the play area outside the school cabin. Jermaine and Derrick are moving the TV set to the porch so we can watch the spacecraft take off. Before we head out the door, let's say a prayer for the astronauts' safe journey to the moon and back."

I stood between the Bernies and Honey Bees while they joined in the prayer. Ruby's voice rang out loud and clear — *Are father, whose arts in heaven, Halloween thy name, thy kingdom come, thy work get done, on*

Earth as a tree in heaven. Give us today our jelly bread and give us our passes, as we forget theys who trespass again us, now and forever, AMEN!

Lady looked at me and rolled her eyes. As I followed the girls to the school cabin, I took a deep breath of fresh air and then another. Even though five tall, rotating fans circulated air in Hippo Hall, the odor of eighty-some sweaty bodies took a few minutes to clear. I thought about my dad and Tommy and how excited they must be to watch the space launch.

The campers hopped from blanket to blanket like they were playing hopscotch or step-on-a-crack. I stood back and watched, amazed at how instantly they made up games. That's when I got an idea. I wanted to run it by Roland, but he was busy fiddling with the TV dials. I felt a warm breath on the back of my neck and turned into Jermaine.

He quietly sang — *Blue Moon, you left me standing alone...*

I hoped he didn't notice the shiver that ran through me. Just then Mary Mac clapped her hands and after a quick glance at Jermaine, I found a tiny corner of plaid blanket not covered with squirming Bernies and sat down. Before I focused on the TV, I sensed someone's eyes on me. I met Turquoise's gaze. I gave her a tight-lipped smile and turned away, but I felt guilty, like she knew about where I'd gone after the *Wizard of Oz.* But how could she know? Lady shook my elbow, frowned like a school teacher, and tipped her head toward the screen.

The grainy newscast showed astronauts in puffy white suits walking toward a tall, white rocket ship. Then the cameras focused on the intense, white-shirted men in the control tower. The next shots scanned the joyous crowd gathered to watch. Mary Mac banged two pots together.

"Campers and counselors, let the littlest ones sit up front. Everyone pay attention. Enough tomfoolery for now — the launch is starting."

The kids squirmed, pushed, and shoved, but then Jermaine stood up and raised his hands like a preacher and a silence — broken only by rustling leaves and a low, woodsy buzz — fell over the campers.

"Quiet now. Time to listen to Uncle Walter," Jermaine announced. When he smiled, his mouth spread wide and his teeth shone white.

What is it about Jermaine? After that night in the woods, I knew I was no different to him than Delia or Daiquiri or Millie or Terrell — whoever caught his fancy. But for those seconds or minutes when Jermaine focused on me, I believed no one else mattered to him — except maybe Turquoise. I thought about what Daiquiri said, *They got history. And you can't change history.* And Lady's words became a silent chant — *Jermaine playin' you.*

Still, I couldn't take my eyes off him. There was a word to describe Jermaine. I tried to remember it — attractive, magnetic, dazzling — something like that. Then it came to me, the word my father used the word to describe John F. Kennedy — *charismatic.* Jermaine had charisma. *That was it,* I thought. At the sound of Ruby's voice, I shook my head and turned my attention to the space launch.

"Who's Uncle Walter?" Ruby called from her seat up front.

"Walter Cronkite," Jermaine answered, "the TV man."

Ruby struck her forehead with her palm.

"He ain't my uncle."

As Jermaine walked through the campers and found a tree along the side to lean on, Roland worked the dials and turned the volume to high. A deep monotone voice started the countdown — *Two minutes, ten-seconds and counting. We are still a go with Apollo 11... Ten-seconds to lift off... two-seconds, one-second, zero... Lift off! We have a lift off!*

With flames flaring, the white spear lifted into the air, cut through clouds, and soared into the blue sky. All around me, campers rose to their feet and cheered.

Oh boy, oh boy, it looks good, a TV voice reported.

The campers crowded close, their mouths and eyes wide open. Tears welled in my own eyes and I was surprised how much I wished I were watching this with my father. I imagined he'd say, *It's a proud day to be an American.* In fact, I did feel proud. The dark faces of the campers and counselors glowed with that same sense of American pride. The hand I felt take mine was Lady's.

"Jonika, you think Mami watchin' this in Haiti?" she asked, a nervous stutter in her voice.

"I'm sure she's watching and thinking of you," I said, and put my arm around her shoulder.

Later that morning, the Andys spilled through the pool gate. Each boy grabbed a kickboard and sat along the edge, kicking his feet.

"Antoine, lead dry-land freestyle stroke for a few minutes. I need to talk to Roland," I called.

Antoine hopped to his feet and, like little soldiers, the Andys dropped their kickboards, formed themselves in a cube, and wind-milled their arms, turning their heads to the side every other stroke. Antoine caught my eye, his expression serious and mature. I knitted my eyebrows, folded my arms across my chest, and nodded my approval. He nodded back and called to the boys, "Thaz good, breathe, uh huh, head down, good Robert..."

Roland and I moved far enough away so the boys couldn't hear us.

"While we were watching the moon launch, I got an idea. What if we make the rest of the week Astronaut Week? Then on Sunday, before the spaceship touches down, we could have pool games, like asteroid toss with water balloons or maybe a limbo moon-walk under the hose, stuff like that. What do you think?"

Roland smiled. "I like it! We could make papier-mâché space helmets at arts and crafts. We'll need balloons for the helmets and the water balloons. I'll talk to Father. Maybe he'll get a helium tank so we can float a balloon into orbit."

"Yes! And maybe this is dumb, but do you think Daiquiri and Turquoise would teach the kids to sing the *Purple People Eater* song? It's fun and sort of related." The more I thought about it, the more excited I got.

"Sure they will," Roland said. "As soon as swim lesson's over, I'll get Lincoln to take the Andys, and I'll go talk to Father Vincent and Mary Mac."

"Jonika! I cain't be doin' all the work," Antoine yelled. His red swimsuit hung low on his tiny hips, and his full hair shimmered in the sun.

Pretty much everyone had let their hair grow. While the girls kept their hair in braids or tied back with bandanas, most of the guy counselors and boy campers sported naturals. A couple boys looked like they belonged on the album cover of *Hair*. I liked the look.

"Bring the swimmers, Antoine," I called.

I jumped in the pool and waited for the kids to take their places along the edge. Before everyone settled, Roland sprinted from the far side of the pool, leapt in the air, and cannonballed in. The kids cheered and splashed until Roland told them, "Fun's fun, but now we swim."

And they did. Antoine directed the boys back to the edge. Then he rolled into the pool using the sitting dive I'd taught them. When he hit the water, he took a stroke and kicked. With his next stroke, he turned almost completely onto his back to inhale, then rolled again to pull and kick. One after the other, the Andys hopped in and tried to imitate Antoine. A bunch of the boys took a stroke or two and then dropped their feet to breathe, but pushed off from the bottom again and stroked and kicked until they needed the next breath. Not Antoine. Antoine kept going. As soon as Antoine touched the opposite wall, I butterflied to him and hoisted him in the air.

"You did it, Twan, you did it!" I screamed.

"Tole you I ken swim," he said like it was no big deal.

It was a very big deal to me. Water streaming down my face covered my tears. Each day, more boys and girls put their faces in the water, pushed off the bottom, and swam two or more strokes before stopping to breathe. In all, twelve campers, thirteen including Antoine, could swim the length of the pool.

By the time the boys had changed and headed out, Daiquiri and Turquoise led in the Bernies and Honey Bees. The boys and girls called out to each other, laughing and touching one another as they passed —

Ooo, Twan wet his pants.

I ain't wet 'em, theys wet 'cause I been swimmin'.

Chubbler.

Don' be making Keesha cry, Boy.

Git out my grill, Shorty.

Yo aight. This boy be splashin' and crashin'.

Don't be hatin', Jabroni.

Before I had a chance to talk to Daiquiri about Astronaut Week, Turquoise lined up the Honey Bees on the edge. When she hopped in the pool, I got in too.

"Thanks, Turquoise," I said, "You're doing all my work."

"Ain't no time for wastin'. I'mma show up to join swim team at school, if you teach us good enough," Turquoise said. The girls laughed and splashed each other.

"Kickboards," I ordered, "let's go."

The girls hugged their boards and kicked down the lanes to the far side. Daiquiri walked along the deck, her eye on the swimmers, while I worked with Turquoise.

"Lean your body on the board. Try to balance. Do you think you can float on it?" I asked.

"Ain't no way to know lest I try," Turquoise answered, her voice determined.

I held Turquoise's hands while she balanced on the board. When I let go, she kicked like crazy and flailed her arms. Every stroke or two, she let her feet drag. Then she launched herself back on the board to start again.

I walked alongside and suggested she put her face in the water. After she worked on it for five minutes or so, Turquoise found her balance on the board and propelled herself forward with increasing speed.

"Try turning your head to breathe when your arm scoops through the water on that side." I demonstrated the rhythm of breathing. "You good?" I asked and she nodded.

I let Turquoise practice while I divided the girls into three groups: those who could swim, those who would swim in a day or two, and the not-yets. Ruby was in the middle group, but Lady stayed in the not-yets. I took that as my failure. While I spent a few moments working with each girl individually, I watched Turquoise out of the corner of my eye. One thing she had plenty of was determination.

After the lesson, while the girls changed into shorts and shirts, I pulled Daiquiri and Turquoise toward the gate. The bushes rustled and a twig snapped. Just outside, Jermaine leaned against an oak, arms folded across his chest, a lollipop stick bobbing between his lips. I waved for him to come on in, but he just grinned and shook his head.

"Jermaine be waiting on me again," Turquoise announced, her voice pleased.

The smile she gave Jermaine lingered when she turned back to me. I felt as if Jermaine and Turquoise had a secret joke about me, but the voice in my head scolded, *don't be pathetic.* Daiquiri's voice brought my focus back to Astronaut Week.

"What you want to talk about, Jonika? Those girls already lining up."

"Roland and I've been talking about doing astronaut and space activities the rest of this week. If Father says okay, on Sunday we plan to have games at the pool. Roland said he can teach the campers to make papier-mâché space helmets. I was hoping you and Turquoise would teach the kids to sing *Purple People Eater.* What do you think?"

I felt pretty nervous. A whiff of chlorine floated in the breeze.

"*Purple People Eater?*" Turquoise said. "That's a oldie, Jonika. But I don't see no reason we can't teach the children your song." She shrugged then called, "Come on, Honey Bees, we rollin' out."

"You best be careful, Jonika. People be thinkin' you like it here — pool games, special songs. How's that go? *Flyin' purple people eater,*" Daiquiri sang.

Down the path, Jermaine walked beside Turquoise. With Daiquiri's voice leading, the Bernies and Honey Bees sang, *Do your ears hang low?*

The next day, during a break from lessons, I headed to arts and crafts to watch Roland teach the kids to make space helmets. As soon as I walked through the door, campers demanded my attention —

Jonika, look here!

How you get to be a astronaut, Jonika?

Girls can't be no astronaut, ain't I right, Nika?

Can you help me, Nika?

At each table, campers and counselors tore stacks of newspapers into strips. While they worked, the kids sang along to songs from the transistor radio Roland borrowed. When *In the Year 2525* played, Antoine shook his head with a disgusted look.

"That's just nasty," he said to murmured agreement.

But the moment *Black Pearl* came on, campers and counselors stopped working, closed their eyes and sang along.

After *Good Morning, Starshine* came on, I walked over to Roland and tried to convince him we should make that the theme song for Astronaut Week.

"It's nice, I guess. But Astronaut Week theme song got to be *Cloud 9*," Roland said in a voice loud enough for the room to hear.

He switched off the radio and sauntered to the front, swaying and clapping. The Andys pushed back their chairs and hurried to join him. As they strutted behind Roland, they sang about doing fine — on *Cloud 9.* I thought they sounded better than The Temptations. I stood and clapped.

"Don't be giving them boys no 'couragement or we never get these helmets made," Daiquiri muttered as she came in the door.

But she added her rich voice to theirs.

The space helmets took a couple days to finish. On Friday, the counselors and the older campers blew up balloons for the entire camp. I expected the kids to pop them, but they held their balloons gently and sat almost still while Daisy and Terrell carried steam-table pans filled with a milky liquid into the arts and crafts cabin, making the air smell heavy and damp.

I found myself watching Terrell. The Bernies loved his nature classes where they learned the names of birds, trees, and wild flowers and the difference between honey bees and wasps. They caught tadpoles in the creek and let caterpillars crawl across their hands.

When he caught me staring Terrell lowered his eyes and moved a step closer to Daisy, almost like a child moving closer to his mother. Something about that step was familiar. I'd seen it before. Then I remembered. If the guys' horsing around got too rambunctious or when a couple of older boys got in a fight, Terrell took a step toward Jermaine. Oh, I realized, *Jermaine looks out for him. Protects him. No wonder he loves Jermaine.*

As Daisy and Terrell started to leave, I called, "Terrell." He turned, his eyes hesitant, his hands drumming against his sides. "Thanks," I said and as he reached the doorway, he smiled.

Across the front, Roland walked back and forth like a preacher. As soon as he stopped and cleared his throat, all talk and chatter quieted.

"Aight now, Space Campers, we got all our supplies ready and today we put them together. First, we gonna dip these newspaper strips in those tubs of gluey water, what Terrell and Daisy made with cornstarch. Look here, you see my balloon? It's gonna be my head. Your balloons be your heads, lest you want me to papier-mâché your skulls. What you do is, take your paper strips, dip one in the tub, then lay it over the balloon, nice and smooth. Then take another strip, do the same. You do that on your balloons 'til they covered all over five, six times. Then we'll keep them here overnight to dry out. Tomorrow, when they're dry, you-alls will paint the papier-mâché. Then later, we'll burst the balloons at the bottom where the knot is. Soon as we pull out the flat balloon, we got our helmet shells."

The gluey water felt warm and thick, but some of the cornstarch settled on the bottom. I swished my fingers through the pan to mix it up again before the Bernies wet their newspaper strips.

Roland walked through the cabin, nodding here, smoothing there, and making *that's good* comments at each table. When campers raised their hands for help, Roland showed them how to flatten wrinkles with their thumbs or pointed out where to add more strips. Every suggestion included a hand on a shoulder and *That's fine.*

When Antoine popped his balloon, he sucked in his breath and held back tears.

"I ain't do nuffin' right," he said, his chin trembling.

"You know the punishment for balloon bustin', right?" Roland asked with his right eyebrow raised.

What punishment? twenty-two quivery voices asked.

"The balloon buster got to sing a song while Jonika blows up a new balloon. Come on, Twan. We all hear you singing in the shower."

Antoine looked around nervously. In a loud whisper, he asked, "What song?"

"Somethin' 'bout a *flying purple people eater*?" Roland opened his hands as if he weren't certain.

Ahh, oh yeah, I wanna sing too — came from the tables.

"Aight, then," Roland said. "I want everyone singing *Purple People Eater* in honor of Twan's balloon bust. But keep working. Look, Jonika already got the new balloon ready."

While they smoothed paper strips on their balloons, the kids sang. Ruby stood on her chair, glanced at me, and sang at the top of her lungs. I walked over to stand beside her, ready to catch her if she fell. But once she belted out — *sure looks strange* — she dropped down in her seat. I moved back to the Bernies' table and put a strip of wet newspaper across my balloon.

"Jonika, what you doing with your balloon?" Lady demanded in an adult voice. "It all wrinkly."

"I know, it's a mess. Yours looks really good, Lady. Can you fix mine?" I passed my balloon to her and checked the square Coca Cola clock on the wall. "I got to get back to the pool."

When she took my balloon, Lady rolled her eyes and muttered, "You want it right, you got to take the time."

After I hopped down the steps, I heard footsteps behind me. A hand landed on my shoulder, and I turned to face Roland.

In a quiet voice he said, "I got time after dinner to help with the pool games. I'll let Father Vincent know Daiquiri and Lincoln will watch the Bernies and Andys at Camp Roundup."

I looked into his warm eyes. *He's so nice*, I thought. *Maybe the nicest guy I ever met.* When he smiled, my heartbeat quickened.

"Okay," I said, trying to be nonchalant, "sounds good."

It sounded very good. *It sounded very good indeed* — as Mary Mac would say.

After Roland trotted back to arts and crafts, I heard a rustle near the schoolroom cabin. A flash of yellow, red, and green disappeared around the building — Jermaine. I had a sick feeling. Whenever I saw him, I felt guilty for following him that rainy night. No matter how hard I tried not to, when I least expected, I'd remember how pathetic I'd been, throwing myself at him. No wonder I pissed off Turquoise. Even today, when I had fun making space helmets and looked forward to coming up with pool games, something simple like the sight of Jermaine's beret, reminded me I was still a loser. As I started toward the pool, I reached down for a pinecone and cradled its rough edges in my palms.

Along the path, insects buzzed and branches rustled. Cornstarch glue crusted on the front of my T-shirt and smelled like wallpaper paste. By the time I reached the pool, I felt fidgety, like there was something important I was supposed to do, but I couldn't remember what. In a couple weeks, camp would be over. Thoughts of home thrummed in my mind like hornets, relentless, troubling, threatening to sting.

I still only knew one way to force those thoughts away.

On moon-landing day, after Sunday Mass, Father Vincent held out his arms with a grave look on his face.

"Boys and girls, all of us are excited for the historic and amazing moon landing late tonight. Most of you will be sleeping, but tomorrow morning we'll bring the television set to Hippo Hall so you can watch the moonwalk while you eat breakfast. I've seen the wonderful helmets Roland helped you make, and we all look forward to games at the pool later on. But before we enjoy this day, I want you to take to your knees to pray for the repose of the soul of a young woman, Mary Jo Kopechne, who drowned Friday night. Children, let us pray — *Hail Mary, full of grace, the Lord is with thee, blessed art thou among women…*"

After the prayer, I walked by Mary Mac and Daisy. Their expressions were grim.

"It's a terrible thing," Mary Mac whispered, "and Teddy Kennedy the driver."

I stopped and stared. "What did you say, Mary Mac?"

"Go on, Jonika, you've plenty to do to get ready for the hordes," she answered, ringing her hands.

At the pool I hosed down the deck, washing away grime and twigs and dead bees. Even before I got the skimmer from the equipment shack, most of the concrete was dry. The sun beat down and I smeared my face, neck, and arms with Coppertone. The lotion smell made me think of the seashore — gritty sand, rough waves, body surfing, the smell of pizza, and the boardwalk crowded with red-faced white people herding their children onto the amusement rides.

Each summer during my family's vacation, there'd be at least one day when a summer school bus from the city pulled up and parked near the beach. As soon as the doors opened, a dozen or more black kids, followed by a few white counselors, scampered across the sand and splashed at the edge of the ocean. While the counselors spread blankets and doled out peanut butter and jelly sandwiches, some families left the beach. Others moved their umbrellas and chairs farther away.

After I connected the hose to the faucet, I filled water balloons for the games and thought about how those city kids felt. Even though they were thrilled to be at the ocean — anyone could see that — they must have known the other beach-goers snubbed them. But I remembered how much fun they had. They built sand castles and ran back and forth between the blankets and the water. Along the shoreline, they sat or lay on the wet sand and let the waves wash over them. Later, on the boardwalk, I'd see them smiling and laughing while they drank sodas and ate slices of pizza.

When I dropped the hose, it wiggled across the deck, spewing water and drenching me. As I turned off the spigot, I realized how brave those kids were. If it bothered them when people stopped to stare, they didn't show it. They didn't let being outsiders ruin their day. They had every right to swim in the ocean, dig in the sand, and walk on the boardwalk and that's what they did. *Why didn't I do that at Redwood? Why didn't I go to classes, go to swim practice, and not care about being different?* I had as much right to be there as anyone. But I wasn't brave. And that, I realized, made me a loser instead of an outsider. I heard footsteps.

"Jonika, you need help?" Roland called from the path.

"Bet your booties, Granny," I called back.

Roland hurdled the gate, chanting, *"Can't get enough of that Sugar Crisp, keeps me going strong."*

At Redwood Academy, the girls made up a cheer from the Sugar Crisp cereal commercial. At games, the cheerleaders yelled — *Offense, defense, our moves are uncanny. Redwood gonna win it?* and the crowd answered — *Bet your booties, Granny.* I didn't know why I said it now, but I liked that Roland got it. What? Did I think black people didn't watch commercials?

"Let's go, Sugar Bear. We got to fill these balloons for the asteroid toss. Where'd you learn to make papier-mâché space helmets? The kids loved working on them," I said. "I did too."

"Ole Sugar Bear got lots of tricks up his sleeve. If you ever took your eyes off Jermaine, you might see some of them." Roland shielded his eyes with his hand.

"My eyes are off Jermaine," I said in a croaky voice.

"What's that mean?"

"What do you think it means?" I didn't bat my eyes, but I wanted to.

There I was, flirting with Roland while Ishmael cooled his tool in prison, and I wasn't entirely sure I was over my crush on Jermaine. Maybe I never would be. Jermaine, I finally understood, was like a light, and I was just one of many moths drawn or doomed to flutter around him. I believe that in his way, Jermaine loved us all. But Turquoise was his spark.

"What?" I asked, when I heard Roland's voice.

"Girl, you on another planet. I asked how you plannin' to run the games?"

We walked to the diving area. On the concrete, with a piece of chalk from the school cabin, I sketched where I planned for each activity to go. "We can do the asteroid toss on land — here — for the younger campers. The bigger kids can have a water balloon fight on this side of the pool — that will be the Meteor Storm."

Roland nodded, his lower lip jutting out. "Over here we could spray water for the kids to jump over into the pool, you think?"

I smiled. "Definitely." *Nice,* I thought.

"Crater hop," he said. His shoulder pressed against mine.

"And on this side we could spray it just over the pool surface and the kids would have to go under or get sprayed in the face." I felt more and more excited.

"That game be called Lunar Limbo."

"We should have stations so the different games can go on at the same time while the cabins go from one to the other like they do for activities."

Roland nodded, "Aight."

"We should have a grand finale. Will this work? We could make four teams for a water balloon relay race, with three campers from each cabin on each team to make it fair. Whichever team wins gets to go first for dinner."

"Dang, Shorty, you been hatchin' this plan for days." Grinning, Roland took my hand and pulled me up. "What you want me to do?"

When I looked into his warm eyes I knew what I wanted him to do.

But instead I said, "Start setting up Asteroid Toss."

After lunch, the woods thundered with stomping feet and reedy voices that rose in bursts of laughter. From the equipment shack, I grabbed my space helmet and pulled it over my head. I'd painted one side pink with a red peace sign and drew the American flag on the other. My head got sweaty, but Moon Girl must welcome the astronauts to Moon Lake.

Ruby led the campers through the gate. Her space helmet, decorated with streaks of blue, green, yellow, red, and black, tipped back on her head. "I'mma first girl on the Moon, Jonika," she declared as she burst into the pool area.

"You are!" I agreed.

I admired each space-helmeted camper who streamed through the gate.

"My space helmet look silly," Lady complained when she passed by. She decorated hers with fat flowers in blue, red, and yellow, drawing long green stalks with tiny leaves.

"I love your helmet. You're the Space Flower Child," I said and touched her chin.

"I'mma Flower Child?" Lady smiled as she waited for me to close the gate after everyone was in.

As she and I approached the pool, Lady stopped and stepped back. A floppy blue sphere dinged my leg, then spattered against the concrete.

"Gotchoo, Jonika," Antoine called.

He wore his silver helmet, with a black blob across the back he identified as an eagle. Three water balloons jiggled against his chest.

"Twan, put those back in the bin. Move on over with the Andys," Roland ordered, his arms folded across his chest. He turned to me and rolled his eyes.

I smothered a laugh.

"Boys," Lady said, shaking her head and looking sad.

"Can't live with 'em, can't live without 'em." I gave her shoulder a squeeze.

"Ain't that the truth?" Daiquiri agreed.

Roland assigned two counselors to each station while Jermaine, in his black helmet with gold stars, was in charge of moving the campers through activities. After Roland lined up the cabins at different events, I joined Mary Mac at the diving well. Once she saw me, Mary Mac climbed the two steps onto the diving board and blew a whistle.

"Attention, campers. The first annual Moon Games are about to begin. Follow directions, do your best, have fun, and take care of each other. Counselors, are you ready for the competitors? Jonika, will you do us the honor of starting the Moon Games with a bang?"

To hoots and cheers, I accepted two trashcan lids from Jermaine. When I slammed the lids together, the bang echoed through the trees.

During the games, I walked around the deck continuously, scanning the pool to make sure heads surfaced after the kids leapt over the stream of water for the Crater Hop or ducked under during Lunar Limbo. Each time I passed Jermaine, he'd smile, or nod, or say, *You did good, Nika*, or, *See you later.*

My pulse quickened, and I couldn't help feeling pleased. Jermaine's shoulders and chest made a V with his tight stomach. As he moved from activity to activity, veins outlined his calf muscles. His dark skin glistened. One time, as I turned my eyes back to the pool, I saw Roland watching me watch Jermaine. My face flushed and I felt guilty and absurd, but I'm not sure why.

After the campers had the chance to try each activity, Jermaine divided up the kids into four relay teams, and then positioned half the kids on each side of the pool. I handed a balloon to the first camper from each team before I whistled for the relay contest to begin.

Each time an older boy received the balloon, he drove through the water like a horse, making waves that threatened to upend the smaller campers. As soon as Antoine was handed the balloon, he jumped in, balanced it on his back, and swam to other end instead of walking. His efficient stroke pulled him close to the team in the lead. As soon as he climbed out, I was waiting to hug him.

"Thaz the way you do it," Antoine said over his shoulder as he swaggered back to his teammates.

When Ruby got the balloon from her teammate, she leaned into the water and forged ahead. In the lane next to her, a big boy pushed past and swamped her. I started to go in, but Lady caught my eye.

"I'm Ruby's buddy," she called.

She hopped in, set Ruby upright, hopped out, and returned to her last-in-line place on her team.

Ruby sneezed water from her nose and bounced the rest of the way until she handed off the balloon to a Bridges girl.

As the last four campers stood on the edge, jiggling and calling for their teammates to hand them the balloons, I thought how well Jermaine chose the teams. Each group was still in contention.

When Lady received the balloon, the other three teams were ahead. With her long legs and thin frame, Lady skipped sideways through the water. When she caught the leader about ten feet from the finish, a cheer erupted from the deck. Lady lunged for the wall and set her balloon on the deck — the winner. I'd never seen anyone move through water like that. Somehow, Lady figured out how to streamline her body against the water's resistance. As she pulled herself out of the pool, the cheers were deafening. With the hint of a smile, Lady glanced at me and skipped to join her team.

Father Vincent climbed onto the diving board and clapped his hands. "The 1969 Moon Games have come to the end. A special thank you to Jonika, Roland, and all the counselors for putting on this glorious competition. Now, boys and girls, retrieve your helmets, line up, and follow your counselors to the cabins to rest for an hour before dinner. Well-played, campers."

Father clapped his hands again, this time above his head. Behind him, Daisy launched six helium-filled balloons, one to represent each cabin, and we watched them float into the air and out of sight.

After dinner, the Bridges sang *I Want a Hippopotamus for Christmas*, and the winning relay team took the stage to lead everyone in *Purple People Eater*. I shook my head to feel my fresh braids swing against my neck. Lady smiled when she saw me, proud of her work. As the campers left Hippo Hall, Mary Mac and Daisy met them with rocket-shaped popsicles. The sun, water, and excitement drained all the energy out of the kids and, sucking popsicles and dodging bees, they dragged themselves to the cabins.

The minute we got back, the Bernies collapsed on their bunks. Daiquiri and I let them go to sleep without changing into pajamas or brushing their teeth. Outside, on the cabin steps, we sat shoulder to shoulder, listening to the radio. By 8 p.m., the veil of darkness began to fall. Days were getting shorter. Crickets buzzed in the woods and the air smelled of sugar and dirt.

"Your Moon Games, they were fun, Jonika. And some of these children be able to swim when they go home." Daiquiri nudged me. "I don't never remember more than one or two campers doing anything but put their face in the water past years. You aight, Jonika, for a white girl."

I felt really happy. Somehow, being here, out in the sticks, away from home and school and everything that made me who I used to be, turned out okay, even good. But when camp ended in a couple weeks, I had to go back. I missed my brother, my dad, even my mother, but I didn't know if I was ready to face them, let alone a new school.

"You run into your *Manetu* boogeyman lately?" Daiquiri asked.

Her smell, of onions and earth, had imprinted me like the baby ducks we learned about in Biology. I hesitated, not sure what to say. But then, I spit it out.

"I saw it again, one night when I was outside alone. I didn't want to tell you."

Daiquiri gave me a sideways look. "When?"

I choked and looked at the ground.

"After the *Wizard of Oz* I went to meet Jermaine at the basketball court, but I was late and missed him. On the way back in the dark, I saw it again."

"I don't know what you saw or think you saw, but seems to me that *Manetu* thing be warning you to stay away from Jermaine. Today when he talked to you I saw you go all googly eyes. Jonika, we like Jermaine, but we know him. He always got to be the center of attention. Everybody got to love Jermaine. Truth is, we'd like him better didn't he try so hard. Now he been talking big 'bout how he likes white bread. Turquoise don't play like that. She told him, make a choice."

My head jerked back like I'd been slapped. I wanted to crawl under the cabin. *Why would Jermaine say those things?*

"Go on. Don't be gettin' all sorry-eyed. Jermaine a lot of fun, but just 'cause you play in the playground don't mean you special friends."

I let out a long sigh. "The way he talked to me, all flirty and sexy, I thought he liked me. And I know this is dumb, but I thought if someone as cool as Jermaine liked me, you know, really liked me, then I would be cool too. And people here would accept me. But I should have known better. I guess the girls at school were right to call me a loser. Even Ishmael — who was supposed to be my boyfriend — lied to the cops to save himself. He swore all the drugs were mine. He threw me under the bus because I'm a loser."

"White people just mean," Daiquiri said. "You different, Jonika, but you no loser."

We sat in silence for a few minutes until Roland came out from the Andys cabin and sat on the step below us.

"You going up the school cabin to watch the moon walk?"

Daiquiri shook her head. "I'm going to bed. All this moon stuff wore me out."

"If you're not going, do you mind if I do?" I asked her.

"Go on, if Roland go with you," she said. "I don't need no scared white girl coming back to my cabin cause the *Manetu* chasing her."

"I'll come get you in a hour," Roland said. "And I'll bring my *Manetu* stick."

After he jogged off, Daiquiri looked at me. "He like you, you know that, right?"

"Maybe," I said.

"Child, you don't know a good one when you see him."

We watched the moon rise and listened to the low drone of insects. From the Honey Bees' cabin, Turquoise's voice drifted out and Daiquiri swayed and sang along — *Sometimes I feel like a motherless child, a long way from home...* When the last notes vanished in the air, Daiquiri sighed.

"Turquoise sings such sad songs," I said.

"Turquoise be singing the blues," Daiquiri said. "That's how she find peace."

After Daiquiri went inside, I stayed on the step. The drop in temperature cooled my skin. I leaned back on my elbows as I listened to night sounds — a distant howl of a coyote, voices muttering in a nearby cabin, a child's quiet sleep cry, faint music from a transistor radio. Soon, I would leave the woods, the kids, the counselors, Father Vincent, Mary Mac, and Daisy to return to my white, suburban life.

Since the day I first came to camp, I'd begun to feel like a real person — one who helped campers learn to swim and cared about their lives. Maybe I made a difference. I knew they made a difference to me. I never wanted to come here. Now, I never wanted to leave.

"Jonika, you sailing away." Roland tossed a pebble toward me and it hopped across the step. "I been standing here waiting so's we can go on up to see the moon walk."

"Just day-dreaming," I said. "I'm ready."

We started up the path. Roland took long strides and I trotted to keep up. The lights from the basketball court made a halo in the sky, and the sounds of voices and a thumping ball filtered through the trees. From behind us, I heard something moving — rustling, crunching — and my heart raced. I lunged toward Roland, caught my sneaker in a root, and plunged forward. My knee burned and my ankle throbbed, the same crappy ankle I injured on the 4th of July. I cried out in fear and pain.

In a heartbeat, Roland knelt beside me. "Jonika, you okay?" In the dim light, his eyes shone.

From behind us on the path, Lady called, "Jonika, Jonika, wait up."

I took Roland's hand to get up and held onto it. "Lady?" I called to the shadow down the path.

From the darkness she appeared, out of breath and trembling. "Jonika, you hurt?" she gasped.

"I'm okay. Is something wrong? Does Daiquiri know you left?"

"Daiquiri say I can watch the moon walk, iffin I can catch you and Roland."

Lady took my other hand and we walked like this until we reached the school cabin, where the TV's blue glow radiated from the window. When Roland dropped my hand before we went in, I felt like I'd lost something.

Inside, Mary Mac greeted us. Over the sounds of talk and laughter, she pointed to the long table in the back of the room.

"Tastycakes and Milky Ways and Hershey bars are on the table. And for those of us who've had our fill of bug juice, Father generously opened up the pantry and put bottles of Coca Cola on ice." She raised her coke. "To the man on the moon. Cheers."

Chocolate — I'd been craving it all summer. The butterscotch pudding, Jell-O, and cookies we had for dessert were no substitute for the tooth-aching pleasure of chocolate. I stared at the candy bowls, catching my breath and ordering myself to maintain control. When Lady grabbed my hand and pulled me to the table, I let out a loud sigh and stared.

"What, Jonika, you don't like Milky Ways?" she said with a look of concern.

"Oh, I like them, all right. I love them."

I reached into a bowl and took two. Then I grabbed a coke and a pack of chocolate cream-filled cupcakes.

Lady shook her head. "No need to be greedy."

While she picked out an orange soda and a pack butterscotch

cupcakes, my mouth watered in anticipation of the taste of chocolate, caramel, and nougat. Just before I turned to look for Roland, I smelled Juicy Fruit gum. Jermaine leaned over me, his body pressed against mine as he reached for a soda.

"When we getting together, Bonnie?" he whispered. "You want we should go for a midnight swim?"

Before I could squeeze away, Lady tugged on Jermaine's sleeve. "Turquoise just come in, Jermaine. She waitin' for you."

"Oh, right, thanks."

Jermaine stepped around me, studied the table, then grabbed two cokes and two Hershey bars before he strolled across the room to Turquoise. Lady turned to me with a furtive look, her lips pursed and her eyes narrowed. "Roland save a seat for you."

She pointed in his direction, then moved away.

"Wait, Lady, aren't you sitting with us?" I called.

"No mind me. I'mma sit with Daisy," Lady said. "I won't leave without you."

I hardly had time to sit down when Mary Mac said in a loud whisper, "Hush. Neil Armstrong's on the ladder."

The room grew silent and all eyes turned to the hazy image on the TV. Just before 11 p.m., a white, puffy, man-shaped figure descended from the module and placed his foot on the moon. Neil Armstrong's scratchy words reverberated like a prayer — *One small step for man, one giant leap for mankind.* The moment felt holy and joyful. On the screen, shots of people watching from all over the world were interspersed with images of Armstrong bouncing on the moon. Another astronaut, Buzz Aldrin, joined him. As they embedded the American flag in the moon's surface, I felt Roland's hand, warm and confident, on my shoulder. I covered his with my own. I imagined my father, upright in his recliner, leaning forward with tears in his eyes, proud to be an American, and my mother, on the sofa, her legs curled under her, worrying about how the astronauts would return to Earth.

When I scanned the room, I felt honored to witness the moon walk here. Father Vincent's enrapt face looked as if he were having a vision. Mary Mac's eyes roamed from the TV to the handful of campers, checking, I was certain, to make sure they were okay. Daisy, kind and comforting, rested her hand on Lady's arm. I studied Terrell, who stood in the doorway, alone and shy, and a wave of sadness rushed over me. I saw myself in him — an outsider, anxious, craving affection. Except Jermaine gave him something I wished I had — someone who, when Terrell stepped toward him, didn't step away.

Across the room, Jermaine sat with Turquoise. He seemed so self-assured, so strong, a natural leader. Yet Daiquiri said they'd like him better if he didn't try so hard. And as I looked at him, I understood what she meant. He wasn't nearly as self-assured as he seemed. He was just a kid like all of us, trying to find his way. I wondered what it must be like for him back in the city — when he shopped in department stores, white security guards followed him, assuming he planned to pocket every tie he held under his chin. Who protected Jermaine from that?

As I studied them, I understood why Turquoise was the right girlfriend for Jermaine. She was tough and smart enough to see through Jermaine's sweet talk and haul him back to Earth. Turquoise was an incredible singer. I wondered if she'd ever get the chance to share that voice beyond her church choir.

I looked over at Lady, her hands on her knees, her head resting on Daisy's shoulder, an eleven-year-old girl who acted so adult — taking care of Ruby, taking care of me. *She's lonely*, I thought, *she needs her mother.* Soon — in a couple weeks — she would tell Mami about the white girl who tried to teach her to swim. When camp ended, I would miss her. She always knew when I came into a room. She never stepped away. Roland squeezed my shoulder.

"Time to go," he said. "I'll get Lady."

We lurched down the path — me with a cranky ankle, Lady mostly asleep, Roland keeping both of us upright. When we reached the cabin, I spilled Lady onto her cot and came back outside to say goodnight.

"Thank you, Roland," I said. "I'll always remember I watched the man on the moon with you."

He leaned over and kissed me. I closed my eyes and kissed him back. And for that moment, nothing else mattered.

Rain fell almost every day for a week, soaking the paths, covering the pool with wind-blown debris, and splattering the campers and counselors with mud. After a week of being stuck indoors, the campers were fussy and bored. Everyone acted depressed, since all activities — finger-painting, potholder weaving, and sculpting with damp, grey clay — were held in-doors.

Finally, on Thursday, the last day of July, the rain stopped. All my camp clothes reeked of mildew and sodden leaves. I dug through my cubby for dry clothes and found the cutoffs and white T-shirt I'd worn the day I arrived. The Bernies' laundry bags hung heavy on their hooks, muddy stains seeping through the thick cotton.

At breakfast that day, while Roland and other counselors ate with the campers, I played cards and smoked cigarettes behind the laundry room with Turquoise, Daiquiri, Jermaine, Lincoln, and Delia. We stopped when we heard the sound of truck brakes squealing. After the growling diesel motor shut off, we continued to play Crazy Eights.

With most of the summer gone, I worried about life after camp. I wondered if as soon as I returned home and started senior year, I'd go back to being a loser with no friends. I just had no idea what to expect. That freaked me out. The truth is, I was pretty surprised I liked it so much at camp. But even though the counselors and kids accepted me, I wasn't part of their worlds. We might act friendly, but we weren't exactly friends. Not really.

Last week, when Roland kissed me after the moonwalk, Daiquiri watched from the cabin window. The next morning while the girls brushed their teeth, she pulled me aside and said, *Look, Joni, we like you. We call you Jonika. We braid your hair and have fun with you. But that don't make you black. You be a fool, first wearing Jermaine's beret and getting all girly 'round him. Now you kissing Roland. He's a good guy and he likes you, but Roland got to watch his step. He knows that. You need to know that too.*

I nodded then, not really sure what I knew. I believed Daiquiri, but I'd just realized how much I liked Roland. I wanted to be with him.

Judge, maybe you think I'm boy crazy. But finally, being with a guy felt safe and real. He knew who I was and I knew who he was. We were different on the outside but not on the inside. Sometimes I felt like I was on a swing. When it went up, I felt happy, when it went down, I was scared. Lincoln threw a seven of diamonds.

My cigarette ashes spattered on my knee. I brushed them away, ground out my cigarette, and concentrated on the card game. Jermaine dropped a seven of hearts. I drew four cards before I got a match and threw down a five of hearts. Turquoise flicked her last card.

"Crazy Eight," she announced and got to her feet.

"You just about crazy as that eight, ain't you?" Jermaine said. "We got time for one more game before they done eating."

Turquoise put her hands on her hips. "Look who talkin' 'bout crazy."

Jermaine shuffled the cards and began to deal when Daisy came around the corner.

"Father and Mary Mac talking 'bout taking the campers to town for a movie. Boys' cabins need to haul up they laundry bags right now to go to the laundry-mat in town. The Bridges' laundry bags can come to me today. Tomorrow, I take care of the Honey Bees and Bernies' laundry. Gonna take all day today and tomorrow what with all these muddy clothes. Go on, now. Father Vincent's Knights of Columbus just delivered a truckload of shorts, shirts, socks, undies, and sneakers from Sears. Everybody get a new set of clothes," she said. Her yellow house-dress swished around her legs as she walked away.

Behind the parking lot railing, we joined the campers and cheered the Sears delivery man as he loaded a dolly with boxes and hauled them into Hippo Hall. We stayed to watch him back up the truck, turn around, and crunch away down the gravel driveway. In front of Hippo Hall, Father Vincent stood on a log and spread his arms as if in benediction.

"Boys and girls, Mr. O'Connell, the manager at Sears, semt donated clothes and sneakers for everyone so we can dry out and look nice for our trip to town."

Campers elbowed each other and jiggled.

"Mr. Melvin, who owns the movie theater, agreed to open this morning just for us so we can watch *The Love Bug.* After the movie, boys and girls who need haircuts will go with me to Mr. Tony's. We want your parents to recognize you when you return home. Mary Mac and our counselors will take the rest of you to St. Joe's, where you can play in the schoolyard or read in the parish hall until we're ready to return to camp. If everyone remains on their best behavior, we may have a surprise for the trip back."

Mary Mac clapped her hands.

"Hurry now. We're on a schedule. Line up for your new clothes, then scurry back to your cabins to wash up and change. The bus will be here in half an hour."

Ruby waved her hand back and forth, dancing in a jig.

"Father, Father," she called.

"What is it, Ruby?" he asked with an amused smile.

"Father, that movie man give us popcorn? 'Cause I don't like no movie what don't have popcorn."

Popcorn. Popcorn. I want me some of that popcorn — campers chanted.

"Popcorn it is. If you promise not to throw it."

Father turned to the counselors and raised his eyebrows.

All along the path to the cabins, the campers sang — *Popcorn, popcorn, I'mma get me some popcorn.*

After the Bernies pulled on their new clothes and sneakers — the sneakers they got when camp started were now ragged, with holes in the toes — we rushed them to Hippo Hall. Daiquiri and I lined up our girls behind the Andys and Honey Bees to wait for the bus. Lady held Ruby's hand, a good thing, because I envisioned Ruby, so excited she couldn't stand still, running away faster than I could catch her.

The kids looked so happy while they waited, my heart broke. I thought about those city kids who poured out of buses at the seashore and scrambled through the sand, thrilled despite white people's stares. Did the theatre owner offer Father a special showing of *The Love Bug* out of the *goodness of his heart,* as Mary Mac was fond of saying, or was it to make sure the campers didn't bother his other customers? People could be good — donating clothes and money so these kids could be at camp. But people could be cruel — assuming black children and teenagers intended to steal from them or do them harm. No one ever suspected I had stolen from Woolworth's. It just didn't seem right.

While the battered St. Joseph's school bus loaded up with campers, I realized I had a lot on my mind. I figured this might be the only time I'd have to myself before the end of camp and I really needed to sort things out. I approached Father Vincent.

"Father, there's all sorts of junk floating in the pool. The filters are clogged and the chlorine levels are all messed up from the rain. Is it okay if I miss the movie?" I asked, fingers crossed.

Father counted the campers as they went up the bus steps, looking around like he'd forgotten something.

"Jermaine, you're in charge of the boys. Load their laundry in the storage compartment under the bus." Father turned to me. "That's fine, Joan, but no swimming when no one's around, agreed?"

"Agreed, Father. And could I bum a couple smokes?"

Father handed me three Marlboros and fished matches from his shirt pocket.

"Keep them," he said over his shoulder as he swung himself into the bus.

Along the path I put a cigarette between my lips and inhaled even though it wasn't lit. As soon as I reached the pool, I realized the amount of debris floating on the water and sprawled across the deck was much worse than I'd imagined. I had hours of work ahead and I wanted to cry. When I dug in my cutoffs' pocket for the matches, I touched a crinkly wad of paper — one of the joints I'd tucked away the morning Father drove me to camp.

I felt a rush of nerves and looked back at the path to make sure no one happened to be nearby. I rolled the joint through my fingers and held it under my nose. Even though the weed was old and dry, its fragrance was spicy and clean — much nicer than the pool's stagnant smell.

Judge, I'm not sure why I didn't tear open that joint and scatter the marijuana in the woods. But as I held it between my fingers, I told myself it would be wrong to waste it. In a way, finding it felt like a reward for making it through the summer and for the hours of work ahead of me to clean the pool. Besides, camp was basically deserted and I doubted I'd ever get another chance to get stoned. I hid the joint on a shelf in the pump room so it wouldn't get wet while I worked.

After I skimmed and vacuumed the crap out of the pool, backwashed the filter, pumped enough HTH into the water to bleach the kids' bathing suits, and hosed down the deck, I retrieved the skimmer and scooped off the debris, determined to get the work done as fast as possible. I couldn't wait to space out for an hour, be mellow, relax, and not think.

A couple hours later, the pump engine rumbled and fresh water splashed into the pool, raising chlorine vapors so strong they wavered over the clear surface. I'd cleared all the leaves and sticks and dirt from the deck, lined up the chairs, hung the lost and found towels and clothes on the benches to dry, and returned the equipment to the storage shed. I was exhausted but happy. *Now or never,* I thought as I grabbed the joint and shut the pump house door.

I was shaking when I looked up the path to make sure no one was around. Then I hopped the fence behind the pump house and spread a moldy towel behind some bushes. Leaves rustled overhead, and I gazed into the trees where a squirrel skittered from branch to branch. The only other sounds came from buzzing insects and chirping birds.

After I sat on the towel, I studied the joint for a moment. My hands trembled when I put it between my lips, but as soon as I lit it, the sweet smell rose like a forgotten perfume. When I sucked in the stinging smoke and held it in my lungs, my head tipped from side to side. My pent up fear and anxiety blew away with each toke. Leaves looked spectacular in their greenness. I stared, transfixed, as a butterfly lit on a bush. Each flutter of its wings made a brilliant fan. Its little black head and dangling antennae seemed a wonder of intelligence. I lay back and blew smoke rings. I felt like I was in the ocean, floating and bobbing on gentle waves.

I had almost fallen asleep when a screech — steel against concrete — jolted me to full consciousness. Someone was at the gate. I crushed the last ember and buried it, then rolled to my hands and knees, terrified.

"Jonika, where you at?" It was Roland's voice.

Why is he here? What time is it? Had I slept all afternoon? Were the kids back? I wondered if I could hide until he went away.

"Jonika?" he called again.

I shook my head to clear my brain. Paranoia wrecked the pleasant buzz. Roland couldn't know I was high. I forced myself to concentrate, then climbed the fence and walked onto the deck from behind the pump room.

From the shallow end, as soon as Roland saw me, he waved. As I came closer, his expression was confused but happy. I noticed he wore his bathing suit.

He draped his white T-shirt and towel on a chair and called, "What you doing back there?"

"Checking the pumps. I thought you went to the movies," I said. In my head, my voice sounded like an echo.

"Nah, I had to patch a hole in the school cabin roof and unclog the boys' shower drain. Looks like you been working too. Pool ready for swimming?" he asked. "'Cause I'm ready to learn."

God, he looked good — his hair a mess of tight curls, his lips slightly open.

"I don't have my suit," I told him, embarrassed to be at the pool without a swim suit.

"Don't be like that. I been waiting for a day when I don't have a audience. Today is the day."

"Well, if today is the day," I said. I turned and walked along the deck to the diving well, hoping my steps didn't look as crooked as they felt.

"Where we going?" Roland asked from behind.

I didn't answer. Instead, I pulled off my old T-shirt and slipped out of my cutoffs and hung them on the fence. If Roland said anything then, I didn't hear it. In my bra and Tuesday undies, I dove in. The cold water shocked me. For a moment, I didn't know which way was up and started to panic, but finally my hands touched the bottom. I turned myself around, pushed up, and broke the surface, gasping. Blinded by the chlorine and the sun, Roland's figure blurred and wobbled. I took a stroke to the ladder, dipped my face in the water, and shook my head. I felt a little straighter.

"You crazy?" he hollered.

He put his index finger against his head and made circles with it.

"You ready to swim?"

I tried to look cheerful and charming — and laid-back. I mean, bikinis don't cover any more than underwear, right? Then for some reason I remembered it was Thursday. I put my hand over the embroidered Tuesday.

When he climbed into the diving well, Roland's eyes were wide. He'd never been in this deep before. He stayed on the ladder with his shoulders above the surface. I paddled over and tread water while I faced him.

"Ready for your lesson?" I asked, grateful the chlorine would explain my bloodshot eyes.

Roland gave me a sideways look.

"How am I supposed to pay attention when you got no clothes on?"

"Hey, I got some clothes on. But I can run to the cabin to get my suit."

I started to laugh and choked on a mouthful of water. Roland reached out and grabbed my arm, and I thought about the night he kissed me. I wanted to kiss him again but I remembered Daiquiri's words — *Roland got to watch his step.*

"Nah, you fine the way you are," he said. "I'm ready, Nika, teach me."

I led him to the shallow end where I showed him the dead man's float. His feet dragged but his head and arms hovered on the surface, sort of. Then I taught him how to rotate his arms for the freestyle stroke. By the time we moved back to the diving well, my buzz was gone. I reached for my T-shirt.

"No need," Roland said, "even though your skin so white it blind me."

"Maybe you need sunglasses," I said.

I left my shirt on the fence. I guess my buzz wasn't totally gone. From the deck, I watched Roland cross the deep water on a kickboard a few times.

"You ready to put it all together?" I asked.

"I give it a try in the three feet," he said, "where I ain't gonna drown."

"I'll never let you drown."

In the shallow water he pushed off the side, flailed his arms, and kicked his legs. Water splashed four feet in the air. Roland moved six feet forward, dropped his feet, and stood to breathe.

"Sister, I don't know how you do it. You make it look too easy."

"It takes practice, lots of practice. We got a week left. I could give you a lesson an hour before breakfast each day and you could practice when you're here with the kids."

"Aight then," Roland said, "now get out the pool and get you some clothes on, Shorty, before I do something I'll regret."

We climbed out and faced each other, water spilling down our bodies. The low forest buzz sounded like it came from inside my head. Lightheaded and hungry, I felt myself sway into Roland. He wrapped his arms around me and kissed me until my heart beat so fast I could hardly breathe. I pulled away and rested my face on his chest, inhaling his buttery smell. His hands ran along my back and settled on my hips. As he held me close, he took a deep breath. I clung to him and we moved in a silent dance.

"I like you, Shorty. You different — like a mystery. You never still. You always jigglin'. You worry all the time 'bout everything."

As he whispered, Roland moved his hips closer and I felt him swell.

"I worry because I'm a loser," I whispered back. I'd never been so excited.

"That's cold, Jonika. That's not right. I think you're special," Roland said, holding me tight.

"But I'm white." I almost sobbed, remembering Daiquiri's words.

Roland's hands relaxed and he eased back to look down at me.

"You kind of... yep, you white, all right. And I'm black. But that don't matter here. Here, we're free."

"But there's hardly any time left before camp ends. And we just, you know, started to like each other."

I wanted him to kiss me but instead he took a step back, a step away.

"I been liking you a little longer than that." He leaned down and brushed his lips on my forehead. "Don't be worryin' all the time. I got to put away the tools before the kids get back from town. I see you at dinner."

He started to go then turned back to say, "We be all right."

Before I left the pool, I pulled on my shirt and cutoffs and tested the chlorine and PH. I wanted to think about Roland, so I sat on the pool's edge with my feet in the water and lit a Malboro. All this time, instead of worrying about Ishmael or chasing after Jermaine, I could have been with Roland. And now camp was almost over.

As I sat there, I couldn't believe I took off my clothes and swam in my underwear. Even though Roland didn't seem too shocked, now that I could think straight, I felt funny about it. It was silly and reckless. But I'm not silly. And I can't afford to be reckless. I mean, what if Father or Mary Mac or Jermaine came to the pool instead of Roland?

I faced the truth — when I stripped to my undies, I tried to be someone I'm not. When I smoked and drank with Ishmael, I tried to be someone I'm not. It wasn't all that different from my parents trying to make me into someone I'm not. I was done with all that.

And I was done with pot, I decided. The risk, the paranoia, and the guilt that came afterward, none of that was worth the temporary high. No more cancer sticks, either. Cigarettes made my breath sour and my lungs tight. I wanted fresh breath for Roland. I wanted to breathe on my own.

As I dipped the cigarette in the water and flicked it away, I felt like I flicked away a loser too.

By the time I reached the cabin, my clothes were dry. The room smelled musty and moldy from everyone's wet things. I went from bunk to bunk, smoothing covers and thinking about each girl. It was strange, but I missed them and wondered when they'd return.

These girls' lives were so much harder and more complicated than mine, but they didn't waste time feeling sorry for themselves. Instead, they laughed, they played, they struggled and learned. I couldn't think of anyone from home who would be as happy to get new sneakers, see a movie, have a picnic, sing on stage, or spend the summer in the woods where they were free. I wanted to be free. I was sick of trying to fit in and sick of being angry when I didn't. I was sick of feeling sorry for myself.

If these campers could learn to swim, I could learn to be myself.

When they returned from town, the Bernies were giggly and secretive. I worried that somehow they knew about Roland and me, but how could they? The girls clumped together in front of Lady.

"Sit down, Jonika," Joyful said with a happy, knowing look. "We got a surprise for you."

Like the Red Sea parting, the girls stepped back and Lady handed me a sack.

"Father brought us to Gino's. We told Mary Mac, Jonika need a hamburger too."

I choked back tears and, while the girls watched, devoured the best hamburger, fries, and chocolate shake I'd ever had. Later, when the girls turned on the transistor radio and danced to the Supremes' *You Can't Hurry Love*, I joined them. When I imitated their moves, they howled with laughter.

"Jonika dance like a white girl," Keesha snickered.

While Lady demonstrated how to move my hips, shoulders, and chest, I understood how the campers felt watching me glide through the water while they struggled with kickboards. Later, Lady and Raven sang Motown songs while they redid my braids.

After breakfast the next day, Mary Mac handed me two shirts, a pair of shorts, underwear, socks, and new sneakers. Back at the cabin, as soon as I changed into new clothes, I jammed everything but my swimsuit in the laundry bag and, with the girls and Daiquiri, dragged it up to Daisy who waited for us outside the laundry room.

August 1st was Friday — only one full week left. I woke early, slipped into my swimsuit, pulled on a new T-shirt and shorts, and walked through the haze. All I could think about was the early morning swim lesson with Roland. I wanted to see him, hear his voice, feel his touch, treasure every moment together. Ahead of me, I heard a hiss and rattle and stopped short, terrified a big snake lay in wait, coiled and ready to spring.

As I backed away, I stole a look toward the sound, not sure how fast snakes move. Two blazing orbs burned through the wavering mist. The headless *Manetu* floated toward me, and suddenly I realized I had to fight this demon or surrender to it. With a fury that astounded me, I reached down, scooped up a handful of dirt and pebbles, and flung them with all my might. *Go* — I screamed silently — *Leave me, now!*

I know this sounds unbelievable, but as I stood there, time slowed. The pebbles floated toward the red-eyed monster like a rolling thundercloud. When they struck, it was like they splashed into muddy water — with soft plopping sounds and little ripples. Before I closed my eyes, the sun rose behind the *Manetu* in ribbons of red, orange, pink, and yellow. When I opened my eyes, the creature evaporated like steam.

My pulse pounded in my ears and my hands trembled. Part of me wanted to believe this was all a figment of my imagination, a waking nightmare. But I know it was real. My body thrummed like an electric power line.

As the sun became a golden ball, color returned to the leaves and trees and chirping birds. I forced my feet toward the pool. There, the water looked as clean and blue as the sky and as I went about my routine, the vise of fear loosened. I checked the big clock on the storage shed and wondered why Roland was late. I wanted to tell him about the *Manetu*. I wanted to tell him I made it disappear.

After a while, I realized Roland wasn't coming. I tried not to be disappointed. I told myself there were a million reasons why he couldn't get away from the Andys. I took a deep breath and sighed.

Trickles of sweat ran through my hair and down my back. *Another hot day.* I hung my T-shirt and shorts on the fence, climbed on the diving board, measured my approach, and sprang up — lifting high, folding into pike position at the peak and unsnapping to enter the water fully extended, hand-over-hand. Under water, I somersaulted and kicked to the surface, cool and clean and composed. I hopped back on the board.

Each time my body rose, folded, straightened, and slid into water, my mind dared to consider the future — a future without Ishmael. The hours we'd spent imprisoned by lethargy in the small room over his family's garage were as inconceivable to me as his hours of confinement at Graterford. I was relieved I'd never again climb the steps to his room.

At camp, I was busy every day. I had responsibilities. Despite being an outsider, I'd earned acceptance, maybe even respect. Each time I entered the cold water, it felt like baptism — with Jonika the given name.

When I returned home, I decided, I'd work hard at school and make new friends. I'd join the swim team, practice twice a day, and swim so well I'd get a college scholarship. I could do it, I could. In college, I'd major in elementary education and get a job teaching poor city kids. My work would matter. No more wasted time. No more listening to people who called me a loser. Time to be real.

When the breakfast bell clanged, I heaved out of the pool. After I dried off, I pulled my T-shirt over my suit and stepped into my new shorts. When I looked up I saw Roland at the gate, his brown skin absorbing the sun, a worried expression clouding his face. He felt bad, I thought, for standing me up.

"Hey," I said, "I thought you wanted private lessons?"

"Yeah, sorry. Had stuff to deal with," he said. "Father Vincent and Mary Mac sent me to find you. They need to talk to you in the office."

"I hope it won't take long. Can't wait for Cheerios, toast, and bug juice."

My newfound determination silenced any wonder about what Father and Mary Mac wanted. Along the path, I trotted to match Roland's hurried strides. He confused me. Yesterday, he kissed me. Today, he missed our swim date and now walked too fast for conversation.

"Catch you later," Roland said when we reached Hippo Hall. I watched until he disappeared inside.

I entered the small office where Father Vincent leaned against his desk and dragged on a cigarette while Mary Mac stared out the window, her hands on the sill and her shoulders hunched. Father offered me a smoke.

"No thanks," I told him, "I decided to quit."

Father motioned for me to sit on a hard-backed chair and Mary Mac turned from the window. Her expression frightened me. When Father stepped away from his desk, across its top I saw my cutoffs, along with a mutilated pack of matches and the soggy remnants of the second joint.

Right away, I realized my terrible mistake. When I pitched my filthy cutoffs into the laundry bag, I forgot about the other joint stashed deep in a back pocket. Blood drained from my face and I sat trembling, unable to meet their eyes. For what seemed an eternity, no one spoke. The sickening silence was penetrated by the buzz of conversations from Hippo Hall and the sulfury smell of scrambled eggs and burnt toast.

"What do you have to say, Joan?" Father Vincent said, catching his ashes in his palm.

I shrugged and looked down. No words could squeeze through my throat even if I had any.

"Is there anything you can tell us to help us understand what you were thinking, bringing marijuana to camp?" he asked.

I shook my head, willing away my tears and biting my tongue to feel the pain.

"Do you know what this means, Child?" Mary Mac's voice cracked.

I nodded, stood up, and grasped the chair to steady my shaking knees. "I'll pack up," I whispered, my voice strangled and hoarse, a throbbing headache blinding me. "I'm sorry," I managed to gasp.

When I tripped down the cabin steps, I felt Mary Mac's hand on my elbow.

"You were doing so well," she said. "And only a week to go."

In the cabin, as I tucked my few things in my swim bag, two red embers smoldered in my brain. Not an hour ago, when Roland came for me, he already knew what I'd done. Now, everyone must know — *Joni the criminal, the pothead who couldn't keep off the dope.* Instead of Montgomery High, swim team, and college, I'd go to juvie. I'd have a record. I'd never be a teacher. My parents would hate me and probably disown me, whatever that meant. I sat rooted to my cot.

My eyes roamed from bunk to bunk and I thought about each Bernie girl. They would return to school with tales of their counselor, Jonika, the white girl who smoked weed, got busted, and was kicked out of camp.

As I sat and sobbed, I heard steps on the wooden floor. It was Daiquiri. I hated for her to see me cry. I wiped my eyes on my shirtsleeve and waited for a blast of scorn.

"They wondering what's taking so long," she said in a soft voice.

"I'm ready," I managed to croak.

"You stupid, Jonika. Why you have to be that way, smoking dope?" she asked, her face screwed up in confusion and anger.

I know my face was all red and blotchy. I took a breath.

"I know there's no excuse. In June when Father Vincent picked me up for camp, on the way out the door I shoved two joints in my cutoffs pockets. It was stupid for sure, but I didn't want my mother to find them. I should have flushed them down the toilet. Then yesterday, when I wore my cutoffs, I discovered them. Since no one was around, I thought, why not? And I smoked one, I did. But Daiquiri, that's when I finally realized all pot ever brought me was trouble and I decided to be done with it for good. I totally forgot about the other joint. I guess it serves me right."

God, I sounded lame and self-serving, the little druggy who swore she'd never use again.

"For real?" Daiquiri asked.

"For real," I answered, "but it doesn't matter. It's too late — I blew it. Tell the girls they made me proud, even though I let them down. They worked so hard to learn to swim."

"I'll tell them."

I kept my head down. I couldn't meet her eyes.

"You best wash your face, get yourself together, and face the music. I'll see you up there," she said as she walked away.

It took another ten minutes to stop crying. With my swim bag over my shoulder, I headed back to face Father and Mary Mac. With each step, waves of exhaustion flowed through me. The scent of pine trees made me gag. When I came out from the trees near the basketball court, the counselors waited in rows along both sides of the path to Hippo Hall. With a sick feeling, I visualized myself running the gauntlet as punishment for my pathetic mistake.

I readied myself to take the anticipated punches and jeers I knew I deserved. With a deep breath, I tightened my stomach and lowered my head as I entered the path where Daiquiri and Turquoise waited like sentries guarding a bridge. From the corner of my eye, I saw Turquoise raise her fist, but instead of a blow, she clasped my shoulder while Daiquiri patted my back.

"You be all right, Jonika," Daiquiri said.

As I moved forward, I turned my head to acknowledge each counselor who whispered something kind and shared a gentle touch. At the end of the line, Jermaine stood across from Roland.

"You be aight, Bonnie," Jermaine said, smiling.

Across from him, Roland nodded. "I be waitin' for you."

Mary Mac took my arm and led me to the office where, I supposed, a police officer waited to haul me away. Instead, inside I faced only Father Vincent and Mary Mac. As soon as the door shut, I raised my head and looked Father in the eyes.

"Father, I want you to know I appreciate all you've done for me and I'm sorry for betraying your trust. The morning you picked me up, I stuffed two joints in my pockets. I forgot about them until the other day when I wore my old shorts. The truth is, once I found them, all I could think about was smoking them. But after I smoked one, I felt ashamed and made up my mind I was done with pot forever. I know it's too late now. This has been the best summer of my life and I wrecked it. But the worst thing is, I let everyone down. I hope someday you'll forgive me."

I sank into the chair then, nauseated and wiped out. As I worked to control my breathing, I wanted to remember every last moment at camp. I treasured the smell of the old wood cabin, Father's cigarette smoke, Mary Mac's lavender soap, and the woodsy fresh air — smells I would soon exchange for the pickled fragrance of sweaty teen girls and the reek of pissy concrete floors.

Father took his seat behind his desk and cleared his throat. He looked at Mary Mac before he spoke.

"After you went to pack your things, I had a few visitors. Your friend Roland took it upon himself to advise the other counselors of your impending expulsion. They banded together and stormed the fortress, as it were. Each of them made a plea on your behalf — *Jonika's the best swim teacher ever, Jonika saved Antoine from drowning, Jonika went into the fire and got burned to save Ruby, the Bernies love Jonika, Lady will be crushed if you kick her out, Jonika's never afraid of work, always willing to help.* It went on and on. I didn't realize you made such an impact, though of course, I should have."

My eyes settled on a black fly trying to escape the cabin. Time and again it bumped the window screen, buzzing and thumping. I knew how it felt, with an almost invisible barrier between freedom and confinement. I forced myself to listen.

"After hearing from the counselors, I turned to my breviary and let it open as it might. There, I read from the letter of Paul to the Galatians — *Brothers, if a man or woman has been overtaken by any offense, you who are spiritual should instruct someone like this with a spirit of leniency.* I believe the good Lord made the breviary fall open to that specific page to guide me. Mary Mac flushed the remnants of your marijuana cigarette down the toilet. You haven't any more contraband, I pray?"

Father took a deep drag on his cigarette, thoughtfully watching the smoke rise and disappear.

"No, Father," I said in a low voice.

"Then go on with you. You have one week to complete your court-ordered service and wipe your slate clean. Don't take this lightly, Joan," Father said.

He raised his eyebrow and offered me a cigarette. I shook my head.

"Thanks, Father. Thank you, Sister Mary Immaculata. I'll never let you down again."

As the sun burned through the morning mist, sunbeams speckled the path to the pool. High in an oak tree, a redheaded woodpecker punctuated its jackhammer, drumming with screeches and churs. From their morning activities, campers' voices flowed and ebbed like a tide going out, fading as I moved farther from camp's center. *How could I have been so dumb? How could I be so lucky?*

My knees shook, and when the antiseptic smell of the pool's chlorine reached me, my stomach lurched and I vomited all over the trunk of a hemlock, the taste foul in my mouth. My stupid decision to smoke that joint nearly ruined everything. My redemption came at the hands of my friends.

Everything confused me — the good stuff as much as the bad. With camp ending in a week, I worried about losing my summer friendships, especially Daiquiri and Roland. What would I do without them? Miles, neighborhoods, and color separated our winter lives.

I crossed through the pool gate into the work I knew — skim, vacuum, backwash, test, teach, swim. After I rinsed my mouth, I felt hungry and faint. I hadn't eaten since yesterday. For now, I gulped water from the spigot and calculated the hours until lunch. Fifteen minutes later, the Bernies swarmed onto the deck. My throbbing headache evaporated and I felt better just to be with these terrific kids.

"Daiquiri say Father Vincent want to fire you," Joyful said, grabbing my hands.

"We thought you going home," Raven said, "thaz no good, unh uh."

"I'm lucky to be here," I said, "and I'm especially lucky to be with the Bernies and Daiquiri."

Lady, smoky eyes glistening and lips pulled tight, glared at me.

"What, Lady?" I asked, anxious and curious.

"I tole Father you can't leave cause you supposed to teach us to swim," Lady stated in her most adult voice.

"We still have a week," I said. "Jump in the water, Bernies."

Before the last Sunday Mass, I pulled shorts and a T-shirt over my swimsuit and trotted along the path to the pool. A light rain sprinkled the leaves, and clouds kept the temperature cool. Whenever I bombarded Daiquiri with plans to get together after summer, she'd shake her head, stick out her lower lip, and say, *Sure, Jonika, 'cause we got so much in common outside camp.* I knew Daiquiri was right as always, but I couldn't imagine my days without her.

By now most of the campers could swim across the pool — some doing doggy paddle, others sidestroke, a few managing freestyle with pauses to breathe. But three Bernies struggled with fear and bashfulness, preferring to avoid failing to swim by refusing to. I tried to think up last-ditch lessons but my mind was preoccupied with concern about returning home. I sneezed a snot rocket into the bushes and wiped my nose with my sleeve. I almost had a heart attack when I went through the pool gate.

"About time you show up for our lesson," Roland said, bare-chested in blue trunks, a towel draped around his neck.

His tight curls glistened. I hoped he didn't see my sneeze — gross — but God, I was happy and surprised to see him.

After everything that happened, I never got a chance to talk to Roland alone. I pretty much assumed I destroyed whatever we had. But here he was, nice as ever. When he smiled, I broke down.

Between sobs, I sputtered, "I'm sorry. I'm so stupid."

Roland wrapped his arms around me and I felt him laughing. He pushed back and smiled.

"You best be sorry 'bout forgetting my lesson. You got your suit on today, right?"

I wanted to capture his smile, to save it forever in my heart. I stepped out of my shorts and pulled my shirt over my head, careful to avoid my snotty sleeve.

"Got my suit on."

As if nothing had happened, we worked on floating in the shallow area and then in the diving well. I showed Roland how to drown-proof by sinking under, then kicking up to take a breath.

When the bell rang for Mass, Roland dried off and shook water from his hair. His eyes were soft as he looked into mine.

"I thought you was a goner when Daisy found that weed in your laundry."

"Me too." I sighed and scratched my arm. "I don't know what I was thinking. But it won't happen again, ever. Thanks for talking Father Vincent out of busting me."

"We all talked to Father," Roland said. "Not just me. You worth it."

Roland looked up the path before he leaned down and kissed me. His hands caressed my back and dropped to my hips. He pulled me close until we were breathless and excited. I wanted to find a hidden place where we could take time to explore each other. When he let me go, I felt flushed and disappointed.

"We got to go, they expecting us," he said, breathing heavily. "Catch you later? Tonight after lights out? Here?"

I nodded, my lips warm and tingling. Did I dare meet him? Other counselors snuck out almost every night to be with each other, but other counselors didn't get caught with a joint in their jeans, other counselors weren't trying to avoid juvie, other counselors hadn't faced the *Manetu*, other counselors weren't white. I dressed and jogged up the path to Hippo Hall for Mass, followed by pancakes for breakfast.

By the time the Bernies and Andys showed up for their lessons that afternoon, I'd thought of a way to motivate the reluctant swimmers. "Friday's the last full day of camp," I explained while they lined up. "Father Vincent agreed we can hold a swim test that day. Campers who swim the length of the pool without stopping get to pour bug juice on me. We'll call it Jonika Juice."

Oh, I'mma get you good. I splash red bug juice all over you head— the kids laughed and bragged about how they would douse me with the sweet, sticky stuff.

During our lesson, all the campers except Lady, even the ones who hadn't before, floated face down, lifted their feet, and slapped the water with their arms. Most would make it across, I believed.

That evening, as Daiquiri and I got the Bernies to bed, I asked Lady to come outside to talk. Her pajama top fit snug across her chest. She had grown this summer, her body stretching to match the adult in her face.

"You're going home real soon," I said, "and you haven't tried to swim. Tell me why."

"I'm scairt," Lady said. "Mami tole me I had a brother what drown when he fell off a raft in Haiti, afore I was born. Mami can't deal with another dead child."

I rested my hands on Lady's shoulders and looked in her eyes. She was almost as tall as me and sometimes the way she acted — so thoughtful and refined — made it hard to remember she was an eleven-year-old girl.

"I'm sorry about your brother, but I'm glad you told me. Lady, I've watched you in the pool, and I think you're ready to swim. But you need to be ready too. And when you are, I'll be right there with you, just like you've been right there for Ruby," I said. "I'll never make you swim if you don't want to, but your Mami might feel better if she knew her Lady could swim."

"I don't want to splash bug juice on you, Jonika," Lady said, her eyes wide and sad.

When she said that, I couldn't help laughing. I hugged her, kissed her forehead, and followed her inside.

Later, as I lay on my cot waiting for lights out, every nerve in my body tingled. When the bell gonged, I jerked like I'd been stung by a bee, unsure about sneaking out. *What if Roland didn't show? What if the red-eyed demon waited for me on the path?* I fumbled for my flashlight and tiptoed toward the door. Daiquiri sat up, her dark face silhouetted in the moon's glow.

"For real?" she said. "For real, you going out?"

"Just to say goodbye. I won't be long. I'll be back in an hour, maybe less," I whispered.

One of the girls stirred and sat up. "What, what?"

"Nothing," Daiquiri said. "It ain't nothing. Go back to sleep."

Along the path to the pool, I aimed the flashlight down, praying no one would see the light. Buzzing and chirping hummed through the trees like electric current. I stopped and decided to turn around, but then the memory of Roland's eyes, his smile, urged me on. My thoughts flipped back and forth like pinballs. Off to the left, wings flapped and an owl hooted. You're more than halfway there, I told myself. Once I smelled the chlorine, I felt safe. When I pushed it, the pool gate crunched over the concrete deck.

I called, "Roland? You here?"

A red orb like a single eye cast a dull glow across the deck and, with my hands shaking, I aimed my flashlight at it. A figure floated toward me and captured me in a one-armed embrace. I breathed Roland's woody smell. The burning punk stick he held in his other hand glowed red. I laughed and swatted him in the chest.

"You scared me,"

"I was scared you wouldn't come."

Behind the pump house, Roland led me to a blanket he'd spread there. I leaned against him to feel his warmth.

"Why did you wait until the end of camp to kiss me?"

"Shorty, you know black boys been hung for messing with white girls, right?"

"But I'm not like other white girls," I said. "I'm Jonika."

We held each other, touching and kissing, our hearts pounding against each other's chest.

When he whispered, "If you want me, I got protection," I pulled him close, nervous but longing to be part of this gentle, loving human being.

I felt as if tonight were my first time, as if whatever happened before wasn't real. Afterward, we held hands in silence and gazed into the sky where Orion brandished his club, the three stars of his belt burning bright.

I broke the silence to ask quietly, "How will I see you after we go home?"

Roland leaned on his elbow and kissed my nose.

"This what we have, Shorty. Right here, right now. No way your parents open the door for a black boy. To tell the truth, my mamma'd clock my head fore she let me go out with a white girl. That's just the way it is."

Before I had a chance to say anything, Roland got to his feet, ran across the deck, and jumped in the pool. I sat on the blanket, unwilling to believe him. We could meet downtown at Wanamaker's or the Art Museum. There had to be a way. Now that I finally found a truly good guy who liked me for myself, I couldn't just let him go.

"Come on in, Jonika. You can tell Daiquiri you took a midnight swim,"

Roland called, his voice distant but strong.

I saw his image shimmering above the dark surface of the pool, and I
leapt in to join him.

After we dried off, Roland draped a leather cord over my head. A
metal disc the size of a half-dollar rested against my skin like a kiss. In the
moonlight, I raised the disc to study it. On one side, Roland had etched the
image of the moon, on the other, the sun.

"To remember me," he said.

With Roland's hand in mine, we walked along the path to the cabins. I
knew I had changed. Because even though I cried, I was happy.

Friday, the last full day of camp, the sun rose in a cloudless sky. Heat
rippled through the air and everyone's clothes stuck to their sweaty bodies.
After breakfast, Mary Mac dragged a wagon filled with gallons of bug
juice to the pool. The swim-suited campers followed in procession.

I sat at the far end of the pool, wearing a white T-shirt and grey cotton
sweatpants over my suit. Daiquiri sat nearby with her feet in the water,
ready to hand cups of bug juice to swimmers who made it all the way. The
other counselors lined up the kids and walked along the deck shouting
encouragement as each camper took a turn.

Michael, who'd turned fourteen at camp, was first. He hopped in the
pool, pushed off the wall, and splashed madly as he paddled his way to
the end. When he climbed out, water sparkled in his hair. He shook it on
me, took a cup of red bug juice, made the sign of the cross over my head,
and dripped the juice into my hair until it ran in rivers down my face and
stained my shirt like blood. After Michael crushed the cup and took a bow,
the campers clapped and hollered. One after the other, campers entered
the water and swam toward my end. Even though twelve or more campers
dropped their feet once or twice or even more times, Mary Mac declared
their consolation prizes were to splash me with half-cups. Only Lady
refused to swim.

Antoine and Ruby waited at the end of the line to go together. They
held hands to jump into the pool, counted — *one... two... three* — and
pushed off the wall. Everyone, including me, stood to watch these two
little kids struggle through the water. When Ruby sputtered with water
in her nose, Antoine floated until Ruby caught up. They kicked their legs
and flailed their arms for almost a minute to cross twenty-five meters in a
triumph of determination more brilliant than an Olympic victory. When

they touched the edge, Antoine's hand a second ahead of Ruby's, a cheer erupted louder than the loudest clap of thunder.

In the pool, the little boy and girl turned their heads from side-to-side, water streaming down their faces, both with wide grins and squinty eyes. Roland pulled out Ruby, and Jermaine lifted Antoine from the water. When Jermaine raised their hands like winners in a prizefight, another round of stomping and cheering erupted. Then Roland put Ruby on his shoulders while Antoine rode on Jermaine's, and they took a victory lap around the deck.

I heard Daiquiri's voice rise above the din. First Turquoise joined in and then the others, clapping and swaying as they sang *Stand By Me*. I was surprised when Daisy took my hand and held it. Lady crossed the deck and took my other hand and together we stood in the sun. When the last notes drifted into the woods, a hush fell over the pool area, the most silence I'd experienced since I stepped out of Father's car and first entered Camp St. Augustine of Hippo. It lasted about a second until Ruby called out from Roland's shoulders, "Antoine and me swimmed the whole pool!"

Daisy dropped my hand and smiled at Lady.

"Go on and play, Child."

Together, we watched Lady take Ruby from Roland's shoulders. After a moment, Daisy took my hand again and squeezed it.

"Jonika, you know I didn't take no pleasure from giving Father that reefer. But I had to do right."

"Maybe this sounds weird, but I'm glad you did," I said. "I can't believe Father let me stay."

"You done a bunch of good, Jonika. That make up for the bad."

Daisy's skin was soft but her grip was firm. I held on.

"I learned a lot from you this summer, Daisy. Will you be back next year?" I asked as the counselors began to round up their campers.

"I been coming here with Sister Mary Immaculata for eight — nine year. I be back if she be back. Been working for the nuns most my life," Daisy told me. "You coming back? You the only one ever teach these childrens to swim."

"I hope so," I said, although the thought hadn't crossed my mind.

"You be all right, Jonika." Daisy squeezed my hand again.

The counselors' voices were drowned in the kids' laughter and shouting. They gathered their campers to line them up for the walk back to the cabins. None of the kids wanted to leave the pool. None of us wanted our Camp Hippo summer to end. As Roland followed the Andys through the gate, he turned and waved.

Red, green, and blue bug juice stained my T-shirt and gummed up my hair, and my sweatpants looked tie-dyed from the sugary goo. I ran to the diving well and flipped into the pool, where the heavy sweatpants slipped off my hips and drifted toward the bottom. After a minute, I dove down, retrieved the sweats, and slapped them on the deck. The Bernies waited with Daiquiri inside the gate. I flung my hair back, pulled myself out and trotted to my girls.

"Lady wants to help clean up," Daiquiri said. "That okay?"

Lady, her wide eyes solemn, looked at me with hope. I thought her hands shook.

"Thank goodness," I said. "I wished someone would help with this mess. Daiquiri, I'll remember the way you sang *Stand by Me* the rest of my life."

"See if you can't get me a audition with Berry Gordy," she called over her shoulder. "Come on, Bernies, we got to get you changed for wiffle ball."

With my arm around her shoulder, Lady and I watched the Bernies disappear on the path, the song *R-E-S-P-E-C-T* bouncing through the trees.

As I unrolled the hose and began to wash down the deck, Lady unwrapped her towel and walked to the pool's edge in her turquoise bathing suit. Without stopping, she hopped in and made sure I was watching. And then, swear to God, she ducked right under water and pushed off. With long pulls and flutter kicks strong enough to keep her feet from dragging, she glided for three or four strokes, changed to a doggy paddle to breathe, then straightened and swam without another breath until she reached the far end. After she touched the wall she got to her feet, panting, water streaming down her face. I leapt in and threw my arms around her shoulders.

"You did it! You did it. You were great. I knew you could swim, Lady," I said. "Why didn't you go with the rest of the kids?"

"I didn't want to pour bug juice on you."

"But when did you learn to swim like that?"

"Every night I practice in my mind what you show us. Today I knew I was ready." Lady took my hand then and asked, "Why you crying, Jonika?" The next day after breakfast, the campers squirmed while they waited on the grassy area near the parking lot. Mary Mac bustled from group to group, checking bags and cleaning jelly-smeared faces with a wet washrag.

Soon, two ancient school buses — their engines spewing dark exhaust clouds — bumped up the gravel driveway and heaved to a stop in the parking lot. Father Vincent climbed the steps to Hippo Hall and clapped his hands.

"Let us end camp with a prayer of thanks to the glory of God — *Our Father, who art in heaven...*"

On either side, Ruby and Lady held my hands. Their voices, Lady's solemn and measured, Ruby's squeaky and excited, joined mine — *...now and forever, Amen.* Father raised his right hand in the sign of the cross and all of us blessed ourselves. I walked Lady and Ruby to the bus lines and felt my heart break. Down on one knee, I put my hands on Ruby's arms and tried to memorize everything about the little girl. Her eyes shone bright behind her nice glasses.

"I'm gonna miss you, Ruby," I said. "You sure did learn to swim."

"I know that, Jonika. I'mma miss you too." Ruby put out her palms and shrugged. "You ain't a cracker, for real."

I rested my face on her head when she hugged me, shaking with laughter and tears.

I turned to Lady, who now stood eye-to-eye with me, and took her hands.

My voice cracked when I told her, "Lady, you helped me more than anyone this summer. In a couple years, you're gonna make a great camp counselor. I know your Mami can't wait to have you back today."

Lady smiled. "I always knowed you was nice, Jonika, no matter what everyone said."

"I don't know what I'll do without you." I pulled her close. "Take care of Ruby on the bus, okay?"

To keep from crying, I took a few deep breaths before I helped Daiquiri get the other Bernies in the right lines. With each goodbye, it became harder to breathe, like wind was knocked out of me.

Beyond the trees, tires crunched across the gravel driveway, coming closer. A red Ford entered the parking area and scraped to a halt. While the campers stared, a white man in dress trousers, a white shirt, and dark tie opened the passenger door for a white woman in a yellow shirtwaist dress. After all the Bernies were lined-up, I followed Father Vincent and Mary Mac to greet my parents. As I walked, my braids swayed.

"Joni, look at you, all tan and healthy," my mother said, a smear of lipstick coating a front tooth. "What happened to your hair?"

In place of a hug, my mother plucked a braid, squeezed it between her thumb and finger, and let it drop. She smelled like Aqua Net.

My father cleared his throat. He patted his shirt pocket and took out his cigarettes.

"Well, Joni, Father Vincent tells us you've done a good job this summer," he said.

From the line entering the bus, Antoine's shrill voice rang out, "Who those white people talking to Jonika?"

I heard Lady's teacher voice — "They her parents."

"Why they white?" Antoine asked.

"Cause Jonika white. You don't know that?" Lady answered.

"I guess she used to be white," Antoine said.

My parents looked startled.

"Jonika, Jonika, bye, bye, bye, bye, bye, bye, bye," Ruby yelled from the bus bi-fold doors.

"Who is Jonika?" my mother asked.

I studied my feet, embarrassed, but Mary Mac answered, "It's the campers' nickname for Joni, all in fun."

"Well, you're Joni to us," my mother said.

Her head went back and forth as she looked from one group of campers to another. My father loosened his tie and tugged on his collar. He opened the car door for my mother and walked to the driver's side.

"Ready, Joni? You must be dying to get out of here," he said.

"Not yet," I called over my shoulder. *I'm dying because I have to leave here,* I was thinking as I ran over to join the counselors who waited for the kids to fill the buses.

"I'll call or write," I promised Daiquiri, her address and phone number magic-markered on the back of my camp T-shirt. "We'll meet downtown, have lunch or something."

"We'll wait and see. You weren't the worst counselor I ever shared a cabin with," Daiquiri told me. "Maybe we do it again some time."

I smiled thinking of it, wanting it to be true. I said goodbye to each counselor. When I reached Turquoise, she opened her arms and hugged me tight, her smell like coffee, sweet with cream and sugar. I hugged her back, my cheek against her neck.

"I guess I was wrong about you, Jonika. You different," she said.

She laughed when I used my best Turquoise voice to tell her, "It weren't no thing."

Jermaine waited beside her. He smiled when I turned to him.

"Yo, Bonnie, you goin' back to your life of crime?"

"Nah, I'm thinking 'bout playing b-ball for the Sixers, now I been taught the moves and grooves."

"I'mma buy tickets for that game," Jermaine said. "Don't be doubting yoself, Nika. You been keeping your head down, hiding out, but you a sleeper. Time to wake up and walk tall. We all seen what you can do. Now go on home and let those white people see it too."

"Thanks, Jermaine. You're the Wizard," I said, smelling his Juicy Fruit breath.

Roland smiled when I approached, but when I reached to hug him, he stepped back and glanced toward my parents.

"This ain't no *Guess Who's Coming to Dinner,* Jonika. You and your folks got enough going on without putting me in it. We know how we feel, we know what we got, and we know how it's got to be." His eyes settled on the pendant around my neck. "Still, every time I look at the moon, I be thinking 'bout you. You special for always."

"Oh, Roland, I'll miss you." I took a breath and held back tears.

"You be all right, Jonika. We be aight." He covered my hands with his for a moment, then let go. "I won't forget."

"Neither will I," I swore.

The bus motors gunned and stuttered. I watched Roland follow the other counselors onto the buses until no one was left but me. As they drove away, kids pressed their faces against the glass and waved. When the second bus passed, Lady leaned out a window and gestured, anxiously, pointing to my parents and shaking her braids. I knew she wanted my parents to like the braids she'd worked so hard on. So I smiled, gave her thumbs up, and threw her a kiss. As the bus pulled away, Lady's image blurred and vanished in the sunlight's glare.

My father held his arm out the window and tapped the Ford's roof while I said goodbye and thanked Daisy, Mary Mac, and Father Vincent one last time. When I jumped into the back seat, Dad swung the car around and sped down the gravel driveway. As we followed the last bus, its taillights glowed like red eyes. But I no longer cared.

Once the Ford turned onto the highway, my father, his eyes straight ahead, his hands stiff on the wheel, said, "Joni, there's something we need to tell you. There's no easy way to say it."

"What?" I asked, convinced from his serious tone that Father Vincent ratted me out after all and I was on my way to juvie.

My mother hunched her shoulders and sighed. Dad took a deep breath.

"It's Michael Reid, Joni. He's dead. Two weeks ago he hung himself in his cell at Graterford. We thought it best to wait until we could tell you in person."

My heart stopped. *Michael Reid was dead.* My father's words echoed in my brain — *dead, dead, dead, dead* — growing fainter until they faded away. His death was incomprehensible and nauseating, but I felt detached and distant. Ishmael, I realized, had died to me that January day we got arrested, and now this death belonged in another dimension, another time, another life — Joni's life — like a movie I'd watched long ago and hardly remembered.

I pressed Roland's pendant to my chest. *Ishmael was dead. Joni was dead. I was Jonika.* My parents accepted my silence for grief. I felt only numb. No one spoke during the hour ride home.

When I entered our house, Tommy came from the kitchen and stopped short when he saw me. He was inches taller and his hair was sun-bleached, but he had the same sweaty boy-smell.

"Joni," he said.

His hug was tentative, like from a cousin I'd only met once.

"You're tall," I said.

"You're dark," he replied.

My bedroom looked sterile and smelled like lemon furniture polish and Lysol. While I was at camp, my mother had touched, organized, and sanitized everything I owned, obliterating the Joni Byrnes who'd lived here. Vacuum cleaner tracks lined the rug. A new blue quilt covered the bed and crisp cotton cases covered two pillows. The dragon lighter, glinting in the sunlight, rested on the nightstand next to a crystal ashtray. When I opened the drawer, the red silk coin purse slid across the smooth bottom. As bad as it was to bring those joints to camp, it was better than leaving them here for my mother to find.

My dresser drawers held Joni's clothes — neatly folded underwear, pajamas, cotton T-shirts, Bermuda shorts, and khaki slacks. My closet had been arranged so that my sweatshirts hung to the right of my sweaters, followed by dresses, then skirts, then blouses. On the closet floor, matched right and left, were bone-colored dress shoes next to saddle shoes, stiff from polish. The stolen Woolworth sneakers, bleached white and shrunken into a cup shape, sat beside the saddle shoes. My records were stacked in one cardboard box and my books and school stuff in another. I flopped on the bed and shut my eyes. When Tommy shook my shoulder to wake me, I had no idea where I was.

"Dinner, Joni. Mom made stewed chicken, special for you," he announced. His voice was different, deeper and more matter-of-fact.

The smell of chicken, onions, and potatoes rose up the stairs and made my mouth water.

"I'll be down in a minute," I croaked.

After I washed up and brushed my teeth, I returned to my room and looked out the window. The grass in Jake and Lisa's yard needed cutting. Their house was dark and sad and lonely. In the backyard, the baby swing moved back and forth with the breeze.

"Joni, dinner's ready," my father called.

I hopped down the steps, not knowing what to expect. I felt like a visitor, but when I took my old seat, my parents smiled. It was like everyone decided to be extra polite and that was okay with me.

"That's enough," I said as my mother filled my plate.

"You look like you lost ten pounds and you didn't have them to lose," Mom said. "I guess you didn't much like the food."

"The food was good. I tried lots of different stuff. I especially liked the collard greens and cornbread."

Mom raised her eyebrows. "Collard greens? Are you sure it wasn't spinach?"

"It was collard greens. Maybe you could make them one night?"

"I'm not even sure where to buy them," she said, "but if that's what you want, I guess I could try."

Dad frowned like he wanted to say something, but his mouth was full from a bite of a roll.

"Thanks for that box you sent," I added. "I really needed all that stuff. And we listened to the transistor radio in the cabin every night. That was great you thought to send batteries too."

Mom's face relaxed into a smile and she let out a breath. I waited for someone to say grace like at camp, but my father and Tommy leaned over their plates and shoved in the chicken. I raised my fork but hesitated.

"Don't you like it?" Mom asked.

She hadn't started eating yet, waiting for me, I guess. I took a bite, then another. The chicken, soft from stewing, melted in my mouth. Little chunks of potatoes and dots of green peas in creamy gravy left a starchy, satisfying taste in my mouth and felt warm in my stomach.

"I like it a lot. It's really good. Even better than collard greens."

My mother's eyes filled with tears. I dipped a roll in the gravy and kept my eyes on my plate.

Early the next morning, when Mom called from the living room that they were leaving for church in half an hour, I groaned, "Sorry, really bad cramps. Don't wait for me."

I pulled the sheet over my head and willed my family to go away. I fell back to sleep until early afternoon, when my door creaked open and Tommy shouted downstairs to my parents, "Do you want me to wake her?"

"What time is it?" I asked as Tommy stepped into my room.

"Like, two o'clock. Sheesh, Joni, you sick?"

"Just tired. I'm getting up now." My stomach growled. "Did you eat lunch yet?"

I dug through my drawers for clothes. Each movement required effort, as if leaving camp and returning home increased the Earth's gravitational pull on my body. The neatly folded cotton shorts and sleeveless tops in my drawers may as well have been baby clothes. The girl who wore them a year ago had moved away. I couldn't bring myself to put them on.

"Tommy," I called, "you got a T-shirt I can borrow? Just for today until Mom washes my camp stuff?"

I pulled my camp shorts off the floor and stepped into them. Tommy tossed me an orange shirt with *The Endless Summer* printed over the image of a guy balancing a surfboard on his head, walking toward two other surfers. When I slipped it on, I felt right again.

In the kitchen, Mom handed me a plate with a Lebanon baloney sandwich on rye, corn chips, and a pickle — my favorite lunch when I was eleven. When I bit into the chewy bread, tasting mayonnaise and mustard with the spicy baloney, I felt sad to think how she must have planned to have my favorite foods ready for me when I came home. She rubbed her hands together and straightened her apron. Her eyes were wary. God, she looked afraid, like she expected me to flip her the finger or something.

"This is great, thanks," I told her. "I can't believe you remembered. It's nice to be home."

Mom's smile made me even sadder. A shiver ran through me. *She has feelings,* I thought, *and I'd hurt them.*

"I have Wednesday afternoon off from Tesses. I thought we could go shopping for your school clothes." Mom's voice was hesitant. "I ran into Sally Fanelli at church and she reminded me public school is a whole new thing for us — no more uniforms. We could go to the mall if you want."

"Yeah," I answered with enthusiasm I knew she hadn't heard from me in a long time. "I went through my drawers and nothing really fits. Did Mrs. Fanelli say anything else?"

"She heard from Father Vincent how well you did at camp. Father promised to write a letter to the Hearing Officer to report on your summer. Sally seemed pleased. Put your dishes in the sink if you're done."

I let out an anxious sigh.

In the living room, my father stared at the TV with an angry look and shook his head. Cigarette smoke curled from the ashtray. He rested a glass of iced tea on his gut. I hadn't watched TV all summer, except for the launch and moon walk.

"What the hell is wrong with people? It's disgusting," he said, shaking his head. "Slashing and murdering those people and that actress, Sharon Tate — she was in that movie your mother liked, *Valley of the Dolls.*"

"What happened?" I asked, covering my eyes at the gory details. The taste of mustard lingered on my tongue.

"They don't know who did it or why. Turn it off, Joni. I can't watch any more of this. I'm going out to the back porch to listen to the Phillies game on the radio. You want to come?"

"Sure," I agreed.

The whole summer, except when we found out Judy Garland died, I never thought about all the bad stuff that happened every day. But as soon as Dad's car pulled away from camp, I learned Michael Reid was dead. Now, those people in California were murdered. Being at camp was like being in another world. I wondered if Roland heard the news. I thought about Lady and wished I'd asked Mary Mac about her grandmother in Haiti. I wondered if Lady might move there with her Mami. At least now she could swim.

It was nice sitting on the back porch listening to the Phillies get beaten in Cincinnati. Even my father's comments — *For crying out loud,* or *For God's sake, catch the ball!* — made me feel like I belonged here, like I was part of this place. Tree branches swayed in the breeze with the smell of onion grass in the air.

"Where are Jake and Lisa?" I asked as I stared at their yard.

"I thought you knew they moved to Pittsburgh. There's a For Sale sign out front — didn't you notice?" Dad asked. "Guess I should go over and mow that lawn."

"Lisa mentioned they might be moving, but I didn't know it was for sure. I'll miss her." I stood up and leaned on the railing. "I was surprised by how much I liked camp."

"They treat you okay?"

"Yeah. Better than the girls at Redwood. The other counselors, the kids, they were just people, regular people. I can't figure out why skin color matters."

He coughed and turned off the radio. "It's just the way of the world."

"Not my world, Dad. Not anymore."

He got up and stood next to me. I expected to see his face red and angry. But it was just sad.

"God help you in your brave new world. You kids have to deal with stuff we never thought about — nuclear wars, race riots, and your own generation spitting in the faces of people who gave them everything."

We stood silently for a bit. I watched a cardinal fly from our tree to one in Lisa's backyard. My father's breaths were heavy. I knew he smoked too much. I wanted to tell him he should quit, but I bit my tongue. After a moment, he sighed.

"Sorry about your boyfriend," he said, his voice low.

"Yeah, well, I hope I'll see him again some time."

I smiled, thinking of Roland.

"Joni, Michael Reid is dead. You won't see him again, ever."

Dad stared at me with a worried look. His sweat smelled like tobacco and Old Spice. My stomach clenched. Already, I totally forgot about Ishmael.

"Yeah, I mean, no. I don't know what I mean. He's really dead?" I gasped, totally freaked out.

I really did feel sad about Ishmael, but it just seemed like so long ago. Still, I couldn't tell my parents about Roland. I had to be more careful. My father surprised me when he put his thick hand over mine.

"I can't forgive him for what he did to you, but I know you cared about him. No one wanted the kid dead. It would be easier on his parents if he died in the war. This way, they'll never get over it. I hope you will, someday."

"The truth is, Dad, even though I feel terrible about the way he died, I did get over Ishmael. I wrote to him once and when he didn't write back,

I figured he didn't want to keep in touch with me. And then I got so busy at camp, I stopped thinking about almost everything except what we did each day."

I paused. My father was looking at me, really listening to what I said.

"Dad, the person I did think about was you. The night of the moon walk, I kept imagining you in your chair, and how proud you must have been when the American flag flew on the moon."

Dad cleared his throat and sniffed. *"One small step for man, one giant leap for mankind.* I thought about you that night too." He reached out to bat away a mosquito. "We worried, you know, that you were too far away, that you wouldn't find your way."

"It was like being on another planet, Dad. I'm not sure I'm ready for Earth."

Both of us were caught off guard by the tears in our eyes.

Those first days back home, I slept until noon or later. Then, after I ate something, usually peanut butter on Triscuits, I took Tommy to the pool. I couldn't get used to swimming with white people. It seemed strange. The only black person at the country club was an old man named Goody who cleaned shoes and golf balls at the pro shop. Whenever I passed him, I stopped to say hello. He nodded but kept to his work. Now, the middle of August, no one came to the pool as often. With a lane to myself, I swam lap after lap, my wind getting stronger each day. I swam without thinking, without counting, not stopping until Tommy told me he wanted to go home.

The day Mom promised to take me shopping, I woke up at eleven. I undid my braids, washed my hair, shaved my legs, and dressed in khaki camp shorts and a blue cotton blouse from my closet. In the mirror, with loose, sun-bleached hair, my face looked really thin. I turned my head from side-to-side and instead of the whip of braids, my hair swung back and forth like I was shaking out a towel. When I heard my mother's car pull in the driveway, I went out and opened the door.

"Joni, you look like a model," she said.

"A model of bad behavior," I answered, raising my eyebrows.

She gave me a sad smile. "That's over now. Give me a minute to check on Tommy."

At Plymouth Meeting Mall, Mom pulled into a parking spot near Strawbridge and Clothier. As we walked through the women's department, she paused to feel the material on a rack of dresses in red, blue, yellow, and green. I tried to walk past but she stopped me.

"How do grown women wear such short dresses?" she asked. "Do you like this style?"

"It's not me. They don't have clothes I like here."

My mother looked concerned. "You need to make a good impression. You want to look nice."

A couple months ago, I would have raged — *What do you know? What do you know about anything?* — and stomped out of the store. Now I smiled, grabbed her sleeve, and pulled her along.

"Mom, *Seventeen* girls wear bell bottoms and embroidered tops. They sell the stuff I like at the Marianne Shop downstairs."

I headed for the escalator. *You too easy, Mamma*, I thought, Jermaine's lispy voice sounding in my head.

At the clearance rack at Marianne, I chose soft peasant blouses, horizontal-striped knit shirts, a loose tie-dye blouse the sales girl called a *kurta*, and a crinkly gypsy top in a paisley print. When I tried on bell-bottom dungarees and pink cords, I liked the way they hugged my hips. The sales girl showed me a leather fringe vest and a sky-blue knit shirt with a peace sign on the front. I carried them over my arm. At the checkout counter, I took a leather headband from the display and tied it across my forehead.

"Really, Joni, you can't go to school wearing hippy clothes," Mom said, disapproval in her voice.

"Ma'am," the sales girl said, "all the girls are wearing these clothes to school in September. You have a lot of good bargains here."

My mother sighed. I lifted a tie-dye scarf from a display and pulled it across her forehead.

"This would look great on you," I told her.

As she counted out fifty-seven dollars, Mom smiled and shook her head. It was so easy to make her happy. I lugged the shopping bag past Woolworth's, where the fake buttery smell from the popcorn machine reminded me of the stuff I stole with Ishmael. It made me feel dirty.

When we passed the record store, I stopped to look at a red poster with a white dove perched on the arm of a blue guitar. It read — *3 Days of Peace and Music August 15, 16, 17 — Woodstock Music and Arts Fair Presents an Aquarian Exposition in White Lake, NY.* Along the left ran a list of amazing bands Ishmael had introduced me to, Grateful Dead,

Jefferson Airplane, Janis Joplin, and lots more.

"Joni, come along," Mom called. "I don't like to leave your brother too long."

Three days of peace and music. Ishmael would have loved it.

On the ride home, I thought about Ishmael. *He hung himself in his cell.* That was so horrible. I know you didn't hear his case, Judge, but did you know he got sent home from the army on a psycho? There should have been a better way to punish him, because he didn't hurt anyone but me. And I forgive him.

I let myself feel sad, but refused to cry.

The next day, before he dressed for work, I followed my father to the shed in our backyard and watched him pour gasoline into the tank of his Sears Craftsman power mower. After he yanked the cord twice, the motor started. He stepped back. A dark oily streak spread across his forehead.

"You sure you can handle this, Joni? Don't run over rocks or big sticks and definitely do not clear out clumps with your hands. Those blades are so sharp, they'd take your fingers off and your mother would never forgive me," he barked over the roar. "Put it back in the shed when you're done. I'll clean it when I get home."

"I'm okay," I shouted as I took the handle, but he'd already started back to the house.

The engine reverberated in my bones as the mower made a curvy path from our yard to Jake and Lisa's. I started on the front, first guiding the mower around the edges to frame the lawn, then moving up and down or back and forth according to my whim. The cut grass had an onion smell and cut pieces stuck to my legs. I was afraid to stop because I doubted I was strong enough to restart the motor. I kept imagining my right hand dangling from my wrist if I tried to clear grass from the wheels.

After I finished the front yard, I bumped the mower along the side, peeking into empty rooms through windows that no longer had curtains. I had so much I wanted to tell Lisa, but now I'd never see her or Natalie again. I never had a chance to say goodbye. It made me sad.

The backyard was about as twice as big as the front, but I worked with determination, starting along the fence and driving the lawnmower in ever-smaller squares. Sweat poured down my face and my legs ached, but the more exhausted I became, the harder I worked. This was my personal penance — for every bad and stupid thing I'd ever done. I imagined the mower blades slicing away the last tendrils of guilt and shame, leaving them to wither and die and blow away. I'd made lots of mistakes this past year. But I'd done some pretty good stuff too. And now I had the chance to start again. I didn't want to blow it.

When I thought about the year ahead of me, I felt as scared as when I faced the *Manetu.* Mary Mac's story of the butterfly and how close she'd come to being dragged into the hedge seemed to be a message to be careful of what I chased after. I summoned Lisa's voice — *Hold on to your dreams, Joni. Don't let anyone steal them.* I thought about the phrase I heard over and over this summer — from Jermaine, Daisy, Lady, Daiquiri, Roland — *You be all right.*

The blades buzzed over the last patch and grass spit out the side. I released the control and the mower sputtered off. I dragged the lawnmower past the Whites' house, across their front yard, and back to our shed.

The next few evenings, I sat in the living room with my father, watching the news. The weatherman pointed out the track of Hurricane Camille, the worst hurricane in ages, as it drove closer to the US from Cuba.

But I was more interested in reports about the huge rock and roll concert. Crowds of kids, far more than anyone expected, created massive traffic jams on their way to a dairy farm outside of Woodstock, New York. Reporters, in stern voices, warned of havoc — *hundreds of thousands of marijuana-smoking hippies took over Mr. Yasgur's farm without sufficient food, bathrooms, or medical facilities to handle the unkempt crowds. Local businessmen,* they reported, *considered the festival a disgrace.*

On Monday, the news reported that thirty-foot tidal waves from Hurricane Camille flattened the town of Pass Christian in Mississippi and washed away 256 lives.

"Terrible," my father said.

Then, Chet Huntley, with black-rimmed glasses and a grim expression, announced, *The rock music festival which brought 350,000 people to a rural area two hours from New York City finally ended.* The screen filled with a guy rocking away on his guitar, playing music that sounded like stars twinkling.

"Turn it off," Dad muttered, cigarette smoke curling through his fingers. He leaned forward and heaved himself out of his chair.

"Tricia Nixon is watching this, and I'm sure she'd want the youth of America tuned in," I told him in my sweetest Tricia Nixon voice.

"What are you talking about? Tricia Nixon isn't watching hippies wallowing in the mud." Dad's voice was suspicious.

I remembered Ishmael once told me Grace Slick went to the same college as Tricia Nixon. We'd fallen on the floor laughing about that. I stared at the TV so Dad couldn't see my smile.

"She really is. Tricia's college friend, Grace Slick, performed at the festival. I bet President Nixon is watching this with Tricia right now."

"You are something else," Dad said.

He sounded amused. He lingered in the entryway, watching. When Tommy burst through the front door, Dad grabbed his shoulder.

"President Nixon is watching this," he told Tommy.

My mother, wiping her hands in her apron, came into the room and sat on the sofa next to me.

"I don't remember the last time we were all together like this," she said and patted my knee.

Frank Reynolds, in his ABC evening news report, turned to Gregory Jackson, on the scene at Monticello, New York. After shots of the empty, muddy fields where shirtless kids dragged trash to help with cleanup, Jackson interviewed a local police officer and shop owners dressed in shirts and ties. My parents leaned forward to listen when the adults reported on the festival-goers' manners — *I think they are really a great group of kids,* the police officer said. *Polite, they were polite kids,* a shop owner added.

"They trashed the place," Dad said, but his voice sounded surprised instead of angry.

"But they did help clean up," my mother said.

"Can I get dessert?" Tommy asked.

My parents followed him into the kitchen.

"You want a cupcake, Joni?" Mom called.

I blurted out what I'd been thinking about since I got home.

"I've been wanting to ask you guys something. Maybe you'll think it's weird, but I really liked the name I got at camp. I mean, I got used to it. Could you call me Jonika? Could you try?" I had no idea what they'd say.

My parents exchanged a glance. With chocolate icing all over his lips, Tommy answered first.

"Sure. Sounds like a French name or something."

"You want a cupcake, Jonika?" my father's voice was a little sarcastic, but he shrugged and smiled.

When Mom handed me a cupcake, she looked at me like we had a secret understanding.

"Would you like a glass of milk with that, Jonika?"

That night after my parents and Tommy went to bed, I came downstairs and went outside. I looked at the moon, a bright sickle-shape, and touched the pendant Roland made — *To remember me.* I shivered.

Next week I would register for senior year at Montgomery High, where I knew no one and had no friends.

So far this year, I'd been arrested. Ishmael died. The Vietnam War raged on. Murderers left the bloody note — *Helter Skelter* — on a mirror. Hurricane Camille swept away 256 lives.

But almost half-a-million kids followed their dreams to Woodstock for three days of peace and music. A man walked on the moon. Ruby wore new glasses. Lady learned to swim. And Roland loved me.

I'd be all right.

Acknowledgments

Family and friends offered encouragement throughout my journey with this novel. I'm especially grateful for the support of the George Mason University community of writers. Kirsten Clodfelter, an outstanding writer and friend, edited the novel. Deb Werrlein offered her keen eye for a final proofread. Chinaka Barbour read an early version and provided valuable insight. Meredith Maslich, my publisher, believed in BECOMING JONIKA. Andrew Devlin, artist and son, created the cover. I'm indebted to them all.

BECOMING JONIKA is a work of fiction. Joni and her family, her classmates, and the characters Joni meets at home and summer camp are constructs of my imagination. The novel evolved after fellow writers encouraged me to develop a short story into a novel, and I thank them for their insight.

My intent in writing BECOMING JONIKA was to represent the confusion and turmoil of the late 1960s through the eyes of a teenage girl whose parents' paradigm collides with the cultural and technological reality she confronts. Joni's personal journey from alienation to authentic existence reflects my existentialist inclinations.

I make no claim of historic accuracy although actual events and cultural allusions are the story's foundation. For these, I acknowledge and thank the Internet universe.